TIMESHIFT

A novel by

D. R. Evans

It is not enough for a patriot to be willing to surrender his life in the service of his country. The true patriot must be prepared to give up his mind as well.

Reichsmarshall Ernst v. Müller
1943

Equivalence Table (Approx.)

Galactic Standard	Terran
Millichron	0·075 seconds
Centichron	0·75 seconds
Decichron	7 seconds
Chron	1·2 minutes
Rotation	23·5 hours
Decarotation	10 days
Cycle	0·90 years
Dern	10 light years

1
RUM-LEM

Rum-Lem's fingers flew as he entered a new command sequence. The Kivran ships were closing quickly. He glanced up at the opnav screen floating before him as he finished entering the maneuvers into the databox. A fourth ship had come into range while he had been working. Like the other three it was a long way behind, but this one was closing even faster than the others.

He commanded the opnav databox: "Check path."

There was a barely perceptible pause before the databox responded: "Jump sequence exceeds safety parameters."

On the opnav screen appeared the codes corresponding to the maneuvers he had entered: CLOAK; REVECTOR BY (15, 95, 3); EXECUTE HYPERSPACE JUMP OF 125·3 DERNS. The revector and the hyperjump were flashing red: the stresses on the ship during the revector exceeded the design limits, and the probability of ending the hyperspace jump too close to a normal-space object was too high.

He frowned and watched the progress of the ships for half a decichron. That fourth ship sure was moving; it had already overtaken one of the others. There was no time to let the opnav system calculate a safe sequence. Even as he reached this conclusion, the blip marking the fourth ship changed color and the weapons system emitted a distinctive buzz.

"Enemy ship within weapons range in five hundred millichrons."

1

He tried to stay calm.

"Opnav override and execute."

The opnav system flashed: SEQUENCE EXECUTING.

The light indicating full cloaking came on, followed instantly by a revectoring that exceeded the limits of the onboard gravity-canceling mechanism. Every object inside the ship, Rum-Lem included, suddenly gained inertia and was thrown sharply upwards and to the left.

Rum-Lem grimaced. He fought to remain conscious as the thrusters whipped the ship around. He could feel the fabric of the restraint belt biting painfully into his shoulder. It was difficult to see properly: his eyes felt like they were being pulled from their sockets. He closed them. The inside of the lids turned red. He could feel the heavy pressure of blood inside his head. His skull felt like it was about to explode. He knew from experience what would come next: he was about to lose consciousness.

At the last possible moment, the forces released him from their grip as the revector ended and gravity inside the ship returned to normal. Almost simultaneously, he felt the juddery tingle in his stomach that indicated a spacetime bubble forming around the ship. A fraction later, a beep sounded: the hyperjump was starting.

He opened his eyes and shook his head to clear it. A tenth of a chron passed before he could see properly, by which time the ship had completed the jump. The opnav screen burst into life as the spacetime bubble collapsed, relocating the ship on the spacetime manifold. He glanced at the damage assessment indicator. It was blank, which meant that either the assessment monitors themselves were damaged or that the ship had passed through the violent maneuver unscathed. He assumed the latter, and relaxed. There was no way he could have been followed through that jump. He had escaped.

Rum-Lem let out a long sigh of relief.

"Opnav, where am I?"

It was a simple question, but one that might take several hundred millichrons for the opnav databox to answer after a jump of that magnitude.

He waited, watching the screens.

Everything appeared normal. There were no other ships within scanner range. Nor were there any substantial sources of spacetime curvature. That meant that he had to be some way from the center of the galaxy, out where the distance between stars was measured in hundreds of milliderns.

"Location calculated," the databox announced, and simultaneously a pair of holographic images appeared in front of him.

Rum-Lem exclaimed in surprise. He was very close to the demilitarized zone. He would have to be careful: there might be imperial patrols out here. But he wouldn't be here long: what he had learned was too important, too unbelievable. He had to get back home and deliver his message without delay. He *had* to.

A flicker of light caught the corner of his eye.

The opnav databox alerted him: "Ship entered scanning range."

The ship identified itself, and for a moment, Rum-Lem could not believe it. One of the ships that had been chasing him before the hyperjump had followed him through it. But that was not possible. No one could have followed him through that jump. Reflexively, he looked up at the cloaking indicator. It was lit.

"Systems databox, independent check: am I cloaked?"

"Affirmative."

A second light flashed on the screen, then a third, and a fourth. Three of the four ships IDed. They matched the ID numbers of the slower three ships that had been chasing him before the jump. The remaining blip was moving faster than the others, and it had failed, illegally, to respond to ID interrogation. As he watched, the anonymous ship passed another of the pursuing vessels. Simultaneously, the weapons databox repeated its warning: "Enemy ship within weapons range in five hundred millichrons."

Rum-Lem looked at the mass of information hanging in front of him. For a moment his mind went blank. He had been followed through an unplanned revectored hyperspace jump while cloaked. Everything he knew told him that was impossible. Yet it had happened, and if he didn't think of something quickly, he was about to pay for his mistake with his life.

He wondered momentarily if he should simply surrender. Once he did that, the Kivrans were legally obligated not to end his life. But a moment's reflection convinced him of the stupidity of that idea. If they had been near the galactic center it might — just — have worked. His surrender broadcast would almost certainly have been picked up and recorded, and the Kivrans chasing him would know that. But out here he could broadcast as much as he liked and the chance of an intercept was negligible.

No, if he surrendered, the legalities would be ignored and he would be killed — or worse — without a qualm. He had no option: he simply had to escape or die in the attempt.

He turned away from the opnav screen even as it showed the unidentified ship passing the last of the other ships. It was still closing. He wondered what kind of ship it was, and who was piloting it. The pilot certainly knew his stuff.

Then he saw the photon missile.

He understood immediately that the unknown pilot knew that the missile would never reach its target; its purpose was not to kill, but to harry. The pilot was even better than Rum-Lem had thought.

"Emergency! New jump sequence. Random revector, jump 500 derns. Full manual override."

The word MANUAL flashed in the air before him. The databox began to speak the word. Rum-Lem's hand pressed the button marked MANUAL SEQUENCE EXECUTE before the databox had completed the first syllable.

The restraining belt bit into his flesh. He closed his eyes, tried to suck in a breath, found it impossible, and simply began to count slowly while his head swam and the inside of his eyelids grew darker and redder. He felt as if the life was being crushed out of him.

He remembered his boast in the simulator: no one could survive accelerative forces as well as he. The boast became a taunt, echoing inside his head. He felt consciousness beginning to slip away.

The force released him and an alarm began to ring, filling the cabin with urgent noise.

"Warning! Warning! Current course will lead to destruction. Automatic override not possible. Spacetime curvature exceeds safety parameters."

Rum-Lem opened his eyes and tried desperately to focus. Everything was a blur, but even through the fog he knew that something was desperately wrong. The holoimage that showed the view in front of the ship was no longer its customary black. Instead it was a glaring yellow.

He barked: "Opnav. Automatic control."

For a moment he relaxed. Whatever the problem was, the opnav databox would take care of it now.

But the databox repeated: "Warning! Warning! Current course will lead to destruction. Automatic override not possible. Spacetime curvature exceeds safety parameters."

Rum-Lem rubbed his eyes and blinked. At last he could focus on the screens before him. The damage assessment screen was flashing in bright red: OPNAV CONTROL INOPERABLE. Of the million-and-one systems that could have failed, he had lost the one he needed most.

He looked at the forward view. Even after the automatic brightness corrections, the yellow was blisteringly bright. But it was not featureless. It had a rice-grain pattern, dark runnels separating bright, elongated patches. He knew what that meant: he was looking at a star, very close, and the ship was heading straight for it.

"Opnav, full manual navigation display and control."

He grabbed the manual flight controls as the screens disappeared. In their place all around him suddenly hung a series of views of the spacecraft and its surroundings. Until now, he had been relying on machines, now it was up to him.

He flexed his fingers as he looked at the screens, assimilating information, trying to remain calm despite the adrenalin coursing through his body. He was closer to this star than he had ever flown, even in simulations. He grabbed the throttle and the revector control and began the delicate job of trying to maneuver out of the star's gravity field without the aid of the opnav databox.

For more than a chron, he concentrated on his task. He did not see the flashing warning lights, did not hear the barrage of complaints from the ship's systems: his whole universe shrank until it encompassed only the holograms floating in the cabin around him and the controls in his hands.

Rum-Lem flew the ship delicately around the star, using the gravity field instead of fighting it, forcing the ship reluctantly into hyperbolic orbit.

As he shot over the pole of the star, the holograms displaying his surroundings shifted to display the new information the sensors had received from the far side of the star. The star was home to a planetary system.

The opnav databox announced: "Warning! Enemy ship closing." At least the warning circuits were still working.

He saw the ship immediately, behind him and closing rapidly along a gravity line that passed even closer to the star than his own. There was no ID associated with the ship.

He swore. How on Dalith had the ship followed him again? It was simply not possible.

He watched the ship. For a moment, it deviated from its course and Rum-Lem felt a ray of hope.

He could guess what had happened. The Kivran ship had terminated its jump even closer to the star, and now it was in real danger of being trapped by the stellar gravity field. He watched grimly as whoever was at the controls of the ship fought to extricate himself from his precarious situation.

The ship disappeared behind the bulge of the star, forcing Rum-Lem to concentrate on his own difficulties. He was moving quickly away from the star. But what should he do now? The spacetime curvature precluded another hyperjump, and he had only a short time before his pursuer came into view — if the pilot escaped the stellar gravity field.

He glanced at the display of the star's planetary system. There were four small planets in inner orbits. The closest two were behind him, in full view of the chasing ship. The other two were more or less directly in front of him, and still hidden from his pursuer by the curve of the star. He gauged the distance to the third planet. He had no choice. He revectored and opened the throttle in a race to reach the planet before the pilot of the other ship could see what he was doing.

He was about halfway there when the other ship appeared around the limb of the star. Instantly, it changed course to follow. It was still gaining. As Rum-Lem approached the planet, the Kivran vessel was no more than a chron behind.

It was going to be a near thing. He looked anxiously at the holoimage screens, trying to judge the outcome of the race. Would there be time for him to find a hiding place on the planet's surface?

He was forced to slow down as he approached the planet, to maintain control as he entered the atmosphere. There was no time to perform more than a perfunctory visual inspection of the planet. It was more than half covered with water; swirling patterns of white clouds hid much of the surface. A single continental land mass was visible on the hemisphere facing him, halfway between equator and pole. The center of the land mass was cloudless and reflected back the brownish color characteristic of desert. That was the place for him: the heat would hide the signatures of his engines.

He angled his craft and plunged steeply downward. As he shot through the atmosphere, the scanners informed him that radio transmissions from the planet filled the electromagnetic spectrum. The planet was inhabited.

Rum-Lem's attention was distracted by the approach of the other ship. He had had to slow down too much as he entered the atmosphere; the other ship would be within weapons range at any moment. He crossed the coastline of the continent and fired his retrothrusters for landing, but as he glanced at the scanners he knew he was too late. The race was lost.

High above, in the cabin of the pursuing ship, a light began to glow steadily on a panel.

"Weapon locked on target," the ship announced.

With immense satisfaction in her voice a woman ordered: "Fire."

2

Hwang Lee

Hwang Lee stepped out on to the decrepit wooden balcony, and the muscles around his eyes tightened at the touch of the frigid arctic air. Most of Hwang's body — in fact, all of it except the area around his eyes — was covered by a heating suit set at a comfortable 296 kelvins. He had purposefully refrained from lowering the visor so that he could see the spectacle before him without the nuisance of intervening plastic.

He closed the door behind him to keep the heat inside the ancient cabin, then turned and looked up at the sky.

He wondered what the aurora had looked like in the old days, when it was a purely natural phenomenon. In those days it was intermittent, of course, and surely it could not have been half as beautiful as it was now, but somehow he could not help feeling that something had been lost when the artificial auroras had been turned on seventy five years ago.

Occasionally, though, the particle injectors were reduced to 10% power in an attempt to give tourists what the North Polar Tourist Agency termed in their vid-ads "a sample of what a natural aurora would look like." Of course, the NPTA never relied completely on nature, for it was far too unpredictable. The last thing the NPTA wanted was the possibility of tourists paying good money to see a disappointing show — or even no show at all.

This weekend was one of the two weekends per year when the particle injectors were throttled down to low power, and it was partly this opportunity to see a more authentic display that had drawn Hwang to his great-grandfather's cabin. The other reasons were more complex, having to do with the intractability of the problem he was facing at work and the fact that Ekbu Tbamti, his group leader at the university, had begun a five-day absence from the lab earlier in the day. Hwang was hoping that a couple of days' solitude in the arctic wastes with only the mute aurora for company might inspire him to a new line of reasoning that would lead to a solution to the instability problem plaguing the quantum bubbles.

The ancient, isolated wooden hut had been built nearly a hundred years earlier. Then it had been a primitive structure; now it seemed positively primordial; perversely, it was this very simplicity that attracted Hwang.

The outer walls of the cabin comprised three wooden layers with nothing but air trapped between the layers to provide insulation, a design that worked far better than Hwang had thought possible until one afternoon he had calculated the thermal properties of such a system.

All power in the hut was derived from old-fashioned synthoil. Hwang knew that he would have to do something about that as soon as he could afford it: synthoil was getting to be expensive these days. But it would cost upwards of 10,000 WCUs to convert the building to use power blocks, and it would be at least another year before he could afford that kind of money.

Considering that the cabin had had virtually no maintenance for most of the past hundred years it was in surprisingly good condition. Up here things decayed slowly; the air was permanently dry and even in the summer with its midnight sun the temperature never rose very high. The cabin made a perfect getaway for Hwang. It was remote, inexpensive, and almost maintenance-free.

Now Hwang stood on the balcony and looked up into the sky, his eyes slowly adjusting to the crepuscule. There were only two distinct auroras visible, a far cry from the usual eight or nine. Directly above was a large, red arc, diffuse and sufficiently dim that Hwang could almost convince himself that he could see stars through its glow. Off to the west was a multicolored, flickering curtain that was considerably brighter.

9

Technically, the local time was shortly after 0800, but time of day was almost meaningless so close to the solstice at these latitudes. The temperature was not cold for the time of year, but even so it would be uncomfortable to remain outside with unprotected eyes for more than a minute or two.

Hwang took full advantage of the short period, gazing in awe at the red arc and experiencing a rare unity with the Universe, losing himself temporarily in his appreciation of the beauty of the almost-natural phenomenon and forgetting his mundane troubles. He watched the display until his eyelids began to hurt with the cold. Reluctantly, he dropped the visor over his face. Immediately he began to feel warmer, but the view of the sky was no longer quite as clear as it had been, and he somehow felt like he was now merely an outsider — an observer, rather than an integral part of the Universe.

His wristcom vibrated.

He tried to ignore the insistent vibration, but the summons had broken his mood. Civilization beckoned, and he supposed he must answer its call.

He lifted his wrist and spoke loudly so that his voice would carry through the microinsulation of his face mask and glove.

"Redirect inside."

He went back into the cabin.

The vidscreen on the wall was lit. "Connection attempt from Ekbu Tbamti," glowed in yellowish letters on a dark green background.

As Hwang removed his outer layer of clothing, he wondered why the group leader was calling him. When Tbamti had left the lab around lunchtime, he had said simply, "See you all in five days." By now he should be relaxing in his Tongan hideaway with his wife and family.

Tbamti deserved the break, for no one at the lab worked harder than its director, who, in addition to supervising a bevy of graduate students and postdocs, was also the lab's chief source of inspiration and principal public relations asset.

Sporadically throughout his career Tbamti had made a point of publishing amusing but scientifically irreproachable papers on some facet of life that was not traditionally the purview of physicists or mathematicians. His papers on such subjects as *The Recipe for the Perfect Ice Cream*; *Bread, Butter and Gravity*; *Why Science Fiction Writers get it Wrong*; and *Camels and Needles: a Study in Wealth* had earned him a large and enthusiastic following among the general public; and, incidentally, a seemingly never-ending stream of grants.

When one added to this his avuncular, larger-than-life personality on the videocasts, the result was a popular, interesting, successful, sought-after man who nursed only one half-secret, unfulfilled ambition: to win a third Nobel.

"Connection attempt from Ekbu Tbamti is being repeated," flashed in a more urgent reddish orange on the dark green background of the vidscreen.

Hwang had removed the insulating suit and was now standing in front of the screen in his ordinary clothes.

"Accept connection," he said.

After the briefest of pauses, the three-dimensional image of his group leader appeared in place of the flat letters.

Hwang recognized the background. The vidscreen was inside Tbamti's Tongan hideaway, and the foreground showed a simply furnished room; through the windows behind Tbamti Hwang could see the blue of the Pacific, the low, early-morning sun reflecting brightly from the undulations of the swell.

Tbamti seemed to fill the hut as he always did, a trick both of his massive frame and the fact that he had a tendency, whether by accident or design, to stand somewhat closer to the vidscreen receptors than most people. He had obviously been wearing a slight frown of anxiety at Hwang's tardiness, but the moment he appeared on the screen the frown was replaced by a hearty smile. His white eyes and teeth beamed delightedly out of the expanse of his enormous black face.

"Ah, Hwang, there you are. I thought for a moment you weren't going to answer."

"Sorry. I was outside, looking at the low-level auroras; they have the injectors turned down to low power this weekend."

"Oh, you're up there are you? Well, rather you than me. Give me sun, sea and sand any day. Anyway, I wanted to let you know that I've been thinking about our stability problem. Have you had any more thoughts?"

It was a measure of the high regard in which Tbamti held the postdoc that he gave Hwang a chance to speak before sharing his own ideas. Unfortunately, Hwang had nothing to say.

"No. That's why I came up here. I thought that maybe if I could get away for a day or two, I might come up with something."

"Well, take a look at this, will you? If you think it's OK, maybe you could give it a try before I come back. It might be the solution we've been looking for. At least it's a possibility."

Hwang noticed for the first time that there were several sheets of paper in Tbamti's hand. Tbamti stepped forward and did something out of the vidscreen's field of view. Immediately, a slot by the side of Hwang's screen began to eject sheets of paper.

Tbamti continued: "I may have come up with a solution; or maybe I've missed something and you'll have the pleasure of pointing out my mistake. Anyway, I'll let you take a look at it. Get back to me with your thoughts."

"OK. Thanks."

"Good-bye, Hwang, and enjoy the auroras."

Tbamti leaned forward and touched something. The screen went blank and then, a fraction of a second later, a holographic view of Denali rising into an azure sky appeared in his place.

Hwang walked to the old table that was one of the few pieces of furniture in the cabin, studying the sheets in his hand. As he looked at them, he yet again appreciated how lucky he was to be working with someone like Ekbu Tbamti. No; he corrected himself, there was no one *like* Ekbu Tbamti. Tbamti was one of a kind.

Just over a year ago, Hwang had turned down a lucrative offer from a high-tech company to join joined Tbamti's élite research team. He had never regretted his decision. In the course of the past year, he had become Tbamti's confidant and, as much as Tbamti had one, his favorite colleague. Neither was afraid to contact the other whenever he was having difficulty with a problem. Working together, no problem had stumped them for more than a few days. Until this past month.

Thirty days ago, Hwang had finally succeeded in creating and confining quantum bubbles.

At first he had been ecstatic. Flushed with enthusiasm he had brought Tbamti down to the lab: a painted room with windows that were permanently shuttered closed on the ground floor of the physics tower at Rabundi University. Wires and equipment of various vintages were strewn all over the floor, giving the impression more of a disorganized storeroom than the laboratory of the world's greatest scientist. The centerpiece of it all, humming quietly in the very center of the room, was a massive metal box — the guidance block — some four meters long, a meter wide and a meter high.

The box sported an array of red lights on its side; the lights flashed on and off in what at first looked like a predictable pattern until one studied it for a while, when one would realize that while each light seemed to obey a simple periodic switch, the pattern of lights as a whole changed chaotically.

But it was not the lights that were the heart of the machine: they were merely indicators of its status. The metal block was topped by a glass cylinder perhaps 10 centimeters in diameter and running the length of the block. Each end of this cylinder was capped with a white plug from which ran a large cable. At intervals of a few centimeters along the length of the cylinder, black collars fitted tightly around the glass. It was within this cylinder that the quantum bubbles were created. Sharing the top of the guidance block with the cylinder was a split-beam laser, used to look for minute changes in the local gravity field.

The purpose of the experiment was the reigning Holy Grail of physics: to provide the first incontrovertible proof of the phenomenon dubbed by the press "antigravity."

Hwang and Tbamti stood in one corner of the room beside the control panel. Hwang flipped a switch to reset the experiment and instantly the lights on the block all went out, except for one in the upper left hand corner.

"Get ready," Hwang warned. "They appear very quickly, and they don't last long."

Hwang pressed a button, and the lights on the side of the block began to flash in a simple, repetitive pattern: two red waves, each commencing at one end and moving towards the center, where they appeared to collide and destroy each other, just as another pair of waves was born at the two ends. A low hum from the equipment grew louder.

Suddenly, the hum changed, and an abrupt, high-pitched tone overlaid the low-frequency sound. At the same moment the left-hand wave dissolved into a chaotic pattern of flashing lights.

Inside the cylinder a blue bubble about two centimeters in diameter appeared and detached itself from the leftmost plug, travelling slowly to the right, along the axis of the cylinder. The bubble vibrated like an unstable soap bubble, although it appeared to be made of nothing more substantial than light. It moved away from the plug, travelling down the length of the cylinder.

The bubble lasted for no more than half a second, during which time it travelled perhaps 25 centimeters down the tube. Then it seemed to dissolve into nothingness. The blueness got fainter and the bubble just seemed to ease itself out of existence, without actually contracting or expanding as it did so.

Just before the bubble disappeared, a similar bubble formed at the other plug. The lights on the right-hand side of the guidance block ceased their wavelike pattern and dissolved into chaos. The bubble detached itself from the plug and moved towards the center, just like the first. This one did not travel as far. Almost as soon as the scientists were aware of its existence, the bubble began to dissolve in the same manner as its twin.

A second and a half later, it was all over. Both bubbles had disappeared and all that remained were the lights, flashing randomly.

A huge smile creased Tbamti's face. "Well done, Hwang. It works!"

"Yes. Sort of. But I can't keep the bubbles stable for long enough. No matter how carefully I set everything up, the bubbles simply will not appear at the same time, and they never make it to the center of the tube. And even if they did, I'm certain I wouldn't be able to control them once they came close to one another. I don't know how to keep them stable. I've tried everything, but nothing seems to work."

"Well, never mind. We should celebrate the progress you've made. We can figure out how to improve things later. There has to be an answer."

But if there was one, it was proving extraordinarily elusive. Tbamti and Hwang had spent a whole month since that first run, trying to understand in detail the dynamics of the quantum bubbles. They had made some breakthroughs: the equipment could now be relied on to create bubbles at the two ends of the cylinder more or less simultaneously, and they had discovered that by shrinking the bubbles to a diameter of no more than a centimeter they were much more stable and often traversed a meter or more before dissolving back into the nothingness from which they had come. But antigravity still eluded them

Tbamti and Hwang were both convinced that the path to antigravity lay in the phenomenon of quantum bubbles, but they also knew that there was no hope of a detectable effect unless they could stabilize the bubbles. The bubbles had to be allowed to evolve without disappearing before there was any chance of an antigravity effect appearing.

After a month without progress, even Tbamti was beginning to become discouraged, and although he had tried not to let his young coworker know how frustrated he was, Hwang understood that the laureate was beginning to think that another major breakthrough would be necessary before they could make any further progress. But perhaps Tbamti had now made the breakthrough they needed.

Hwang's brow furrowed as he tried to follow Tbamti's miniscule script. According to Tbamti's calculations, their problem lay in trying to constrain the quantum bubbles too tightly. The collars along the length of the cylinder were fed with radio energy at a frequency of precisely 14·025 megahertz, which Tbamti's calculations had long ago indicated was what he called the "frequency of optimum coupling."

But his new calculations suggested that, for the quantum bubbles to maintain their integrity, they had to be allowed to evolve for short periods without being affected by external constraints. Counterbalancing this was the fact that, if the radio energy was cut off completely, the bubbles would simply evaporate into nothingness.

Tbamti was proposing a simple, almost a trivial, modification of their present experiment. He proposed that the radio energy should be switched on and off several times per second.

Hwang sat at the table and considered Tbamti's notes carefully. At first he was dubious that such a simple change could possibly make any real difference, but the more he thought about it, the more excited he became.

The basic idea was very simple. When the radio energy was not turned on, the bubbles would evolve naturally, following their tendency to return to the nothingness from which they had been created. When the energy was available, they would be constrained and would extract energy from the radio waves. By alternating between the two states while the bubbles were being driven forward by a directed impulse, then it seemed possible that the bubbles could be made to drift down the column until they came close enough for them to interact. And it was this interaction that was the whole point of the experiment.

Hwang's stomach rumbled. He glanced at his wristcom and discovered that he had been engrossed in Tbamti's equations for more than three hours. It would be late evening by now back at the university. If he were to leave immediately, it would be the early hours of the morning before he arrived.

Hwang did not stop to think. He had to know whether Tbamti's changes would work.

He bundled Tbamti's papers under his arm, recovered the things he had brought with him for the weekend, grabbed a package of food from the refrigerator, and hurried to the garage that abutted the cabin.

His skycar looked newer than it was. It was nearly twenty years old now, not that much younger than Hwang himself. It had a ceiling of fifty kilometers and a cruising speed of only 5,000 kph. Still, it was reliable and cheap to run, and met Hwang's limited needs. The skycar would last him a few more years yet. He clambered into the plastic shell, sealed the door, and started the ground motor.

As always, the launch was a little jerky. There was a problem somewhere with one of the detonation thrusters, a sticky valve perhaps, but Hwang's practical expertise in such matters was limited, and the jerkiness had not yet reached the point where it was worth the expense to have it fixed; so the craft shuddered slightly as it lifted from the ground. Then it smoothly reoriented itself for the journey and began to gain both speed and altitude.

As the airspeed indicator moved through 500 kph, the frame of the vehicle began to rattle as it always did. The rattle was always worse up here in the arctic, accentuated by the slight shrinkage caused by the cold arctic air. As the car accelerated through 1,000 kph, the rattling gradually faded away and was replaced by the gentle drone of the turbopulse engines.

Hwang switched off the cabin lights and began to eat. He glanced at the course chart: his route would take him close to the pole and then south across Scandinavia, central Europe, the central Sahara and thence to Rabundi. Estimated total flight time was almost exactly three hours.

Now that he was airborne, Hwang's excitement faded and he suddenly felt exhausted. It had been a long day. Within moments of finishing his food, he leaned back, closed his eyes, and dozed.

When he awoke, he was passing over northern Africa. The Time To Landing indicator was down to forty five minutes. He could see little through the window, but in the distance was an enormous agglomeration of lights. Even without the navigational screens to tell him, he would have realized that he was flying over the Sahara, one of the few remaining unpopulated areas in the world. The distant lights were from Kalhad, the second-largest city in Africa.

He settled back and enjoyed the view as the onboard computers guided the skycar towards its destination.

16

The skycar began its long descent and the blackness below gave way to a vista of lights as the desert fell behind. Below him now was jungle; unlike the desert the jungle was populated, and there were dense clusters of lights now in all directions. The car made a few adjustments, guiding him around the major population centers, and it was not long before the bright lights of Africa's largest city lit the horizon. Ten minutes later, he was on the ground in the skycar park at Rabundi University.

It was a little after three in the morning, and the city was as quiet as it ever was. He saw no more than a dozen people as he walked to the stop for public ground transportation.

He signaled his presence and about three minutes later a robotbus trundled up to take him to the university. According to his wristcom, it was half past three when Hwang submitted to the retina scan and the doors of the physics tower slid open to admit him.

He went immediately to the lab. The equipment was all there, just as he had left it yesterday. He checked the energy in the power cube — it was still more than three quarters full — and switched on the computers.

The changes that Tbamti had suggested should be simple to implement: a few minor alterations in the control program should be sufficient.

He finished making the changes shortly after five.

Hwang debated whether he should wait until someone else was present before running the experiment. Tbamti always wanted at least two people present when the experiment was running, as a precaution against accidents. But the computer controlled everything, and the minor changes Hwang had made to the program could not possibly cause an accident. And anyway, if anything did go wrong, the computer would simply shut everything down.

He began to apply power.

He switched on the reference laser and its detectors. The beam from the laser split into two parts. One part was reflected by mirrors so that it traversed the top edge of the guidance block. The other part went directly from transmitter to detector, passing above the center of the cylinder, where the two bubbles were supposed to meet. A computer compared the signals from the two lasers and produced a readout that was continuously updated. Right now, there was no deflection: both beams matched their calibration. Full gravity was acting along the entire path length of the beams.

The computer confirmed the integrity of the operational circuits and Hwang pressed the button for the run to begin. He was sweating. For the first time, he found himself thinking that this time there was a real chance the experiment would work. This time, antigravity might really be created and Tbamti might be about to get his third Nobel. Hwang, if he was lucky, might be about to get his first.

The red lights along the side of the block began to ripple in unison, starting at the edges and then sweeping slowly inward to collide and disappear at the center; then they reformed at the edges and repeated the sequence.

Hwang counted the sweeps and watched the digital meters on the screens. On the tenth sweep, the meters, as they always did, briefly indicated the formation of quantum bubbles. They swept into existence for a fraction of a second, the only visible confirmation a slight kick on the meters.

On the eleventh sweep, the kicks were more pronounced. This time, Hwang could convince himself that the nearer of the two bubbles had lasted long enough for him to see it.

On the twelfth sweep, there was no doubt. The bubbles were definitely visible. Still too unstable to be picked up by the waves as they passed down the cylinder, they shivered unsteadily for several seconds before dissipating.

On the thirteenth sweep, the bubbles appeared and phase locked themselves to the sweep of the lights. Slowly, they began to drift towards each other.

The drift was painfully slow. The sweep of the lights towards the center was much slower than before the bubbles had formed. The meter indicating deviation from gravitational symmetry stayed in dead center. The hum of the power transformers switched on and off several times a second, like a burst of high-speed, old-fashioned Morse code. And still the bubbles remained intact. They continued their stately progress towards the center of the cylinder. They travelled farther than they had ever done before. Hwang's heart was racing. This time it really was going to work.

Something changed as the bubbles came within about a meter of each other. A vibration, too low to hear, began to shake the room. The energy being consumed by the experiment increased, and the bubbles began to become oddly indistinct.

For a moment Hwang thought that the bubbles were becoming unstable, but then he realized that they were oscillating, too rapidly

18

to see clearly, but slowly enough that somehow the oscillations were producing a sound wave that filled the room — even though the bubbles existed in a vacuum.

He could not quite hear the note, but he could feel it, shaking the lab. A few seconds later he began to hear something. It was deep, a veritable proslambanomenos of a note. As the bubbles continued to drift closer, the frequency of the note increased. He covered his ears, keeping his eyes fixed on the bubbles, which were now beginning to glow brightly.

Any second now....

When it happened, it was not at all what he and Tbamti had expected. Instead of creating a tiny volume in which gravity could not propagate, the bubbles began to spin around one another like a pair of miniature orbiting binary stars. Simultaneously, the noise abruptly ceased. Hwang removed his hands from his ears. The power meter had gone crazy: the experiment was suddenly consuming an unbelievable amount of energy.

Before Hwang could react, the electric current pouring from the power cell melted a bus-bar, cutting off power to one half of the experiment.

The two bubbles shivered momentarily, and then they touched.

The collapse of the physics tower greeted the early-morning arrivals at the university. Later, there was unanimous agreement that there was no explosion. The building simply collapsed, without warning and seemingly without cause. The only oddity, insisted on by a pretty young undergraduate who had been passing the building a couple of minutes before its collapse, was that she had felt the ground trembling as she had walked by.

The university security computer indicated that the only person in the building at the time of the collapse was Dr. Hwang Lee, a postdoctoral student working with Professor Ekbu Tbamti.

Lee's office was on the fifteenth floor, but generally he worked in a laboratory on the ground floor. He could have been in either place, or anywhere in between. In any case, it was hardly possible that he could have survived the building's collapse. He would either have fallen to his death or been crushed. Still, until a body was found there was always hope, and lifting machinery was quickly brought in to try to sort through the rubble to look for Dr. Lee.

The pretty undergraduate was certain that no lights had been on when she had passed, and Lee's office was on the side of the building that would have been visible to her, so the Disaster Relief Team dug through the debris toward the shattered laboratory, whose shutters would have prevented any light escaping.

It took them more than six hours to reach the laboratory. Ekbu Tbamti was there, freshly arrived from Tonga, when a worker came over to him and said, "OK, sir, I'm sure we've reached it. But it doesn't look anything like you said it would."

Tbamti cursed with frustration and after donning protective gear followed the worker through the precariously shifting rubble to what remained of his laboratory. His description of the lab had been complete and precise; was it possible that these fools had been so stupid as to excavate the wrong part of the building?

But Tbamti immediately recognized the remnants of his laboratory. There were the single-event holograms of Tonga on the wall; there were the conduits that brought the utilities into the room. There could be no mistake: this was his laboratory all right. Except that two things were missing. There was no sign of a body. But neither was there any sign of the experiment. Hwang and all the apparatus associated with the quantum bubble experiment had disappeared.

3

LYSTRA TEN-WER

The woman sat upright in bed, her arms clasped around her knees as she rocked slowly backward and forward. She looked to her right, where her partner breathed easily in deep, relaxed sleep. Until late last night, she had been expecting that they would reregister as partners for another cycle when the current registration ended in just a few rotations. But now that expectation had been reversed, and her mind was filled with a storm of conflicting thoughts and emotions.

The trouble, as she freely admitted to herself, was that for the first time in her life she had permitted herself to fall in love with her partner. It had happened gradually, almost imperceptibly, and it was only recently that she had begun to come to terms with the new emotion that had slowly been stealing over her. She had even had thoughts about making the relationship permanent, although she had not said anything out loud for fear of scaring him away. Men generally were reluctant to certify relationships as permanent. But he, too, was in love with her; she was sure of that.

It seemed like a perfect match, the kind the holoimage broadcasts were always pushing to the masses as the ideal for a happy life. It seemed perfect at all levels: physical, emotional, and even, to the extent that she thought in such terms, spiritual.

But everything had turned to disarray with his quiet confession this evening after they had coupled and then separated for sleep.

She was on the verge of sleep and his words were spoken quietly, so that she had heard them but not fully understood their import.

"Darling, I must tell you something," he had said. "I don't feel like I can continue our relationship unless I share this with you."

Her response had been a wordless grunt as she hovered just this side of sleep.

"Please, don't think of me any differently. But you need to know this. I'm not really from Kivra. I'm a Dalithian spy."

Somehow, incredibly, the news had not jerked her into wakefulness. Perhaps it was the bland emotionless tone in which the planet-shattering information had been imparted. Perhaps she was just too relaxed after their coupling. Whatever the reason, her brain had simply noted the information and then slid into sleep.

It was only later, in the middle of the night, when she woke from a bizarre, disturbing dream which featured the ominous blue sky of Dalith, that she remembered his confession. As she came fully awake, she discovered that sweat was dribbling down her body despite the carefully controlled climate of the apartment.

Unable to sleep, she sat rocking gently backwards and forwards, trying to come to terms with her partner's confession.

There was no question of them staying together now. Obviously he hadn't realized that, otherwise he could hardly have been so blasé about his announcement. But it was impossible: a rising star at the Ministry of Peace and Security could not cohabit with a confessed Dalithian spy.

No, the the question she was wrestling with had nothing to do with whether they could continue to cohabit. It was a much simpler one: would she tell Supervisor Qwilm when she reported for work in the morning?

She regarded the sleeping form at her side. She would be betraying him. If she told her supervisor, at the very least her partner would "disappear". He would never be heard from again. Quite possibly it would mean his death. Was she capable of sending her partner to his death?

He had trusted her by telling her his secret, obviously thinking that while she might have to wrestle with whether to continue the relationship, the secret itself was safe with her. But was it?

They had been together for nearly a full cycle, and it had been the happiest cycle of her life. He had been like a breath of fresh air in the stale ordinariness of her existence. That freshness was now explained, of course. He could hardly help being different. He was from Dalith. She wondered how a Dalithian had managed to fool the authorities and lead an apparently normal life here at the very heart of the Empire.

She considered this problem for several chrons, as an alternative to wrestling with the decision that confronted her. Eventually she gave up. She could think of no way in which a citizen of Dalith could possibly take a functioning place in Kivran society without being detected.

Yet apparently he had succeeded. As she considered this, she began to realize the implications. He had admitted that he was a spy, but the ramifications of this statement had not at first been obvious. Yet the more she thought about it, the more it struck her that the Dalithians must have gone to immense trouble and surmounted many obstacles in order to place him here without being detected. Surely they would not go to such lengths without a purpose. But what could that purpose possibly be?

Could it be that their meeting towards the end of last cycle was not an accident? Had it all been arranged that they would meet and that he would then play on her emotions? Had their cohabitation merely been part of some complicated design? Surely not. After all, although she did work for P&S, nothing of any real importance was entrusted to her. She merely monitored security reports from the robotships in the demilitarized zone, hardly something that would interest a Dalithian spy.

And anyway, surely the Dalithians, contemptible and stupid though they undoubtedly were, knew better than to expect her to share even what little she did know with a partner, especially in their first cycle together?

Even more strange, why had he chosen this moment — almost on the eve of the new cycle, after they had all but agreed to renew their relationship — why would he choose this moment to jeopardize that relationship by making his confession?

She stretched out a hand to wake him and ask these questions; but something stopped her, and she withdrew her hand and instead continued to rock and hug her knees and ponder her questions.

She considered another side of the matter.

Rather than try to understand his motives, she simply accepted his statement as fact. He was a Dalithian spy. Did that really matter?

She certainly owed him a lot, for he had made her very happy, but did she not owe the Empire and its society far, far more? For this was the society that had accepted her when she had arrived from her backward world to attend the Kivran Imperial University. This was the society that had given her a job and a purpose in life. She looked across the room to the far wall where a small holoimage of the emperor hung, looking benevolently out over the bed with unseeing eyes in which she was sure she could detect both kindliness and justice.

She owed the emperor everything, really. Not personally, of course, for she had never met him and never would. He did not even know of her existence. She was merely one of his 100 billion subjects, of no real importance in the grand scheme of things. But still, as she looked at those intelligent green-brown eyes smiling at her out of the handsome, middle-aged face, she knew where her allegiance lay. Almost without knowing it, she had made her decision. She would inform Supervisor Qwilm in the morning.

She momentarily considered warning her partner about what she had decided, but she immediately dismissed the thought. That would be the act, not just of a traitor, but of a *cowardly* traitor. She tensed reflexively at the thought. If there was one thing Kivrans could not be accused of, it was cowardice. They had always stood firm in the face of Dalithian aggression and duplicity. Kivrans were never cowards.

She remained upright in bed for a while, motionless now and silent. Then she threw a tiny, tight, thin-lipped smile at the holoimage of the emperor, released her knees, and slid down once more into the warmth of the bed.

Firstmeal would have been a tense affair, except that, as usual, her partner had left early without disturbing her. His job as a manual worker in the palace gardens required that he work long hours, but it also meant that his body was always healthy and strong, unlike her own, which always seemed vapid and easily tired.

She ate her meal mechanically. She gave no thought to reconsidering her decision. In fact, she gave little thought to anything at all. Her mind was made up; now it was merely a matter of going through the motions.

After the meal, she left the apartment and lined up with the other occupants of the apartment block as they awaited the hoverbus to take them to their workplace. The line, as always, was long.

The hoverbus arrived on time. She climbed aboard and took a seat. A man seated not far away looked at her with concern, as if her troubles were somehow written on her features. She made an effort to rid her face of all emotion.

Fleetingly, she wondered whether the man might be available for the next cycle. She saw him every day, although she knew nothing about him. He was dressed casually in loose clothes, indicating that he had a low-level job. Perhaps, like her partner, he was a gardener. He had that weather-beaten, browned visage that one associated with an outdoor occupation. Maybe she would ask him in a rotation or so if he was available. He had an understanding, caring look, as if he realized that she was in some sort of trouble. He looked like he wanted to help.

She looked away and gazed mindlessly out the window as the bus made its way along the tree-lined hover route towards the center of the city. The journey lasted no more than fifteen chrons, then she was disgorged into the docking corridor along with most of the other passengers. She walked along the corridor and into the building, where she took the elevator to the 91st floor. She stopped at the receptionist's desk.

"I'd like to see Supervisor Qwilm at his earliest convenience."

The receptionist, a young female, looked up at her and smiled a pitying sort of smile.

"He's already made an appointment for you. You may go straight in."

Ordinarily, this coincidence would have struck her as bizarre. Whole cycles went by without people of her grade being invited to a supervisor's office. Yet, this morning of all mornings, he had obviously been expecting her. She headed for Supervisor Qwilm's office.

The pore pattern on her cheek was scanned, and the door of the supervisor's office slid silently open.

Supervisor Qwilm's office was not much larger than her own, in keeping with the relatively minor distinctions between social classes mandated by the emperor. His holoimage screen, though, was considerably larger than the hers — this one filled the whole of one wall — but its contents were no different from those in any worker's office. His chosen scene was of the inside of a wood. The sky was invisible, hidden by a canopy of overlapping leaves that made the wood dark and a little eerie. There was the sound of a stream not far away, but the only movement on the image itself was from a slight wind: the gentle movement of small branches, the occasional fall of a leaf. She could almost feel the wind brushing her face.

"Good morning, Lystra Ten-Wer. You have something to tell me?"

Her eyes moved reluctantly from the holoimage to meet those of Supervisor Qwilm. She wondered briefly how much he knew about her. After all, he was responsible for nearly a thousand people, of whom she was merely one, and not a particularly important one at that. He was smiling at her: a jovial, apparently genuine smile of friendship. He went so far as to stand, a traditional mark of respect rarely seen any more, and one that made her feel a distinct warmth towards him.

"Yes," she said. "It's about my current partner. He told me last night after coupling that he is a Dalithian spy."

The words came out fluidly and effortlessly. The hard part had been making the decision; once that decision was made, it was surprisingly easy to go through with it.

The supervisor's smile broadened. He seemed unsurprised by her revelation. She tried to read the strange expression that now appeared on his face, but it was some time before she identified it: Supervisor Qwilm was looking at her with pride. She wondered fleetingly if this had all been some sort of a test, but the thought was smothered even before it could be fully formed.

"Thank you," said Supervisor Qwilm. "Could you give me his name, please?"

She stopped, overcome by a sudden panic. It was a simple question. She had lived with the man for nearly a whole cycle. They had shared their deepest secrets and their greatest desires. Yet now, all of a sudden, she realized that she did not know his name.

―――――――――――

A gentle, hummy sigh of contentment escaped her closed lips. She was leaning against something hard, seated on something soft. Even with her eyes closed, she knew that the hardness was a tree trunk and the softness a bed of leaves lying atop spongy, fertile soil. There was a warmth to the day — not the sterile warmth of an office, but the honest, natural warmth of the open air. Her eyes were closed. It was too much effort to open them. She relaxed, and went back to sleep.

When she awoke, nothing had changed except that the tree trunk now dug into her back, slightly hurting her. She leaned forward, her eyes still closed, and reached back to rub the area between her shoulder blades.

"Can I do that for you?"

She opened her eyes and found herself looking into the empathetic eyes of a tall man about her own age. He was standing in front of her, looking down at her with a smile.

"Yes, please. If you would."

She turned slightly and the man stepped forward and knelt down to rub her back. It felt wonderful. She closed her eyes and shivered at his touch.

Nothing changed for several chrons; then eventually, he asked, "All right now?"

"Mmm, yes, thank you."

"May I sit with you?"

She opened her eyes. "Yes, please do."

As the man seated himself beside her, she examined their surroundings.

They were in a wood. The trees were tall and sparse, but the leafy canopy was so dense that the sky was invisible. Occasionally, just for a fraction of a second, an intense burst of oddly yellowish sunlight would penetrate the greenery, only to be immediately obliterated by the gently moving canopy far above their heads. The ground sloped away towards a declivity to her right, from which direction came the sound of running water.

At first, that was the only sound she noticed, but as she listened she realized that the air was filled with birdsong. She did not recognize any of the tunes, but she tried to guess what each bird would look like from the sound it made.

There was a soft *chrrr-chrrr* that she thought must come from a small bird. She imagined it as yellow and blue, scurrying around on the ground, looking for worms. And a *pibbitt-pibbitt-pibbitt*, more strident and almost raucous, the sound of a large bird, high above in the greenery somewhere. And a whistling song, like a maestro on a flute-like musical instrument but pitched impossibly high and playing the notes staccato and in frantic haste, obviously the sound of a small songbird.

"You got the last one right, at least," the man said, reading her thoughts.

"It changed notes so quickly, you see; it has to be a small bird."

"Yes, I see." The man nodded in understanding. "Nice here, isn't it?" he asked a moment later.

27

"Mmm, yes."

"Ever been anywhere like it before?"

"No. Is it always like this?"

"Oh, yes. Always."

They remained silent for some time. At length the man spoke again.

"I'm Rum-Lem," he said. "What's your name?"

"Lystra. Lystra Ten-Wer."

"It really is nice here, isn't it? So peaceful."

"Yes, it's wonderful."

He looked at her with such evident absorption that she felt bound to reciprocate. She examined his face. He was a handsome man. His face was soft and gentle, his eyes large and almost liquid. It was a kind face. He was smiling at her.

He said, "Forgive me. It's rude of me, I know. But I can't help it. It's just that I feel like I've seen you somewhere before."

Lystra continued to examine his face carefully, trying to remember. She felt certain she would have remembered if she had ever seen him before. She shook her head.

"No, I'm sorry. I don't think so."

He shrugged. "Never mind. Just a fancy. Lystra; it's a nice name. Were you named after someone?"

"Yes. According to the records it was the name of my birth mother's mother."

"Tell me more about yourself."

She shrugged. "There's not much to tell. I'm not a very interesting person."

He laughed. "Now that's not possible. Someone as pretty as you is interesting merely by virtue of your existence."

Lystra tried hard not to blush, but didn't quite succeed. It was a long, long time since someone had paid her such a compliment. Part of her brain dived deep to find the last such occasion. It was when she was still undergoing her formal education. A young man had said something very similar. After a short time, they had agreed to an unofficial pairing. It hadn't lasted long and they had never seen each other since.

"You look like you're remembering. Tell me about yourself. Tell me everything."

Lystra's cheeks flushed again.

"You're not really interested."

"On the contrary, I can think of nothing I'd rather do than sit here and while away the afternoon listening to you talk about yourself."

"Well, really there's nothing much to tell, but if you insist...."

She smiled a smile of happy defeat, and began to reminisce.

"I was born on the planet Eb. You've probably never heard of it. It's a small, mostly agricultural planet on the outskirts of the Empire, one of the Outer Planets, not far from the demilitarized zone.

"I was born in the main birthing hospital in Eb-wan, which is the largest city on Eb. I was the result of a coupling between a maintenance engineer on a farm and a bureaucrat in one of the government offices. I guess I was some sort of a mistake. The records don't show that permission was ever given for my conception. Normally I would have been aborted, but my birth mother applied for exemption under the Desirable Errors Decree, and she was granted permission to carry me to term. The scans showed that I would be intelligent and therefore worth saving.

"It was good of her to keep me; I don't think most people would have done that. I've met her a couple of times, secretly" — Lystra was slightly surprised that she felt no qualm of embarrassment at admitting this illegality to a man whom she had only just met — "and she seems quite pleased at the way things have turned out. As am I, of course."

"And I." He flashed her a smile of encouragement. "Carry on."

"Well, it's all rather boring, really. I was educated on Eb. I did well academically, as the pre-birth scans had predicted. My adoptive parents loved me and were very proud of my achievements. They died in a crash just after I was accepted at the Kivran Imperial University. I still miss them.... Anyway, I did well at university, and when I graduated I was offered a job in the Ministry of Peace and Security. I've been there more than five cycles now."

"Do you intend to make a career out of P&S?"

She shrugged. "I guess so. They tell me I have an aptitude for the work and mostly I enjoy it. It's quite interesting."

"What kind of work do you do for them?"

She hesitated a moment before answering. "Monitoring work."

"What kind? Domestic, Remote or Space?"

"Space. Occasionally a bit of Domestic. Nothing important, though. But I'm not allowed to talk about it."

"Come on, you can tell me. I'm your friend. Do you deal with intercepts from Dalith?"

She said nothing.

"The demilitarized zone?"

She remained silent.

"I bet that's it. You work on monitoring intercepts from the demilitarized zone, don't you?"

"I'm sorry. Let's talk about something else."

"Do you like it here?"

"Yes. I wish I could stay here forever, just like this."

"For ever and ever?"

"For ever and ever."

"What about partners? How's that side of your life?"

Lystra shrugged. "You know, the usual. I had a few partners when I was at university. None lasted very long."

"Nothing since then?"

"No. Too busy."

"Any regrets?"

"No, not really. That's the way of it, really, isn't it?"

"Don't you sometimes hanker after a stable many-cycle partnership? A proper pairing?"

"No, I think that would get boring. And it wouldn't do my career any good. They tend to view long-term relationships with suspicion at P&S."

"But there are more important things than your career, though, aren't there?"

Lystra thought for a moment, then shook her head. "No, I don't think so, not really."

"You enjoy your work, then?"

"It gives me great satisfaction."

"But you like it better here?"

She looked around, drinking in the peaceful tranquillity of the woods.

She said, "It *is* nice here, isn't it?"

"Yes, it is. You know, you could stay here forever if you told me a bit about your work. I could stay with you if you'd like that."

"No," Lystra shook her head. "My work is my life. And anyway, like I told you, I'm not allowed to talk about it. I could never betray the trust they place in me."

"Never?"

"No, I don't think so."

"Well, let's just enjoy this afternoon. Lean back and close your eyes."

She did as he suggested. The tree pressed itself once more between her shoulder blades. She fidgeted a little to get comfortable. Then she relaxed. Within moments she was asleep.

From somewhere beyond her consciousness a voice, clinical and female, said, "OK. That's the end of the run."

4
HWANG

Hwang Lee gradually clawed his way to consciousness. For a while, he was aware of only two things: the air was hot and heavy with humidity, and he was lying face-down on something quite hard.

He remained unmoving, his eyes closed. Gradually, he became aware that he was out of doors — either that or there were open windows nearby, for he could hear a veritable cacophony of birds. There was also something that sounded like the movement of branches high above.

He drifted back to sleep.

When he next woke, the air was distinctly cooler. Sweat had dried on his face and the light filtering through his closed eyelids was less bright than it had been. He rolled over on to his back and opened his eyes. Then he struggled to sit up. He hurt, but nothing seemed to be broken. His only visible injury appeared to be a long scrape along his arm that was sealed by a layer of dried blood.

He looked around.

The only recognizable objects were the remnants of parts of the lab. Through a fog he tried to remember. Gradually, it came back to him. He recalled receiving the notes from Professor Tbamti, then the long journey back to Rabundi from his great-grandfather's cabin. He remembered entering the physics tower in the middle of the night and the tedious job of reprogramming the computers.

He had started the experiment, and everything had seemed to be going perfectly, more perfectly than ever before. The quantum bubbles had formed and slowly migrated down the guidance cylinder. He remembered a moment of surprise when the bubbles had begun to dance around one another instead of coalescing and destroying themselves in the antigravity surge that he and Tbamti had predicted. That was all. The next thing he knew was when he had woken here.

But where on Earth was he? Most of the lab appeared to be here, but it was hardly how he remembered it. A couple of walls had caved in. Or, rather, they had simply collapsed. Ceiling tiles had fallen on some of the equipment. The large, rectangular guidance block seemed relatively unscathed, although it now stood inactive, just a dormant mass of metal, glass and unpowered electronics. The computer console at which he had been standing was nearby, dead. Several other ancillary pieces of equipment were visible, all of them lifeless but apparently unharmed.

But it was the environment itself that was the most puzzling of all.

Gone was the physics tower. Gone, indeed, seemed to be the entire city of Rabundi. In its place was a high, airy canopy of trees. A low sun sent a few struggling slanting rays through the greenery high overhead. Even as he watched, the hidden sun must have dropped below the horizon, for the green of the canopy suddenly turned several shades darker and the cavernous interior of the natural cathedral acquired a sudden gloominess.

Simultaneously, the jungle seemed to come alive with enthusiastic sounds. The noise of insects became almost painful as the air was filled with the screeches, tones and buzzings of an uncountable population of small, nocturnal creatures.

Hwang tried to ignore the cacophony and to concentrate instead on formulating a theory to explain what had happened.

The conclusion was obvious, albeit distasteful, for this was a possibility that neither he nor Ekbu Tbamti had ever considered. But it was the only plausible explanation. Obviously, the effect of the quantum bubbles had not been simply to nullify gravity in a small volume surrounding their interaction, but somehow the bubbles had caused their entire environment to be physically transported some distance from Rabundi and into the central African jungle.

He could not have been transported very far. The heat and the vegetation, as well as the rapid onset of night (which was already almost complete), told Hwang that he was still near the equator, which ran just a few kilometers north of the city. The surroundings looked like typical rainforest vegetation, not that he was an expert in such matters. There was luxuriant growth everywhere. Vines climbed the trunks of the enormous trees and covered much of the ground. The very air seemed dripping with life.

Well, it should be easy to get help — his wristcom would give him his location and allow him to call for help.

He looked at his wrist and saw with a momentary pang of concern that the device seemed to be broken. Even its simple timekeeping facility was impaired, for the screen was blank. He wondered for a moment if perhaps the canopy above his head was blocking the satellites' signal, but he dismissed that as impossible, for local retransmission of the signals in Rabundi — in whichever direction it lay — would surely overcome any such blockage.

He tapped the wristcom. "Connect to Ekbu Tbamti."

Nothing happened, and after a while the words *Unable to complete connection* flashed on the screen.

He thought for a moment. "Connect to Rabundi General Hospital."

The screen went blank again. After a few seconds, the screen repeated: *Unable to complete connection.*

"Huh?" grunted Hwang, not yet worried, but certainly annoyed. The wristcom was definitely damaged.

He commanded its self-test function. After a few moments, the wristcom informed him that all circuits were performing normally.

Hwang shrugged in exasperation. Obviously, the self-test was not working properly either. He gave the wristcom up as a bad job and examined his surroundings more carefully.

The cacophony had not lessened. If anything, it had intensified. And it was getting so dark under the canopy that it was becoming difficult to see much of anything at all.

The trees were enormous, and their trunks at ground level were widely separated. It was only high above his head — how far? fifty meters? it was too dark to tell now — that the trees branched out like green umbrellas and formed an almost unbroken surface, blocking the view of the sky above.

A new sound suddenly intruded amongst the high-pitched noises. Not far away, a large creature was moving through the trees. He could not see it, but he could hear its growl. It sounded almost like a lion or a tiger — he remembered hearing the feral growl of a tiger at the Beijing zoo when he was a child — but what species of big cat still survived in the wild? There were certainly no large wild animals anywhere in the vicinity of Rabundi.

He felt a frisson of fear. Perhaps he had been transported farther than he had thought. Perhaps he was in the Central African Jungle Preserve, where a few large animals were allowed to roam free.

But almost immediately he felt a wash of relief. There were no dangerous animals in the preserve, just a few harmless gorillas and large apes that might give him a bit of a shock if he were to encounter them; but they would not harm him as long as he kept his head.

The growling sound came closer. He had almost, but not quite, argued himself out of his fear. The growling ceased, and Hwang held his breath, facing in the direction from which the sound had come. After perhaps ten seconds, the sound started once more, and Hwang silently exhaled. The creature, whatever it was, was moving away.

He was glad that he would not have to be out here for long; the rescue parties should find him soon.

Then, with a shock, he realized that when he had begun the experiment it had been just before dawn. Yet now it was past sunset. He must have lain unconscious on the jungle floor for more than twelve hours. And in that time no one had rescued him.

It dawned on him that if his wristcom was broken, then a search party would not be able to home in on its signal.

With a shiver he realized that there was a distinct possibility that he was going to have to spend the night in the jungle. The situation was ridiculous. He could not be more than a few minutes by skycar from civilization, and yet he could think of no way of signalling his presence to the search-and-rescue teams.

He stopped himself. He had just made an unwarranted assumption. Perhaps no one was searching for him. No one could expect that the experiment could have gone so badly wrong. If they were looking for him, it would be in the physics tower, for surely that must have collapsed when the experiment and its surroundings had suddenly been transported into the jungle. They certainly wouldn't be looking for him out in the middle of the Central African Jungle Preserve — if that was indeed where he really was.

His head was beginning to ache. *Calm down*, he told himself. *Just take everything slowly and you'll be fine. First things first. Try to find somewhere safe for the night and then worry about getting out of here in the morning.*

Even though he had just slept for more than twelve hours, he felt physically drained. Whatever his body had gone through, it was demanding more sleep.

Hwang considered his options. He could think of only two: either he could try to climb one of the trees and spend the night out of reach of the larger ground animals, or he could build a fire. Neither of these was a very attractive proposition. On the one hand, the trees seemed to have precious few crannies where he might safely sleep, and they all seemed to rise at least ten meters above ground level before providing any sort of handholds at all. And in any case he was not at all sure that his body was capable of making the effort needed for tree climbing.

On the other hand, he had no materials with which to build a fire. There were twigs and branches littering the vine-covered jungle floor, but they were all sodden, either from recent rain or simply from the heavy wetness of the air. The vines themselves were thick, wet and sinuous. They looked virtually unbreakable, and in any case were surely too wet to burn.

He bent down, lifted a tendril that trailed in front of him and tried to snap it. It oozed a wet, sticky substance, but refused to break. Building a fire was not going to be easy. And even if he did manage to get a fire going, he had no way of keeping it under control.

What should he do?

And at that moment, the large animal returned. Hwang had been too engrossed in his thoughts, or perhaps the animal had been more silent this time. In any case, he jumped in fright as the low-pitched growl sounded no more than five meters to his right.

He spun around reflexively, and saw a dark, shadowy form. Its eyes, which were set close together, were looking forward, providing the brain behind the eyes with clear stereoscopic vision: the creature knew exactly how far away Hwang was. The two stood, unmoving, looking at one another.

Hwang wished desperately for more light, so that he could see the creature. Of one thing he was sure: it could not possibly be as bad as it appeared in the crepuscular dimness under the canopy.

The thing looked like an enormous shadowy man, fully three meters high. It was standing on two legs, like some kind of massive gorilla. Except that it was larger than any gorilla he had ever heard of. And it was studying him with something that looked a little too much like intelligent belligerence.

Hwang tried to convince himself that, despite the appearance of the apparition before him, gorillas were not dangerous as long as they weren't threatened. And the thought that Hwang could threaten this creature was clearly preposterous. A charging bull would have posed no threat. The creature came a step closer. Hwang was convinced that he could see both purpose and menace in its eyes. He quickly corrected himself; he was ascribing human emotions to an animal that, at worst, might be a little curious about a creature it had never seen before.

It took another step closer, and Hwang was forced to tilt his head back to keep his eyes on its face. The creature stopped. It was no more than two meters away.

Now he could see its face more clearly. It was not the face of a gorilla. The creature had only narrow slits for eyes; its nose was large and protuberant; a massive mouth in which a line of teeth, pointed and adapted to the task of ripping meat, filled the bottom third of the face. If this was a gorilla, it was unlike any gorilla of which Hwang had ever heard.

For a space that seemed an eternity, Hwang and the creature simply looked at one another.

The creature was the first to move.

It put out a massive arm and rested it against the trunk of a tree. Then the arm straightened and the creature let out a deep grunt of effort. For a second the tree resisted; then, with a loud splintering crash, it moved. The canopy overhead burst open as the upper branches were pushed to one side. The creature turned and applied a second arm to the trunk. It was Hwang's chance to escape, but he watched transfixed at the power of the creature as splintering sounds filled the air. With an almighty *crack!* the trunk split.

The upper branches landed with a thud that shook the surroundings. Then the creature turned to look at Hwang. It almost looked like it was smiling. Hwang received the distinct impression that the creature had been simply demonstrating both its strength and the futility of opposition. Then it emitted a loud, satisfied bellow.

Hwang turned and fled.

Aching muscles were forgotten as he tried to distance himself from the monstrous animal. He ran between trees and jumped over dead vine-covered branches as he tried to ignore the crashing sound of the creature lumbering after him.

Hwang was not particularly fit, and he soon began to pant. For perhaps as long as half a minute, he increased the the distance between himself and the creature, but after that his lungs began to scream for relief and he started to stumble as his aching muscles refused to obey his brain's commands.

The creature began to gain on him.

It's only a matter of time, Hwang thought as he desperately pumped his legs.

On he ran, driven by the sounds not far behind.

And then Hwang pitched forward. Unable to see clearly where he was going, he tumbled as the ground disappeared from under his feet. For a fraction of a second he flailed in mid air, and then there was a splash as he hit water.

He struggled to the surface and looked desperately around.

The sky was filled with coruscant stars; the towering trees formed a wall behind him. He had fallen into a wide, slowly moving river. He swam a few strokes, moving away from the bank. Part of his mind was comforted to see Orion lying on his side exactly where he should be. He had been right: he couldn't be far from the equator.

Then his attention was drawn to the bank where the creature suddenly appeared and in its headlong pursuit fell into the water, just as Hwang had done.

There was an anxious moment as Hwang wondered if the creature would swim after him, but after surfacing and looking around in consternation, the creature turned away and pulled itself heavily on to the safety of the bank. It turned towards Hwang and let out a bellow of rage. The creature pulled at a tree trunk and lifted it out of the ground, then threw it after Hwang in what was unmistakably a fit of anger. The tree hit the water about halfway between them.

Hwang relaxed. He was safe.

Safe, of course, was a relative term. He dare not return to the bank, for fear that the creature, or one like it, would find him once more. But he could not stay out here in the river for long. For one thing he was too tired to stay afloat for more than a few minutes; for another, who could say what kind of animals might live in the river? No doubt a crocodile would look upon him with just as much relish as the gorilla — or whatever it was — had done. And a crocodile would give no warning before attacking.

He looked around and saw, not far downstream, a small, low island roughly in the middle of the river. He struck out for it, ignoring his protesting muscles.

A couple of minutes later he hauled himself out of the water on to the gently sloping shore. Then, exhausted, he laid his head in the crook of his arm.

He slept.

5

LYSTRA

The mandatory mindprobe was the only thing about her job that Lystra Ten-Wer really detested. There was nothing she could do about it, of course. Although mindprobes had been made generally illegal several hundred cycles ago, their use was mandated for government employees with access to sensitive information. Unfortunately, her promotion half a cycle ago had elevated her to a grade where she would now be probed at least once every cycle.

After the probe she felt weak, tired and nauseated — a not uncommon reaction. Lystra was driven home and provided with a sedative tablet to help her sleep. Then she was left alone for the rest of the rotation. She took the sedative and stumbled to bed. Her sleep was deep and dreamless.

Lystra awoke late next morning feeling much better. The aftereffects of mindprobes could sometimes cause unpredictable behavior and employees were encouraged to take a full rotation off work, so she got out of bed, waterdoused, dressed, and made herself a light firstmeal. Only occasionally was her equanimity upset as she momentarily recalled some event that had occurred under the probe.

Lystra had no desire to remember the scenarios that had been implanted to test her reactions. She knew some people who could recite exactly what had taken place while they were being probed. For her, memories of the probe were just snapshots, brought to consciousness only by some triggering event that might occur many rotations later.

She spent the morning tidying the apartment and watching the news on the holoimage screen. Nothing very interesting had happened. The main item was a groundquake on Klivliviv which had killed a hundred thousand people and left some three million homeless. But Klivliviv was a long way away, and Lystra felt no real empathy for its inhabitants. She switched off the news, then remembered with a sudden burst of pleasure that she had prepared something special for this period of ennui which she had known would follow the mindprobe. With a step that was almost sprightly she returned to her bedroom.

As she glanced towards the bed, she had a momentary recollection that in one of the mindprobe scenarios she had been paired. The idea was so unlikely that she had to smile. She had never officially paired with anyone, and had never felt any great inclination to do so.

She picked up a vidbook from the table beside her bed. It was the story of Var-Lem. She shivered. That had been perhaps the most dangerous event in recent imperial history. The emperor could so easily have been killed. It was only thanks to the quick reactions of a minor security guard that he had been saved and the spy taken into custody. She smiled wryly. That minor security guard was now the Minister of Peace and Security, with a seat on the Inner Council. Indeed, it was commonly believed that Amril Gdrena, the heroine of the Var-Lem saga, was now the second most powerful person in the Empire, after only the emperor himself.

It was strange the way things had turned out. Within half a cycle of Var-Lem's abortive attempt to assassinate the emperor, the emperor had died anyway, the victim of a trillion-to-one accident in which his space ship had been penetrated by a meteor immediately after completing a hyperjump. His son was the current emperor.

She glanced at the holoimage on the wall. The eyes of the emperor looked down on her with their eternal deep pools of kindness and understanding. She felt a calm peacefulness steal over her. The Empire was truly fortunate. The current emperor was the latest in a long line of wise and benevolent leaders. The thought that someone would want to kill an emperor was incomprehensible. But then, Var-Lem had been a Union agent, and nothing the unionists did made much sense.

Even the Union's style of government made no sense. Instead of a kindly leader who possessed absolute power and was advised by a wise

Inner Council of ministers, they were led, if that was the correct term, by a figurehead who was chosen to fill that position for a period of only five cycles at a time, after which a new leader was chosen by popular referendum of all citizens of the Union. How could such a system ever have evolved? It was plainly ridiculous; could the unionists not see that the strength of a leader lay in his ability to encourage people to act in the long-term interests of the Empire — or, in their case, the so-called Free Union — instead of their own selfish short-term interests?

But it had been that way for a long time, ever since the War of Secession. The current state of distrustful peace between the two powers — the Status Quo — had prevailed for some five hundred cycles.

The vidbooks explained it all; although, naturally enough when dealing with matters of ancient history like the origin of the Empire and the Union, matters were sometimes sketchy, and occasionally the vidbooks even contradicted one another.

She put the vidbook entitled *Var-Lem and Amril Gdrena — Assassin and Savior* into its place on the shelf and removed the one she had saved for today.

It was an oldstyle vidbook, of the kind that had not been manufactured for several hundred cycles. Larger and heavier than modern vidbooks, the book had an integral flat, gray screen on which small, jerky images appeared. The images were two dimensional, unlike the three dimensional holograms that floated above modern vidbooks.

She settled herself comfortably on the bed and pressed the button to start the book. On the screen appeared words that Lystra (being an educated person) had little trouble reading, although they scrolled out of view quickly and she had to concentrate to keep up with them. Fortunately, there was a simultaneous spoken commentary.

"This is item number 165-67409 of the Kivran Central Library and Repository. This is a controlled-access item. If you do not have clearance to consult this item, you are required by law to cease its operation now. Failure to comply with this regulation carries severe penalties."

There was a pause of a quarter of a chron while viewers were supposed to wrestle with their conscience. Then the voice — low, male, authoritative — continued.

"This item is for research purposes only. It contains information that is not necessarily sanctioned by the emperor. Neither the emperor nor the government of Kivra and the Empire vouch for the truth of statements made herein."

The screen faded to gray, then the face of a man appeared. His image was blurred. The background was a monochrome of pinkish green that bled into the white of the man's face, giving it an unhealthy, cadaverous pallor. The man began to speak in a voice that was at first difficult to understand; the words were Galactic Standard, but his pronunciation and manner of speech had a quirky character that made him hard to follow.

"Hello. Welcome to this vidbook. We hope you will find it informative. If so, we urge you to purchase other copies for your family and friends. This vidbook is one of a series from Cashews of Kivra, publishers of fine educational materials. Cashews vidbooks are available wherever fine books are sold. We have stores and outlets on all the 250 planets."

The talking head continued. Lystra found it easier to lean back, close her eyes and simply listen to the man's strange speech.

"This is vidbook number 6 in the Cashews series *Facts About the Universe*. This book is entitled, *The History of the Kivran Empire*. We invite you now to watch and enjoy the book as the history of civilization unfolds before you."

Lystra kept her eyes closed. She had no interest in the animated graphics and jerky images that accompanied the narration.

There were a few moments of silence, and then the sound of quiet but appropriately majestic music issued from the book.

"The beginnings of our history are shrouded in mystery," the commentator began. "There is almost no fact about our past that has not been attacked or questioned by modern historians. However, over the cycles, a consensus has been reached about the most important features of galactic history.

"The planet Kivra is a relatively old planet. For the details of planetary formation and the physical evolution of the Universe, we commend to you number 3 in this series, *The Physical History of the Galaxy* and number 2 in the series, *The Physical History of the Universe*.

"Kivra is what is known as a late third-generation planet. It orbits the star Halbrann, which is a large, red-orange star approximately one third of the galactic radius from the central black hole. For reasons that are unknown at this time, intelligent life appeared on Kivra before it developed anywhere else in the galaxy. In fact, nowhere has indigenous intelligent life been discovered except on Kivra, the Mother Planet.

"At first, evolution on Kivra proceeded slowly, but a chance supernova explosion some 6 derns distant irradiated the gene pool of the planet's evolving population, giving rise to explosive progress, the culmination of which was ourselves: intelligent humanity...."

Lystra Ten-Wer's breathing deepened. She was asleep.

6
STRENK

Dalith, arguably the second most powerful planet in the galaxy, is slightly smaller than Kivra, the Mother Planet, but it is also denser, so that its surface gravity is $1 \cdot 02$ standard. Nearly a third of the planet's surface is open water, and it is a young planet, so that its atmosphere tends to be damp and free of the desert dust that pervades Kivra's upper atmosphere. The Dalithian star is G-class, in contrast to the Mother Planet's old, cool, orange-red star, with the result that the sky on Dalith is an odd blue color, rather than the friendly pink of Kivran skies.

Dalith was not the first planet to be colonized, far from it, but its remarkable abundance of raw materials — so different from mineral-poor Kivra — and especially the plentiful veins of high-grade pluridium ore, brought it quickly to a prominent position in the Empire. Pluridium in its pure form lies at the heart of the process for manufacturing normal-temp superconductors, and of course the Empire has always relied heavily on the ready availability of inexpensive normal-temp superconductors. It was only natural that, because it was both far from Kivra and richly endowed with a raw material for which the Empire had an almost insatiable appetite, the inhabitants of Dalith soon came to resent the fact that their planet was ruled and exploited by a distant, manipulative and apparently uncaring imperial power.

As cycles turned to decacycles, the government of Dalith slowly became more and more recalcitrant in its dealings with Kivra. Simultaneously, it pursued a policy of supporting neighboring planets whenever disputes arose with the Mother Planet. Dalith encouraged free and strong trade amongst the nearby planets, helping their economies far more than did faraway Kivra, and gradually Dalith assumed the rôle of protector and leader for a large fraction of the galaxy. In this way, Dalith forged a substantial, although untested, power base.

Eventually the inevitable happened and the Dalith system requested full independence from the Empire, the first system with the temerity to do so.

At first, the emperor seemed not disinclined to agree to Dalith's request. Encouraged by this benign response, the governments of several other planets with close ties to Dalith also requested independence.

Negotiations began and seemed to progress satisfactorily, albeit with considerably less speed than the Dalithians and their neighbors desired. But at last the documents were signed and independence was granted.

On the return journey from the signing ceremony, the ship carrying the jubilant delegates was attacked and destroyed by a Kivran fleet. The Dalithian defense system provided Dalith only five hectachrons' warning that an armada of imperial ships was hurtling across the galaxy in a series of well-planned hyperspace jumps with the obvious intention of teaching upstart Dalith and its friends a lesson they would never forget.

What followed was, from the Dalithian point of view, nothing short of a miracle. Every ship capable of fighting or harassing the oncoming fleet was launched, not just from Dalith, but from more than twenty other nearby worlds. The two massed fleets met on the outskirts of the Zveng stellar system. The Empire arrived with ten times as many ships as the small fleet that had coalesced under the banner of "The Dalithian Union of Free Planets." Or at least so the Kivrans thought. But as soon as battle was joined, it became clear that the true situation was quite different. The Kivran Minister of Peace and Security had made the mistake of thinking that the Empire was united in its desire to crush the rebellious spirit of Dalith. He now learned the magnitude of his error, for large numbers of imperial ships whose commanders and crews were from the region of the galaxy near Dalith began to defect to the Dalithian side.

The Empire made its first retreat less than a rotation later, bloodied beyond anything it could have expected.

Thus began the War of Secession. The unofficial Dalithian Union of Free Planets quickly renamed itself the Free Union of Independent Planets, and the Union and the Empire found themselves engaged in a long and bloody war.

Eventually, the Union won its freedom from Kivra and the Treaty of Empire and Union was signed, establishing the Status Quo. Since then, Dalith's benign rule has extended over a full third of the galaxy.

All this is well known, of course. Every child in the Union learns these facts in elementary school.

But for the first time since the signing of the Treaty of Empire and Union, the Status Quo was at risk. And the fault belonged to just one man.

————————

Tcharn's normally relaxed face was tense; lines etched themselves around the corners of his mouth as his teeth involuntarily came together in a clench. Normally easy-going and companionable, the stress of the past few rotations was beginning to take its toll. Deputy Strenk's words were only adding to that stress.

Strenk sat awkwardly in the chair across the desk from his superior, unable to get comfortable, fidgeting and causing the chair to move under him every few decichrons.

Strenk was in a difficult position. He had agreed to, and even supported, Operation Kālek, but that was before President Rahl had been elected.

Part of him was chagrined that such a well-planned operation could have gone so badly awry. But part of him, he had to admit, was pleased to see Tcharn's evident discomfiture, for Tcharn, so long Strenk's protégé, had finally overtaken his mentor and now Tcharn was in charge; for Strenk in particular the adjustment had not been easy.

Deputy Strenk looked across the pawlwood desk at the furrowed brow of his superior. Tcharn was worried, as he had every right to be. Tcharn opened his mouth to speak.

"You're sure about all this, Strenk?"

"Certain, sir. The message came through late yesterday, encoded with Val-Dor's personal cipher, on the link reserved for priority traffic. And the expedition I sent out confirms it. Everything fits."

Tcharn shook his head wearily.

"Run it by me again, Strenk. One last time. Maybe I can see a flaw."

Both his voice and his face told Strenk that Tcharn was clutching at straws. There was no flaw in their reasoning, and they both knew it. But Strenk went through it all again. He tried to speak evenly, but it was difficult given the gravity of the situation.

"Rum-Lem made his attempt on the fifteenth rotation of this month. On that rotation, the databoxes estimated the probability of success at 99.35%. One could not hope for better odds than that."

Tcharn nodded.

"We have only a sketchy report of what happened. As Per-Lem had indicated, the warning systems in the residential wing of the palace went down for 99 millichrons for a maintenance switch-over precisely at noon. Val-Dor was watching as Rum-Lem entered the palace in the moment the system was down. There was no alarm. That was the last time Val-Dor saw Rum-Lem.

"We know that Rum-Lem failed. The emperor has appeared on a several live holoimage broadcasts since the fifteenth. But we don't know *why* he failed, and until Val-Dor's report arrived, we had no idea what might have happened to Rum-Lem.

"Val-Dor waited two rotations before going to the spaceport. When he got there, Rum-Lem's ship had gone. That's all we knew until this latest report came in."

The deputy paused.

"It could just be a coincidence, you know."

Tcharn shook his head. "We both know it isn't. Continue."

"Well, there wasn't much Val-Dor could do except remain undercover and keep a lookout for anything suspicious. If Rum-Lem had been captured, then neither Val-Dor nor Per-Lem had any realistic hope of escape. But it seemed very unlikely that the Empire had caught Rum-Lem. Rum-Lem was under strict orders not to allow himself to be taken alive, and...."

"I know, I know. Don't remind me."

Strenk moved on.

"Anyway, Per-Lem sees all the reports from imperial monitorships in the demilitarized zone. She has informed Val-Dor that a cryptic signal came in from a ship designated 35/CW. That ship is a chronon monitor, in orbit around a system containing the inhabited planet

Tirsh. There is a regressed human population on Tirsh, and the
monitor is there in case they discover how to timeshift, at which point
presumably the Empire will move to annex the system, although why
they would want another backward and doubtless rebellious planet I
certainly don't know."

"No political commentary please, Strenk. The facts alone are bad
enough."

"Sorry, sir. Anyway, from Per-Lem's report we know that a chronon
burst was detected by 35/CW approximately seventy five chrons after
Rum-Lem entered the palace. The timing is consistent with the
possibility that he was running back to Dalith. The signature reported
by 35/CW matches precisely what we would expect if a timeshift
weapon had been fired at a large object somewhere in the vicinity of
Tirsh. And by 'large object,' I mean something...."

"...roughly the size of a spaceship. Yes, I get the picture."

"On my own authority, I dispatched two ships fully loaded with
instrumentation to take a discreet look at the Tirsh system. I know
it's an illegal act, but I told the pilots to be careful and to get out of
there if there was any sign of trouble; I felt that we could always come
up with a plausible cover story if things got out of hand. Anyway,
when they reached Tirsh there was no trace of any imperial ships. But
there was still some residual from the chronon burst. They measured
it and their numbers were consistent with Per-Lem's report.

"The pilots searched for tachyon signatures in the vicinity of 35/CW.
They found no inward jumps, but there were tachyon traces corresponding to four outward jumps. All appeared to be jumping back
towards imperial lines. The jumps occurred shortly after the chronon
event."

"So you're postulating that Rum-Lem was trying to escape, that he
was followed by four imperial ships, at least one of which was armed
with an illegal timeshift weapon, and that they caught up with him in
this out-of-the-way system in the demilitarized zone, where he was hit
with the timeshift weapon."

"That's my reading of the facts, yes, sir."

"Then tell me this, Strenk: why use an illegal weapon when they
could simply have blown him to pieces with photon missiles? If they
were close enough to timeshift him, they were certainly close enough
to destroy him."

"Because that would have left traces, sir."

"So did the timeshift weapon. It left the chronon burst."

"Only because we knew where to look. If it hadn't been for Per-Lem and Val-Dor, we'd never have known about it. And if we hadn't dispatched the ships to investigate immediately, we still wouldn't have found anything. The chronon burst had already decayed to almost nothing. If they had blown him apart with a photon missile, the evidence would have been there for rotations."

"OK. Maybe. But why isn't there any evidence for any inbound jumps? If you're right, five ships entered the system and only four left. But you haven't found any entry tracks. Those tracks should be easy to spot."

"Yes, sir, and I've been puzzling over that. The only thing I can think of is that the ships might have exited hyperspace very close to the system's star. The emissions from the star would hide the evidence of their arrival — remember, sir, how Tel-Villard used that trick once in a simulated battle? He evaded the defense team's monitors by exiting hyperspace next to a star. They had no warning of his attack, and he won the game. Perhaps Rum-Lem remembered that trick. Or perhaps he had no time to plot a good jump, and simply exited hyperspace close to the star by chance. The others would have been following him. In that case, none of them would leave any trace of an inbound jump. And if he completed a jump close to the star he would have had to run for it, because the spacetime curvature would be too extreme to allow him to jump again. And if the imperial ships were faster than Rum-Lem's, or if their weapons had a sufficiently large range...."

"Yes. All right. You've made your point. There are a lot of ifs, but I suppose it's at least possible. At the very least we have the evidence of the chronon burst. So we have to assume that Rum-Lem has failed and that he's floating around in some other time, or wherever you go after you've been blasted with a timeshift weapon."

"Yes, sir. I'm afraid I think that's about right."

Tcharn suddenly looked much older than his 55 cycles.

"Well," he said heavily, "I suppose I have to accept that. But now we are left with another problem. What do we do about Per-Lem and Val-Dor? Do we leave them in place? Is there any point to that? Might we get another chance at the emperor? Or do we try to get them out?"

Strenk did not answer. This was not his decision to make. For once he was grateful that Tcharn and not he was in charge.

7

HWANG

Hwang Lee awoke with an ache in his bones, a crick in his neck, and an uncomfortable, dirty, wet feeling all over the lower half of his body. Slowly, he drew himself to a sitting position and looked around.

The sun was high in the sky and the day was equatorial-hot. He was sweating, and dribbles of perspiration tickled his cheeks.

He was sitting on the muddy periphery of an island. The river moved sluggishly past. The island was almost in the middle of the river, which was perhaps a hundred and fifty meters wide at this point. Lining both banks was an unbroken wall of trees.

To the northwest a line of distant, haze-wrapped hills was visible above the trees. Not far away to the west was a single tree-covered hill.

Hwang sniffed the air. There was a faint odor, something undefinable and unrecognized. He remembered the odor from last night, although it seemed fainter now. Looking across the water towards the nearest bank there was no visible sign of animal life, but he could hear the screech of birds coming from the jungle.

Hwang dragged himself to his feet.

Slowly, he made his way around the circumference of the island. It did not take long. The island was about fifty five paces long and about a third as broad, with its length aligned along the course of the river. There were a few trees, reaching to a height of perhaps six meters, but most of the island, which nowhere extended more than a meter above the level of the river, was covered by a virid carpet of broad-leafed grass. There was a large clump of bushes at the northern end, weighed down with orange berries that might or might not be poisonous. Tentatively, he nibbled half a dozen to assuage his hunger. They tasted good, but he dared not eat any more in case they were toxic. There was no sign of animal life anywhere on the island.

While he was exploring, Hwang periodically tried his wristcom without success. He looked up at the sky, and suddenly he realized something that had been niggling at the periphery of his consciousness. It was not possible, of course, but it was hard to argue with the evidence of his eyes.

He shielded his eyes and examined the sky meticulously. There was not the slightest trace of a skycar. Not one. He suddenly realized that the same had been true last night. In his momentary glance at the night sky he had been so relieved to see Orion recumbent overhead that he had given no thought to the absence of lights from skycars.

It made no sense. It was simply not possible, at any time of day or night, to look at the sky anywhere in the world and fail to see the evidence of people journeying from one place to another. There was nowhere on the face of the Earth — and that went especially for places near mega-cities like Rabundi — where the sky was not perpetually marked with the evidence of mankind scurrying overhead. Lights at night, contrails during the day: there was no way to avoid them; they were ubiquitous. And yet, last night he had seen not a single moving light in the firmament. Just as now there was a similarly impossible lack of contrails. The sky was deep, blue, neverending... and empty.

Hwang shook his head and methodically searched again, starting close to the horizon in the south and ending a couple of minutes later low in the north. There was nothing. Simply nothing.

Suddenly, a loud *crack!* rent the air: the sound of wood splintering somewhere on the bank where he had fallen into the river last night.

A flurry of brightly colored birds rose from the trees, screeching raucously. They circled noisily a couple of times, then formed themselves into a small flock and flew across the river with slow, heavy flaps of distended wings. They disappeared into the foliage on the far bank. Whatever had disturbed the birds remained hidden.

Hwang tried the wristcom yet again, but his mind was busy grappling with the problem of the empty sky. The train of thought was simple; its ramifications were terrifying. If there were no skycars overhead, then perhaps there were no satellites. And if there were no satellites, then perhaps there were no cities. And if there were no cities, then perhaps there were no people....

He shook himself, then sat down in the shade of one of the trees. The wristcom gave its tedious *Unable to complete connection* message and Hwang held his head in his hands and tried to think.

What was the last thing he remembered before he woke up last night in the jungle? That was easy. He had gone though it all once already, before that gorilla-creature had found him. But he forced himself to walk through it again, in case there was something he had forgotten the first time.

He had started the experiment in the ground-floor lab of the physics tower. The quantum bubbles had been created, just as they always were. They had begun to move together, just as they always did. But this time there was something different. The change that he had made to the control program had had the intended effect. This time, the bubbles had been stable. Instead of disappearing into nothingness, the bubbles had maintained their integrity as they moved towards the center of the guidance cylinder. As the bubbles had approached one another there had been a surprise, something that neither he nor Ekbu Tbamti had expected. Instead of coalescing and destroying one another and thereby creating a short-lived region free of gravity, the bubbles had instead gone into orbit around each other. Had the orbit been stable? Had it decayed quickly, to be followed by the expected coalescence? Hwang furrowed his brow, but he could not remember. The next thing he knew was when he had woken up sprawled on the floor of the jungle.

He tried to approach the problem differently. All right, so he knew how he had got here: it must have been an unexpected side effect of the experiment. But where exactly was *here*?

He was close to the equator, there was no doubt about that. The river looked similar to the Rabundi River, which ran northward through the city not far from the university campus. Of course, the Rabundi River had long ago been tamed and bridged. There was no jungle near that river, for Rabundi was a modern, gleaming metropolis that straddled both its banks and extended many kilometers into the surrounding jungle.

He stopped as the beginnings of a horrifying thought began to coalesce about the germ of an idea. It was a very odd coincidence. If it was a coincidence.

About a kilometer from the physics tower was a bridge across the river. The Rabundi River was broad and sprawling, and its bridges required several support posts to span its width. But there was one bridge that was different from all the others. Its central column did not disappear into the slow-moving, murky waters of the river. Instead it stood on the firm ground of a small island, an island that gave the bridge its name: the Murinni Island Bridge. Murinni Island was only a small thing, hardly worthy of being called an island. It must be about fifty or sixty paces long. And maybe twenty paces across. And less than a meter high.

Hwang looked across the water toward the small hill to the west. It was a gentle rise that rose perhaps thirty or forty meters above the level of the surrounding terrain. He tried to imagine what the skyline must look like from Murinni Island if one could somehow eradicate all signs of civilization. Yes, it was entirely likely that Government Hill would lie in that direction. And the line of hills in the distance to the northwest: they could easily be the Scipatti Mountains, couldn't they?

He tried to remember how far he had run last night when he was trying to escape. It was impossible to be certain — he had been running for his life — but it was all too plausible that he had run exactly the distance between the physics tower and the Murinni Island Bridge.

He groaned, because now he knew exactly where he was.

For several seconds, he felt nothing but a terrible, empty despair. He brought his emotions under control. It was too early for despair. He was not powerless, not yet. He was an intelligent, trained physicist, one of the brightest people in the world — the thought that perhaps he was the *only* person in this world was rejected even before it could percolate into his consciousness — and if anyone could understand how he had got here, and how to get back, it was Hwang Lee. He just needed to think logically. There was some way back. There had to be.

All right, he thought to himself, he knew where he was: on Murinni Island. So now the question was: *when* was he?

The question was perplexing, because it was one that theoretically should never have to be asked. Although Hwang could not remember all the details of the proof, he knew the results that mattered.

It was obvious that he was not in the future. Any amount of time sufficient to remove all traces of Rabundi City would be more than enough to change drastically the geography of the area. The course of the river would alter; Murinni Island itself would be washed away or left high and dry. And anyway it was inconceivable that *all* traces of the vast metropolis of Rabundi City could be completely erased. He couldn't be in the future.

So could he somehow be in the past? It would not have to be a very large leap into the past, for this part of Africa had remained undeveloped until little more than a century ago.

But there was a powerful and convincing reason why that was impossible. Romig's Second Law of Information Flow, formulated two hundred years earlier and experimentally verified hundreds of times, stated that time travel into the past was impossible.

He corrected himself. Romig's Second Law said no such thing. What it did say was that information could flow in only one direction along the time quasi-continuum; in fact, the direction of information flow was, *inter alia*, an indicator of the direction of the flow of time in any sufficiently large multi-dimensional closed system. There were two major consequences of this theorem, along with a whole host of minor ones. The theorem's principal lemma was that one could learn only about events in the past, never about ones in the future; and the corollary of this lemma was that if time travel were possible (Romig's Laws said nothing about the feasibility of time travel), then it was a one-way process: transportation to different points in the timestream, if it was possible at all, could occur only into the future, never into the past. So he could not be in the past. But he already knew he was not in the future.

And yet the only other hypothetical eventuality was equally impossible. It had been known for almost as long as Romig's Laws that there was no physical reality to the idea of parallel worlds, even though the notion of such worlds ("parallel timestreams," they were usually called) was one that was useful in performing certain calculations in quantum probability. A long time ago, fictional stories about people who had slipped from one timestream into a parallel one had been quite popular, but these had gradually slipped out of vogue as slowly the notion of parallel universes became merely an abstract, somewhat abstruse, calculational tool in advanced quantum physics. While it was theoretically possible that parallel timestreams existed, it had been proved conclusively that it was not possible for an event in one timestream under any circumstances to affect events in any other timestream. Thus, travel between streams was not possible.

But suppose theory was wrong and he *was* in some sort of a parallel universe. The bifurcation between his own world and this one must have occurred a long time ago, for there was no trace of a city here; there was no trace of worldwide wristcom communication; there was no trace even of air travel.

It occurred to him that this evening he should make a point of looking carefully for artificial satellites when the sun set; that would be a good test of the level of technology in this parallel universe — if that indeed was where he was.

He was somewhat cheered at this idea. Partly because it gave him something to look forward to, and partly because he found himself comforted at the thought that he had probably solved his problem. It was obvious that he was not in the future. And Romig's Second Law was so well tested that it was unbelievable that it contained an error. Therefore, he *must* have moved into a parallel timestream. There was no other sensible explanation. And surely it was impossible that he could have travelled to a parallel timestream whose course had bifurcated from his own timestream so long ago that there would be no artificial satellites. Technological invention always proceeded quickly, and that would surely be true in any parallel timestream, including this one.

Cheered at the prospect that tonight he would receive incontrovertible confirmation that he was not alone, Hwang looked with renewed hope at his surroundings.

The sky was beginning to cloud over. The clouds expanded as he watched. Within an hour or two, they would grow to enormous thunderheads which would deluge the forest. The cycle would be repeated most days until the end of the rainy season.

He stopped. It had been getting towards the end of the rainy season in Rabundi. Hwang shivered at the thought that perhaps, in a parallel timestream, exactly the same clouds were forming over the splendor that was Rabundi City.

He turned away from the sky and looked instead across the river towards the near bank. He should go back and check on the equipment. The bank wasn't far away. It wouldn't take long to reach it, especially if he removed his clothes for the swim.

He immediately began to suit the action to the thought. For a moment he hesitated when he reached his underpants, then he realized what a false modesty it was, and removed them as well. He gathered his clothes into a ball and tied them around his neck.

He looked up and down the river. He couldn't remember if the Rabundi River had ever been infested with crocodiles or hippopotami or other dangerous animals. Most likely it was, long ago. But there were nothing in sight right now; slowly he slid into the water.

He swam breast stroke, moving with an economy of effort and making as little noise as possible. The river carried him some way downstream, but after a couple of minutes he reached the shore without incident and pulled himself out of the water. He dressed and then began to pick his way through the trees.

The forest was dense at the water's edge. A wall of greenery stretched from high above his head all the way down to the surface of the river, so that even though he knew he was no more than ten paces from the river, it was both invisible and inaudible. As best he could, he headed for the place where he reckoned the physics tower lay in his own timestream.

The jungle was a noisy place. Trees groaned as they grew. Twigs made sharp scuttering sounds as they fell from high above. There was the chatter of small animals coming from somewhere not far away, and from everywhere came the high-pitched call and stridulation of insects. Above all these were the neverending calls of unseen birds.

The air under the canopy was still, heavy and sodden. He was moving through a strange, almost surreal greenish twilight, even though beyond the canopy it was early afternoon. Vines meandered incessantly across the jungle floor and extruded thick, snake-like tendrils that wound up the trunks of the trees.

At last he saw the imprint of his own footstep in a patch of mud. The vines here had been trampled down, making a kind of path. He began to follow the trampled vines.

A few minutes later, he reached what remained of the quantum bubble experiment. He looked around suspiciously, looking for the animal — whatever it was — that had caused him to flee last night. Apart from its massive footprints on the ground near the equipment, there was no sign of the creature.

Hwang began to check the equipment for damage. Then came the first distant rumble of thunder, and a new worry gripped him.

In a short time, perhaps only a few minutes, it was going to rain. The equipment was designed to function in a carefully controlled, air-conditioned environment. Who could say what might happen to it if it were exposed to an equatorial rainfall? It had already been exposed to the sodden air for a day or more. Looking carefully, he could see tiny spots of rust on the surface of the guidance block. A downpour might easily ruin the equipment forever.

He looked around for something to cover it. The vines were too tough: although the leaves were a good size, they were almost impossible to break off. On the ground were some old, dead leaves, large but brown and brittle, which would be difficult to keep in place but might be of some use. There was nothing else at hand.

Working quickly, he manhandled the rest of the equipment so that it was gathered against the guidance block; then he began to cover it with the brown leaves. It was a frustrating affair: the leaves tended to slide away from where he placed them unless he weighted each one individually with a small rock, and there were precious few of those to be found. The leaves were too brittle to be folded to conform to the contours of the equipment or to be jammed into spaces to supply anchorage. After about ten minutes, he stood back to survey his work, puffing with exertion. It would not do: the rain would seep through the gaps between the leaves in no time. He had accomplished nothing.

Thunder, which had been rumbling sporadically in the distance while he worked, suddenly crashed nearby. The canopy overhead was as opaque as ever, but the small gap created by the gorilla's display of strength showed an ominously dark sky. Did he have thirty seconds, or five minutes, or half an hour? He had no way of knowing, but in any case he could not afford to wait. He had to get the equipment covered.

He removed his clothes and stretched them over the most sensitive equipment. Almost all of the large guidance block was still exposed, but there was nothing more he could do.

He turned and, naked except for his shoes, ran as quickly as he could back to the river, following the trail he and the gorilla had made.

At the riverbank there was a break in the trees where he and the gorilla had crashed through. Through it, he could see the sky. Dark clouds loomed, and lightning flashed intermittently.

He began ripping at the large leaves that grew here in abundance. There was one kind of tree in particular that had leaves similar to those of a banana. The leaves broke off easily, and in little more than a minute he had as many as he could carry. Clutching the bundle of leaves, he headed back to the equipment. The first heavy drops of rain hit the canopy above.

He reached the equipment just as the first drops began to seep through the canopy and fall to the ground. Flinging the leaves into a pile, he began to jam them into angles in the equipment, bending and molding the leaves to the contours of the electronic gear. By the time he finished, a downpour was in progress.

Thunder crashed in sharp cracks. The rain fell in a hard sheet. Instead of giving the air a fresh, clean scent, the rain seemed to emphasize the smell of decay, so that the air was filled with the pungent aroma of rotting detritus.

Naked except for his shoes, Hwang stood in the middle of it all. There was nowhere to shelter. Rain was falling everywhere. He sat on the damp ground and waited for the storm to pass.

After perhaps an hour, the rain began to abate. The canopy brightened as sunlight began to shine on the far side. The rolls of thunder weakened. Hwang got to his feet and brushed off the dirt that clung to his body. He tentatively lifted one of the leaves covering the equipment and felt underneath. There was a layer of dampness, but nothing more. He sighed audibly, relieved that a possible disaster had been averted.

Suddenly, there was a flash of motion in the corner of his eye. He turned sharply to face it.

The force of the impact flung him sideways.

There was a hideous, eldritch caterwaul near the left side of his face, as if an immense cat had decided to exercise its vocal chords directly into his ear. A moment later, something thudded into his left shoulder. He lost his balance. As he hit the ground there was a blur on his left. Simultaneously there was an agonizing pain in his shoulder.

He had been attacked by a species of large cat. One outstretched claw was buried in Hwang's shoulder, ripping the flesh. The cat thrust its face forward and opened its mouth, exposing two rows of vicious teeth. Hwang pulled his head away just as the cat's jaw snapped closed. One of the cat's teeth left a trail of blood on his cheek. If he had been a fraction slower, Hwang would have lost part of his face.

There was no time to think. Acting on instinct, Hwang jumped to his feet, the cat swinging from his shoulder, its claws grabbing a deeper purchase in his flesh. Hwang balled his right hand into a fist and smashed it down on the creature's skull. He screamed in pain as the animal contracted its claws. Hwang ran to the guidance block, the cat hanging crazily in front of him, and he smashed the cat between himself and the unyielding metal, pounding his fist again and again against the animal's skull.

The screeches from the animal were horrific as Hwang pounded, swaying backward and forward, crushing the animal against the metal, then moving away, then crushing it again. Suddenly the claws retracted and the animal dropped to the ground. Hwang kicked out and caught the cat a glancing blow on the shoulder. The cat lashed out at his leg, leaving a series of deep, parallel cuts. Hwang kicked out again and this time, more by luck than judgment, his shoe connected with the animal's jaw.

The cat's forequarters were lifted from the ground by the force of the kick. When it landed, it took a step backward. Hwang moved forward and kicked again, pressing his advantage. The cat leapt backwards, dodging the kick. It hissed ferally one last time and then suddenly turned and trotted off silently into the trees. In moments, it was gone.

Hwang leaned against the guidance block and slid, exhausted, to the ground.

He remained this way for some time. Blood seeped from his shoulder. The cuts in his leg were narrow but dangerously deep. He realized that he could not afford to fall asleep, much though he wanted to. If he slept now, he might never wake up.

With his left hand he pressed the wounds in his leg closed, and the flow quickly congealed and stopped. His right hand he clamped against the torn flesh of his left shoulder. Here he was less fortunate: the blood continued to flow.

Wearily, he clambered to his feet. Now he recognized for the first time the precariousness of his situation. He felt ominously light-headed. On the ground where he had been sitting was a small pool of blood, seeping into the jungle floor. He began to lurch in the direction of the river.

Never had a kilometer seemed so far. He lost track of time as he stumbled forward. It occurred to him that he could have used the leaves that were protecting the equipment as a sort of bandage or tourniquet, but when he had the thought he was already a hundred meters from the equipment, and in his confused state it seemed to him that it would be easier to continue walking until he reached the river than to turn around and to try to dress the wound.

It was fortunate that the cat did not return, for Hwang made an easy target as he dragged his feet ever more slowly in front of each other, stopping frequently to rest against the trees. His legs wobbled and he fought to stay upright, for he knew that if he once collapsed, it would be that much harder to get up again.

All logical thoughts receded. His mind was filled with only one idea: to reach the river. What he would do when he got there was something he was incapable of considering. His whole purpose in life now was simply to reach the water.

On and on he went.

At last he arrived.

His hand was caked to his shoulder. His neck was stiff and he could not turn his head. The bleeding at his shoulder seemed to have stopped, but he did not dare to move his hand in case it reopened the wound. He stood for several seconds on the bank of the river, confused, looking out across the water toward the island, trying to think. At length he sat down on the bank and eased himself slowly into the water until his shoulders were awash.

He rested with his back against the bank and his feet buried in mud to act as anchors. The water was marvellously cool. It was the most wonderful thing he had ever felt. He closed his eyes.

The next thing he knew, he was suddenly chilled. Opening his eyes, he saw stars burning brightly in a clear sky. He felt distinctly better. His head was no longer filled with wool; he was going to live.

Venus hung over the river to the west, casting a silver glow over the landscape. Looking up at the familiar constellations, he remembered his self-appointed task for the evening. For a long time he remained where he was, in water up to his neck, gazing at the sky, searching for the telltale motion of an artificial satellite. He saw two meteors race across the sky. But there was no other movement.

Strangely, he was not worried. It was somehow better to know the truth. And anyway right now he had more pressing problems to deal with. His right hand was still caked to his shoulder. He eased his hand free. Fresh blood began to flow, dribbling down and mixing with the river water. He cleansed the wound and then climbed up on to the bank, where he leant against a bush and considered his position.

His stomach contracted painfully.

When had he last eaten? He couldn't work it out, but he knew it was a long time ago. He tried to remember whether he had seen anything that might be edible, but his memories were fuzzy and confused. Even if he found food, what then? How long could he survive? And was survival even worthwhile? Was he trapped in the middle of an unexplored continent, the nearest civilized humans thousands of miles away? Or were there no civilized humans here at all? Had he somehow jumped timestreams and landed in a parallel universe in which humanity did not even exist?

He shifted his position, trying to get more comfortable. He willed himself to think other, more useful thoughts. Simply staying alive was going to be difficult unless he brought some sort of order to his life. He needed an encampment, some place he could defend against predators like the cat and the enormous creature of last night. The island was the obvious place. Yet then he would not be near the equipment, and if he really was located in a parallel timestream his only chance of return was to reenact the experiment in the hope that he might transfer to some other timestream in which humans had at least reached this part of Africa. But before he could do that, he needed to understand what had happened to him, and that would take weeks — if not months — of concentrated effort.

Perhaps, if he could understand what had happened, he would be able to change the parameters of the experiment so that he could return to his home timestream. Perhaps.

He would need the computers for that. Tomorrow, he would see about getting power to them. He realized that he had not even looked at the power cube. Was there even enough power left to run the computers?

Part of him wanted to get up right now and go back to the equipment to check the status of the power cube. But he was tired, and still weak and lightheaded. He curled into a fetal position, clutching his knees to his stomach. For a while he listened to the sounds of the jungle; gradually he slipped into sleep.

8

LYSTRA

It was the morning of the second rotation following the mindprobe, and Lystra Ten-Wer awoke feeling much better. Gone was the uncomfortable, quasi-drugged feeling of lassitude, and she jumped out of bed and waterdoused quickly, keen to start the day. The waterdouse seemed more than usually refreshing, as if it were removing the last particles of the dirty feeling in her mind along with the sheen of perspiration from her body. Things were back to normal. It was going to be a good day.

As she dressed she called out, "News, please," and listened to the morning's reports from around the Empire.

Nothing of import had happened overnight. The governor of Sylra had been killed in a freak accident while travelling to Kivra for talks to settle the dispute regarding the Sylran contributions to the imperial defense fund. The groundquake on Klivliviv that had been reported yesterday had turned out to be only a precursor to a major quake that had struck overnight; there were now an estimated 50 million dead or injured and twice as many homeless. Kivra had filed a formal (but predictably futile) complaint against Dalith protesting an unauthorized entry into the demilitarized zone. The Dalithians had responded by filing a similar complaint against Kivra. In short, there was nothing of interest.

She went into the kitchen for firstmeal. She bolted the food as soon as it was disgorged from the machine, anxious to get back to work and deal with the backlog that undoubtedly had built up. She hurried from the apartment as soon as she had finished eating, eager to beat the rush of workers who would soon be clogging the hover-routes.

Lystra joined the line at the hoverbus stop outside the building. She experienced a momentary flashback to something that might have been a dream but wasn't. During one of the mindprobe scenarios she had been waiting in the hoverbus line, just as she was waiting now. She closed her eyes, shook her head, and tried to think of something else.

When she opened her eyes, a couple of people in the line were looking at her curiously.

"Mindprobe flashback," she explained.

They nodded their heads sympathetically. They understood.

The hoverbus arrived, as punctual as ever. As she was taking her seat she felt a momentary inexplicable surge of adrenalin. She cast her eyes around the bus, trying to discover what had caused it. It was several moments before she saw the man sitting on the opposite side of the aisle. She did not know his name, but she knew that he too had been in the mindprobe scenario, although what his part had been she could not remember. He was dressed casually in rough workclothes and his face was sun-browned, from which she deduced that he was some sort of manual laborer who worked out of doors, perhaps in the gardens of the imperial palace.

She felt an odd movement in her lap. Looking down, she realized that her hands were trembling. She looked at the man again to see if he was watching her; but no, he was looking out the window, oblivious to her presence. Whoever he was, he had not even noticed her. She began to feel calmer. It was all just a trick of the mindprobe. In another few rotations there would be just a few forgotten memories buried deep in her unconscious. Until then, flashbacks and sudden surprises were to be expected.

Lystra made an effort to forget about the gardener (or whatever he was) and to concentrate instead on the view out the window as the hoverbus headed for the city center.

By the time the hoverbus reached the Ministry of Peace and Security, Lystra had forgotten about the man. She disembarked into the docking corridor. Together with more than a hundred others, she walked briskly towards the enormous bank of elevators that served the three-hundred-story structure.

An elevator whisked her up to the 91st floor where the floor receptionist greeted her with a warm smile as Lystra placed her thumbprint on the pad of the work-recorder.

"Good morning, Lystra. We missed you. Glad to have you back."

"Good to be back, Ven. Take my advice: don't ever take a job where you have to be mindprobed. It's not fun."

"Too late for that. My next probe is scheduled for fifty rotations from now."

"You mean you have to be probed too?"

"Sure," said the receptionist. "Everyone who works on this floor gets the pleasure of a probe once per cycle. Even the janitors. Too many secrets, I suppose, not that I ever see any of them. Still, I don't suffer too badly from probes; it doesn't affect me like it does some people. I'm always back on the job next rotation."

Lystra laughed. "Well, if you ever want to change places with me, let me know. I hate the thing, it makes me feel so..." — she paused, trying to think of the right word — "...sullied," she eventually concluded. "You know what I mean?"

"I suppose so. Still, it doesn't hurt, and it doesn't take too long; at least that's something."

"I suppose. And it's better to be safe than sorry, I guess. Although what a spy could hope to learn from DI-1 I certainly don't know. Well, Ven, it's good to be back, but I can't stand here chatting. All those reports need my attention, and I'd better attack them before I'm inundated with new work. I'll see you later."

Lystra paused outside her office and placed her thumb on the entry pad. The door slid open. Everything was exactly as it always was: the walls bare except for the holoimage screen which she kept switched off, preferring dull gray to the distraction of moving images, no matter how serene. The only items on her desk were the databox and a small voice recorder into which she dictated notes. The room was a model of efficiency, and contrasted sharply with the offices of the few co-workers whom she occasionally visited. Were it not for the case of vidbooks that lined one wall and the mug on the desk one might be forgiven for thinking that the office was unused.

Lystra started the databox. She sighed when she saw the work that had piled up. It was worse than she had expected. It was amazing how many reports had come in in the past couple of rotations.

Putting everything else out of her mind, she set to work.

Lystra Ten-Wer's official job title was "Intercept Intelligence Officer — First Class — Demilitarized Zone." Its subtitle was "Head Officer — Sector QA-11." All told there were nearly a thousand people in her division, DI-1, most of whose job it was to collate, analyze and archive the continual stream of data coming back from the robot monitorships in the demilitarized zone. Lystra was the youngest of the fifty two people who headed the groups responsible for individual sectors. The sector that was her responsibility, QA-11, was located some two thirds of the galactic radius out from the central black hole, in one of the spirals. She had been in the job half a cycle. She had applied for the post with no real expectation of success (she was too young) but to her surprise Supervisor Qwilm had offered her the job on the strength of her performance on the aptitude test.

Scattered throughout sector QA-11 were more than two hundred monitorships. This was more than usual, for two reasons. Firstly, one of the systems in the sector had once been colonized. The planet Tirsh was one of the half dozen or so planets that had regressed after colonization, so that although there was now a thriving human society on Tirsh, there was no collective memory of Kivra, hyperspace travel, or anything concerned with the fact that it had once been a colony. Seven monitorships circled Tirsh's star, monitoring radio transmissions from Tirsh and retransmitting them back to Kivra along pencil beams.

The second reason for the relatively large number of ships in QA-11 was that the far end of the sector abutted Union territory. Most of the two hundred monitorships were at the distal end of the sector, eavesdropping on communications within the Union and providing a stream of information to be processed by the databoxes of the workers whose job was to monitor QA-11.

Lystra's job involved a certain amount of direct monitoring, but the major part of her responsibility was to review the daily reports from the other workers in the sector.

She spent her morning reviewing reports. A few, as usual, called either for investigation or independent verification. Those that warranted investigation she forwarded to Supervisor Qwilm. Those that needed verification she marked and put to one side so that she could examine the databases for collateral evidence once she had completed her backlog. One monitorship had apparently malfunctioned, causing her to sigh in exasperation. Monitorship failures were rare, but the ones at the far end of QA-11 were always especially troublesome to repair because of the proximity of the Union boundary. Any repair ship sent that far into the demilitarized zone would have to be met by a Dalithian ship and then escorted to the repair site. The repairs would be carefully inspected and verified by both parties. It was a tedious process, and it would be many decarotations before monitorship 4/RS would be functional again.

She broke off for secondmeal, and then returned for another stint at the databox. Lystra was determined to finish the reports before she went home, even if she had to work late.

It was not until late afternoon that she saw the red report.

She had just started to look at the reports that she herself was responsible for screening. The moment she brought up the overview on the databox, she knew that something unusual had happened.

The databox screen presented her with a listing of the night's reports. There were about fifty of them; at the top was a single red line. Red reports were very rare. She had seen only one before. The memory caused a momentary flicker of annoyance. On that occasion she had forgotten to forward the report to her supervisor as regulations required, which had led to a painful interview with Supervisor Qwilm and the only negative entry in her file. She would not forget this time.

She touched the line and the report expanded. It was from monitorship 35/CW, which, she recalled, was the same source as the earlier red report.

The report was terse and incomprehensible. It contained two lines:

$$3546285 \cdot 12, \ 5 \cdot 2, \ 7 \cdot 159$$
$$19764 \cdot 3217 \ 361 \cdot 47$$

The numbers meant nothing to her. But she didn't need to understand them: her job was simply to forward the red report to Supervisor Qwilm. She returned to her work, and by the time she left work late that evening she had almost forgotten the report from monitorship 35/CW.

9

HWANG

The pain in Hwang Lee's leg was getting worse. Although the wound in his shoulder where the cat had dug into muscle and sinew was much deeper than the light scratches along his leg, it was the leg that was festering.

The pain had travelled downward to his ankle and he was having difficulty walking; his entire leg was beginning to swell. He had managed to swim back to the island, where he was at least relatively safe; but if his leg continued to worsen he might soon be marooned, and there was not enough food on the island to keep him alive for long.

Water was less of a problem: he could drink the foul-tasting river water as he had been doing for the past... how long was it? two days? three? He looked at the sun, which was falling towards the forest on the far bank. Three days, he decided, fighting waves of light-headed confusion.

He felt his brow. It was hot and filmed with sweat. He wondered if his sickness was from the wound, or was it associated with the acute diarrhea that had plagued him for the past day or so?

And to cap everything, there was the reptile. He could not see it at the moment, but he knew it was not far away: a giant crocodile-like creature at least five meters long, which periodically cruised by the island, thrusting its way through the water with nonchalant flicks of its enormous tail. The crocodile would pause as it passed, regarding him malevolently. The croc clearly understood that if it was patient, Hwang would weaken.

Hwang's stomach wrenched. He stood painfully and shuffled a few steps to distance himself from the small area where he had made his camp. He squatted and tried to empty his bowels. There was almost nothing, just a few wet dribbles. He passed his hand over his brow again. He was trembling.

He sat down on the grass, his head throbbing, his leg aching. He touched the skin near the long parallel claw marks on his leg, and yelped in pain.

The sun set, and the abrupt coolness revived Hwang a little. In his low fever, everything seemed slightly surreal, not quite believable.

The jungle was filled with the calls of millions of insects. He drifted into sleep.

When he awoke, he felt much better. A cool breeze had sprung up, and a dark shadow in the north indicated the presence of a massing cloud blotting out the stars. He could smell rain on the air. The jungle was noticeably quieter.

He touched his leg. The pain was not as bad as it had been earlier. He looked towards the shore, and as he did so, his stomach growled in hungry complaint.

On the spur of the moment, he made a decision. He couldn't afford to stay here. He hobbled slowly to the water's edge.

Easing himself into the warm, muddy water, he struck out in a feeble one-legged breast stroke towards the closest shore. He was halfway there before he remembered the giant crocodile. He pressed on. His mind seemed detached, as if he were in a dream and the worst that could happen was that he might wake up. Maybe the croc was just a figment of his imagination. Maybe he was delirious. His hand brushed against something, and he realized that somehow he had reached the shore. Grasping a root, he hauled himself up on to the bank.

He sat panting for several minutes. There was a rumble of thunder not far away. A minute later several flashes of lightning were followed by a nearby crash and then by the patter of rain.

Drops plopped heavily into the river. Within seconds, the rain became a downpour. Drops thudded on to his head. He hauled himself wearily to his feet and made his way into the shelter of the jungle.

After a couple of dozen paces, he sat down, his back against a tree with a wide umbrella of branches. He closed his eyes, and listened to the sounds around him.

The insects were all but silent, their high-pitched calls replaced by the continuous rumble of distant thunder and the occasional sharp cracks of its closer counterpart. The air was sweet with moisture and life.

He must have nodded off for a while, for suddenly the storm was over and the air was heavy with the incipient heat of a new day. Enough stray light percolated through the canopy to tell him that beyond the trees the sun had risen.

He pulled himself to his feet. He tried his weight on his bad leg. It didn't seem any worse. He decided that he would spend the day gathering whatever edible fruits, berries and nuts he could find, then carry them somehow back to the island. If he could gather enough food to keep from starving for a couple of days perhaps he could give his leg enough rest to recover completely.

Cheered that he had a positive plan, he made his way back to the river.

The sun was — as always — hot, even though the day was young. He was thirsty, and he momentarily contemplated drinking from the slow-moving, muddy river. His stomach, like his leg, was improving, but he decided to wait for a while in the hope that he would be able to slake his thirst with fruit or berries instead of river water. Maybe the water was the cause of his diarrhea.

He headed upstream along the bank until he reached the trail back to the equipment.

When he reached the equipment, he saw that vines were already beginning to encroach on it. Rust spots had appeared on the guidance block and a layer of aluminum oxide covered much of the exposed metal.

After recovering his clothes and putting them on, his first task was to examine the power cube. Without power, he was lost. Nervously, he opened the hinged door to the compartment in which the cube resided. His heart sank. The cube was 90% depleted.

Ten percent should be enough to run all the equipment, but it probably wasn't enough to replicate the last run. There had been a tremendous power surge just before everything had gone wrong. Another surge like that would deplete the cube in moments, before the experiment could run its course. If only he could figure out what had actually happened during that last run. Perhaps that was where he should start. There was enough power to run the computers for a long time — years if necessary — and with their help surely he ought to be able to understand what had gone wrong.

But then, with a sinking feeling, he realized that even with power, the equipment would not work for much longer. The humid heat of the jungle would see to that. A few rust spots hardly mattered, but their presence indicated that inside the guidance block the delicate electronics were being attacked by the hot, moisture-laden air. It would not be long before the equipment was reduced to a pile of useless metal, glass and plastic.

But maybe he would be able to solve the problem quickly. It might take only a matter of days, not the months that he feared. If he could accumulate enough food to be able to work without distractions for a few days, perhaps he could figure it all out; and then he might be able to find his way back. Perhaps. If the equipment still worked by the time he had finished. And if there was enough power in the cube.

He tried not to think about how unlikely it all was, how small the likelihood of success. Instead, he began to roam the surrounding jungle, picking all the fruit that looked edible and stashing it in his pockets and an old bag that had survived the explosion, until he could carry no more. He took the food back to the equipment and added it to a growing pile, then repeated the exercise.

He continued in this way all day, careful not to overexert himself, although gradually the work took its toll, so that by mid afternoon he was using a stick for support, which severely restricted the amount of food he could carry. Yet he continued doggedly on. There were nuts in profusion under a species of tall tree with a broad canopy of leaves. On smaller trees bushes he found several varieties of succulent, sweet fruit that slaked his hunger and quenched his thirst.

As the afternoon wore on, the sky began to cloud over, although the only indication of this under the canopy was a gradual deepening gloominess. By late afternoon his leg was hurting too much to continue. And he had yet to think of a way to get any of what he had collected safely across to the island.

The air, always hot and humid, seemed to carry an extra burden of moisture. He forced himself to take deep breaths, pulling the heavy air reluctantly into his lungs.

With no warning the storm broke. A flash of lightning illuminated the canopy and he began to count, gauging the distance. Thunder shook the ground just as he reached "two."

The next flash was even closer. Somewhere nearby a flock of birds rose screeching raucously from the trees.

In less than a minute, Hwang was soaked. Trees rocked wildly in all directions as violent swirls of wind pulled them first one way and then another. The sun may or may not have set; darkness had certainly fallen, but whether it was caused by the setting of the sun or the violence of the storm it was impossible to tell. Rain fell heavily into the soft, half-rotted floor of the jungle with thumps that coalesced into a ponderous rumble.

He tried to move his cache of food so that it was sheltered by the equipment. It was so dark, except for those moments when lightning flashed, that he worked mostly by touch.

He caught his leg on the sharp edge of a piece of equipment and cried out in sudden pain. He touched the wound, and his hand came away wet — not with the clean wetness of rainwater, but with the sticky, viscous wetness of blood.

Enough! he decided.

He sought shelter on a small shelf that ran the width of a metal cabinet. Curling himself into a fetal position, he could just fit himself into the small cavity, where he was reasonably protected from the rain. His teeth, despite the warmth, began to chatter. He closed his eyes.

Somehow, he drifted off to sleep.

He awoke once in the night. The storm had worked itself out. He tried to unroll himself from his fetal ball and gasped sharply in agony as his cramped muscles protested. At last he managed to stand, and he hobbled across the sodden ground, his feet squishing in mud, to the guidance block. He climbed painfully on to its surface, then stretched out on the hard metal, one hand dangling over the side, the other resting against the glass of the cylinder in which the quantum bubbles formed. Slowly, his muscles relaxed. He forced himself to take slow, deep breaths, and after a while he drifted back to sleep.

He awoke with a scream, his universe filled with sudden, excruciating agony. He jerked upright. In the gray-green of a new day, Hwang could see the jungle cat hanging from his side. Its long, bared teeth were clamped to the skin of his torso. From the cat's mouth issued a feral whine of bloodlust. Blood, Hwang's blood, stained the fur around the cat's mouth.

Hwang clenched a fist and drove it as hard as he could into the side of the creature's head. The cat rolled with the blow, but its teeth remained tightly locked about Hwang's flesh. The cat pulled and Hwang's tissue gave way, ripping open and exposing a rib.

For an instant, the cat's eyes met Hwang's. In them, Hwang saw a disconcerting trace of intelligence, as if the cat was merely toying with him, testing him to see how he would defend himself against attack. Without thinking, Hwang lowered his head until it was only centimeters from the cat's face and then, with every ounce of his strength, he screamed directly into the creature's left ear.

The startled animal released its hold. Dropping to the ground and backing away, its whine became a throaty roar. It shook its head several times, as if it had been temporarily deafened. Hwang climbed off the guidance block and dropped to the ground close to the cat; but his leg buckled as his foot hit the ground and he fell forward. For a moment, their eyes met. They were both on all fours, separated by no more than half a meter. Hwang thought he saw uncertainty in the cat's eyes. He lunged forward, screaming. It was enough. The cat turned tail and disappeared into the jungle.

Hwang collapsed spread-eagled on to the muddy ground, tears of pain rolling down his face, dirt entering the massive wound that the cat had inflicted.

The next few hours were the worst that Hwang had ever experienced. His mind was filled with a haze of pain from which there was no escape. He was no longer capable of coherent thought and he knew it, like a man who is unpleasantly aware of his own drunkenness. For a while he remained prone on the jungle floor; but eventually the thought percolated into his consciousness that he was too exposed and it was only a matter of time before some creature found him; and when it did, he would be unable to offer any defense. Somehow he had to retreat to some place where he could rest and regain some strength.

He crawled to the cache of food. Much of it had been spoiled by the downpour, and a layer of mildew had already formed, but he stuffed his pockets with nuts and as much of the soft fruit as he could carry. He ate from the pile of berries, ignoring the dank flavor of mold, until he could eat no more.

The only place where he would be safe was the island. Dribbling berry juice from the corner of his mouth, he began to crawl in the direction of the river.

Never had a thousand meters seemed so far.

Hwang forced himself into a rhythm: he counted to five, then dragged himself forward half a body length; then he stopped and counted to five; then he dragged himself forward again.

His lacerated side screamed at him to stop. He tried to crawl with only one hand, limiting the dribble of escaping blood with the other. His leg screamed its protests, but slowly the equipment fell behind.

It was mid afternoon by the time he reached the river. He almost slithered headlong into it as he lifted handfuls of the muddy, silty water to his lips, long past caring about diarrhea.

He rested, but not for long. The sun was already halfway to the horizon. If he did not leave now, there might be no second chance. He had left a trail of blood and sweat a kilometer long for animals to find. If he did not reach the island, he would never survive the night.

He wondered how far he would be carried downriver. With the water flowing faster now because of last night's storm he was not at all sure that he could reach the island before being swept past. But he could not face the thought of dragging himself farther upstream. He lowered himself into the river and sighed in temporary pleasure at the revivifying coolness.

He experimented for a couple of minutes, trying to find the least painful way to propel himself forward. He settled on a kind of sidestroke on his left side, using only his right leg to propel himself forward.

He moved slowly away from shore. Just as he had done earlier, he settled into a rhythm: *one* and kick and *one* and kick. Every stroke took him a little farther from the shore, a little closer to the island. But all the time, whether he was kicking or not, the current was carrying him downstream. All too soon, he was nearly level with the upstream extremity of the island, and he knew that if he did not swim faster he would be swept past.

He started counting more urgently, forcing himself to ignore the pain: *one*-kick-*one*-kick-*one*-kick. He tried not to watch the island moving past, but it was impossible to ignore. He was more than halfway there now, yet the island was already at its widest part. Every moment now he was carried a little farther downstream, and the island became a little narrower, and he had to swim a little farther to reach safety.

There was only one chance.

Refusing to acknowledge the pain, he rolled on to his front and began to swim an untidy, splashing crawl. He pulled air into his lungs, then expelled it in an agonized underwater shout, then desperately sucked in more air.

With every stroke now, he was moving closer to the island. A shadow passed overhead, darkening the water all around, but he was too busy to pay it any attention. He reached out with his arms, kicked with his legs, sucked in air, and expelled it underwater in an excruciating rhythm that was his only hope of survival.

Moment by moment, the island came closer. He was winning the battle. He tried to pull even more strongly, increasing his tempo. Now he could see the downstream end of the island every time he came up for air. He was so close now, so close. Four more pulls, three..., two.... The very tip of the island was in front of him now, just out of reach; beyond the sliver of land, the width of the river stretched away an impossible distance to the far shore.

His left hand touched something at the nadir of a stroke. He lowered one foot and it caught in the muddy bottom of the river. He lowered the other foot. For a moment there was a tug of war as Hwang leant into the current, trying to push forward while the river tried to drag him downstream, away from the island. He pushed, and gained a few centimeters. The island rose out of the water no more than a couple of meters in front of him. One and a half meters. One. He fell forward. The water was only knee high. He crawled the last half meter, finally escaping the river's watery grasp. Then he collapsed.

A motion caught his eye, and he looked up to see, no more than six meters away, the monster crocodile whose existence he had completely forgotten. Its eye glinted, and it took a step closer.

There was nothing more he could do. He had given his all. He had nothing left.

His head fell to the ground and he watched helplessly as the crocodile took another step closer.

10
TCHARN

Deputy Strenk was sitting opposite Chief Tcharn.

Tcharn said, "You're quite sure you've told me everything?"

"Quite sure, sir."

The defense chief nodded slowly. "Because if there's anything — anything at all — you haven't told me, now's the time to do so, before I go before the president. I have to know everything if I'm to handle this properly."

It was common knowledge that the erstwhile friends were poles apart on the issue of the Status Quo, but even so it shocked the deputy that Chief Tcharn could suspect him of withholding information. After all these cycles, did Tcharn not know him better than that? Strenk might not share his superior's quasireligious fervor for the Status Quo, but he would no more have thought of hiding something than he would have thought of..., well, than he would have thought of committing any other crime that might endanger the Union.

Tcharn continued: "As I assured you at the beginning of this conversation, Deputy Strenk, the recorders are, unfortunately, malfunctioning this morning." Tcharn smiled briefly before spelling it out. "So anything you tell me now will be unverifiable."

He paused for a moment, took an audible breath, and continued, "And I give you my word that anything you say will bring no retaliation from me." The chief of defense smiled tensely at the man whom he had once considered his friend and mentor, and was now his heir apparent. "I need to be sure that I know everything; that's all. I'm sorry. I have to ask."

Strenk looked at the man on the other side of the pawlwood desk. Tcharn was not actually sweating, but he looked as if it were a close thing. It occurred to Strenk that he was seeing something new: Tcharn, perhaps for the first time in his professional career, was truly worried. Strenk had known his news was bad, but only now did he begin to realize just how bad it was. Perhaps the débâcle that Operation Kālek had become was even enough to bring Tcharn down.

Taking everything into account, it was possible that the president might even be pleased. President Rahl's election platform, for the first time since the Status Quo had been instituted 500 cycles earlier, had included a commitment to increased openness and communication with the Empire. President Rahl's landslide victory had been in large part due to his enlightened attitude on the subject of defense; but since his election his promises to seek to normalize the Union's relationship with the Empire had been strangely unrepeated, even though the polls continued to indicate that it would be a popular move. It was possible, even likely, that the president's reluctance to move forward was due to Tcharn's uncompromising stance against any change.

But when President Rahl heard the latest news, surely he would demand Tcharn's resignation.

To replace Tcharn President Rahl would doubtless choose someone considerably less fanatical about the Status Quo; he would choose someone with a reputation for reasonableness; he would choose someone, in fact, like Deputy Strenk.

Strenk suddenly found the room uncomfortably warm. He realized that Tcharn was watching him and, try as he might, he discovered that he could not hold his superior's gaze. His eyes slid away and he found himself looking through the large window of Tcharn's ninety-fifth floor office, focussing on the distant blue sky.

"There's nothing else to report, sir," Strenk said. "Operation Kālek was implemented exactly as you planned it. You know I would never endanger your...."

Tcharn nodded. "All right. Of course I believe you, Strenk. But I had to ask. The safety of the Union depends on how we respond to this, and I have to know everything that might be relevant."

Tcharn's face suddenly cleared, as if he had seen the way through to the solution of a knotty problem.

"You are dismissed. I must prepare for my meeting with the president."

Chief Tcharn stared at the door for some time after it had slid closed.

It would be difficult to imagine two more different people than Chief Tcharn and his deputy. Tcharn was fifty five, and at the height of his career. He was round-framed and red-faced, with thinning hair and a ready smile. Strangely, he had reached his current position by earning the trust and friendship of the man who had just left his office.

At sixty two Strenk had a body that would be the envy of many men little more than half his age. Wiry and lank, with a shock of gray hair, he moved with a nervous jerkiness that contrasted with Tcharn's smooth, relaxed, fluid motions.

It was Strenk, then merely Deputy Section Head Strenk, who had first recognized Tcharn's potential. Thirty cycles ago, Tcharn was merely a security advisor on Qintir. During a routine tour of inspection from headquarters, Strenk had been so impressed by Tcharn's drive and intelligence that he had offered him a promotion to return to Bureau headquarters on Dalith as Strenk's personal adjutant.

Tcharn had accepted, and as Strenk rose through the bureaucratic hierarchy, so did Tcharn. But Tcharn was not just a mouthpiece for Strenk: he had his own opinions about defense and was not afraid to share them with anyone who cared to listen. He was hawk to Strenk's dove, and the pair made a formidable combination in presidential briefing sessions.

It was widely assumed that it was only a matter of time before Strenk was appointed chief of defense. Tcharn, naturally, would be his deputy. But it had not turned out that way. President Sar-Lon had been so impressed with Tcharn's uncompromising insistence that only by maintaining a constant vigilance could the Empire be kept at bay that when the post became vacant it was Tcharn, not Strenk, who was appointed chief. Strenk had been forced to swallow his pride by agreeing to serve as Tcharn's deputy.

Since then, it was no longer true that the two were close friends. A hint of guilt on Tcharn's side, and a jealousy that refused to die on Strenk's, saw to that. But until candidate Rahl's election manifesto was published, there had been no great rift between them. Rahl's manifesto emphasized their one real difference: Rahl, like Strenk, felt that the Status Quo had lasted long enough, and it was time to begin talks with the Empire with a view to dismantling the centuries-old barrier between the two powers. To Tcharn, such talk bordered on treason, and when candidate Rahl became President Rahl, a deep wedge had been driven between the chief and his deputy. Both men were aware of the fact; neither was entirely certain what its eventual outcome would be.

Tcharn removed a couple of items from a drawer and placed them in a pocket; he gazed briefly out the huge window, then he turned and strode purposefully from his office.

The air traffic databoxes cleared the lanes so that Tcharn's hovercar could proceed at full speed. Within moments, the hovercar reached its cruising speed just below the speed of sound.

The hovercar's windows darkened automatically under the intense ultra-violet of Dalith's G-class sun, turning the sky dark blue, almost an imperial indigo, and accentuating the grays and browns of the city that reached to the horizon.

The sun glinted off the myriad planes of the city below. Telborn, the largest city in the Free Union of Independent Planets was home to nearly half a billion people.

The hovercar was already over what had once been the residential outskirts of the original city. Now low buildings and high-rise offices bedaubed with the multicolored logo denoting government buildings were intermingled with the blighted edges of an impoverished residential area. A short distance ahead was the immense green area that had once lain beyond the city's perimeter and in which stood the original governor's residence — now a museum and preserved historical site — and which more prosaically acted as Telborn's major park and recreation area.

It took nearly a full chron for Tcharn's car to cross Telborn Park, before greenery was replaced once more by the metallic gleam of civilization. Now the buildings were relatively modern. Expensive living quarters climbed high into the sky next to new office buildings and small industrial parks. Telborn had become over the years a tight confederation of quasi-autonomous boroughs each of which housed, more or less, a million people. From the air it was impossible to tell where one borough ended and another began.

Tcharn turned away from the window, glanced at the clock, leaned back more comfortably in his plush chair, and closed his eyes. He nodded off for a chron or two. His eyes flickered open when the descent warning sounded. A glance outside confirmed that he was approaching the small hoverport reserved for high-ranking ambassadors and bureau chiefs on urgent government business.

The hovercar landed and, even before the warning lights had been extinguished, Tcharn was on his feet. He stepped through the ship's exit and on to the plush carpet of the VIP entrance lounge. Five guards bowed deferentially.

"Follow me, sir," one of them said.

The president's office — "The Study" as it was universally known — was located some distance from the hoverport. Tcharn and his guide walked down two hallways, rode an elevator up two floors, walked down a short corridor and then halted before an enormous door on which the presidential insignia of indigo and gold was lightly embossed. The guard stood to one side, bowed deeply, and invited the Union's chief of defense to enter.

Tcharn stepped forward. The invisible security devices scanned his body for concealed weapons and his face was checked with infrared lasers to confirm his retina and pore patterns; then the door slid open. He entered the Study, head lowered, looking at the deep-pile maroon carpet into which the presidential insignia was woven. Halting inside the doorway, he made a stiff, formal bow. As yet he had not even looked up to see if the room was occupied.

He remained stationary for a long moment, putting himself entirely at the mercy of his superior, indicating that he was the president's to command, symbolically inviting the president to kill him instantly should he so desire. The president, of course, did no such thing.

Instead, he simply said, "Well, Chief Tcharn, so here you are. Sit down."

Tcharn looked up.

The president was seated behind the ancient desk that had been hewn from a single massive pawlwood tree, a gift to the man who had served as the commander in chief of the rebel forces in the early days of the War of Secession and who had been elected first president of the Free Union of Independent Planets before the war was half a cycle old. The effect was calculatedly impressive, but it was lost on Tcharn.

The president gestured irritably at the seat in front of Tcharn.

"Sit down, Tcharn, and tell me what's been going on. Everything. I need to know."

"Sir?"

President Rahl lost his temper. The president half stood, leaned forward, and pounded the desk. His face reddened as he shouted.

"You know exactly what I mean, Tcharn. You — or someone — authorized a covert operation in imperial territory. A man named Rum-Lem was involved. I was never informed. I never authorized it — and you know I never would. Tell me about it. Now. All the details. Everything. Then we'll decide what's to become of you."

As he regained his seat he was breathing heavily.

Tcharn was unmoved by the president's outburst. He answered calmly, as if he were explaining a technical point to a none-too-bright youngster who by some quirk outranked him — which, more or less, was exactly how he viewed the situation.

"Mr. President, your statements are not entirely correct. When you took office, you signed a blanket authorization that all defense operations were to continue until completion or until their annual review, whichever came first. You made no exception for this operation. Its annual review is not due for another quarter cycle. You *have* authorized it, at least until then."

"Don't play the lawyer with me, Tcharn."

Tcharn shrugged. "It's called Operation Kālek, sir."

"Kālek?" The president looked blank.

"Yes, sir: Kālek. It's a tree indigenous to the planet Qintir. The kālek is an odd-looking tree that has unusually deep roots and lives for a very long time; it seemed appropriate.

"The basic idea behind Operation Kālek is fairly simple, albeit extremely dangerous.

"We sent an operative undercover to work in the Empire's Ministry of Peace and Security, which, as I'm sure you know" — Tcharn knew that it was highly unlikely that the naïf president really did know this — "operates the Empire's covert operations. The agent's brief was to intercept information that might be useful to us."

He paused, giving the president an opportunity to refute this statement. How much did the president really know? The president remained silent, and Tcharn relaxed. The president apparently did not know the real objective of Operation Kālek.

Tcharn continued. "Unfortunately, our agent Rum-Lem was discovered. We don't know how. But we do know that he tried to make a break for it and return to Union territory. He left Kivra hotly pursued by imperial ships.

"He must have made several hyperspace jumps, hoping to lose them. Eventually, he jumped into the demilitarized zone, probably hoping that his pursuers would not follow, but apparently they did. They caught up to him in the Tirsh system, which is close to our border with the zone. He nearly made it home, sir, but not quite. We monitored a transmission from an imperial reconnaissance satellite in the Tirsh system."

Tcharn paused once more and scrutinized the president's face. He wanted to see what effect his next words were going to have on the leader of the Union.

"Apparently, sir," he continued, "they used a timeshift device on Rum-Lem. He no longer exists in our timestream."

Tcharn fell silent. There was nothing more to say. There was only one reaction possible to this revelation: blazing fury mixed with a desire for retaliation. The Empire's use of a timeshift device on a fleeing spy signalled a willingness to abandon the terms of the Treaty of Empire and Union. And that could lead to anything. Even war.

He waited for the president's anger to flare. But there was nothing. Nothing! At most, there might have been a slight tightening around President Rahl's eyes. But he remained silent. The president simply sat behind his desk, looking at Tcharn as if he were waiting for more. But what more could there be? Use of a timeshift weapon changed everything. Didn't the president realize that?

Tcharn found himself wondering how the president would have reacted had he known the true nature of Rum-Lem's mission. He probably would have sided with the Empire. The thought chilled him: it was becoming more and more clear that the president's campaign rhetoric was not something merely to enthuse the masses, but actually reflected his beliefs. Apparently, the president was willing to hand the Union over to the Empire without a fight.

But before he could do that, he would have to remove Tcharn from his post.

The silence continued, each waiting for the other to break it. At last, the president said, "So? What else do you have to tell me?"

"Sir? I don't think you understand."

Tcharn would explain it in the simplest possible terms. Perhaps President Rahl simply did not grasp the ramifications.

"Timeshift devices are explicitly banned by the Treaty of Empire and Union. It is one of the few clauses in the Treaty that, so far as we know, neither we nor the Empire have ever breached. There have been controlled tests, of course, and both sides have maintained timeshift capability, but the fact that one side has now seen fit to fire a timeshift weapon on the other fundamentally alters the relationship between us. We cannot simply proceed with business as usual."

"You mean to tell me that you're honestly concerned about the Empire using a proscribed device, even though, it seems to me, we gave them ample provocation? I will not discuss the matter further. It is obvious to me that you have outlived your usefulness, Chief Tcharn. I expect your resignation in writing on my desk first thing tomorrow. I shall appoint your successor immediately."

And now Tcharn understood. This meeting had little to do with the loss of an agent, the use of a banned weapon, or even whether the Status Quo should be maintained. It was about the president's need for an excuse to remove a defense chief with whom he fundamentally disagreed. What the president had seen in Tcharn's explanation of events was not an unconscionable violation of the treaty, but simply an opportunity to rid himself of Chief Tcharn.

Well, if the president wanted to play rough....

The president said, "This interview is terminated, Tcharn. Leave."

Tcharn remained in his seat and raised a quizzical eyebrow as he shook his head.

"Mr. President, I will not submit my resignation."

"Then you are fired, as of right now. Get out of here before I call a guard. You no longer hold a position in my government. You will be escorted to your office and observed while you remove your personal effects."

Tcharn stood. The president leaned back and smiled weakly.

But instead of turning to leave the room, Tcharn felt in his pocket, then gently placed a kill-gun on the pawlwood desk.

For several moments, neither man moved.

"It's not loaded," the president eventually declared.

"Quite so," Tcharn agreed. "You know it can't be loaded because the security scanners would have detected it if it had been, and of course your guards would never have allowed me to walk in here with a loaded weapon."

He paused for a long moment, his eyes firmly on the president's face. The president's eyes flickered between Tcharn and the kill-gun. He looked nervous. As well he might.

Tcharn continued, "Yet you aren't quite sure, are you? The security system should have detected the weapon even though it isn't loaded. And the guards should have taken it from me, shouldn't they?"

"Get out of here before I have you arrested."

The president began to reach for the button under his desk that would bring the guards.

Tcharn snatched up the kill-gun and aimed it directly at the president's chest.

"Lean back, sir, away from the desk. I'm afraid I cannot permit you to call the guards yet."

The president halted, his hand half way to the button. He weighed the situation then began to edge forward.

"As you yourself said, it isn't loaded."

Tcharn pointed the weapon, and squeezed.

There was a dull thud and a large fragment of the president's desk was transformed into a splintered mass of wood.

The president leapt backwards. The barrel of the kill-gun followed him.

Tcharn reached into his pocket and withdrew a small golden cube, perhaps half a thumb's length on a side. He held it up for the president to see, then slipped it back into his pocket.

"To put it crudely, Mr. President, it's a wideband jammer. It enables me to walk through the most sophisticated security detection devices while carrying a loaded weapon such as this. It also permits me to speak freely, knowing that your recording devices are incapable of recording anything that happens in this room while I am carrying the jammer. Now," he adopted a conciliatory tone, "I suggest that we both take our seats and continue this discussion in a more friendly atmosphere. Believe me, sir, I have no desire to be confrontational. After all, we are both working for the same side. Please sit down, sir." His voice was honeyed with sincerity and reasonableness.

He gestured towards the president's chair as he eased himself into his own seat. Tremulously, the president sat down.

Oozing lenity, Tcharn continued, "Sir, you must understand: I have only the interests of the Union at heart. Not your interests, not even my own interests, but the Union's. You must believe me when I say that, to put it bluntly, the Union cannot afford to be without me in this crisis. Whatever your other advisors are telling you, I can assure you that there is absolutely no chance for a peaceable relationship with the Empire. In fact, in my estimation, we are closer to all-out war than at any time since the Status Quo began. Their use of the timeshift weapon is only one indication of that, but it is an important one. You must realize that not only did they use it, but they must have known there was a good chance we would find out. They will be watching now for our response. If that response is for you to ignore it and to go to the emperor with a request for increased trade and closer links, they will interpret that not just as weakness but as idiocy. They will be delighted to enter into extended negotiations; then, whenever it is convenient, they will launch everything they have. And we... how would we be able to respond if that attack came a few cycles from now? What are your plans for defense, sir? No, there's no need to answer, we both know. You want to wind everything down quietly, canceling a contract here, weakening our defenses a little there. A few cycles from now, if Amril Gdrena's generals attack us with a fleet of ships — especially if those ships are equipped with timeshift weapons — they will be able to blast their way in here and take whatever they want.

"Sir, I know how the imperial mind works. And I certainly under-stand the mind of Amril Gdrena. I've studied her for many cycles. I'm not scaremongering. I simply can't let you play into her hands. It's true that you are the president. But you are *only* the president. The Union is more important than any individual, even a president. I know you mean well, and I wish I could let you proceed with your grand plans for galactic peace, I really do. But I'm sorry, I just can't."

"I will have you killed for this, Tcharn."

The president, predictably, had not been listening.

"You could try, sir, indeed you could, but I advise you strongly to think about the consequences. Consider this: presidential security guards are appointed by my bureau. Every presidential security guard has a subliminal command burned into his subconscious before he is permitted to serve. If I am removed from office involuntarily, you will be killed, sir, by a member of your élite guard. The same is true if I die under suspicious circumstances. And, in addition, there are other precautions I have taken but which I am afraid I cannot reveal. You *would* die if you killed me, sir. You have my word on that."

The president hunched in his chair, suddenly a beaten man. It was all too much. He had known that Tcharn was not to be trusted, but this? This was unconscionable. When he finally spoke, it was in little more than a mumble.

"But why, man? You've had a good, some would say a great, career. Why not just leave peacefully? There's no need for any of this... this... treason."

He gestured vaguely towards the part of his desk that the kill-gun had destroyed.

"It's simple, sir. You are the first president in my lifetime who honestly believes that the way to security is through friendly relations with the Empire. But I know that, on the contrary, that is the way to destroy the Union. I cannot afford... no, the *Union* cannot afford for me to allow you to remove me from my post, leaving you free to give it to someone who thinks that in weakness lies strength. That is politicians' talk. You may love the Union passionately. I'm sure you do. I'm not questioning your patriotism as you are questioning mine. But I am more than questioning your judgement; I am refuting it and will continue to do so as long as I live. While I am alive, the Empire will always know that the Union is strong, so strong that it would be madness to attack us."

"But you just told me they used a timeshift weapon. Is that not an attack, or at least the threat of one?"

"No, it was a test."

"A test?"

"Certainly. They wanted to see how we would react. And I will initiate an appropriate response in due course. Now, sir, with your permission, I will leave, and we shall hear no more talk about resignations or dismissals. Understand?"

The president nodded reluctantly. "For the time being, Tcharn, you will remain in your position. About that I obviously have no choice. For now, you have beaten me. But only for now. You will regret this, Tcharn, I promise you that."

Tcharn considered this for a moment, then nodded. It was enough. Without another word, he turned and walked to the door.

"Tcharn?" the president called after him.

Tcharn turned to look at the president.

"You've made a powerful enemy today, and you will live to regret it."

Tcharn did not reply. The door slid open and he left the Study.

As the door closed behind him, Tcharn had already put the confrontation behind him. He was consumed by two questions: who had given Rum-Lem's name to the president, and why had that person waited half a cycle to tell the president about him?

11

TCHARN

Tcharn entered his well-appointed apartment in Telborn's exclusive Borough 32. He poured himself a drink and stood for some time at the window of the penthouse apartment, looking out over the city as dusk fell. Lights came on. Five hundred million people, all gathered in one place. It was hard to credit it. The largest city in the galaxy, larger even than Kivra City on the Mother Planet. Five hundred million people going about their lives — eating, sleeping, working, procreating — and hardly one of them giving any thought to the possibility of war with the Empire. The Status Quo had lasted so long now that it was taken for granted; the possibility of war was almost unthinkable.

But if President Rahl had his way, there would soon come a day when they would all have to think the unthinkable, a day when young men and women would once again be called to die for their freedom. Unlike his president, Tcharn understood Amril Gdrena: the moment she thought the odds were stacked sufficiently in her favor, she would attack.

There was a sudden sharp cracking sound, and Tcharn looked down to see he had been squeezing so hard that he had crushed the cup, cutting his index finger. A drop of blood began to swell at the cut; he hurried to the kitchen before it dripped to the floor.

It was not worth using the healing unit for such a minor wound, so he simply wrapped a clean handkerchief around the cut as a makeshift bandage. He disposed of the broken cup and selected a replacement. He was on the point of pouring himself another drink when the security computer announced: "Deputy Chief Strenk to see you."

Tcharn halted. Strenk lived in the same building, but social calls between the two men were now a rarity. Tcharn pondered for a moment before deciding that Strenk was probably simply impatient to discover what had happened at his meeting with the president.

"Let him in," he called, and the door slid open to admit his erstwhile friend and mentor.

For a moment the two stood facing each another. Unlike Tcharn, Strenk did not smile; his lips were compressed in a tight line.

"Come in, come in, Strenk," Tcharn said cheerily. "You'll join me in a drink?"

"Do the facts call for one?"

"You mean: do we still have our jobs? Or are you asking if the president had converted me to pacifism? The answer to the first is: Yes, at least for now; and to the last: No. But perhaps you're right. Even a little alcohol muddles one, and now you're here I have no excuse not to try to get to the bottom of everything. Perhaps you can help me decide what to do about the situation. Take a seat."

He waved airily around the spacious living room, and Strenk settled himself comfortably in a chair that silently conformed itself to his contours. Tcharn plopped down heavily opposite his deputy.

He took half a chron to compose himself, then he said, "The question is, what do we do now?"

"About?"

"About Operation Kālek. It's falling apart at the seams. Until now, I've been prepared to let Per-Lem and Val-Dor remain in place, but I'm beginning to think that's too dangerous."

"Why now in particular? Is it something to do with the timeshift weapon?"

"Partly, yes. Has there been any progress on getting confirmation?"

"Yes. They're still working on reducing the error bars, but so far the chronon burst is still consistent with a timeshift weapon being used in the Tirsh system."

"And it's true, isn't it, that the only thing we know of that can cause a chronon burst is a timeshift field?"

"Yes. I've had one of our technical people look at the profile of the chronon burst and he says that if it came from Tirsh, then it must have been a fairly small field."

"How small?"

"He wouldn't commit himself. You know what these techs are like. But he did say he was pretty sure it wasn't big enough to timeshift anything as large as a ship."

"So... smaller than the first burst half a cycle ago?"

"Yes, definitely."

"I don't understand what Amril Gdrena thinks she's doing. It's clear enough, I suppose, why they didn't simply blow up Rum-Lem's ship as he was trying to escape. If they'd done that, we would have immediately broadcast the news that they had killed a citizen of the Union who had mistakenly wandered into the demilitarized zone. But why didn't they just let him come back? He was only a gardener; he didn't have access to any secrets. All he'd done was make an unsuccessful attempt on the emperor's life. If they'd been able to capture him alive, he'd have been invaluable, if only for propaganda purposes; but dead or timeshifted he was worthless. And Gdrena must have known she was running a grave risk of detection when she used a timeshift weapon." He shook his head. "It was a pointless escalation, an unnecessary change in the Status Quo. For five hundred cycles neither side has used a timeshift weapon. Now she's used two in half a cycle. Why? And what was she firing at this time? None of it makes sense."

"Perhaps she's testing us."

"That's what I told the president: Amril Gdrena showing her strength. He bought it. But I don't.

"If she *is* testing us, she's chosen a particularly stupid time to do it. She has to know that President Rahl was elected on a peace platform. Why would she jeopardize that? She should be overjoyed at the prospect of peace. As I keep telling everyone — not that anyone seems to listen — peace talks are the best thing that could happen as far as she is concerned. Peace would make us easier prey than a sleeping vagren."

For a while neither of them spoke. Eventually, Tcharn sighed and said, "I think it's time to recall Per-Lem and Val-Dor."

"Why? They're still sending us good information. I may support the idea of peace talks, but I don't see why we should withdraw our best assets."

"This second chronon burst has me worried. Amril Gdrena is up to something, and I don't know what. That makes me nervous. I don't like being nervous, especially where Amril Gdrena is concerned. Remember, Rum-Lem was a gardener in the imperial gardens, and so is Val-Dor. If someone launches a sufficiently thorough check into Val-Dor's background, they'll find enough holes that they'll begin to suspect him. They may not give him time to commit suicide when they move in. And if Val-Dor is caught, not only would we be unable to get Per-Lem out, but Val-Dor would give everything away the moment he went under the mindprobe. He wasn't conditioned to resist like Per-Lem was. We'd lose both of them as well as Rum-Lem — and, worse, Amril Gdrena would learn everything they know. It would take us decacycles to recover from that kind of setback.

"For all practical purposes Operation Kālek is dead now. We should cut our losses and get them out. The information we get from Per-Lem is interesting, but hardly important; she's not high enough in P&S. And if she or Val-Dor is discovered, the cost to the Union will be far greater than any gains we might make if they remain in place. At this point the risks far outweigh the possible benefits. I'll tell Val-Dor to close the operation at the earliest opportunity."

Strenk nodded. "I'm sorry it had to end like this. Even if I didn't agree with it, it was a good plan, Tcharn."

The chief grunted. Tcharn's normally jovial face was grim.

"You don't look very happy about your decision," Strenk ventured.

"Oh, it's not Per-Lem and Val-Dor that are really bothering me. It's not even yesterday's chronon burst that's the real problem. The real puzzle is something much closer to home. And I don't like the conclusion I keep reaching."

Strenk raised a quizzical eyebrow. "What's the problem?"

"Operation Kālek. How many people knew that we had agents in place in the Empire?"

"Five, if you include Per-Lem," Strenk answered promptly.

"And those people are?"

"You, me and the agents themselves."

"Exactly. Neither President Rahl nor his predecessor was told anything about Kālek, even though I told the president this afternoon that his predecessor sanctioned it. Kālek is buried so deep that no one should have been able to find it."

"You mean someone else knows about it?"

"The first thing the president said to me was: 'Tell me about the covert operation you have taking place in imperial territory.' It's true that he didn't know very much. I only told him about Rum-Lem, whose name, incidentally, he knew; he didn't seem to know that Rum-Lem was only part of the operation, though. He certainly didn't know Rum-Lem's real mission, or that he was timeshifted half a cycle ago. Or that he was my son.

"But you're right, no one else knows about Kālek. So the question is: how did the president find out anything at all? I know that I haven't told anyone."

Tcharn shifted slightly. His arm rose, and Strenk discovered that he was looking at the mouth of a kill-gun.

"So, Strenk, whom have you told?"

12

LYSTRA

Lystra Ten-Wer awoke from an uneasy sleep with an uncomfortable premonition that this was going to be a difficult rotation. Her sleep had been disturbed by disquieting dreams that fled as she awoke, leaving only a vague, uneasy sense of inanition. It was not a good start to the rotation.

The red report was the cause of it all, even though three full decarotations had passed since it had appeared on her databox and she had forwarded it to Supervisor Qwilm. She *had* forwarded it to her supervisor. She *had*.

But Supervisor Qwilm had never received it. A routine audit of her work had turned up the discrepancy: she had received a red report and, for the second time since her promotion, failed to forward it to her supervisor. Qwilm had called her into his office for an explanation, and was understandably dissatisfied with her insistent pleading that she had forwarded the report as required. Her only explanation was that there must have been a databox programming error — but they both knew how unlikely that was, and at their last meeting just the rotation before Supervisor Qwilm had no qualms about putting her on indefinite leave until the technicians had confirmed that such an error was impossible.

In the meantime, she was finding it difficult to sleep.

She got wearily out of bed and slowly began to prepare for the rotation ahead.

After waterdousing, she moodily prepared firstmeal, then toyed with it, then threw most of it away uneaten.

She switched on the holoimage screen, hoping to find something to dispel the ennui, but neither the news videos nor the entertainment channels held her attention for long. She looked over her library of vidbooks, but even these held no attraction.

She gazed out across Kivra City. From her south-facing seventieth-story apartment, she had a good view over much of the city.

Suddenly, her whole environment seemed oppressive and burdensome. She felt like screaming into the heavy silence of the apartment.

Normally, Lystra felt a degree of pride that she lived here at the very center of the Empire's power, almost within sight of the emperor's palace itself. Today, she felt merely depressed that life was so meaningless. She found herself wondering what everything was about. Surely there had to be some point to it all?

She shook herself and said out loud: "Pull yourself together, woman, this is not like you."

Which was true enough, for usually she was so immersed in her work that she had little time for pointless speculation and self-analysis. Questions about the meaning of life were the province of philosophers and other academics who contributed nothing to the Empire. She tried to convince herself that her job was important, that *she* was important. Normally, this would have been an easy task, but today she failed.

A ponderous movement in the distance attracted her attention. At the spaceport, a ship had lifted off. It was a large ship, its gray-red sheen dully reflecting the color of the sky. It labored skyward, and almost half a chron passed before the ship disappeared into the clouds: a transport ship, fully laden, making its neverending circuit, ferrying goods from one planet to another. Laden though the ship looked, it must have been even more so when it arrived, for Kivra imported almost everything necessary to its survival and exported little except regulations and bureaucrats.

Her eyes remained listlessly on the point where the ship had disappeared into the clouds.

You need a vacation, Lystra Ten-Wer.

The thought came without warning, but she found herself giving the idea serious consideration. It was a strange notion, almost an alien one, for never before had she felt it necessary to escape her quotidian existence. But the more she turned the thought over in her mind, the more attractive a short vacation seemed. She would do it. A couple of restful rotations at some pleasant resort where she could get away from the city and the gloomy Kivran weather: that should put her right.

Lystra turned away from the window. She had automatically dressed in her P&S uniform, but now she returned to her closet, undressed, and began with an odd cheeriness to sort through her clothes, looking for something that would be appropriate for a vacation.

She discovered that she was humming.

She arrived at the spaceport with no destination in mind. For a while she watched the comings and goings, realizing with some surprise that this was the first time she had visited the spaceport since her arrival on Kivra more than ten cycles before. A greater contrast with the spaceport on her home planet could hardly be imagined.

Eb was a small, unimportant, mostly agricultural planet, one of the group condescendingly known on Kivra as the Outer Planets. Eb was self-sustaining, but lacked sufficient population to produce much in the way of exports. Consequently, the spaceport on Eb was a small affair, little more than a massive paved area on the outskirts of the capital city, Eb-wan. Every rotation, a single passenger liner landed. Most of the time, no more than a handful of passengers joined or left the ship. Several small freighters left Eb every rotation, carrying the planet's meager exports to hungry markets. There was almost no military traffic, and what little there was was insufficient to merit a separate spaceport, so the few military ships that visited the remote outpost were forced to share the commercial spaceport.

How great was the contrast with the Empire's busiest spaceport. As Lystra stood watching, there was not a moment when she could not see at least one vessel hanging in the sky, either taking off or landing. Frequently, there were several craft in motion at once. And this was only the civilian traffic: there was a separate military spaceport on the other side of the city.

The ground rumbled as a passenger liner lifted off. A skyscraper in flight, it slowly gathered speed as it climbed into the air, its atmospheric thrusters whining at full power. The craft disappeared into the cloud layer.

95

Lystra entered the terminal.

It was cavernous. Counters around the periphery represented upwards of fifty different spacelines. For no particular reason, Lystra began to walk towards a counter with the legend *Galactic Destinations* in rather plain lettering that neither moved nor changed color. Behind the counter stood an unoccupied tall woman with long, yellow hair and piercing black eyes. Lystra had never heard of Galactic Destinations; presumably, it was a small spaceline serving only a few systems, hence the lack of busyness on the part of its representative and the plainness of its sign.

"Good rotation. May I help you?"

The woman spoke Galactic Standard in an off-world accent that Lystra could not place.

"I apologize if this is an unusual request, but I'd like to take a vacation for a couple of rotations. I just want to go somewhere unspoiled and with not too many people. Is there anywhere you can recommend?"

The woman's smile widened. "What kind of environment would you prefer? We can offer mountains, lakes, beaches, anything you want. Soam is famous for all of them."

"Soam?"

"Yes. It's quite close to the Prantys system, but it's such an out-of-the-way place that there's no direct flight from Kivra, and we are the only line that flies there. You take a passenger liner from here to Prantys, then a small ferryship from Prantys to Soam. It sounds just the place you're looking for. Hardly anyone goes there, but I think it's beautiful, especially at this point in its cycle. I spend all my vacations there."

"Tell me more. Kivra City is beginning to overwhelm me, I think. I want to spend a couple of rotations somewhere with plenty of vegetation, a reasonably pleasant climate, and not too many people. It would give me chance to be alone for a while and enjoy some fresh air."

The woman's smile broadened even further, until it was almost a grin.

"Then I can recommend Soam without reservation. It's the only inhabitable planet in its system, so few people go there. For some of its cycle the climate is not very attractive: hot and wet; but at the moment it's at aphelion and the skies should be clear almost everywhere. It has everything you might want: jungles, forests and even a few open areas of grassland. It does have a blue sky — you don't mind that, do you?"

"No, I guess not."

"Good. There are no civilizations on Soam, and the only settlements are a few small research communities."

"But there are hovercars available? I will be able to get away from the settlement?"

"Oh yes; certainly. There's a even small tourist center where you can stay. I can make a reservation for you if you like, although it's hardly necessary. I've never known it be more than half full. Hovercars with planet-wide range are available at the spaceport. There is the usual system of orbiting beacons and transponders, so you can't get lost."

"It sounds marvelous; exactly what I'm looking for. I'll take a ticket for the next available ship, and I'd like to return late the rotation after tomorrow, if that's possible."

"Certainly. If you would give me your card?"

Lystra handed over her currency card while the woman elaborated. "As I said, there are no direct flights from Kivra to Soam. You need to transfer at Prantys. The next passenger ship for Prantys leaves in twenty five chrons, so you should just be able to make it. There will be a short wait at Prantys before the ferryship leaves for Soam. You should be on Soam by mid afternoon, which will be early evening local."

The transaction was quickly completed. A couple of chrons later Lystra was making her way towards the departure gate for the flight to Prantys. As she walked, she caught herself humming an old tune that had been popular back when she was a student.

Passengers were already boarding, so she immediately entered the ship and found a seat. The ship was a medium-sized passenger liner, with a capacity of about five hundred. The flight was a little over half full, and Lystra chose a seat near a window so she could enjoy the views. Most of the passengers were businessmen or bureaucrats in government uniform.

The ship lifted off on schedule. She had a brief view of Kivra City before the ship penetrated the cloudbase. Within moments, the ship shot out into the beautiful light pink sky in which hung the reddish-orange orb of Kivra's K-class sun. The ship continued to accelerate, and Lystra was pushed firmly into the depths of her seat. The sky turned a deeper shade of pink, then red, then black. The bright cloud deck fell away and the horizon curved as the ship climbed. The curve began to close in on itself. Within a couple of chrons, she was looking at Kivra from near space.

The liner pulled away from the planet, still gaining speed. The ion drive took over from the thrusters; acceleration increased but was mostly compensated by the anti-grav field. The Mother Planet fell quickly behind.

This continued for some thirty chrons as the liner moved to a point sufficiently far from Kivra that a hyperspace jump could be initiated. Lystra occupied the time looking out the window at the stars that filled the sky. She had forgotten how peaceful space was. The Mother Planet was about one third of the way out from the galactic center, so the view out the window was of a breathtaking array of multicolored pinpricks hanging motionless in space. Only a few objects were close enough to move: Kivra itself, Kivra's star, Halbrann, and Traal, Kivra's solitary natural satellite. For a while she watched transfixed as Traal's pock-marked, orange-tinged disk moved against the background of stars. Then, like the parent planet, it was left behind.

An automatic announcement came over the cabin intercom.

"Ladies and gentlemen, this liner will make a hyperspace jump in one chron. Please do not be anxious; there is no danger. If you have never experienced a hyperspace jump before, you are warned that the windows will be automatically blanked while the jump is in progress, in order to spare you the disorientation and nausea generally produced by viewing a jump. However, there is nothing inherently dangerous in viewing the jump and if you desire you may do so if you are seated adjacent to a window. Simply press the yellow button under the window panel and it will revert to transparent mode. All passengers are assured that there will be only minimal discomfort as the ship performs its jump."

After a brief pause the intercom announced: "Prepare for a hyperspace jump in ten centichrons. Thank you."

The star-filled sky suddenly disappeared as Lystra's window turned opaque. Almost simultaneously, she felt a disconcerting wrenching in the pit of her stomach. Her entire body began to tingle. She realized that she was gripping the armrests of her seat tightly; she tried to relax and to breathe normally, but it was difficult to ignore the fact that she was being wrenched out of the continuum in which the entire Universe had its existence.

The jump was quickly over. Less than a chron elapsed before the voice of the computerized announcer said, "Ladies and gentlemen, we have completed the hyperspace portion of our journey. Now, please relax. We shall be on Prantys in a little over thirty chrons. And may I take this opportunity to thank you for travelling on a StarJumper Series 47 passenger liner."

Lystra's window was transparent again. The plethora of stars had disappeared. Prantys was well away from the galactic center and between the spiral arms: stars here were mere occasional dots in an otherwise black sky.

The disk of the planet slid swiftly across the window as the ship maneuvered for entry into the atmosphere. A short time later it landed at the planet's principal spaceport.

Lystra disembarked along with most of the ship's other passengers, feeling a frisson of adventure.

The spaceport was much less impressive than the one in Kivra City. The passenger terminal was squat and decorated in abstract patterns with a desert motif in which a friendly pastel orange predominated. Large windows looked out over the landing/launch area, where half a dozen craft were parked. The building was busy, with most people wearing relaxed, brightly colored, civilian clothing. With a start, Lystra realized how used she had become to the drab uniforms of government employees. One tended to forget that away from the Mother Planet government employees were the rare exception rather than the rule.

She interrogated a wayfinder box about her connection. The machine dispensed a guidance wand and she held it in front of her. Immediately, a series of arrows lit up on the floor, showing the route she should take. She followed the arrows, which one by one flickered out as soon as she passed them, while new ones lit up to point the way ahead.

She reached a small boarding gate at the end of a long concourse and returned the wand to the closest wayfinder box.

It was as she turned away from the wayfinder box that she saw him. She halted and caught her breath with a start.

His eyes were on the arrows on the floor that marked his route. He was making directly for the very machine beside which Lystra herself was standing.

More than ten billion people lived on the Mother Planet. Yet here she was, standing at the gate for a small ferryship that would carry her to a sparsely-populated wilderness planet, and the person approaching her with his eyes on the floor was someone whom she recognized. She could hardly believe the coincidence.

She watched the man approach, wondering if perhaps she had made a mistake; had a similarity of features deceived her?

No; now she was certain: it was the man on the hoverbus she took to and from work, the man whom she had decided was probably a gardener.

There was something else about him too, some other memory, that remained just out of reach. It niggled at the back of her mind, as if it was something that, if not exactly important, was something that she *should* remember. But the memory remained stubbornly inaccessible.

As he reached the machine their eyes met. He nodded hesitantly, one Kivran greeting another on a distant world. There was no sign of recognition on his face.

The man surrendered his guidance wand to the machine and offered a brief greeting.

"Good rotation."

"Good rotation. You're from Kivra City, aren't you? Don't I recognize you?"

"Do you?"

The man looked momentarily confused. Then his face lit up in recognition.

"Oh, yes, I remember you. The hoverbus. I didn't recognize you out of uniform. You work for P&S don't you?"

Before Lystra could reply, their conversation was interrupted by an announcement: "Would all passengers for the ferryship to Soam please move forward for embarkation. The ferry will be leaving in five chrons. Boarding is about to end. I repeat, would those passengers taking the ferryship to Soam please board immediately. The ship will depart shortly."

"My ship," the man said, gesturing vaguely towards the gate. He began to edge towards the ragged line of passengers. Lystra moved with him. She still could hardly believe the coincidence.

They joined the end of the line. As the line moved forward, she told him her name and a little about herself. The man reciprocated as their tickets were checked and they walked through the gateway and into the ferry. With no pause in their conversation, they found two seats on the left side of the ship and sat down.

The man's name was Teberill Gandeer. It was a strange name, and he explained, perhaps a shade too defensively, that he was from the Outer Planets, near the demilitarized zone. By what process he had come to Kivra he did not say. His was a strange and esoteric profession. Just as Lystra had guessed, he was a gardener, helping to maintain the vast imperial gardens that surrounded the emperor's palace in a state, as Teberill put it, "worthy of the greatest man in the galaxy."

They waited for liftoff, and in the silence that fell Lystra found herself studying her companion.

He looked to be roughly her own age, or perhaps a few cycles older. His skin had been browned and his hair bleached by the sun. There were the hints of crows' feet around the corners of his eyes, and the thick skin of his brow was furrowed deeply even in repose. His eyes were muddy brown, but something about them, a strange habit of seeming to focus in the middle distance perhaps, made her think that behind those eyes was a brain operating much more quickly than one at first thought.

Suddenly she remembered what had been bothering her: this man had appeared in one of the scenarios in her last mindprobe. She could not remember what part he had played, only that he had been present; but how odd it was that this man, whose name she had not known until a few moments ago, who was now seated beside her, joining her in a journey to a planet of whose existence she had been unaware only a short time before, had appeared in a mindprobe scenario. She looked out the window, puzzling over the unsettling coincidences.

Outside, a steady rain was falling, and the dull gray of the spaceport was rendered dismal by the wet sheen that covered everything. There was a brief delay while a young man in P&S uniform boarded the ferry late. He looked harried as he scanned the cabin in search of a seat. Lystra felt more pleased than ever to be escaping work for a couple of rotations.

A cabin announcement warned that liftoff was imminent. Less than a chron later, the ship emitted a deep rumble and the infrastructure all around them began to vibrate disconcertingly.

She must have looked anxious, because Teberill leaned towards her and said soothingly, "Don't worry. These primitive ships are much safer than they appear. They're designed for carrying freight, and some of the niceties like thruster suppressors generally aren't added when they're converted to carry a few passengers. But they're really quite safe."

The ferry was indeed quite unlike the plush passenger liner on which Lystra (and Teberill, she assumed, although she had not seen him aboard) had arrived. The ferry was a working ship, transporting goods and a few passengers among the planets of the widely spaced systems in this part of the galaxy. It was an older ship, much used. Lystra's seat was stained, and around it hung the stale aroma of a thousand prior occupants. The window was deeply scratched, and here and there throughout the cabin she could see exposed unpainted rusting metal. The passenger cabin provided seating for about a hundred, and was little more than a third full. She glanced around it. Several people looked nervous. She wondered if the same tension was etched on her own face. It probably was, for despite Teberill's claims it was hardly unknown for ferries such as this to fail to reach their destination. She looked once more at the gardener. His eyes were closed, as if he intended to doze for the duration of the journey to Soam.

There was a distinct shudder as the ferry left the ground. Lystra's gaze returned to the window. She swallowed hard, then tried to persuade herself that there really was nothing to worry about. There were thousands of these ferries scattered around the Empire, and fatal mishaps occurred no more than once or twice per cycle. After all, pilots would hardly agree to fly such ships if they were unsafe, would they? This ferry alone doubtless visited five or six planets every rotation. The probability of an accident occurring on this trip was almost infinitesimally small. Yet even so her hands tightly gripped the armrests of her seat.

The ferry climbed into the gray Prantian sky. It was quickly enveloped in cloud. When the passenger liner from Kivra had landed, it had passed through the cloud layer in moments; the ferry took almost half a chron to pass through the same layer.

Eventually they emerged into the transparent, pinkish sky of Prantys. As on Kivra, although much more slowly this time, the horizon curved and began to bend back on itself.

"There really is nothing to worry about, you know."

Lystra turned and flashed Teberill a defiant smile. She had thought he was asleep.

"I know," she said. "At least," she added, "my mind knows that. It's my stomach that isn't quite convinced." Her smile became wan and apologetic.

"I know what you mean. Sometimes just knowing something to be true isn't quite enough, is it?"

Lystra shook her head. "Sorry. It's just that I've never travelled on a small ferryship like this."

"Oh, you get used to them in my profession. We are always stocking new plants in the emperor's gardens" — he imbued the word 'emperor' with an aura of magisterial dignity — "and it's part of my job to observe the natural habitat of species we're thinking of importing, to be sure they'll grow properly on Kivra."

"So you're used to this, then. Sorry, that sounds so superior of me, as if I always travel on passenger liners. I didn't mean it to sound that way. In fact I haven't been off-planet in almost a decacycle. I'm strictly desk-bound at P&S."

"No offense intended, and none taken. You're a bureaucrat; there'd be no need to apologize even if you continually roamed the galaxy in luxury. But tell me: why is a P&S bureaucrat on a ferry to an out-of-the-way place like Soam?"

"It's a vacation. Just for a couple of rotations. I just needed to get away, go somewhere where I could relax and forget the pressures of work."

"A woman of the moment, one who isn't afraid to do something unusual." Teberill's face was a broad, pleasure-filled smile. "I like that, it's so rare in people these days, especially bureaucrats."

Lystra blushed at the implied compliment, and also at the sudden feeling of guilt it engendered — after all, this was her first unpredictable act since... when? She couldn't remember ever doing something so spontaneous.

Teberill's smile was warm and friendly. There was nothing overt, just a suggestion that if she was willing to admit to herself that she liked him, this could be a very unplanned vacation indeed. In the flustered confusion that suddenly overwhelmed her, she was thankful for the announcement that crackled through the cabin.

"This is the pilot speaking. It will take us a while to get far enough from Prantys's gravity field to make the hyperspace jump. For now, I suggest you relax. We should be ready to make the jump in about fifty chrons. There will be another announcement just before we jump."

The fifty chrons passed in inconsequential chatter. Teberill's journey, it seemed, was not official. He told Lystra that he had heard of some interesting ferns indigenous to Soam, and he wanted to spend his rest period there to see whether they might be worthy of a place in the emperor's gardens. He said that he had once briefly lived at a research station on Soam, and while the ferry made its way to the jump point he told her some of the basic facts about the planet.

103

Soam was almost uninhabited. It was also small for a life-sustaining planet. Its gravity field was considerably less than standard, so that it was barely able to maintain a tenuous grasp on an atmosphere that had originally been heavy in carbon dioxide and nitrogen. Plants had evolved, breathing in the carbon dioxide and expiring oxygen, so that now the mix of gases was capable of supporting both plant and animal life in profusion.

The planet's eccentric orbit and highly inclined axis gave it a complicated annual weather cycle, the only stabilizing force being the relatively large percentage of the planet covered by salt-laden oceans. None of the five continents was large, so the effect of the oceans was manifest even in the interior of the largest continent. There were a few mountains and rifts, but none were particularly spectacular. The planet had long ago cooled to the point where there was little geologic activity. Most of the mountain ranges were now little more than hills, worn away by the powerful erosive forces typical of planets with high rainfall. Only the highest peaks of one range, the Skyward Mountains, reached above tree line and were capped permanently with snow and glaciers.

Teberill told Lystra that there were small settlements on all Soam's continents, but all except one were research stations, and were closed to the public. The only settlement at which visitors were permitted to stay was Marsûk, which was also home to the planet's only spaceport. Marsûk boasted a permanent population of about a thousand, with beds for almost five hundred visitors in the tourist center.

Teberill promised Lystra that she would not be disappointed by the scenery around Marsûk — the area, while hardly spectacular, had a gentle unsullied beauty that was exactly what an over-stressed, nature-starved bureaucrat from Kivra needed.

By the time the pilot announced the hyperspace jump, Lystra felt like she knew everything worth knowing about Soam. She also felt like she had known Teberill Gandeer far longer than a few tens of chrons.

The hyperspace jump passed without incident, although it took considerably longer than the jump on the passenger liner. The windows had no blanking mechanisms. Outside was a strange and nauseating sight: rapidly shifting, pulsing lights seemed to spin and gyrate crazily against the dim gray-blue background of hyperspace. It made her want to vomit. She closed her eyes tightly. The gardener grasped her hand. He said nothing, but his gentle squeeze communicated more than anything he might have said.

When the jump was finally over, Lystra ventured a look outside and saw that Soam was indeed a beautiful planet. The blue of its oceans complemented the green of its continents and the glaring white of its clouds and ice caps in a dazzling synergy of color. Lystra had never seen a planet that looked so delightful.

She said as much to Teberill, who agreed but added, "Of course, most of the time it doesn't look like this. You must remember that you're seeing it at its best. It's only because it's nearly at the extremity of its orbit that it's like this." He paused, then added, "But you're right. Right now, it *is* beautiful, one of the most beautiful planets in the galaxy."

The ferryship landed safely. Lystra had to suppress a momentary disquiet at the unaccustomed blue of the sky. Hanging in the blueness were puffy white water clouds, moving slowly from west to east. It was strange, but it was also, in its own way, undeniably fascinating.

They disembarked, then went in search of food. A snack bar overlooked the landing area, and there they ate a meal of imported food — which was all that was available, although Teberill told Lystra that she would be pleasantly surprised by the local fare when she got the chance to try it. While they ate the ferry lifted off. Lystra watched the ship climb into the blue sky. It threaded its way between clouds, leaving a white contrail that remained for a while after the ferry itself had disappeared. The spaceport was now empty except for a cluster of P&S vehicles on the far side.

After they had eaten, Teberill rented a hovercar and took Lystra on a tour of Marsûk's surroundings. The area was filled with gently rolling hills that were thickly covered with trees. Here and there the trees broke to reveal wide rivers that reflected back the blue of the sky and the yellow of Soam's G-class star. Lystra thought that everything looked so peaceful and natural that it was almost as if they were the very first people ever to explore the planet.

The more time Lystra spent in Teberill's company, the more impressed she became. Along with his other talents, he even piloted the car expertly; he flew manually and with barely a glance at the instrument control panel, almost as if he were flying by instinct and the hovercar was merely an extension of himself. At times he flew high, so that Lystra was treated to a panoramic view of the untouched green and blue world spread out below; at other times they were barely above the treetops, so that she felt almost as if she were some giant winged creature skimming perilously over the surface of the planet. She had never seen a pilot so much at ease with his vehicle.

All too soon the journey was over, and Teberill touched down back at the Marsûk hoverport.

They registered at the tourist center. Lystra was quietly surprised when he requested separate sleeping quarters; she had assumed that they had formed a tacit agreement to couple, yet it seemed that Teberill had no such thoughts. As they walked towards their rooms, Lystra almost suggested that they spend the night together, but before she had quite made up her mind they had reached his room and he was wishing her a good night.

Maybe he was right. Light was already fading. Soam rotated quickly, and the journey had been more tiring than she had realized; it occurred to her that if they were going to couple, it would be best to do so after the short night, when they were refreshed and relaxed. So she bade Teberill goodnight, but extracted a promise that he would wake her in the morning.

She waterdoused quickly and then went directly to bed. As she relaxed, she entertained warm thoughts of the gardener from Kivra, but only for a very short while. Very soon, she was asleep.

She was woken by a quiet tapping dragging her from the mists of sleep. Someone was at her door.

"Who is it?" she called. A warm feeling flooded over her as she remembered Teberill.

"It's me, Teberill Gandeer. I hope I didn't wake you. I was just about to go to the restaurant for firstmeal, and you did say that you wanted to join me."

The room was still dark, the blankable window keeping out the light. The clock on the wall indicated that she had slept for about 400 chrons, which meant that it was already morning outside.

"No, I'm awake," she called. "Thank you. I'll be right out."

Lystra leapt out of bed. As she washed — more quickly than she had done in cycles — her mind wandered fleetingly back to yesterday morning in her apartment, when she had dispiritedly watched the freighter lifting off from the Kivra City spaceport. She could hardly believe that now she was on a beautiful, sparsely populated planet, and standing on the far side of the door was a man who, before the rotation was out, would almost certainly become her lover. For the third time in less than a rotation she noticed that she was humming.

They ate firstmeal together, and Lystra could hardly believe the taste of the local food: it almost exploded in her mouth, treating her taste buds to combinations of sweetness and astringency and tartness and smoothness that she had forgotten existed after living for so many cycles on the Kivran diet of preserved and synthetic food.

After they had finished Teberill purchased food for later, then they walked together to the hovercar park.

They lifted off and, with barely a glance at the opnav computer, Teberill piloted them over a large lake and headed out over thick forest. Lystra's gaze wandered down to the greenery racing past below, her mind considering happy possibilities.

Her reverie was rudely interrupted as without warning the car dropped like a stone and simultaneously turned sharply. Teberill accelerated and in moments the car was racing at full speed at treetop height along a trough between two ridges, at the bottom of which a wide blue river wound leisurely. The arboreous slopes extended high above them. She felt a frisson of fear. Teberill's face was tense with concentration as the car raced along the gully. Suddenly, it rose high and changed direction, arcing to the left. They flew over a ridge, and plunged, momentarily weightless, down the other side.

Lystra let out an involuntary scream, then sheepishly apologized: "Sorry. You surprised me. You don't need to impress me, you know. I'm already impressed."

He smiled at her.

They followed the downward slope on the far side of the ridge. In the distance, a deep blue ocean reflected the yellow of the sun. Before them the forest petered out, leaving a wide, grassy plain between the hills and the ocean. Teberill began to throttle back, and they dropped towards the edge of the forest. The car settled on the grass at the very edge of the trees. The engines stopped, and silence fell.

The view was gorgeous. The plain stretched out before them to the distant sea, interrupted only by the occasional stand of trees and a couple of low, undulating hills. Here and there in the distance were black dots: local beasts cropping the virid grass.

"You're quite a pilot, you know that?" Lystra said.

For a moment, she thought he was going to kiss her; but in the end he just said, "I love this place. It's such a beautiful spot just to relax for a while."

She felt happier than she could remember.

———————————

They lay in the sun, their bodies close but not touching. Lystra was on her front, looking out over the plain towards the distant, glistening sea. Within touching distance, Teberill lay on his back, stripped to his waist to reveal a bronzed chest covered with a fuzz of blond hairs; his eyes were closed and he was breathing deeply. The only sounds were the occasional chatter of a bird in the trees and the drone of insects flying among the tiny flowers that were almost hidden in the grass. A soft breeze off the distant sea caused the trees to sough gently.

Lystra closed her eyes and felt the gentle caress of the breeze as it played over her back. She fell asleep.

She woke to a nightmare.

13
TCHARN

When the chief of the Bureau of Defense of the Free Union of Independent Planets requires assurance that someone is telling the truth, there are several means open to him. Each has its pros and its cons, and the one Chief Tcharn used on any given occasion was dictated by circumstances rather than considerations of efficacy, for each method was guaranteed to be reliable.

Most often the choice was a simple selection between truth drug and mindprobe. But there was a third method, more discreet and less invasive. It was this method of interrogation that Tcharn had chosen for Deputy Strenk.

They were seated in a bare room. They were comfortable enough: the room was at a pleasant temperature and the soft chairs were conformed to the contours of their occupants. Strenk was seated in the center of the room, Tcharn near one wall. The floor was bare wood, the walls and ceiling painted a particularly insipid color that might have been gray or, possibly, brown. The only decoration, if that is the correct word, was a spotlight in the ceiling between the chief and his deputy. The spotlight lit Deputy Strenk's face, blinding him so that he could make out nothing in the gloom of the room beyond the glare of the beam.

Invisible to Strenk, although the deputy knew that he was present, was a third man, seated in a corner facing him. The man's name was

109

Dunnis Delrun; his title as it appeared on the roster of Defense Bureau personnel was "Verification — Head of Department." He was the bureau's most skilled aletheologist: that is, Dunnis Delrun determined the truth of a person's statements by observing that person's body language.

At this moment, Dunnis Delrun was watching Deputy Strenk — technically his immediate superior — as the deputy prepared to answer the questions that Tcharn was about to ask. As the interrogation progressed, Delrun would tell Chief Tcharn whenever the deputy lied or paltered.

Tcharn began the interrogation simply, to provide Delrun with a baseline sample of Strenk's body language.

"Deputy Strenk, you are as familiar as I am with the techniques of body language interrogation, so I need not go into the usual details. We will run a short calibration series first. I shall ask you four simple questions. These questions are not designed to entrap you. You will answer two of them truthfully, and two of them with lies. Do not tell us which is which. You understand?"

Tcharn tried to keep all traces of inflection out of his voice, but he was not quite successful. Subjecting his deputy and mentor to an aletheologist's gaze had a trace of the surreal to it. He was already sure that he knew how the interview would end, but if Strenk was not the one who had leaked information about Operation Kālek, how on Dalith had the president ever found out about it? No; the source had to be Strenk. Which meant that Strenk was in league with... whom? Just the president? Or Amril Gdrena? Was that possible? Could Strenk be, if not exactly a spy, perhaps a sympathizer?

"I understand," Strenk replied.

Unlike Tcharn, he made no attempt to hide his feelings. His voice was like ice, his lack of inflection reprimanding the chief for his suspicions.

Tcharn posed the first question: "How old are you, Deputy Strenk?"

A pause while Strenk decided whether to tell the truth or to lie.

"Fifty five cycles," he said.

"Do you currently have a partner?"

No hesitation this time. "I do not."

"Have you ever killed a human being?"

Strenk laughed drily. "Not directly, no."

"And what color is the sky on Kivra?"

"How should I know? I've never been there."

110

In a voice tinged with anger Tcharn said, "You're supposed to answer the questions, Strenk...."

"Sir?"

The voice from the corner was quiet but firm. Tcharn stopped in mid-sentence.

"Deputy Strenk answered the first and third questions with lies. The second and fourth questions were answered truthfully."

Tcharn regarded Delrun skeptically.

Delrun continued quietly, "Deputy Strenk, you heard what I just told Chief Tcharn. Am I correct?"

"You are not," said Strenk.

Dunnis Delrun guffawed.

"I always thought you had a sense of humor, sir, even though you try to hide it. Now I know it for a fact." Delrun turned to Tcharn. "He lies," he said simply.

Tcharn looked from one to the other in exasperation. "Are you two playing games with me?"

"I'm sorry, sir. I couldn't resist," said Strenk. "This whole thing is so ridiculous, ever since the moment you pulled a kill-gun on me. I don't know how the president found out about Kālek. *I* didn't tell him. I didn't leak anything about the operation to the president or to anyone else. I thought you knew me better than that. I'd never do anything to endanger any bureau operation, even one I didn't personally support. Neither would I knowingly endanger bureau personnel. Especially these particular personnel. You should know that."

There was a long silence.

"Sir, I think he's telling the truth. You haven't told me what the point of this interrogation is, and I haven't heard of Operation Kālek before; neither do I know what the president does or does not know about it, but I *am* fairly certain that Deputy Chief Strenk is telling the truth. If you would like to put a couple of direct questions to him, it will remove any doubt."

"Deputy Strenk," Tcharn said, "have you ever discussed Operation Kālek either directly or indirectly with anyone other than myself and the operatives involved?"

"No, I have not."

"Never?"

"Never."

"Is there any circumstance in which you might do so?"

Strenk considered the question. "I cannot say I would *never* leak the information, but I can think of no circumstance in which it would be likely."

"Would you do it to save the lives of one or more of the operatives?"

"No. Would you? — I'm sorry, sir. That was uncalled for. I withdraw the question. No, I would not reveal the existence of Operation Kālek, even to save the lives of one or more of the operatives involved."

"All true, Chief Tcharn," said Dunnis Delrun.

Tcharn made a motion with his hand, and the spotlight abruptly went out, to be replaced with a pleasant yellowish light emanating evenly from ceiling and walls.

Tcharn and Strenk looked at one another, the same thought uppermost in both their minds.

"But if not you, then who else is there, Strenk?" Tcharn asked. "How did the president find out?"

"I don't know, sir; I don't know."

14
Amril Gdrena

Amril Gdrena was a young operative in the Ministry of Peace and Security when the chance to prove her superiority came her way.

In those days, the emperor had seen it as his duty to travel widely throughout the Empire, greeting the crowds that gathered everywhere with a smile, showing that he was one with the people whom he ruled, and readily accessible even to the most distant of the imperial worlds.

Wherever the emperor went on his travels, he was accompanied by a detachment of guards from the Ministry of Peace and Security. To be chosen as a member of the imperial guard was regarded as something of a vacation, a welcome break from the monotony of the daily routine, but when Amril Gdrena heard that she had been chosen to join the detachment which was to accompany the emperor to Klivliviv and several of the Outer Planets, she felt that an awesome responsibility had been placed upon her young shoulders.

Perhaps it was because she alone took the task of protecting the emperor seriously — or perhaps it was because her conviction that she was better than everyone else was in fact true — but whatever the reason, it was she who spotted the man in the crowd of well-wishers on Klivliviv. She had her eyes firmly on the man as his hand slid under his clothes and began to withdraw a kill-gun. The stun-gun was in her hand and she had fired even before she was aware of what she was doing.

Normally, the matter would more or less have ended there. The emperor would probably never have been told of the failed attempt on his life; the man would have been picked up and quietly disposed of following interrogation; Gdrena would have been promoted one or two grades; and her career would have continued its predictable but slow upward climb.

It was the interrogation of the would-be assassin that changed Amril Gdrena's life.

Under the mindprobe the facts quickly came out. The man, whose name was Var-Lem, was not a citizen of the Empire. He was a Unionist from the planet Qintir who had sneaked across the demilitarized zone with a single task in mind: to kill the emperor.

Qintir lay just beyond the demilitarized zone, in Union territory. Like many of the people living on the outskirts of the Union — the so-called Fringe Planets — Var-Lem was a poor farmer, struggling to survive under the twin burdens of heavy taxation and poor soil. Under such circumstances, he might ordinarily have been expected to harbor ill-will toward the Union, but an event in his childhood had caused his hatred to turn instead toward the Empire.

When he was ten cycles old, Var-Lem's parents had been killed in one of the border incidents that had been common in those days. Ever since, he had nursed a deep hatred of the Empire. Probably nothing would ever have come of this were it not for the fact that the harvest on Qintir had failed for two consecutive cycles, causing Var-Lem to take out two mortgages on his farm, gambling that the harvest would not fail for a third cycle in a row.

It did.

Protests to the government on Dalith failed to bring relief and the banks threatened to repossess his farm. Instead of taking his anger and frustration out on the most obvious targets — the implacable Union and the mercenary banks — he had somehow concluded that the Empire was responsible for all his troubles, and so he had decided to take out his helpless frustration on the Empire in the most dramatic way he could think of.

He had sneaked across the demilitarized zone, making more than a hundred short hyperspace jumps in his battered old ship, landing on a remote planet and then begging and stealing his way to Klivliviv, where the emperor was scheduled to visit. Then he waited for his target.

If it had not been for Amril Gdrena's alertness, Var-Lem would probably have succeeded in his self-appointed mission and thereby thrown the Empire into chaos.

As a reward for her actions and the efficacy of Var-Lem's interrogation, Amril Gdrena, despite her youth, was named to head a committee charged with the task of making recommendations to ensure that no such thing ever happened again. Half a cycle later, the committee submitted its report, which mostly consisted of recommendations that existing defenses should be strengthened and the security around the emperor when he travelled should be tightened. The report was accepted *in toto* by the Minister of Peace and Security.

What was known to only Gdrena and the minister was that along with the committee's official report Amril Gdrena had submitted a private communication of her own. This communication began defiantly:

> *Attached hereto is the final report of convened committee 3214 of the Ministry of Peace and Security, "Committee to recommend steps to increase the safety of the Emperor when away from the imperial compound, with particular regard to the prevention of attacks by Unionists."*

> *The committee's report is bureaucratic and political, and is essentially useless, since it entirely fails to address the fundamental problem of imperial security. The permanent solution to the problem is as simple as it is obvious....*

The minister did not immediately follow the recommendation contained in Amril Gdrena's communication — not because her solution was unworkable, but because it required more political courage and power than he had at his command. What he did do was to transfer her to his personal staff. And then he began to prepare the ground.

The first step was to isolate the emperor from his people. This was childishly easy. A series of hypnotic implants caused a minor official to make a failed attempt to assassinate the emperor, thereby rendering the imperial leader receptive to the suggestion that he curtail contact with his subjects. Almost overnight, the emperor retired from the public gaze. No one was permitted access; even the holoimage cameras were kept at a distance. An impermeable cocoon was woven around the emperor. That, the minister decided, was enough for the present.

It was Amril Gdrena herself, some fifteen cycles later, after her own appointment as Minister of Peace and Security, who finally unveiled the Gdrena Plan in all its horrifying simplicity.

Initially, the Gdrena Plan garnered support from only three other members of the Inner Council.

There, by tradition, the matter should have rested. Once a negative decision had been reached on a motion put forward by any member, tradition said that the matter could not be revisited unless circumstances changed.

But then ministers began to die.

She was careful. The three deaths were freak occurrences, with nothing in common. One was a spaceship accident; another was a rare and virulent virus contracted on one of the Outer Planets; the third an unfortunate incident with a jealous lover. None of the dead ministers had been among those most violently opposed to Gdrena's plan. They had simply voted against it.

At the next meeting a quarter cycle later, there was a noticeable tension in the air. Nothing specific was said, but when Gdrena asked with a smile, "Anyone want to revisit the idea I put forward last time?" several people looked at her meaningfully. An uncomfortable suspicion was beginning to form.

No one answered Gdrena's question.

Her smile simply broadened and she continued, "All right. I just wondered. Then I think we'll move on to the next item of business."

By the time of the next meeting, two more of the naysayers were dead and there was an almost palpable sense of confrontation in the air as the ministers filed into the meeting room.

As they took their seats, Gdrena leaned towards the man on her left, the Minister of Human Resources, and said quietly, "You're next."

The minister, an overweight, bald man who had been the staunchest opponent of the plan, pretended not to hear. But a sheen of sweat appeared on his face.

As soon as the meeting came to order, the Minister of Human Resources said, "I've been thinking about that plan of Gdrena's about imperial security. Perhaps" — and here he turned to her and shot her a broad, friendly smile as good as the best of her own — "Perhaps she would be good enough to go through it once again for the newcomers amongst us, and those of us who perhaps did not think about it carefully enough before. I've been thinking that we might have been a little hasty in rejecting her idea."

The Gdrena Plan was adopted without debate. The emperor, of course, was not informed. Half a cycle later, the plan was executed.

Amril Gdrena was now 52, and long acknowledged as first among equals. She was without a doubt the most powerful person in the empire, although that fact was known only to herself and her twelve colleagues on the Inner Council.

She was as brilliant, as driven, and as uncompromisingly ruthless as ever. Augmenting everything was a streak of good fortune that had made her believe that she was invincible. And so she had been. Until half a cycle ago, when she had made the only important mistake of her career.

As Minister for Peace and Security, Amril Gdrena was responsible for security inside the imperial compound. Therefore it reflected badly on her when that security was shown to be lacking, even though no one outside the Inner Council would ever know that a breach had occurred.

The palace recorders had captured everything. The spy had entered the palace in the moment when the security systems were being switched. Someone in P&S must have leaked the exact time.

The spy had wandered the rooms in the emperor's private wing with a kill-gun in hand, looking for the emperor. Instead, he had found the empress. The intruder's interview with the empress had lasted less than five chrons, but her words had sealed the empress's fate. She had contracted a bacterial infection and died the following rotation.

The empress had been a popular figure and her untimely passing was mourned by the whole Empire, most of all by the emperor himself, whose great love for his life partner was well known. An enormous audience had watched the private memorial service on the holoimage newscasts, and many had cried along with their beloved and obviously grief-stricken emperor. Amril Gdrena was justly proud of the whole thing.

The Union spy had escaped before the security guards could intercept him, and when he fled the building he carried with him the most dangerous secret in the Empire.

Before he could be stopped, the man had reached the spaceport and left Kivra in his own private ship.

Amril Gdrena was in her office in Kivra City when she was alerted to what had happened. She recognized the danger instantly: if the spy were able to transmit what he had learned to the Union, it might mean the end of the Empire. At the very least the Empire, and possibly the Union as well, could be stressed to breaking point by the uncontrollable forces that would be unleashed.

She ordered, "Destroy the ship. If you can't do that, render it inoperative by any means at your disposal. Failure is not an option."

Three Black Ships were housed in the military spaceport on the opposite side of Kivra City; the fourth stood at the end of a hallway that connected directly to the minister's office. A launch corridor was permanently open for the ships, which were the first line of attack against the Union, to be launched at the first indication of a hostile act by the enemy. They were also the only ships in the imperial fleet permanently armed with timeshift weapons, whose use was banned by the Treaty of Empire and Union.

The three ships lifted off almost simultaneously. Each was equipped with weapons and advanced navigational and engine systems that none but Gdrena and the ships' pilots knew about. Not even the other members of the Inner Council were aware of the full power of a Black Ship.

Amril Gdrena stabbed a communicator button.

"Brynt Veel. In my office. Now."

Half a chron later her door slid open. Inside stepped a muscular man of about thirty. He looked at Gdrena without speaking.

He was tall, dark-haired and coldly handsome. Something about his eyes radiated a cold, impersonal malevolence. Perhaps it was because they were black. Perhaps it was because they seemed never to blink.

She had first seen him while making a tedious inspection of the Kivra Space Military Academy, some eleven cycles earlier. He had been the academy's star pupil, and General Poltven had been keen to show him off. He had taken the minister for a spin in one of the holosimulators, just the two of them, while he had engaged the simulated enemy in a series of dogfights from which he had emerged unscathed and breathing only slightly more deeply than usual. Gdrena had come out of the simulator bathed in sweat.

A rotation later, Brynt Veel left the academy. Shortly after that, all evidence that he had ever attended the military school was expunged from the records. Now Brynt Veel was Amril Gdrena's confidant and right-hand man. He was the only person in the entire galaxy outside the Inner Council and the imperial family who knew of the Gdrena Plan.

"I just launched the other Black Ships. They're chasing a Union spy. He has to be stopped."

Veel did not smile.

"I'm better than any of the pilots on the Black Ships, minister."

"Prove it."

The Black Ships were the most advanced ships ever constructed by the Empire. To chase and destroy a lone private vessel should have been ridiculously easy; but it was as well that Gdrena decided to launch the fourth ship, for without it the spy would never have been stopped.

The story that Gdrena conveyed to the Inner Council in the subsequent emergency meeting was simple. It was also inaccurate.

Gdrena told the Council that warning had come too late to stop the spy from reaching his ship and blasting off into space. By the time the Black Ships had reached near-space, the spy had been able to get far enough away from Kivra that he was able to make a hyperspace jump. This much was true.

Gdrena told them that the Black Ships had followed, quickly blasted the ship out of existence, and returned home. End of story. This was not true.

Only Gdrena and the pilots knew how close the chase had been.

The difficulty lay in the fact that although the spy's ship had the appearance of a rather pedestrian craft, it was in fact the most advanced ship that the Union was capable of building.

The two sides were remarkably well matched. The hyperspace drives in the imperial Black Ships were somewhat more advanced than the one in the Union vessel, but the databoxes aboard the latter were significantly more powerful. Additionally, the illegal timeshift weapons carried by the Black Ships added significantly to their inertial mass. So it was a very close thing. A very close thing indeed.

The first three Black Ships leapt from their launch pads less than a chron after the minister's order to deploy. The name "Black Ship" was well deserved, for the surface of the ships was a uniform matte black; the ships carried no markings whatsoever. Only the automatic identification transponders betrayed them as imperial craft.

The three ships raced up through the atmosphere and into space faster than any manned ships had a right to do.

Nearly a chron later, a fourth ship lifted off. Unlike the others, this ship carried no automatic identification transponder.

The Black Ships were flown by two-person teams: a pilot responsible for the actual flying of the ship and a copilot responsible for navigation and weaponry. Copilot One, the copilot of the lead ship, was the first to recognize that the task they had been set might not be as simple as it had appeared. His scanners locked on to their target as they climbed through the Kivran atmosphere. He arched an eyebrow in surprise when he saw its speed. This was no ordinary ship.

The scanners confirmed that it carried a single human. Then the scanners lost synchronization lock.

"He has some sort of jammer," Copilot One said.

"What do you mean?"

"Ship coming up fast behind us," interrupted Copilot Three.

They were not even out the atmosphere yet, and already things were going wrong.

The opnav displays confirmed Copilot Three's words. Something was coming up through the atmosphere behind them. But nothing else in the Empire could accelerate as rapidly as a Black Ship.

An ice-cold voice broke in on the communications channel.

"This is the minister. I am aboard the fourth ship. We will intervene only if you fail in your mission. I assure you, this is not a test. That ship must not be allowed to escape."

In the other ships there was no time to react to this news. By now all the copilots had seen that their scanners had lost lock on the spy's ship.

"What sort of jammer?" shouted Pilot One.

"How on Kivra should I know?"

This was not the way it was supposed to be. Up, shoot, and down again, all in less than ten chrons; that was what should have happened. But without a solid lock it was going to be tricky to fire before the spy jumped.

"We can't lock on to him," Copilot One said with a tinge of desperation. "I can tell roughly where the ship is, but the opnav system isn't giving me any velocity vector at all. We'd be shooting blind if we fired now."

Pilot One swore. "Let me see the screen."

His copilot pressed a button and the view floating in front of the pilot changed. He could see the target, but instead of a clear, steady image, there was only a diffuse blob, to which no velocity vector was attached. The pilot made a minor correction to his course, trying to calculate an intercept path by eye.

"Bastard's moving, isn't he?"

The copilot did not answer. He was concentrating on the blob that represented the spy's ship. It had reached a position where a Black Ship could safely make a hyperspace jump. Was the spy's ship also capable of making a jump so close to Kivra? The blob trembled momentarily, and then disappeared into nothingness.

Copilot One swore out loud.

"He jumped. Everyone, try to read his course and follow. Switch to hyperspace contact. Keep in close communication. He's going to get away if we're not careful."

At the back of his mind, he remembered that observing every move was the minister; if the spy really did get away, all their lives would be forfeit.

There was a flurry of activity as the three copilots tried to calculate the course the ship had been taking just before it jumped. If they knew its precise position, velocity and acceleration vectors, the onboard databoxes would be able to tell them fairly accurately where the hyperspace jump would end. Under normal circumstances, the databoxes would have been keeping close track of precisely these parameters, but circumstances now were far from normal. Everyone aboard the Black Ships knew that if the Unionist was a halfway decent pilot he would have performed a maneuver at the last possible moment. Such a maneuver — a turn or a sudden acceleration or deceleration — could shift the end of the jump by more than a dern. And perhaps worst of all, the jump had been made well inside Kivra's gravity field, so that the only way to follow the ship with any precision was to jump from the same point and with exactly the same velocity and acceleration vectors.

Their only chance was to analyze the tachyon signature left by the ship as it jumped; but to analyze that would take a chron or more, even with the ultra-fast databoxes aboard the Black Ships.

"We'll have to use the tachyon signature; we'll never find him otherwise," said Copilot Two.

121

Everyone knew he was right. The Black Ships slowed while their databoxes analyzed the signature of the tachyon leakage from the spy's jump.

Almost a chron passed.

"Got it," shouted Copilot Three, simultaneously transmitting the data to the other ships.

Within moments all four ships thrust themselves through the interstices of hyperspace.

It was a short jump. The spy would never have dared make a long jump under such conditions; but as soon as they emerged from the jump the pilots realized that the spy had already jumped again. This time the tachyon trail was much clearer, for now they were in interstellar space, free of the distorting effects of spacetime curvature.

They understood the spy's strategy now: he would make a series of short jumps, hoping to keep one jump ahead of the Black Ships. It was a good plan, but it assumed that the Black Ships were no faster than his own ship, which was unlikely.

The Black Ships jumped, and it was immediately obvious that again the target had already jumped. They followed. With each jump the pursuers closed the gap slightly.

The spy began to make mistakes; there was insufficient time for his opnav system to plot the hyperspace jump accurately, and his course began to deviate from a line pointing at the demilitarized zone. The pursuers' task was simpler than the spy's. They did not need to calculate the parameters for a safe jump; they could simply follow their man, and as long as he jumped in interstellar space, the tachyon trail was clear enough for them to follow.

With every jump, the Black Ships were gaining. But were they gaining fast enough?

Amril Gdrena looked at Brynt Veel. They were approaching the demilitarized zone and her face was drawn into a crag of tight lines.

"They've had long enough, Veel. We'd better show them how it's done."

Veel smiled a rare smile. "My pleasure, madam minister. Or perhaps you would prefer to pilot?"

There was a barely perceptible pause before Amril Gdrena replied: "Yes, thank you, Veel. I think I will."

And before Veel could wipe the surprise from his face, the minister grabbed the controls and the ship leapt forward.

The spy's ship jumped, and within moments all four Black Ships followed in its wake. The minister's was the last to materialize, but her ship raced forward, passing one of the imperial vessels.

"We're very close to the demilitarized zone," said Veel quietly.

"Within photon missile range in five hundred millichrons," barked the opnav databox.

"He's cloaking," said Veel.

"Too late. He's dead," murmured the minister.

"There he goes."

The minister stabbed at buttons and leaned on controls. The ship vectored into hyperspace.

They entered normal space. The minister raced past the second of the Kivran ships.

"Within photon missile range in five hundred millichrons," the opnav databox repeated as it re-acquired the spy's ship.

"Fire one," ordered the minister.

"But we'll never hit...."

"Fire it," she shrieked. "I want him rattled."

Veel pressed the button, and a photon missile launched.

The spy ship jumped.

The imperial ships followed.

As soon as they materialized, all the Kivrans knew that their target had at last made a fatal mistake. They had materialized far too close to a star. Emergency systems kicked in, working overtime to protect them from the radiation.

Pilot Two swore loudly.

Gdrena leaned forward and switched off the communicator. Veel nodded his approval. It was impossible to concentrate while idiots babbled in one's ear. He looked at Gdrena's face. She did not notice: she was absorbed in the opnav screen floating in front of her.

It was difficult to see the Union ship: the efflux of charged particles from the star interfered with the scanners. But those same particles also interfered with the jamming system on board the Union ship, as well as all their guidance systems. This close to the star, not even a Black Ship could make a jump into hyperspace: the spacetime curvature was simply too great. If Gdrena could pilot their ship safely away from the immediate vicinity of the star, it would be a simple chase until she drew close enough to finish off the spy ship.

"We're inside the demilitarized zone," said Veel.

Technically, all the ships were now violating the Treaty of Empire and Union, but no one gave the violation a moment's thought; they were all too busy plotting safe courses around the star.

"Don't talk," the minister said. She was dropping closer to the star and accelerating, trying to close the gap.

Veel allowed himself a smile. He knew what Gdrena was doing. She knew that if Veel had been piloting their ship, the spy would have had no chance of getting away, and she was desperate to prove that she was as good a pilot as he. She wasn't, of course. But, he mused, she was certainly better than any of the others. And she was probably good enough. She was forcing the craft into a fast, low line, not quite as close to the surface of the star as he would have gone, but close enough. They were going to catch their man.

Gdrena wrestled with the controls, her eyes flicking over the opnav display. She lost sight of the spy's ship as the bulk of the star intervened. But it hardly mattered now. There was nowhere for the spy to run. His only chance was to try to reach a planet.

"The system. How many planets?" she barked.

Veel was momentarily flustered. She had caught him out. He had been so busy watching her, evaluating her skill at the controls, that he had forgotten that there were things he could be doing to help her. He spoke rapidly to the mapping databox. A moment later it responded.

"Nine," he said. "The third is inhabited by humans, uncivilized but advancing when last checked. We have several chronon monitors orbiting the periphery of the system, so someone must have thought it worthwhile to keep an eye on them."

Gdrena nodded. "That's where he'll go."

The ship began to pull away from the star, arcing high over one of its poles. Through the interference caused by the stellar particles, the screen showed the blurred, jittery image of the spy ship heading for a planet. The planet itself was not yet visible, but the computer displayed its predicted position, directly in the path of the ship.

"That's the inhabited one," Veel said. "Planet number three. It's called Tirsh."

Gdrena nodded. For a moment she took a hand away from the controls and stabbed at a single red button.

Even though she was not looking at him, she knew that Veel had seen what she had done, and now was gazing at her incredulously.

"I've armed the timeshift weapon because if he makes it to the planet, we don't want to hit him with a photon missile. And if he doesn't reach it, we don't want to leave evidence all over space for the Union to find. This way it will be nice and clean."

She stopped. Why was she justifying her use of the banned weapon to Veel? Was it because she was really justifying it to herself? She shrugged the questions aside. She was Amril Gdrena, and she answered to no one. She simply did whatever was necessary, and that was an end to the matter.

The two ships raced toward the planet, barely a chron apart. The interference from the solar particles diminished. The spy's jammer began to function once more, but by now the heuristic artificial intelligence circuits in the surveillance system had learned how to combat much of the jammer's effectiveness.

The imperial ship was the faster of the two, and the gap continued to decrease. Moments before reaching the third planet, the Union ship finally came within range of the Black Ship's photon missiles.

"Transfer surveillance program to armed photon missiles," the minister ordered.

Veel spoke quickly, downloading the program that had learned how to combat the jamming mechanism into the memories of the photon missiles. Amril Gdrena was not going to let the spy get away. If the timeshift weapon failed, a veritable swarm of photon missiles would obliterate the spy's ship, whatever the consequences.

The Union ship entered the atmosphere surrounding the third planet and applied full reverse thrust.

Still outside the atmosphere, the minister's ship closed.

The half of the planet they could see was covered almost entirely with water, with just one large land mass, not far from a large white polar cap.

"Timeshift lock," said Veel as the Union ship raced across the boundary of the continent and began to head inland toward what looked like a large desert.

"Fire," Amril Gdrena said.

There was a momentary hiccup in the display hovering before them. The signal disappeared.

The two scoured the display, looking for any trace of the ship they had been pursuing. There was none. The ship was now (whatever "now" meant) in another time continuum. The information its occupant had been carrying could never reach the Union.

125

So the threat had been dealt with, but as Brynt Veel piloted the ship back to Kivra, the minister's brow was clouded with thought.

If the Union had been capable of placing one spy so close to the very heart of the Empire, then surely they could place others. Tcharn would have to be a fool not to have sent in at least one more agent; and if there was one thing she knew about her opposite number in the Union, it was that he was not a fool.

As the ball of the Mother Planet filled the opnav display she pondered two questions: how many more deep-cover agents did the Union have on Kivra? and how long would it be before another attempt was made on the emperor's life?

15
HWANG

Hwang struggled to consciousness and tried to scream, but his teeth barely parted and what came out was little more than a feeble groan. He thought about opening his eyes, but the effort of just thinking about it was too much. He slipped back into unconsciousness.

The next time he awoke, the pain was less. It was still too much effort to open his eyes, but at least his brain was semi-functional.

The last thing he could remember was that he had been lying face down in mud while a massive crocodile looked across the short distance that separated them with an unmistakable malevolence.

But he was no longer on his stomach: now he was lying on his back on something that most definitely was not wet mud. He felt almost as if he were floating on a bag of air. He shifted his weight slightly; whatever he was lying on gave, accommodating the movement.

The air, too, smelt distinctly odd: quite different from the raw, natural, moist smell of the jungle. The overall impression was of civilization, of technology.

With a pleasurable feeling of relief he realized that he must somehow have returned to his own time. The quantum effect was only temporary, and now he was safely back in a hospital in Rabundi City, being attended by professional physicians. The thought relaxed him. He was warm, and comfortable, and sleepy....

The next time he awoke, he knew that he had slept for a long time. The air was cool and comfortable; and now he realized that there was a gentle pervasive humming just on the edge of perception.

He opened his eyes.

He was in a small room, so small that it was almost cramped. Apart from himself and the bed on which he lay, there were several machines crowding along one wall. He could not guess their purpose: they were simply gray surfaces on which what appeared to be buttons were strewn haphazardly; here and there were rectangles that might have been gauges of some kind. He and his bed were enclosed in a translucent bubble that arched perhaps half a meter above his head. A white sheet was draped over his body from the clavicle down. He was alone.

Several things about the room immediately struck him as decidedly odd.

It was too small for a hospital sickroom, and the usual accoutrements of such a room were entirely absent: there were no drip feeds, and no monitoring devices were connected to his body. Even the machines hugging the curved wall looked somehow too utilitarian to be concerned with life-support.

The room was curved: the ceiling meshed with the wall beside his bed, forming a single continuous smooth surface, as if he were enclosed in part of an enormous egg. The other three walls were completely undistinguished, except that in one was a large, white rectangle that might have been a door of some kind, although it was unlike any door that Hwang had ever seen. From his horizontal perspective there was something disquieting about the proportions of the putative door. It seemed somewhat taller than was strictly necessary.

Then there was the lighting. There was none. At least, there was no source of light that Hwang could immediately discern. The entire room was swathed in a gentle glow whose source was apparently the walls themselves.

The walls were a sort of russet color, except for the vertical wall that contained the door, which was instead a deep shade of green that clashed hideously with the other walls. There was nothing on the walls: no pictures; not even a vidscreen; nothing.

The floor was maroon, and made of some seamless material that glinted dully; it appeared to be stippled.

But something else was even stranger, and it took Hwang several seconds to realize what it was: he was no longer in pain. There was just the barest twinge of something in his chest where the massive cat had ripped his flesh open and exposed a rib.

He moved the sheet to look. All that remained of the wound was a barely-discernible yellowish scar.

Suddenly, there was a movement in the opposite wall.

The white rectangle *was* a door. It slid open soundlessly and a shadow stepped into the doorway.

At first, Hwang could see only a silhouette of a tall man. The man paused in the doorway for a few moments before stepping into the room.

He reached the bed in two strides, then looked down at Hwang, and smiled. The man's head nearly brushed the ceiling.

All Hwang's misgivings about where he might be were doubled, then redoubled.

In the diffuse light from the walls, Hwang could see the man well enough. His clothes glistened metallically in a manner that was unsettlingly unlike any clothing Hwang had ever seen. But it was the man's features that were the most disturbing. The man's face was smooth — too smooth. He had a clear, high forehead that was topped by a thatch of brown hair. A few crows' feet around the corners of the eyes gave an impression of age distinctly at odds with the youthfulness of his skin. The man's lips were thin almost to the point of nonexistence, and they were a kind of dark brown rather than any shade of red. His eyes were almost black, so that it was difficult to tell where iris ended and pupil began. His skin was sallow, its shade not dissimilar to Hwang's own.

The thin lips were curved into a hesitant smile, but there was no smile in the man's eyes. It was hard to read his expression, but Hwang thought hopefully that it contained a trace of anxious compassion.

Whoever the man was, it was obvious that Hwang owed him his life. He returned the man's smile.

The man made an ambiguous motion with his hand, then turned to the gray machines. He fiddled for a moment at one of them, then turned to face Hwang. The shield enveloping the bed seemed to move and fold in on itself and, in a few seconds, had completely hidden itself somewhere under the bed.

The odors in the air suddenly became stronger — and now, unmistakably, there was something cold and distant and alien about them. Suppressing the disturbing and quite fantastic possibilities that were flitting through his head, Hwang spoke.

"Thank you."

He sounded unnaturally gruff, and he cleared his throat and repeated his thanks.

Wordlessly, the man held up his hand, then gently lowered it to rest on Hwang's chest. Hwang could feel the pressure of the man's hand through the sheet. There was no pain, none at all.

"Vrsanith," the man said, seemingly to himself.

His smile was now echoed in his eyes, and Hwang had no difficulty in recognizing the man's satisfaction at a job well done. The man stepped back, and from somewhere produced a small circular object.

"Ghtrznk klnk," the man said, offering the device to Hwang.

Hwang's eyes widened in surprise: it was his wristcom. He slipped it on to his wrist.

"Ghenn smwub," the man said, turning and beckoning for Hwang to follow.

For several moments Hwang remained unmoving on the bed, fingering the wristcom and staring down at the scar on his chest. He placed a finger on the scar and pressed, gently at first and then firmly, but still he could feel no pain. He looked up; the man was waiting in the doorway.

Hwang slid out of bed and was momentarily embarrassed to discover that he was naked. He looked around, but could see no clothes. The man beckoned once more for him to follow.

The floor's stippling was revealed as thousands of tiny bumps of some soft, rubbery material. It was quite pleasant to walk on, although slightly strange. He crossed the small room, and then followed the man through the doorway.

He stopped in shock.

For a moment he thought that he was going to faint, for it was now no longer possible for some part of his mind to argue that he was in some kind of esoteric recovery area in a hospital back in Rabundi City. Now it was obvious where he was.

He was inside a spaceship.

It was a small ship, that much was obvious from the cramped quarters. In front of him was a bare area delimited by several of the green walls with white doors. The floor was a continuation of the maroon stippling; the ceiling was a squat purple dome. The horizontal distance from the center of the dome to the wall beside the bed in which he had been lying was no more than five meters. Assuming that the ship was symmetric, then its diameter could be no more than about ten meters. The distance from the floor to the highest point of the dome was about three meters.

He and the "man" — who he was now sure was not human — were standing in a central area from which led several doorways. The doorway through which they had come slid silently closed and seemed to merge with the wall, betraying its presence only by the difference in color.

"Pvranti," the man said.

Hwang turned and saw that one of the other doors had opened and the man was stepping into the room beyond. Hwang followed into a small room, the mirror of the one in which he had first awakened. There was a bed in the room, along the curve of the far wall. The only other item was a closet, whose door slid open in response to a gesture from the man. He began to rummage inside.

There were no machines in this room. There was not even a table or any kind of a chair, just the bed and the closet. The room betrayed no individuality: just like the room in which Hwang had awoken, there was nothing on the walls or floors to provide any clue about the personality of the person who slept here.

After perhaps half a minute, the man turned to Hwang with several garments on his arm. He placed them on the bed, made a putting-on motion, and then retreated from the room. The door slid closed with an unnerving lack of sound.

Hwang looked at the clothes. They obviously belonged to the man — or perhaps he should call him "the alien" — and so were quite the wrong size for Hwang. They had the same shiny metallic sheen as the clothes the alien was wearing, and when Hwang stretched out his hand to touch them he expected them to feel cold and impersonal. Instead they were warm and soft.

He lifted one of the garments, a kind of tunic, and examined it in the light from the wall. No matter how closely he looked, he could see no trace of either weave or seam. The garment seemed to have been fabricated from a single piece of some quasimetallic substance. Hesitantly, he put it on. The sleeves drooped a good six inches beyond his fingertips, and the tunic came so low that it covered his private parts. He knew that he must look ludicrous. But the alien had seemed to indicate that he was to wear these clothes, so, slowly and aware of how ridiculous he must look, he donned the other items.

When he had finished, he could barely walk, for the legs of the pants made it difficult to take a step without tripping. Nevertheless, he carefully made his way to the doorway. He halted, wondering how to open the door, but it suddenly slid open of its own accord.

The alien was outside, apparently waiting for Hwang to emerge. It was obvious that he suppressed a laugh when he saw Hwang.

For a moment, Hwang was annoyed. What had the alien expected? He must surely have known that his clothes would not fit.

The alien stepped forward; then he reached out and began to stroke Hwang's right sleeve gently with one hand. Hwang felt a strange movement, as if the sleeve had been imbued with a life of its own. After several seconds, the man took his hand away and Hwang looked in amazement at the place where the man had touched the garment: the sleeve now fitted his arm perfectly. The man pointed to Hwang's other arm. Hwang began to stroke it as the man had done. He felt the sleeve moving of its own accord and after a few moments the movements stopped: that sleeve too now fit perfectly. The alien smiled broadly.

"Itvik nbrzhnz," he said.

Working together, the two of them had Hwang's clothes fitting perfectly in less than two minutes.

"Thank you," Hwang said when they had finished.

"Dethersnz mobritz."

There was an awkward silence while they regarded each other. They had to learn to communicate. Unless the alien had some other tricks up his mobile sleeves, that would take much longer than simply fitting Hwang with a new suit of clothes.

Hwang pointed to himself and said slowly, "Hwang Lee." He repeated his first name several times, enunciating clearly: "Hwang, Hwang, Hwang."

The man did not react. He neither repeated Hwang's name nor did he tell Hwang his name. Instead he simply looked at Hwang. He did not furrow his brow, but Hwang had the distinct impression that nevertheless the alien was deep in thought.

Then the alien slowly leaned forward. He lifted his hands slowly to Hwang's face. Hwang looked uncertainly at the approaching hands, then drew away, fearful of the alien's intentions.

The alien stopped, and pondered for a moment. Then he lifted his hands to his own face, separated his lips with his fingers, and opened and closed them several times. A stream of gibberish poured forth.

Hwang looked at him in puzzlement. What was the alien trying to tell him?

The alien leaned forward again and slowly raised his hands to Hwang's face. The alien's hands were smoother and distinctly warmer than ordinary human hands. One hand rested on Hwang's chin and one on his upper lip — there was a bristle of hair in both places. Hwang wondered tangentially how long he had been asleep. The alien forcibly opened and closed Hwang's mouth several times.

The alien said, "Ghstnrti vwolok persinad," and withdrew his hands.

Hesitantly, Hwang tried to repeat the words: "Ghstnrti vwolok persinad."

But it was obvious that this was not what the alien wanted. And in any case, the words sounded quite different when they came out of his own mouth; there were nuances in the alien's speech that he could not reproduce. And there were probably other subtleties that had completely escaped him.

Hwang shrugged, then pointed to himself and said, "Hwang."

The man stared at him for several seconds then said, "Hwang."

The man pointed at Hwang, repeated the name several times, then paused as if waiting. He looked, thought Hwang, distinctly bored.

The two regarded one another for some time. The alien's expression was unreadable. The negricity of his large eyes made him seem to be staring wide-eyed at Hwang.

Hwang felt unnerved by the alien's gaze. It was obvious that the alien was frustrated by Hwang's inability to grasp something simple. But what? Hwang could not imagine what the alien expected of him.

Knowing that this was not what the alien wanted, he tapped his chest several times and repeated, "Hwang."

The alien looked distinctly unhappy.

Eventually, the alien repeated the word: "Hwang."

Aware that he had somehow disappointed the alien, Hwang tried to comfort himself with the thought that at least communication had begun.

16

AMRIL GDRENA

Amril Gdrena tried to put herself in Tcharn's position. He must have a contingency plan in case his spy was caught or killed. But what could that plan be?

She started with one of the few facts of which she was certain: Tcharn's spy had been employed as a gardener in the imperial gardens.

It was a clever choice of occupation. An imperial gardener could gain unauthorized access to the palace more easily than almost anyone else. Also, the background checks to which gardeners were subject were far weaker than for most governmental positions, because gardeners typically came from the Outer Planets, where backgrounds were notoriously vague.

The spy's apartment was ransacked, but the gardener had cleaned it out. That told the minister something important: the attempted assassination was not the result of some sudden, unexpected opportunity; it must have been a carefully premeditated act.

It was impossible for the spy to remove all traces of his presence from the apartment, though, and the forensic specialists found plenty of samples of his skin and hair. From these, the spy's DNA was extracted, and then began the long process of matching these against the Empire's DNA bank.

The DNA of most imperial citizens for the last two centuries had been digitally encoded. There were still some parts of the Empire where the reporting of DNA was incomplete — the Outer Planets were notoriously lax about such matters — but even so the bank held the digitized DNA for over three hundred billion people, living and dead.

Amril Gdrena ordered the spy's DNA to be checked against the database. When the report reached her desk, it contained a surprise.

The databoxes concluded that there was a 99·2% probability that the spy who had been timeshifted was the grandson of the man whom a young Amril Gdrena had shot while protecting the emperor on Klivliviv.

The minister pondered the coincidence. Why, of all the people available to him, had Tcharn chosen Var-Lem's grandson to execute the task in which Var-Lem himself had failed?

She had a great deal of respect for her opposite number — far more than she had for any of her colleagues on the Inner Council. More than once she had mused that if Tcharn and she had chanced to be on the same side, together they would have ruled the galaxy. It was a silly idea, of course. She already ruled one third of the galaxy, and she was intelligent enough to know that if the two of them had really both been on the same side, one of them would long ago have met with a fatal accident. She smiled wryly. She wondered which of them would have survived.

Tcharn operated at a severe disadvantage compared to herself. The Union's head of state was elected by a Union-wide vote every five cycles, and Tcharn served only at the pleasure of whoever happened to be the current president. Policies changed with every new incumbent, and she recognized that it must be difficult for Tcharn to plot a consistent course through the ever-changing and sometimes stormy seas of Union politics.

At the moment, the poor man was saddled with the most inept and naïf president ever elected to that position. She almost felt sorry for Tcharn. President Rahl actually believed that a long-lasting, galaxy-wide peace based on mutual trust and cooperation was attainable. He wanted desperately to increase ties between the Union and the Empire, and had made deep cuts in the Union's defense budget as a gesture of good will towards the emperor. She wondered how Tcharn was coping with the novel idea that the greatest threat to his beloved Union was not the Empire but its own president.

After gloating idly for a few moments, the minister wiped the smile off her face. Tcharn might be in difficulties, but he was still a worthy opponent. He must surely have placed more than one spy on Kivra, but how could she find the others? And what about the strange coincidence uncovered by the DNA database? Surely it could not be just chance that the two Unionists who had tried to kill the emperor were so closely related?

The juxtaposition of these apparently disparate thoughts triggered an idea in her mind.

Tcharn was not the only one with spies. And so the minister instigated enquiries inside the Union about the family of Var-Lem, the man who long ago had tried to assassinate the emperor on faraway Klivliviv. What, she wanted to know, had happened to Var-Lem's family?

It was nearly a third of a cycle before she received an answer. As she read the report, she began to salivate.

Var-Lem had been survived by a woman with the official status of "spouse," meaning that the two had pledged themselves to each other for the duration of their natural lives. When Var-Lem left Qintir on his ill-fated expedition to the Empire, there was one living child, a girl, Tan-Lem, roughly ten cycles in age.

Tan-Lem had grown up on her home planet of Qintir. In her youth, she had apparently garnered something of a reputation as a firebrand (with a penchant for robbing banks, Gdrena noted with amusement) and she had moved briefly in the higher circles of Qintirian society, apparently welcomed as a kind of celebrity rebel.

In her early twenties, she dropped out of sight and little more was known of her. She had apparently lived the rest of her life in obscurity, probably in one of the impoverished villages that dotted the planet, but nothing was known for sure.

Only one other fact was certain: around the time she disappeared, Tan-Lem had given birth to twins, a boy called Rum-Lem, and a girl named Per-Lem. From that point on, no one seemed to know anything about either the children or their mother.

Gdrena's informant reported that Qintir was a primitive planet on which reporting and record keeping was lax. While it would be possible to instigate a full search for the children and their mother (if she was still alive, which was doubtful given the short life expectancy on Qintir), to do so might raise suspicions, for strangers were not welcomed in such places.

As Gdrena read the report, she became more and more certain she could fill in the blanks: Var-Lem's daughter Tan-Lem had been brought up by her mother, who had inculcated into the child a hatred of the Empire, a hatred having its origin in the long-ago border incident in which the parents of her spouse, Var-Lem, were killed, and fed by the loss of Tan-Lem's father after his failed attempt to kill the emperor.

Tan-Lem, for whatever reason, had decided against taking personal revenge against the Empire, preferring instead to raid the banks which had repossessed the family farm after her father's death. But she had coupled, and two children had been born and, like her mother before her, Tan-Lem had indoctrinated her children with a deep hatred of the Empire.

The minister drew a chart:

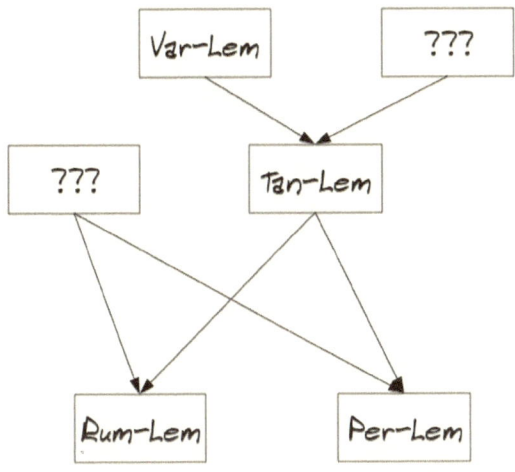

At some point, the existence of the children had become known to Tcharn — perhaps they had even volunteered their services — setting into motion this second attempt to rid the Empire of its figurehead.

It was a tenuous chain of logic, but it explained the relationship uncovered by the DNA databoxes: the spy was Rum-Lem, Var-Lem's grandson.

But this theory left one question unanswered: the grandson was gone, thrust into a time continuum from which there was no escape; *but where was the granddaughter?*

Was Per-Lem as carefully hidden somewhere inside the Empire as her brother had been? And if so, how to find her?

Gdrena began with the imperial gardeners. Of the slightly less than a thousand gardeners, about a quarter were women. She considered bringing them all in to be mindprobed, but rejected that idea as untenable. Per-Lem would be doubly careful since Rum-Lem's disappearance. She would be on the lookout for anything out of the ordinary, and at the first sign that the gardeners were being mindprobed she would go to ground or flee, and Gdrena would never find her.

Instead, the minister instigated secret background checks on every gardener, male and female. It would take time, perhaps more time than she had, but it was the only way to proceed without alerting Var-Lem's granddaughter that Gdrena was looking for her.

Backgrounds were examined, DNA tested, records of employees and their parents checked and rechecked, looking for any inconsistency. There were none; everyone passed — except one man.

Records for a man named Teberill Gandeer were almost complete, lacking only a sample of his birth DNA, which was not an uncommon omission in the case of workers from the Outer Planets. But there was a more glaring problem. The DNA he had provided when he had joined the government's employ could not possibly have come from a native of Whidden, the planet that was supposedly his birthplace.

Further investigation increased her suspicions: the records indicated that shortly after Teberill had left Whidden as a young man, the farm on which he had been raised had burned down, killing both his parents. He had no other relatives.

She initiated a search, trying to find someone who had known the gardener as a child, someone who would be able to tell them whether the man now living under that name was indeed the real Teberill Gandeer.

After the Gandeer farm had burned, its land had been purchased by the owners of an adjacent farm. The old couple from that farm remembered the young Teberill well, and informed the P&S investigator that he had had only one close friend as a child: their own son Distren, who had long ago moved away to the Olberon system.

Distren was located, picked up, and brought to Kivra, where he was ushered into the minister's office. She gave him a glass of pazen juice to calm his nerves, then showed him a holograph.

"Do you recognize that man?"

Distren shook his head. "I don't think so."

"Look carefully. Your childhood friend, Teberill Gandeer, perhaps?"

For a long time Distren looked at the holograph, viewing it from several angles, his brow furrowed in concentration.

Eventually he said, "Well, it's difficult to be sure. It's been fifteen cycles since I saw him last, but I don't think that's Teberill. The eyes are somehow wrong — too far apart, perhaps. But I wouldn't want to stake my life on it."

"Tell me," Gdrena asked Distren with a quiet, confidential air as she leaned comfortably back in her chair, "was there something you used to do with your friend Teberill when you were children? Some game you used to play, perhaps? Or was there some event, perhaps an embarrassing one, that both of you know about but which neither of you would ever share with someone else? Something that was completely private between the two of you? Is there something that Teberill could not possibly have forgotten, so that if he met you now, and you referred to it, he would react in a way that only you could predict? Or perhaps there was some secret password or phrase that used to have a special meaning to just the two of you? The name of some club that you and he invented?"

Amril Gdrena waited patiently. The man was nervous, but that was understandable. This was a moment he would remember for the rest of his life. Give him time, he'll remember something. He was bound to; there was always *something* to remember.

The man's face broke into a hesitant smile.

"There was something," he said. "Please forgive me, but this is going to sound awfully stupid."

"You were children. Children never do anything stupid." Gdrena spoke softly, as if she were stating an obvious truth that she believed with all her heart.

"There was a game we used to play when we were counting the vagren in the fields. We invented our own way of counting, using made-up words for numbers...."

"Go on." The minister smiled her encouragement.

"We would count like this:" Distren continued, "yan, tan, tethera, methera.... We had numbers all the way up to four hundred, although I don't think I could remember them all now. It was a decimal system, just like ordinary numbers, because back then we did not imagine there could be any other way of counting. We built larger numbers using the smaller ones, like saying 'ten and one' for eleven. It got a bit unwieldy once we reached a hundred and eleven."

Gdrena nodded, the friendly smile still on her face.

"I see. So you are telling me that if someone went up to Teberill Gandeer and said — what was it? — 'Yan, tan, tethera...,' Gandeer would either respond with the word 'methera', or he would at the very least want to know where the person had learned those words?"

"Yes, I think so."

"I see."

Gdrena paused for a while, lost in thought. Distren waited, sipping his pazen juice.

"OK," she eventually continued, "what we'll do is this. We'll arrange for you to meet the man in the holograph apparently by chance in the imperial gardens. You will say, 'Yan, tan, tethera.' We will watch his response. If he does not react in a way that you think is reasonable, simply ignore him and continue on your way. If he does respond the way he should, then greet him like the old friend he is. Tell us anything that seems unusual, but otherwise you will be free to return to Olberon once you have done this small thing for us."

So the meeting was orchestrated. And Teberill Gandeer failed the test.

––––––––––––––

Teberill Gandeer's specialty was ferns. So when someone reported that a cluster of ferns in a secluded part of the public portion of the gardens was dying, it was his responsibility to investigate.

He squatted on the ground, examining the sorry-looking plants, trying to understand what could have caused such an unhealthy brownish tinge. It was a puzzle; he had seen nothing quite like it before. It was almost as if something was poisoning the plants. He pulled out a small kit to take a soil sample.

His attention was momentarily distracted by a solitary stranger approaching along a nearby path. The man was pale and walked quickly. Teberill Gandeer's attention returned to the ferns.

Perhaps it was too much phosphorus in the soil? But that didn't explain the fact that the plants seemed to have been thriving until recently. Could something possibly have been added to the soil?

"Yan, tan, tethera."

The gardener looked up, annoyed at the interruption.

"I'm sorry? What was that?"

The stranger had halted nearby. He had been smiling in a friendly manner, but now the smile was suddenly wiped off his face. In its place was something that looked almost like fear. The man was trembling slightly. He spoke again, his words falling over themselves.

"I'm sorry. I said: 'yan, tan, tethera.' It's a way of counting, like 'one, two, three.' I'm sure you've never heard of it. It doesn't mean anything. Sorry if I interrupted you."

And the stranger moved off, walking even more quickly than before.

The gardener watched the stranger. A hidden holographic vidcam caught his frown as he returned to his work.

Amril Gdrena smiled at the vidcam image. She did not know yet how the gardener fitted into Tcharn's scheme, but she was sure that somehow the man who called himself Teberill Gandeer was connected to Rum-Lem. Whoever the man was, he wasn't the real Teberill Gandeer.

The gardener finished his work, then picked up his tools and walked quickly away.

Gdrena refrained from taking precipitate action. Now that she had her man, she was satisfied simply to watch and to wait. She did not understand the links among Rum-Lem, his as-yet-undetected twin sister Per-Lem, and the man who called himself Teberill Gandeer, but she was certain that somehow they were connected. If only she waited, the puzzle would unravel itself of its own accord.

While he was at work, the gardener's apartment was searched, but it betrayed nothing. A DNA sample was matched yet again against the sample from the man who had originally been hired under the name of Teberill Gandeer, some ten cycles earlier. It matched. Whoever he really was, he had been in place for a very long time — just like Rum-Lem.

More and more, the minister found herself brooding about Tcharn's plan.

Why had Rum-Lem remained in place for so long before acting? He could just as well have attempted to assassinate the emperor long ago. What had changed half a cycle ago?

She could think of only one possibility, although that possibility seemed so unlikely as to be barely feasible. Was Tcharn so prescient that he had foreseen long ago the possibility that a weak and peace-loving president would one day be elected to head the Union? Could he possibly have rationalized that were such a thing ever to happen, his position would be under threat — and the best defense would be to increase tensions between the Empire and the Union? Was that the whole point of Tcharn's operation? To nullify President Rahl?

Or was she on the wrong track entirely? Was she overestimating her opponent? Or did he have some goal that she had not yet uncovered?

She picked up a communicator and threw it across the room. It shattered with a satisfying crash against the far wall.

For five rotations following the meeting with Distren Teberill Gandeer was watched. For five rotations nothing happened. For five rotations Amril Gdrena was unnaturally tense.

On the morning of the sixth rotation, Amril Gdrena attended a meeting of the Inner Council; and that morning the gardener calling himself Teberill Gandeer varied his routine.

It was the start of a personal three-rotation rest period, and shortly after firstmeal he took a taxi to the spaceport. There he purchased a ticket for Soam, connecting via Prantys.

The surveillance team, whose brief covered surveillance only while the subject was on Kivra, called in for instructions.

But the minister could not be reached, and, in the absence of specific orders, the leader of the surveillance team decided that it was safer to let the subject go than it was to exceed his authority and follow the subject off-planet. That decision cost him his rank. The passenger liner for Prantys left shortly afterwards with the gardener on board, unwatched.

As Amril Gdrena emerged from the conference room, Brynt Veel approached and thrust a memorandum at her.

"You won't like it," he predicted.

He was right. She was furious, but there was nothing she could do about it except to have the idiot in charge of the surveillance team demoted so quickly that his head swam.

The minister ordered an immediate check on the passenger manifests of all ships arriving on Prantys within the last two rotations, including ones still in flight. The results arrived less than twenty chrons later, and a coincidence was immediately obvious: travelling on the same liner as the gardener, and also bound for Soam, was a mid-level member of her own ministry, a woman by the name of Lystra Ten-Wer.

Amril Gdrena consulted her databox, sure that she was on the verge of something important. Lystra Ten-Wer's file appeared on the screen. Born and raised on the planet Eb — yet another of those backward Outer Planets with an agricultural economy and on which the imperial presence was nominal. Parents dead — how convenient. Graduated with highest honors from Kivra Imperial University. Applied for a position with P&S. Offered the job, which she accepted. Since then, climbed the bureaucracy with almost undue haste. Half a cycle ago promoted to Grade 15. Half a cycle ago.... The minister checked the date. Lystra Ten-Wer had moved to her new position only three rotations before Rum-Lem had made his assassination attempt. Coincidence?

Her eyes ran to the detailed entries from the last half cycle:

Case 67-4521-41   *Citizen 465-987-098-125*
                                     Lystra Ghetrol Ten-Wer
                                     Supervisor: Visik Qwilm

Subject interviewed with regard to failure to forward a red report from chronon monitorship 35/CW. Subject admits negligence by failing to follow Standard Order 723-A.

Action taken: Punitive 2% decrease in salary. Warned that a repetition will precipitate immediate investigation with view to demotion to Grade 14, along with any other appropriate disciplinary action.

Secret audit of subject's performance by monitor oversight team to be performed regularly, at periods not to exceed four decarotations.

Disposition: closed.

Note 67-1151-4652   *Citizen 465-987-098-125*
                                       Lystra Ghetrol Ten-Wer
                                       Supervisor: Visik Qwilm

Mindprobe report: Subject passed all scenario tests. In accordance with Order 327961, subject was exposed to scenarios 721A and 721B, with the following results:

721A: subject betrayed Dalithian spy to the subject's supervisor; subject did not recognize gardener Teberill Gandeer;

721B: subject did not recognize Rum-Lem; subject was unfamiliar with Dalithian and Qintirian birdcalls; subject refused to discuss her work with Rum-Lem.

Then Gdrena came to the most recent entries. She read them quickly.

Case 67-4521-80   *Citizen 465-987-098-125*
                                     Lystra Ghetrol Ten-Wer
                                     Supervisor: Visik Qwilm

Subject interviewed with regard to failure to forward a red report from chronon monitorship 35/CW. Subject insists that the report was forwarded in accordance with Standing Order 723-A, but databox records indicate that report was deleted by subject and was not forwarded.

Action taken: subject placed on indefinite leave, pending a thorough check by technicians regarding the possibility of databox programming error, as suggested by subject. Subject continues to protest that report was forwarded in accordance with Standing Order 723-A.

Disposition: Case remains open.

There was a brief addendum, added the evening of the rotation before:

Case 67-4521-80

Technicians find no evidence of databox error. To the contrary, records show that the red report was deliberately deleted by subject.

Detailed examination of subject's databox reveals unauthorized access to records from imperial palace security databoxes on date 2657-215.

Action taken: none at this time; will schedule interview with subject at earliest possible opportunity, to be followed by possible mindprobe.

Disposition: Case remains open.

The minister was certain: Lystra Ten-Wer was really Per-Lem. The evidence from her personal databox clinched it: the date 2657-215 was just prior to Rum-Lem's attempt to kill the emperor. She had accessed the imperial palace security databoxes and passed to Rum-Lem the information that had allowed him to enter the palace. Amril Gdrena did not know how she had fooled the mindprobes — that was supposed to be impossible — but somehow it had happened. Lystra Ten-Wer was Per-Lem, brother of Rum-Lem. And now she and Teberill Gandeer were on a ship bound for Soam. Doubtless their journey wouldn't end there. They were running for home.

She pressed her communicator.

"Veel, come here; we're going on a trip."

When he arrived, Brynt Veel knew better than to ask where they were going. He followed the minister to the docking port where her hovercar awaited. Veel slid into the pilot's seat.

"The military spaceport," the minister ordered.

Gdrena's official ministerial ship was not a Black Ship, but it was the next best thing. They lifted off as soon as they were aboard, heading for Prantys.

They exited hyperspace near Prantys fifty chrons after the liner carrying Teberill Gandeer and Lystra Ten-Wer had landed. Gdrena spat out her orders to the local P&S outpost via commlink.

"I want to know what happened to two people who arrived on the recently-landed passenger liner from Kivra: Teberill Gandeer, male, and Lystra Ten-Wer, female, both with tickets for Soam. Where are they now? And are they together?"

The answer arrived as they were making their final approach for landing: Teberill Gandeer and Lystra Ten-Wer were aboard a ferryship that had just been sealed preparatory to lifting off for a string of nearby planets: Soam, Printir, Deleron, Mark and Bithîk.

"Are they seated together?" Gdrena asked urgently.

Yes.

"Unseal the ship. I want someone on board, watching them."

She turned to Brynt Veel. "They're trapped. They can't escape now. Tcharn has been too slow this time. The only trick will be to take them alive."

Veel nodded, and a rare smile crinkled his face.

17

AMRIL GDRENA

Technically, Soam was not an imperial colony; its official status was merely that of a research base. There were no permanent communities on the planet, and it did not engage in trade. Soam was simply a scientific outpost which permitted a small amount of tourism in order to lessen the drain on the imperial purse. Soam's entry in the records was correspondingly brief, and by the time her ship landed, Amril Gdrena had absorbed everything the records contained about the planet.

She wasted no time dealing with the Outpost Officer, who was officially responsible for maintaining law and order on Soam. She knew the kind of person who was typically appointed to such a position: some hanger-on who had once done someone a favor, and whose reward was to oversee a small colony of scientists whose last thought was to give the governing authorities any trouble.

Instead, she established a secure link back to the head of the Law Enforcement section of her ministry back on Kivra.

Section Head Tril snapped to attention when he saw who was at the other end of the incoming commlink.

"Madam minister, what can I do for you?"

In his consternation, he knocked a pile of reports to the floor. He pretended not to notice.

"Section Head Tril, I am about to land on a planet by the name of Soam."

Tril looked even more flustered. He had never heard of the place, and he was afraid that the omission would be interpreted by the minister as a lack of dedication.

Amril Gdrena elaborated: "It's a minor research outpost not far from the demilitarized zone, close to the Prantys system."

Tril nodded enthusiastically. At least he knew where Prantys was.

"I want a full communications blackout zone established around Soam in less than fifty chrons. Put the barrier up outside the navigation satellites, so that only communications beyond the planet are affected."

"Yes, madam minister; immediately, madam...."

"And I want fifty of your agents to report to me on the surface in forty five chrons. Jump to it."

The minister abruptly closed the link.

"Get this ship down as quickly as you can, Veel," she ordered.

"Yes, madam minister," he mimicked the obsequious manner of the section head.

Gdrena glared at him, then smiled. Veel's insubordination was unimportant. Tcharn's agents were trapped.

Section Head Tril did a commendable job. Soam was electronically sealed from the rest of the galaxy in precisely forty two and a half chrons. It took slightly longer for the fifty operatives to arrive on-planet, but Amril Gdrena was quietly pleased as she reviewed the team now standing before her at the edge of the Soam spaceport with uniformly grim expressions.

Her orders were simple.

"There are two people, a male and a female, registered in the names of Teberill Gandeer and Lystra Ten-Wer, at the tourist center at Marsûk. They are in separate but adjoining rooms, at least for the present. You are to place them under full covert surveillance. At the first suspicious sign from either of them, they are to be stunned and brought to me. The same goes if the surveillance is compromised. Under no circumstances is either of them to be allowed to regain consciousness if it is necessary to stun them. They are suspected Union agents of the highest caliber, and they will certainly kill themselves rather than permit themselves to fall into our hands. You are not to let that happen. I want these people alive, but I also want to observe them for as long as possible before we make a move. Do I make myself clear?"

147

Fifty heads nodded.

"And I don't think I need tell you what the penalty is for failure?"

The operatives remained motionless, but adopted even grimmer expressions.

"Right. Get to it."

By the time the short Soaman night began, imperial agents were installed in all the rooms near to those in which Lystra Ten-Wer and Teberill Gandeer were sleeping.

The following morning, the spies ate firstmeal together in the restaurant. In a corner a mismatched couple, a woman in her early fifties and a tall, unsmiling man dressed in black and more than twenty cycles her junior, kept a watchful eye on them.

Their meal concluded, the gardener and the P&S bureaucrat ambled to the hovercar park, where they boarded the car they had rented the day before. They lifted off and headed northeastward.

Amril Gdrena and Brynt Veel followed in an unmarked hovercar, keeping their target just in sight in the distance.

They had not gone far when Veel said with a note of alarm, "They've just disappeared off the scanner."

"What do you mean?"

"Exactly what I said," snapped Veel. He swore.

The spies' hovercar was a barely-visible dot in the sky ahead of them; it should have been clearly visible on the scanner. But there was nothing.

"They must be carrying some sort of jammer."

"So, Brynt Veel, we know you're the best pilot ever to sit in the control seat of a space fighter, but how are you at piloting a mere hovercar? Are you going to let them lose you?"

Veel slammed the throttle forward. He and the minister were rammed deeply into their seats.

For perhaps half a chron, Veel closed the gap. Now they could make out the outline of the hovercar ahead. Without warning, it suddenly plunged towards the green canopy of the jungle far below. As it plummeted, the hovercar disappeared against the dark background of the jungle.

"I can't see it," Veel said angrily.

This was a trick he had not thought of. He raced downward, trying to bring their target above his horizon.

"Surely you're not going to let some gardener from the imperial gardens lose you? I expected better than that from you, Veel. I could have you killed for less, you know."

Veel could not tell if Gdrena was serious, but in any case there was nothing more he could do. He was a fighter pilot, not some gutless hovercar taxi driver.

By the time he arrived at the point where he had last seen the spies, he knew he had been beaten. The other vehicle was nowhere to be seen.

He piloted their craft in tight circles, searching the sky for some trace of a moving black dot.

"He's lost you, hasn't he?"

Veel nodded. He expected an outburst, but Gdrena simply laughed.

"All right, go back to the spaceport. At least you're man enough to admit when you've been beaten. We'll take our ship into orbit and wait for them to break cover. They can't transmit a message and they can't leave. They obviously knew they're being watched, but it seems they don't intend to commit suicide, so it hardly matters what they get up to until we find them again."

Veel turned the hovercar and headed for the spaceport.

Forty chrons later, the minister's ship was in a high-inclination orbit around Soam, circling the planet every 60 chrons. On board, the minister and Brynt Veel watched the scanners, waiting for the spies to break cover.

They waited all day. Twilight was falling at the tourist center when a hovercar suddenly appeared from nowhere over the sea, heading for Marsûk. It IDed as the gardener's hovercar. Not far away, a hovercar flown by P&S operatives turned to intercept. It fell into place behind the gardener's vehicle, trailing it closely; they weren't going to lose him a second time.

The gardener landed at the center, and moments later an operative transmitted an urgent message.

"Madam minister, the man, Teberill Gandeer, just returned to the tourist center. I just saw him leave his hovercar."

"And the woman?"

"Madam minister, she is not with him. He is alone."

"Don't let him out of your sight. And don't let him leave Marsûk again. Stun him if necessary."

She flicked off the communicator and looked at Veel.

"All right, Veel, Soam is only a small planet; it shouldn't take us long to find her. Take the ship down into the atmosphere."

The minister turned on the life detector, adjusting it so that it would register only humans.

"Go to the place where we lost them this morning," the minister ordered as the ship plunged through the rarefied upper layers of the atmosphere. "Then fly outward from that point in a spiral. There's nowhere she can hide from us. The detector will find her. If she's still alive."

18
HWANG

To talk for an hour, or even for two or three hours, is not a particularly arduous task. To be forced to continue speaking for three days — especially when one's audience comprises an individual who rarely responds to one's words — is strangely humiliating, difficult and tiresome.

At first, Hwang thought that it wouldn't take long. He moved quickly through the ship, naming things out loud — at least the things he could identify. Then he led the alien outside and pronounced carefully the names of everything he could see from the small island in the middle of the river on which the ship had landed.

In the process, he naturally learned much about the alien vessel. The ship was an ovoid about ten meters in its longest dimension. There was only a single level, with the floor exactly midway up the vessel. Presumably the lower half housed the propulsion and other vital systems. The ship was cramped, apparently designed for just one occupant; presumably other ships (for surely there must be others) might be much larger.

The central area beyond the room in which he had awoken was surrounded by four vertical walls, each with a single white door. The doors had some way of sensing one's approach — it was only later that the idea came to him that it was the stipples on the floor that did the sensing — and opened automatically to let one through. Two of the doors led to rooms that he had already seen. Another led to the largest room on the ship, in which there was a machine that dispensed what passed for food, as well as flavored water. In the center of this room was a kind of table and a couple of chairs. There was also a small subsidiary room leading off this dining area, which turned out to be a bathroom and toilet.

The last room was the control cabin. This looked like nothing Hwang had ever seen before. It was the smallest room of all, excepting the bathroom, and the lighting was so subdued that it took a while for his eyes to adjust to the gloom.

At first, all Hwang could make out was a pair of seats and a blank console with a few indentations and bars that looked like they might be lights, although they were unlit.

The alien gestured for Hwang to sit in one of the chairs, and when he did so he was momentarily discomfited to find that the chair not only conformed to his body but also raised itself slightly off the ground, so that it hung in the air a short distance above the floor without any visible means of support. Simultaneously, several colored bars and panels appeared on the console in front of him. There was also a faint hum. He stretched out a hand to touch the control panel, but the alien thrust out an arm to stop him.

"Trwsqk vladik," the alien said with a wide smile on his face, which Hwang took as a friendly warning not to touch the panel.

"Panel, light, chair or seat," Hwang said, naming the objects as he pointed to them, wearily returning to his task.

After finishing with the control cabin they went outside where the ship was unexpectedly unimpressive. Its color was mostly a dull, dark maroon, with here and there symbols of various sizes rendered in a kind of muddy blue.

The hull was slightly stippled, rather like the floor inside, although it seemed to be constructed of some kind of metal instead of the rubbery substance of which the floor was made.

There was no obvious means of propulsion. There were only three small breaks in the entire surface of the ship, all on the outermost rim, beyond his reach above his head. Each appeared to be a round, black hole no more than a few centimeters in diameter, but it was impossible to tell if the holes were narrow tunnels that led to the interior of the ship or were simply black circles on the surface.

Hwang turned away from the ship. "River, sky, jungle...," he continued his litany.

Every now and then he looked intently at the alien for some indication that he was being understood. But the alien's face remained as inscrutable and inflexible as a mask, except for occasional smiles of encouragement whenever Hwang got bored and stopped talking.

Several times, Hwang pointed to something and repeated its name: "Elbow, elbow, elbow." Then he waited for the alien to repeat the word back to him. Eventually, the alien would understand what was expected of him; but Hwang could not escape the feeling that the alien had no interest in this exercise. He seemed to be merely humoring Hwang in order to encourage him to move on to the next object.

Before long Hwang began to feel frustration and even a degree of anger at the alien's apparent stupidity and inability to learn. Hwang became even more annoyed when, as a kind of pop quiz, he pointed to his elbow and waited for the alien to say the word he had learnt just a few minutes earlier. The two of them stood looking at one another for a long time. The alien seemed to be waiting for Hwang to say something. Hwang exploded, his frustration getting the better of him.

"What's wrong with you?" he shouted. "I just taught you that word not quarter of an hour ago. It's an elbow, you dummy, an elbow. Can't you even remember things for a moment? Say it: elbow."

The alien looked at him impassively, with a vague smile on his face.

"Elbow. Say it. Elbow, elbow, elbow." Hwang was screaming. He wanted to grab the alien and shake some sense into him.

"Elbow," the alien screamed back at him.

Hwang shook his head. One of them still was not getting it. Was the alien really as dimwitted as he seemed? Or was Hwang the dimwit?

He took several deep breaths to calm himself, then began again. "Knee. Foot. Floor."

And so it continued for the remainder of the day. They ate a tasteless supper of a chewy bar and a fruity drink. Hwang was tired and listless.

"Food, drink, cup," he recited, but his heart was not in it and mostly they ate in silence.

Next morning Hwang had an idea. He had been trying to teach the alien nouns. But perhaps alien brains were wired differently from humans'. Hwang had started attaching names to objects without giving the matter any thought; but perhaps to an alien mind it was verbs, or even adjectives, that were the foundational blocks of language.

So over breakfast — which was another tasteless chewy bar dispensed from the machine, along with a container of flavored water (with a different flavor from last night, he noticed) — he tried a new tack.

"Eat, drink," he tried, suiting the actions to the words. "Stand, sit."

The alien gave him a wide smile, which Hwang took as an encouraging sign. But even so his frustration returned when the alien refused to repeat any of the words until Hwang had demonstrated them several times. The alien parrotted the words without their accompanying action, so that Hwang was uncertain whether the alien really comprehended their meaning at all.

With an ever-increasing sense of frustration, Hwang continued all day in this manner, mixing nouns and verbs now, along with the occasional adjective. By nightfall he was exhausted, and after another parsimonious and unsatisfying meal of the chewy substance that was more and more reminiscent of cardboard and a container of yet another flavor of water, he went to bed tired and angry.

Even though he was exhausted, his seething frustration kept him awake.

What more can I do? he wondered. *I'm doing everything I can think of. What does he want? Adverbs? Prepositions?*

But no answer came, and eventually he slid into an uneasy sleep.

The third day was more of the same, until mid-morning. And that was when Hwang received a shock.

They were outside, sitting on the grass near the shore. Hwang had just gone through the same litany for what seemed like the hundredth time: "The sky is blue. The grass is green. Green grass. Can you say that? No, of course you can't. You don't understand a word I'm saying. How much longer is this going to go on? A day? A week? A month? Forever?"

Somewhere toward the end of the prior day, he had found himself conducting a running conversation with himself, decrying the alien's inability to understand. After all, if the alien couldn't understand even simple words, it hardly mattered if he spoke in complete sentences, did it? And it went at least some way toward venting his frustration.

And then the alien spoke.

"You say not year."

Hwang's mouth fell open.

"Wh... what?"

"Day, week, month, year. You say: day, week, month, forever. Forever is not year. You speak sentences. Long sentences I not not understand."

The alien waited. His benign smile had not changed, but now Hwang suddenly realized that the smile signified not stupidity but a patient intelligence.

"You want me to talk in sentences?"

"Speak normal. Talk ordinary. Long words. I learn."

At last Hwang understood. All this time the alien must have been just as frustrated as Hwang. He didn't want nouns or verbs or adjectives, or even adverbs or prepositions. He didn't want single words at all. He wanted ordinary speech. From that, he would deduce everything.

"I'm sorry. How could I have been so stupid? All this time I thought you were the stupid one, and really it was me who was the idiot." He laughed, his frustrations replaced by an eruption of relief. "You want me to talk? I'll talk. Let me tell you the story of my life. And after that, maybe you'll tell me yours...."

He related everything he could think of about himself, and then about the history of the Earth, and then about society in general. He talked for the whole of the day, and next morning he continued where he had left off. All this time the alien simply listened. Every now and then, Hwang would stop to reassure himself. "Are you understanding what I'm saying?" he would ask.

"I understand. Talk more," the alien would respond, and on Hwang would go, talking and talking and talking.

Late the next morning, they were seated in the shadow of the ship. Hwang was in the middle of a monologue about animals when he suddenly halted, looking at the unblemished but very dead carcass of the crocodile not far from the ship.

"I never thanked you for saving my life, did I?"

"No, but it's not necessary. It was the least I could do," the alien replied.

"Well, anyway, I...." Hwang stopped, and looked at the alien.

"You have done a good job. You don't need to talk any more for now. We can communicate, at least at a basic level. We will need more, but that will come quickly and naturally. It is fortunate that you are well educated. Languages have many nuances, and the more intelligent the teacher, the better the details are learned. I thank you for being such an excellent teacher."

The alien offered a slight bow.

A strange emotion flooded over Hwang. At first he thought it was simple relief: relief that at last he could end his meandering, interminable monologue; relief that now there was someone with whom he could communicate. It was several moments before he realized that the feeling was something much stronger than mere relief. It was an attachment, almost a kinship, a kind of friendship with this alien who, having nursed him back to health through some process at which he could not even guess, had now gone to the effort to learn to communicate with him. Hwang felt his eyes beginning to moisten.

"It's all right. Emotion is to be expected," the alien said. "Until this moment you have been alone. Now you have realized that whatever happens, there is someone with whom you can share your thoughts. It is natural; don't be embarrassed. But I am afraid that your joy will be short-lived once you realize the seriousness of our situation. It is not exactly 'out of the frying pan and into the fire' as your saying goes, but more 'out of one fire and into another.' But at least we have each other, and your ability to understand technical matters far surpasses my own, even though your basic knowledge of technology is less developed than mine. So perhaps, after all, there is a trace of hope for us. Yes, perhaps just a trace."

"What do you mean?"

"I am afraid this will come as a shock to you," the alien said. He paused for a moment to think, then continued, "I will tell you as much as I can of our situation. And perhaps you can explain more completely how you came to be here, for this planet was not known to have" — the alien searched for the right word — "I don't know your word for it; this planet is not known to be able to move people out of their own stream of time."

So it was true: despite the theoreticians' belief that it was impossible, Hwang had somehow slid into a different timestream. He discovered that he was trembling.

The alien continued, "My name is Rum-Lem. No doubt you have many questions, and I will do my best to answer them in due course. There will be no shortage of time for us to learn about each other, for in the entire galaxy, indeed, the entire Universe, we are the only beings of our kind. I don't know how you came here — that is a puzzle — but I must tell you that it is very unlikely that you or I can ever return to the time from which we came.

"But I get ahead of myself. First let me tell you who I am, and something about the galaxy beyond your planet Earth, which we call Tirsh. Then I will explain our situation.

"The galaxy contains many inhabited planets. At last count there were well over two hundred planets that support what we call 'civilized' life. By 'civilized,' I mean human life that has the ability to travel between star systems. There is also a smattering of planets such as your own, which are inhabited by humans who have forgotten their past and are in the process — some slowly, some more quickly — of rediscovering the lost secrets of technology.

"All human life in the galaxy sprang from a single planet, the planet Kivra, sometimes known as the Mother Planet. After the Kivrans mastered hyperspace travel, which was long, long ago, most of the galaxy was quickly colonized. The colonization was haphazard, and more than a few planets were colonized by groups of dissatisfied humans who wanted to begin a new life away from the Mother Planet. Most of those thrived and later joined one of the two great confederations that came into existence after a long and bloody war. The populations on a handful of planets regressed, losing the technology that they once had, and forgetting their true origins. Your planet, the one you call Earth, is one of these. On a few planets, human life died out completely.

"As is so often the case, the civilized planets found it impossible to maintain friendly relations, with the result that the galaxy is now divided into three roughly equal zones. The oldest is the Empire, which covers what you might call the eastern third of the galaxy. The central band, the one in which your Earth is located, is regarded as neutral territory and is, at least nominally, demilitarized. The remaining third is the Free Union of Independent Planets, or simply the Union. There is an uneasy state of peace known as the Status Quo between the Empire and the Union.

"I am an agent of the Union, a spy you might call me, and for many years I have been working undercover in the Empire. I had a mission, a very important mission, but it turned out to be impossible to carry out, for reasons that no one in the Union had ever suspected.

"But before I could transmit this information back to the Union, I was chased by imperial ships here into the demilitarized zone. I made a hasty hyperspace jump and found myself trapped by the spacetime curvature surrounding your star, the Sun. I was trying to hide on your planet when the Empire used a..." — he sought the correct word, could not find it, and offered a substitute — "...time-jumping device. Such weapons are banned by the treaty between the Empire and the Union, but it is quite understandable why they used it, because what I learned is enough to destabilize, and possibly even to destroy, the Empire.

"Probably what saved me from being simply blown to pieces was the fact that Earth was inhabited. If they had fired on me, your planet would have become aware of the fact that other, more advanced, civilizations exist, and the cultural anthropologists have been telling us since records began that such knowledge is almost certain to destroy any civilization that gains it before it independently learns the secret of interstellar travel. In any case, firing a photon missile here would have been regarded as a very serious violation of the treaty. It was much less risky for the Empire to use a time-jumping weapon. Even though it was illegal, it is unlikely that the Union ever found out about it.

"Now, I am sure you have many questions; but first, please tell me how you came to be here. I don't understand it. You don't have the technology."

"I don't understand it either," said Hwang, "but I'll tell you what I know, and perhaps together we can work it out."

Hwang related the details of the quantum bubble experiment. Rum-Lem occasionally interrupted to ask questions — which was difficult because his technical vocabulary was limited — but eventually Hwang, describing the experiment's last run, arrived at the point where the two bubbles had gone into orbit around one another.

"The next thing I knew was when I woke up in the jungle, about a kilometer from the river," he concluded.

"Yes," said Rum-Lem. "I have not been trained in such matters, but I do know that antigravity and temporal jumps are somehow related. There's a reference computer on board and we can consult that later. The two concepts are somehow, in some way I don't understand, two different aspects of the same thing."

"Like electricity and magnetism, or space and time, or particles and waves?"

"Yes, I think so. Gravity can be thought of as curvature in spacetime, and the act of forcibly flattening that curvature removes gravity but also allows the movement of objects through time."

"But what about the temporal paradoxes? Our physicists proved long ago that time travel is possible in only one direction: forward.

But I can't possibly have moved forward through time. We would be surrounded by ruins from the city that occupies this place in my time. The stars have barely moved, the constellations — the patterns in the sky — they are just as I have always known them, yet constellations change over time. If I had really moved very far into the future, it would be obvious from the changes in the sky."

Rum-Lem shook his head. "No, you do not quite understand. It is difficult for me to explain, partly because I do not have the words in your language — indeed, perhaps the words do not yet exist in your language — but also because I am not a physicist and I have only a layman's understanding of these matters.

"A temporal jump is not the same as time travel, not the same thing at all. Perhaps... perhaps 'timeshifting' would be a better word. Time travel is believed by our physicists to be impossible — except, as you say, in one direction — but timeshifting is something quite different. You see, you and I have been exposed to something I will call a timeshift field. That field caused us to move forward in time, but probably not by very much. Possibly by only a few seconds. Perhaps not even that. But the amount of the shift hardly matters. What does matter is that for us time advances exactly as it does for everyone else; it is just that we exist slightly in their future. And because our time advances at the same rate as theirs, we remain, always and forever, slightly in everyone else's future. The Universe in which we are now located is, in one sense, almost identical to the one in which your Rabundi City exists. Our stars and planets look the same as theirs. Many of the plants and animals are the same; yet things have evolved differently here. Whatever it was that caused humanity to arise on the Mother Planet apparently never happened in this slightly altered universe. And so we are alone. There are no other humans." The alien made a gesture with his hand. "I am sorry. It is not a good explanation, but it is the best I can do. Later we can consult the reference computer and I can try to translate some of what it says, and you will understand more fully what has happened."

Hwang's face was furrowed in a deep frown.

"Yes," he said slowly, "Yes, I think I understand, at least partially. You are saying that we are in the future, but only a short time in the future, maybe one second, maybe a minute, maybe a year, but whatever the amount, it will remain constant. It's sort of like a parallel universe, but not quite. Yes, I think I understand that."

"Yes, that is right. But I am sorry. It is not good news."

"Then has no one ever come back after being timeshifted?"

The alien looked forlorn. "No. You must understand that throughout the galaxy timeshifting is regarded as a weapon; indeed, it is in some ways the most powerful weapon ever devised. When the timeshift effect was first discovered, only inanimate objects were exposed to the timeshift fields. Then we used animals and then, fully aware of the risks they were taking, several scientists were sent forward. It is not known whether anyone survived. Some theoreticians believe that the forces involved are sufficient to rip molecular structures apart; other scientists believe that this is not so, that objects survive the timeshift field essentially intact. Of course, you and I now know that these latter scientists are correct — we both survived. But it was long ago agreed that timeshifting is a one-way trip, that the same theory of temporal paradoxes that prevents time travel into the past also prevents a negative timeshift. I think there was once, many centuries ago, some debate about the matter — and it is not now a subject of research, since timeshift weapons have been banned — but as I understand it, there is no way for us to return."

Hwang felt a sinking feeling. For a while he had felt a surge of hope. Now it was replaced by despair. He nodded unhappily.

"I think I understand. But I would very much like to work with your reference computer, to try to understand properly. Perhaps, since we seem to be stuck here, I can learn your language."

The alien made a motion with his hand. "Possibly, although it is undoubtedly simpler for me to translate for you. If I had the skills, I could input the knowledge of your language I have acquired into the computer so that it could translate for you, but I am not trained for that."

"Can all aliens do what you did: learn a language simply by listening to it? If so, it is an impressive skill that somehow we have lost."

"Oh, no. It is quite a dangerous procedure. It was part of the consequence of my decision to become a spy. We have a device that you might call a... mindprobe. If used with sufficient care, it can rewire parts of the brain. In my case it was deemed important that I be provided with enhanced language skills in order to support my cover; I was supposed to be from the Outer Planets, where many dialects of Galactic Standard are common."

Hwang nodded, suddenly pensive. He shivered. The thought of a civilization in which a person's brain could be rewired to enhance one's abilities — and in which someone would willingly submit to such a procedure — filled him with a cold fear.

19
VAL-DOR

The gardener counted down the moments. As noon approached, Teberill Gandeer raised his head from the flower-bed at which he was working and looked across the lawn to the palace.

Rum-Lem was walking towards one of the many undistinguished doors in the rear of the palace. He halted, waiting for exactly the right moment.

Precisely at noon, Rum-Lem opened the door. Teberill Gandeer held his breath momentarily. No alarm sounded. Per-Lem had done her job. In a moment, Rum-Lem was inside the palace and the door had closed behind him. Teberill Gandeer allowed himself the briefest of smiles, then returned to his work.

It was eerie going home that evening, watching the faces of everyone on the hoverbus, knowing that in all probability the emperor was now dead and he was one of the few people in the galaxy to know it. Nothing had been announced, of course. If Rum-Lem had succeeded — and he remembered with satisfaction the probability of success that the databoxes back on Dalith had calculated — then Amril Gdrena and the Inner Council would need to act quickly to come up with some explanation for the emperor's sudden demise. Certainly they would never admit the truth: that he had been killed by a Union agent. It would take a rotation or two for them to come up with a consistent cover story before they broke the news to the hundred billion people who revered the emperor.

He watched the evening newscasts for signs of anything unusual. The only mention of the emperor was brief, to the effect that he had spent part of the morning in a holographic commlink meeting with the governor of Klivliviv. There was no indication of how he had spent the afternoon.

There was, however, an odd addition to the late-evening broadcasts: the empress had been taken ill, and her condition was cause for concern.

The following morning there was still no news about the emperor, but apparently the empress' condition had worsened overnight and was now quite serious. Val-Dor wondered if her illness had something to do with Rum-Lem. Perhaps Rum-Lem had done better than expected, and had killed both the emperor *and* the empress.

Later that rotation, Val-Dor went to the spaceport to inspect the area where Rum-Lem's ship was usually parked. The ship was gone. Val-Dor could not suppress a small smile of satisfaction: the plan called for Rum-Lem to return to Dalith as soon as his mission was accomplished. Val-Dor and Per-Lem were to remain in place for a short while, to observe how the Inner Council handled the emperor's assassination. Then they would be recalled. As he left the spaceport, Val-Dor was certain that it would not be long before the trio would be reunited back on Dalith.

His euphoria was short-lived.

That night the broadcast channels were filled with subdued announcers mourning the Empire's beloved empress, showing vids of her life and repetitively emphasizing how much she would be missed. And then the emperor himself made a brief appearance. He looked gaunt and tired but otherwise normal. He thanked his subjects for their concern, eulogized the empress briefly, and announced five rotations of official mourning. As the emperor's image faded on the vidscreen, Val-Dor swore. Something must have gone wrong, and instead of killing the emperor, Rum-Lem had managed to kill only the empress.

But his ship had gone. Did that mean Rum-Lem was under the misapprehension that he had succeeded? Or had he aborted the mission after killing the empress, in order to escape while he still had the chance? Val-Dor watched the rest of the news, waiting for some mention of an accident in space, or the arrest of a Union spy, or any other item that might possibly relate to Rum-Lem's fate. There was nothing.

Val-Dor considered whether he and Per-Lem should stay in place. The only way they could hope for another chance to kill the emperor was to remain undercover on Kivra. But if Rum-Lem had been captured... but no, that couldn't have happened. If Rum-Lem was in the Empire's hands, they would have put him under a mindprobe, and imperial agents would already have come for Val-Dor and Per-Lem.

So it made sense to stay in place, and await developments.

Next rotation, as usual, he saw Per-Lem on the hoverbus. She stroked her eyebrow, indicating that she needed to be debriefed. They met in the garden that evening, but instead of news of Rum-Lem or the emperor, all she had was a red report from a monitorship. But he was glad of the excuse to make a transmission back to Dalith. He sent the details of the red report, along with an addendum: "What happened R? R ship gone. Do we remain?"

The chilling answer came next rotation: "R lost. You stay."

So Operation Kālek had failed: the emperor still lived, and Rum-Lem had been killed — or worse. But Tcharn obviously hadn't given up hope that the mission could still be accomplished.

Sometimes, though, Val-Dor wondered if Operation Kālek was worth its cost.

For half a cycle, nothing changed. Val-Dor continued his usual routine. The emperor lived on, appearing in news broadcasts, although less frequently than usual since he was in mourning and obviously deeply affected by the loss of his dearly beloved empress.

Val-Dor continued to speculate whether the empress' death had really happened at Rum-Lem's hands. But the empress, although popular, was essentially a nonentity. Everyone knew that her sole rôle was to raise the emperor's child. Val-Dor could not imagine Rum-Lem settling for her death as a kind of consolation prize.

He continued to debrief Per-Lem periodically, sending back reports to Dalith. There was no further news about Rum-Lem.

Only one event stood out in the half-cycle since Rum-Lem had been lost. It was almost inconsequential — except that for an agent operating in enemy territory, nothing out of the ordinary could ever be dismissed as unimportant.

It occurred one afternoon when he was working on some sick ferns in a secluded part of the palace gardens. A nervous stranger had approached and uttered an odd phrase in a manner that suggested that it was a password of some kind.

"Yan, ten, tethera", the man had said.

When Val-Dor did not respond, the man hurried away.

After that Val-Dor was especially cautious; he did not contact Per-Lem, and watched for signs that he was being followed. But he saw nothing and relaxed again. If he was under suspicion, surely he would have seen some evidence of it.

A few rotations later Per-Lem stroked an eyebrow, telling him that she needed to be debriefed.

Debriefing Per-Lem was always a traumatic experience.

Firstly, there was always the possibility, no matter how remote, that they would be discovered. The place where debriefing occurred was a quiet, rarely-visited arbor in the public portion of the imperial garden. The session rarely last more than twenty chrons, but still there was always a chance of discovery. But worse even than the fear of being discovered — much worse — was the emotional strain.

Once, long ago, they had pledged themselves to one another, using the words of the ancient ceremony: "for as many cycles as we shall both live." But the woman known as Lystra Ten-Wer had no recollection of that oath. Her past held no memories of the time they had spent back on Dalith when their lives stretched before them and they were young and the entire galaxy seemed to be in their grasp.

As he approached her, she would be sitting alone in the arbor, unaware even that she was waiting for someone. He always had to steel himself for what was about to happen. He would quietly say the code phrase, causing her to enter a hypnotic trance in which she would tell him details of the reports she had seen and the gossip she had heard at work, while his heart felt like it was bleeding.

Tcharn must have known that Val-Dor was weak, that if there was some way he could free his lover from the shell who sat before him divulging its exiguous secrets, then he would long ago have broken down and done so. But there was no way: only the technicians back on Dalith could do that.

So Val-Dor was powerless. He listened, and when it was all over, he spoke another phrase, and then he left her, his heart full of lead. And that night he would not sleep.

There was no way to know whether the information Per-Lem gave him was important or trivial. He simply forwarded it as quickly as possible, trying to rid himself of responsibility and involvement. Until the next time.

He debriefed her as usual. She reported that a signal had been received from monitorship 35/CW. She gave him the numbers from the red report, and that evening Val-Dor transmitted them back to Dalith. He added a brief appendix: "Do we continue to stay in place?" It had been half a cycle now since Rum-Lem had been lost. Surely it was time to go home?

The reply came next rotation: "Both return earliest opportunity. Kālek aborted."

It was as if an enormous weight had been lifted from Val-Dor's frame. He dwelt lovingly on the word "both." It was over. Time to go home. Time to resume ordinary lives. Time to get to know one another all over again.

He applied himself to the happy problem of the logistics of their return to Dalith. But next rotation Per-Lem boarded the hoverbus and stroked her right eyebrow with her left hand three times: "I think they may be on to me."

It was more than enough for Val-Dor. Time to go, never mind about covering their trail. He rubbed the fourth finger of his right hand across his lips: "We are pulling out. Leave tomorrow."

The sequence had been planted in Per-Lem's brain long ago. She would wake up next morning with a niggling dissatisfaction at life on Kivra. By midmorning, the dissatisfaction would resolve itself into an urge to get away from the Mother Planet for a vacation. She would go to the spaceport. Once there, she would be attracted to the booth of a small line that journeyed to the Outer Planets. She would hear of Soam, find it appealing, and purchase a round-trip ticket.

That was as far as the implanted commands went. After that it was up to Val-Dor to find a way to get her safely back to Dalith. An escape ship was already in place, hidden in a cave in the Skyward Mountains. All he needed to do was to get her on to the ship. Which should be easy.

And then, once they were back on Dalith, Lystra Ten-Wer would cease to exist. She would become Per-Lem once more. They had been assured that the operation would be safe, although of course Per-Lem would have to be watched for some time afterward to ensure that she was stable. The psychoanalysts had been quite clear about what would happen if by some freak accident Per-Lem's memories were to be released in Lystra Ten-Wer's mind. "Immediate schizophrenic psychosis," they had warned. "In layman's terms, she'd go instantly insane. The conflict between the two personas inhabiting the same skull would result in the destruction of both. To restore Per-Lem, we must make sure that the memories of Lystra Ten-Wer are completely eradicated. It's the only way to be sure."

Val-Dor knew that even though their work on Kivra was over he would not rest easy until they were back on Dalith and he and a restored Per-Lem were lying together in one another's arms.

Val-Dor watched discreetly from behind a parked hovercar as Per-Lem disembarked from the taxi at Kivra City spaceport. She hesitated outside the terminal, looking up at the ships taking off and landing. When she entered the terminal, he did not immediately follow her. Instead, he waited and watched. No one was tailing her. Good. That would make things easier.

He travelled to Prantys on the same passenger liner, taking a seat near the back of the ship where it was easy to see without being seen. No one was paying her any attention. He began to relax and to think about how he was going to entice her into the ship that was hidden in a remote cave on Soam, waiting to take them both home.

He engineered a meeting at a wayfinder box on Prantys, and ensured that they sat together on the ferryship to Soam. And then, as they waited for liftoff, came the first hint that perhaps after all she was being followed.

At the last moment, after the doors were sealed and the launch sequence was under way, the procedure was suspended and a young man dressed in a P&S uniform came on board. Wherever one went in the Empire, young men in P&S uniforms were more or less endemic, but even so Val-Dor was suddenly alert. The rules at spaceports were rigorously enforced. Countdowns were suspended only in the case of an emergency. To suspend a countdown simply to permit a passenger to board was unheard of. No doubt things were a little looser out here on the fringes of the Empire, yet even so the delay caused by the young man's arrival would force a complete recalculation of the ferry's trajectory. Whoever the young man was, he could not be simply one more young P&S operative.

The man chose a seat behind them, so it was difficult to keep a watch on him without being obvious. The only safe thing to do was to assume that Per-Lem's cover had been blown — which meant that he too would come under scrutiny, since he was seated next to her and the two were obviously on good terms.

He spent most of the journey to Soam pondering their situation, but it was only after they landed that the true extent of his difficulties was revealed. Parked at the far end of the spaceport was a ship in the colors of the Ministry of Peace and Security and sporting the maroon, black and gold insignia that marked it as the minister's official vessel. Beside Amril Gdrena's ship were two others in official P&S livery. The man in the P&S uniform hurried towards the ships. It was obvious that he was going to make a report.

Val-Dor convinced Per-Lem to share a rented hovercar, and she agreed enthusiastically to his suggestion that on the morrow he would show her some of the beauty of Soam.

As the short Soaman day came to an end, they registered at the Marsûk tourist center. He found it increasingly difficult to ignore the uniformed P&S operatives who seemed to be more and more in evidence. He was surprised that Per-Lem — no, she was Lystra Ten-Wer, with no memories at all of her life as Per-Lem, he kept reminding himself uncomfortably — made no comment; but perhaps she was so used to P&S uniforms that she gave them no thought. Without comment, he got them separate but adjoining rooms.

He escorted her to her room for the night, then retired to his own room. Outside he could see, in the spill of a light, two men in P&S uniforms watching their rooms.

Had Amril Gdrena already sealed Soam? That's what he would have done in her position. He tried to initiate a commlink back to Kivra.

After a few moments, the holoimage screen flashed: "We apologize, but the system is unable to complete the requested connection. Please try again later."

He waited ten chrons, then tried again with the same result.

He went to bed, but for a long time he simply lay there, pondering the situation.

Shortly after dawn, he knocked on Per-Lem's door and offered to accompany her to firstmeal. He ignored the uniformed P&S operative lounging not far away against a tree. It was somewhat more difficult to suppress his surprise at the sight of Amril Gdrena in the corner of the tourist center restaurant, eating her firstmeal with someone whose back was towards him.

If Amril Gdrena herself was still on Soam, that meant she was certain that one or both of them were agents for the Union — nothing less could have kept her on such an unimportant planet.

"Is something the matter?" Lystra Ten-Wer asked with concern.

"What? No, sorry. Just thinking, that's all. Have you finished? Are you ready to go? I'll pick up some food to take with us. I know a delightful spot for a picnic with a wonderful view of the grasslands and the ocean. If you're looking to lower your stress level, I can't think of a better place anywhere in the galaxy."

He forced himself to smile.

"Sounds wonderful. Let's get going."

Lystra's smile at least was genuine.

As they lifted off from the hovercar park, Val-Dor watched the opnav display. He noticed with grim satisfaction that behind them another hovercar lifted off and followed on an identical track.

He checked in his pocket. The short-range jammer was safe. It wouldn't delay them long, but it would give him a chron or two. He flew higher, and the Soam landscape spread out below them. The other hovercar followed.

"Hang on," he said, and suddenly they dropped like a stone. He reapplied full power when it seemed like they were certain to crash, and the hovercar shot forward, forcing the breath from its occupants as the trees flew past a short distance below them.

He flew expertly over a slight ridge and dropped into an enormous green canyon carved by a wide river. He turned and they raced along the river, skimming the surface of the brilliant blue water, walls of greenery rising on both sides.

His hand momentarily slipped into a pocket and slid a switch on the jammer.

He grinned at Lystra. "I thought you'd like to see the planet close up. It's a wonderful place at this point in its cycle, probably one of the prettiest in the entire galaxy."

His calm words seemed to reassure her, and she smiled before turning to enjoy the sight of the blue and green world flashing past.

He opened the throttle, watching the speed indicator carefully, until he was flying just below the speed of sound. Any faster, and the sonic boom would give him away, but at this speed the car was all but silent as it raced upriver.

Val-Dor's mouth was drawn into a thin line of concentration. The river began to meander, and he increased altitude slightly so he could fly in a straight line, cutting off the corners of the river's curves.

A range of hills appeared on their left; he banked sharply and began to gain altitude, following the slope. He raced over the top of the ridge, and let the car drop in free fall on the far side, so that for perhaps a tenth of chron he and Lystra experienced a feeling of weightlessness. Lystra yelped in surprise.

She looked at him sheepishly and said, "Sorry. You surprised me."

He smiled warmly and re-applied the throttle; weight returned.

The jungle thinned ahead of them. Not far ahead, almost at the bottom of the slope down which they were racing, the trees gave way to a wide swath of grass; in the distance, the ocean sparkled with a serene blue, reflecting the odd-colored sky. Here and there dots on the grass showed where the large ungulates of the Soaman plain were grazing.

Val-Dor landed at the very edge of the trees. As he cut the motor Lystra looked at him; her was chest heaving.

"You're quite a pilot, you know that?"

Her smile was almost too much for Val-Dor. For a long, dreadful moment he wanted to throw away all the cycles of training, separation and loss — anything to hold her safe in his arms the way he had done back on Dalith before her mind was invaded by Tcharn's machines.

Was it really true what they had assured him time and time again: that she remembered nothing at all of those times? Was there not even the slightest vestige of Per-Lem inside Lystra Ten-Wer's head?

But he knew it had to be true. Not once had Lystra shown by a moment's hesitation or a wrinkled brow that she was trying to place a memory that didn't fit. He looked away.

"Beautiful, isn't it?" he said. He had to say something. "It's the perfect place just to relax for a while."

They disembarked and he led her a short distance into the shade of the trees.

They ate, and talked about nothing in particular, and he could almost see the peacefulness descending on her. He knew that he was making a mistake, that he should be hurrying things along, that at any moment Amril Gdrena's hovercar might come roaring over the plain. He had taken the precaution of erecting an invisible force field around them, so they would be invisible to most detectors, but even so it was only a matter of time before they were found. Yet it was so wonderful just to be with her again....

Her body language was inviting him to couple, and he desperately wanted to succumb, to take her in his arms and say the things he had said to her back on Dalith when they had pledged undying love.

He leaned forward. She closed her eyes to receive a kiss. And then, with infinite regret, he drew back. This was not the time. Sometime soon, this dangerous charade would all be over, but until then he could not afford this.

Lystra was still waiting with her eyes expectantly closed. When she realized that the kiss was not to coming, she looked at him in puzzlement.

Val-Dor made a peculiar rubbing motion with his left hand on his brow.

Oh, my darling, he thought, *you've no idea how sorry I am that it has be this way. One day soon maybe we can regain our innocence and just be ourselves again. But for now I have no choice; this is the way it has to be. I'm so sorry.*

A strange expression came over Lystra Ten-Wer. She looked disoriented, as if she were suddenly unsure of where she was. She swayed as if she was about to collapse. Then she suddenly righted herself; her face cleared, and lost all trace of expression. Her eyes were on the distant glistering ocean, but it was obvious that she could not see it. She began to speak in an emotionless monotone.

"My supervisor has detected the subterfuge with the red reports from monitorship 35/CW," she began.

She went on to describe a meeting in Supervisor Qwilm's office. Occasionally, Val-Dor interrupted to ask a question, but for the most part she spoke without pause, explaining what had alerted her subconscious to the possibility that she had fallen under suspicion.

When she finished she gazed silently at the distant sea. Val-Dor looked at her, thinking furiously.

Of one thing there was no doubt: Tcharn had been right: it was time to end Operation Kālek and to return to Dalith.

His basic task was to lure Lystra Ten-Wer, that model citizen of the Empire, on to the ship that would carry them back to Union territory. That should not be hard, given her obvious feelings for him. But there were other, more challenging difficulties. Soam was surrounded by a communications shield; it was highly likely, therefore, that there was also a ring of ships circling the planet to ensure that no one left.

When this part of the mission had been mooted, they had all thought that nothing had been left to chance. Tcharn had chosen an obscure planet, Soam, for the rendezvous, and a cave had been secretly hollowed out in a remote mountainside far from the tourist center. In that cave was their escape ship.

The plan was simple: Val-Dor was to lure Per-Lem to the cave by any appropriate means. Once there they would board the ship and steal away from Soam. Since Soam was relatively close to the demilitarized zone, it would be a simple matter to execute a series of jumps across the zone to reach Union territory. The whole thing shouldn't take more than a few hundred chrons. But they had reckoned without Amril Gdrena. The minister would never let them leave Soam alive unless they were in custody.

Leaning forward, he softly caressed Per-Lem's face; then he gently guided her to the ground. She closed her eyes. He kissed her upturned cheek and spoke a few words. Her breathing deepened. She was asleep.

"I'm sorry, my darling. This will all be over soon."

He pulled a vine from a nearby tree and carefully bound her hands. Then he scribbled a note and placed it between the vines and her wrist.

He took a field generator from his pocket and carefully buried it close to the sleeping form of Per-Lem. With one last look at his wife he clambered into the hovercar. Moments later, he lifted off and the hovercar climbed steeply into the sky.

20

Rum-Lem

It did not take long for Hwang and Rum-Lem to decide on a rough plan. What occupied them for the better part of two days was putting it into practice.

While Hwang had been teaching Rum-Lem his language, he had given his lab equipment scarcely a thought, partly because he was so caught up in his task and partly because he had assumed that the alien would know of a way to return him to his own time. It was only after Rum-Lem had explained how they were both trapped in what he called "forward time" that Hwang realized that his equipment was going to be needed if they were to have any chance of returning home.

Hwang had no idea how long he had been aboard the ship recovering from his wounds. But all that time the equipment had been protected from the elements by only a meager covering of leaves.

"How long was I aboard your ship before I recovered?" he asked, half afraid that Rum-Lem was going to tell him that he had been unconscious for weeks or months.

"While I treated you with the life-support machine, you mean?"

"Yes. How long?"

"A little more than a day. Your wounds were very bad. You were almost dead. For a while I thought I was going to lose you."

A day! And only a few more days had elapsed since then. Less than a week had passed since he had been mauled by the cat.

173

"Listen," Hwang said, "we've got to try to bring the equipment from my experiment aboard. The climate here is attacking it, and from what you've told me it sounds like we're going to need that equipment if we're to have any chance of getting back to our own time."

Rum-Lem made a gesture with his right hand that Hwang had come to recognize as the alien's equivalent of a shrug.

"I really don't think there's much chance of return, Hwang."

"Listen. We know that you arrived here in forward time because you were fired on by a timeshift weapon, even though I don't yet understand how such a weapon works."

Rum-Lem nodded.

"But we also know that I arrived here because of something that went wrong with my quantum bubble experiment. The device that sent you here is out of our reach, in some other time, but the one that sent me here is sitting in the jungle, no more than a kilometer away. It's protected, but not very well, and if we leave it much longer it will be ruined beyond repair. It might already be. Maybe you're right: maybe there's no way home; maybe we won't be able to modify the equipment so that it sends us back. But we won't know for sure until I've had a chance to study your computers so I understand how timeshifting works, and that will take weeks or months, and by then it will be too late, the equipment will be damaged beyond repair. So we need to rescue it now and bring it aboard while we still have the chance."

"All right," said Rum-Lem, although the look on his face made it obvious that he thought it pointless.

Recovering the equipment proved to be far from easy. It was large and it was heavy, which meant that it was impossible to move. Instead of bringing the equipment to the ship, they quickly realized that they would have to take the ship to the equipment.

But the equipment was under the canopy of the jungle, so it was impossible to land the ship nearby without first clearing a space in which to land.

Hwang led Rum-Lem along what remained of the path from the river. Even though it had been only a few days since Hwang had last come that way, already the jungle had almost reclaimed the path, and when they reached the equipment, Hwang saw that tendrils were encroaching on that as well.

They cleared the vines and leaves away and Hwang inspected the equipment carefully. Much of the metal casing of the guidance block was pitted, but it was not as bad as he had feared, although there was no way of knowing if any of the electronics inside had been damaged.

While Hwang inspected the equipment, Rum-Lem marked out an area on the ground large enough to accommodate his ship. The area contained three fully grown trees; all three would have to be removed. Although there were several weapons aboard the ship, and many tools designed for all manner of contingencies, there was nothing they could use to remove the trees. The hand-held weapons operated only on animal life, and the more destructive large weapons were not delicate enough to be sure that the trees could be felled without damaging Hwang's equipment.

They talked the problem over, and eventually they hit upon a solution. It would be slow, but it should work.

For the next day and a half, sweating profusely in the jungle heat and taking frequent breaks for rest, they separated long lengths of vines, removing the tendrils to leave long, pliable — albeit weak — ropes. Then they pleated together over a hundred of the prepared vines until they had three separate lengths of tough, pliable rope, each nearly sixty meters long.

They pulled the vines back to the island, where Rum-Lem attached one end of each rope firmly to an immovable fixture inside the ship, leaving the rest of each rope to trail out through the open doorway.

While Hwang returned to the equipment, Rum-Lem flew his ship into position over the area they were trying to clear. He descended until the ship was almost touching the canopy. The vines trailed down, out of sight through the trees, reaching all the way to the ground.

Hwang knotted the vines firmly around the trunk of one of the trees. Then Rum-Lem slowly ascended, ripping the tree from the ground. The whole thing thing was over more quickly and easily than Hwang had dared hope.

In this manner the trees were cleared, allowing the ship to land no more than twenty paces from Hwang's equipment.

Now came the second major problem: how to move the gear aboard. There were a few small pieces of equipment that they could manhandle on to the ship, but most of it was far too heavy to move.

Eventually, Hwang decided that there was nothing for it but to dismantle the experiment into manageable pieces, carry the pieces on board, and then reassemble the experiment inside the ship.

The whole exercise took two full days, but at last it was done, and the ship's central area was filled with Hwang's equipment. The guidance block was so large that the door to the dining area was permanently open, the last half meter of the block obtruding into the room.

"Will the ship still be able to fly with all this weight on board?" he asked.

Rum-Lem smiled. "If there was some way to put a mountain inside this ship, it would still fly. Don't worry."

He also reassured Hwang about another point. Hwang was worried because the power cube for the equipment was ninety percent depleted. Rum-Lem explained that the ship used electricity to power most of its circuits and he could supply any amount that Hwang could possibly need; they simply had to build a device to transform it to the voltage and frequency used by the experiment, which shouldn't be difficult.

"Do you think you can make your experiment work again?" Rum-Lem asked over supper.

"It won't be easy, but yes, I think there's a good chance."

Rum-Lem nodded. "Then our next priority must be to help you understand the timeshifting process. I'm not sure how much the reference computer will tell us, but I hope it will be enough. Once you understand how timeshifting works, perhaps you'll be able to think of a way to make it work in reverse — always supposing that's possible, of course."

"Right," Hwang agreed. "But just at the moment I need a rest. My arms and legs ache, and I'm exhausted. Anyway, I've been waiting for an opportunity for you to show me what this ship can do. Besides which, I have an idea that may save us some time."

"An idea?"

"Yes. You mentioned that others have been sent into forward time. Maybe we can find them. Or at least traces of them. You said that the early volunteers were scientists. They must have tried to find a way back. If we can find their calculations, it might save us a lot of time and effort. The scientists wouldn't have been able to return to normal time themselves because they had no equipment. But they were scientists, so they must have tried to discover whether return was theoretically possible."

And there was another possibility.

"Do you happen to know if the scientists were of both sexes?" he asked.

Rum-Lem did not know, but it seemed likely. On Kivra there were as many female scientists as male, and as far as he knew it had always been that way. He did not know exactly how many scientists had risked their lives by entering those early timeshift fields, but Hwang's idea that the descendants of those early scientists might still be alive in forward time was an intriguing possibility.

Except that Rum-Lem already knew that there were no such descendants.

For some time after his ship had been hit by the timeshift beam, Rum-Lem was disoriented and confused.

Initially, the only indication that he had been hit came from the onboard chronon detector, which gave a single brief warning shriek as the ship was thrust forward through time. Rum-Lem was too busy looking for somewhere to hide the ship to notice it.

Almost half a chron elapsed before Rum-Lem realized that something was seriously wrong. He slowed to a halt, hovering high over the desert, and began to probe the surroundings with the onboard scanners.

There was no trace of the ship that had been chasing him. For that he was thankful, although it was puzzling. Then he observed that the scanners were no longer detecting any indications of human activity on the planet. There was no pollution, no electronics, no electromagnetic radiation, nothing. But just a few moments ago the scanners had been full of such indications.

He commanded the databoxes to replay the data from the last chron. This time he saw it, and he stopped the replay as soon as the chronon detector shrieked its warning.

There it was, unbelievable but also unmistakable: a burst of chronons, lasting no more than a centichron. It could mean only one thing: something in his vicinity had been exposed to a timeshift field. And as he looked at the blank detector screens, he knew what that something was.

At first, he was relieved to discover that both he and the ship seemed to have survived the shift through time without damage. He ran a complete series of diagnostic tests on the ship's internal systems. They all passed. The self-regenerating circuitry had even repaired the damaged opnav system. Everything was working perfectly.

He called up the entry on timeshifting in the onboard reference databox. It did not say much. Timeshift weapons had been banned under the terms of the Treaty of Empire and Union, although it was suspected that both sides retained limited timeshifting ability. The timeshift effect had been discovered long ago, before the War of Secession, at the research facility at Tel Dahn, in the remote deserts of Kivra. Nothing that had ever been exposed to a timeshift field — including several scientists who had volunteered — had ever returned to normal time, and it was now thought by most scientists that a return was theoretically impossible. Other physicists thought that the stresses associated with the timeshift process would destroy anything so delicate as a living being.

That was the extent of the databox entry. Not very interesting, and not at all helpful.

Rum-Lem spent a fitful night turning over his options in his mind. Rum-Lem was no scientist. Perhaps there was some way to get back to ordinary time, perhaps not; but the first necessity was to find someone with whom to discuss the problem. Shortly after dawn he lifted off and began the first of a series of hyperspace jumps that would take him across the demilitarized zone back to Dalith.

He proceeded carefully, because he had no way of knowing how accurate his gravity-field maps were in forward time. After making a couple of short jumps, he compared the position of a nearby star and its retinue of planets with the position predicted by the opnav computer. The match was exact. After that he was more confident, and he increased the length of his jumps. Evidently, objects in forward time occupied the same position that they did in normal time.

When he reached Dalith, though, he found a planet that had never been colonized. The only large land-based life forms his scanners detected were unthinking, ponderous ungulates. He scanned for communication links, but there were none. He scanned for artificial electromagnetic radiation: none. He scanned for pollutants: none. Humanity had never come within a hundred derns of this place.

Now he began seriously to worry about his situation. How could it be that in a galaxy apparently identical to his own, humans had never come to Dalith?

The obvious place to look for an answer was the Mother Planet. He set out on a series of jumps that carried him three quarters of the way across the galaxy.

When he arrived, it was quickly obvious that there were no people on Kivra either.

He spent the next few rotations skimming the surface of Kivra looking desperately for any indication of human life. It was only after he had scoured the entire planet twice that he at last admitted to himself what until now he had refused to accept: he was alone in the Universe. The planets that in normal time were home to billions were here completely devoid of human life.

He set out on a wild search. He knew he was wasting his time, but he also knew that he could not be completely sure until he had looked everywhere. One by one, he visited every planet that had ever been colonized.

He found no trace of humans.

It was only when he had run out of places to look that he returned to the planet designated JG-1275-3 [Tirsh], where the imperial ship had catapulted him into this nightmare. There was no logical reason for his return except a vague hope that maybe some sort of barrier had been breached by the timeshift field, and so perhaps it would be easier to return from here than from anywhere else.

The rational part of his brain knew that such thoughts were a ridiculous chimera, but how could he live without hope? He could not afford to be entirely rational, because that would force him to admit that his situation was hopeless.

He landed on a small island not far from the northernmost coast of the smallest continent-sized land mass — the one over which he had been flying when he had been timeshifted. And there he tried to make some sort of home.

At first his rhythm was that of Kivra, whose inclination and periods of rotation and revolution set the calendars and clocks for the rest of the galaxy, even the unionist planets. But as time passed Rum-Lem gradually started to ignore what the instruments were telling him, and he settled into a life regimented by the orbital motion of Tirsh.

Gradually, he became accustomed to his daily routine. After a while, he even began to enjoy it. Only two things stopped him being happy: he would never see another human again for the rest of his life; and he had failed in his attempt to deliver what he had discovered to the Union. If it were not for these, he could have been reasonably content with his new life. The climate of the island was equable, and there seemed to be no dangerous lifeforms either on the island itself or in the lagoon that was formed by a substance that, on investigation, showed itself to be constructed by the skeletons of billions of tiny creatures that lived in the warm, salty waters surrounding the island.

There were numerous harmless small animals on the island and in the surrounding water. Rum-Lem was particularly enamored of the many birds with brightly colored plumage whose loud cries frequently filled the air as they flew overhead in large, particolored flocks.

He experimented with eating fruits and nuts from the indigenous plants. He learned that red berries were generally poisonous, but many of the fruits were wholesome and tasted quite good, although on the whole he preferred the taste of bars from the synthfood machine. His favorite was a large brown nut that grew near the top of a species of tree whose trunk grew almost straight up and sported leaves only at the very top. He discovered that if he broke such a nut — for which he had to use a sharp rock or metal tool — he would find inside a delicious white, sweet milk. If the nut was overripe, the milk dried into a strangely textured solid that tasted quite different from the milk but was equally satisfying. Occasionally, by way of variety, he would shoot one of the small mammals that inhabited the island and roast it over a fire.

More than a hundred rotations passed, and Rum-Lem's thoughts of returning to his own time became gradually less and less frequent as he began to accept the constraints of his new life.

Then everything changed.

He was just finishing his final meal of the day. The planet's star had set not long before, and a gentle breeze was drifting across the ocean, carrying the pleasant, tangy scent of salt. Several of the brighter stars were visible in the dusk, and Rum-Lem was seated on the grass, looking out across the ocean to the place where a line of white marked the reef. A solitary bright planet hung in the sky not far above the horizon. He was eating a vagren-flavored synthfood bar and drinking the milk from one of the large brown nuts. Nearby, the access door to the ship was open. In a few chrons, he would finish his meal; then he would enter the ship for the night, close the access panel, and go to bed.

A sudden loud wailing from inside the ship rent the serenity.

Rum-Lem dropped the nut, spilling its milk on the grass. What could possibly have caused one of the automatic warning systems to go off? Before he could decide which warning it was, the sound stopped.

He jumped to his feet and dashed up the ramp and ran into the control cabin. He felt a surge of adrenalin. It couldn't be, could it?

It was.

He stopped in front of the control panel. The panel was quiescent, simply monitoring the environment for any sign of danger, gray-black except in one place: the chronon monitor was flashing urgently.

Without pausing to think, he dropped into the leftmost seat. It lifted into the air and the control panel lit up. His hands began to move quickly, pressing buttons as he barked commands. His eyes flashed over the panel and the holoscreens that appeared before him. The access panel closed. Less than a chron later, the spaceship lifted off.

As the ship arced upward, he ran an integrity check on the chronon monitor. Surely it had malfunctioned? That was the only sensible explanation. But the integrity scanner showed nothing wrong.

So it was true: a flux of chronon particles had passed through the ship. Even though Rum-Lem was no scientist, he knew what that meant.

Chronons do not occur naturally. Not even in the earliest moments of the Universe has a naturally occurring chronon particle existed. It is not possible to create a chronon particle, even in the most advanced particle-creation machines. Chronons can only be released, never created. And there is but a single known circumstance in which chronons are released to propagate freely: when a timeshift field is generated. Whenever an object is timeshifted, the shift is accompanied by a flux of chronon particles escaping from the timeshift field. The flux is always brief, typically a centichron or less in duration, and the chronons soon decay into ordinary matter-antimatter pairs, with a half-life of approximately thirty chrons*, so after a short time all traces of the chronons disappear.

Rum-Lem understood that chronons were somewhat analogous to those more common particles known as tachyons. Just as tachyons inhabit the world of hyperspace and leak into normal space whenever a ship performs a hyperspace jump (thereby rendering the details of the jump vector computable by someone observing the jump) so chronons inhabit a region that is briefly exposed during a timeshift. Somewhere nearby a timeshift field had briefly existed.

He accelerated quickly up through the atmosphere and shot into space, keeping an eye on the chronon indicator. But it remained silent. The chronon burst was over, and it seemed that there was not going to be another, at least for a while.

Once he was in orbit, he called up the data from the burst. The chronon peak was broad and weak. That was odd. Chronon bursts usually showed sharp, well-defined peaks characteristic of the beamed

---

* To be precise, this figure has long been debated, since chronons are superluminal and therefore violate causality constraints.

field from a weapon. This burst had apparently been generated by an uncollimated field. But who would ever generate an uncollimated timeshift field? And why?

Uneasily he waited, hoping for a repetition.

He remained in orbit for two full rotations of the planet Tirsh, but detected no more chronons.

A disturbing possibility struck him. He was assuming that the chronon burst could not have been a natural phenomenon. It was known that chronons could not occur naturally in normal time. But he was not in normal time. Here in forward time, might such bursts not be a natural phenomenon? Perhaps there was some sort of inherent instability in forward time that produced occasional leakages of uncollimated chronon particles?

It was a worrying thought, and it had a disturbing ring of plausibility. But he wasn't ready to give up yet. Maybe the burst profile could tell him something useful.

He displayed the profile of the burst again, and commanded the databoxes to examine the profile for any deviations from its theoretical shape. The databoxes meticulously examined microscopic distortions in the shape of the chronon burst, and informed him that there was a slight shortfall compared to the theoretical best-fit. Rum-Lem smiled excitedly, his heart suddenly beating faster. There was a simple explanation for the shortfall: of the several hundred billion particles in the burst, a few had been absorbed. The databox computed that this suggested that the source of the burst was on the opposite side of the planet. A few chronons had been absorbed while passing through Tirsh.

He adjusted the ship's life detector, switched on several other detectors that might prove useful, and dropped out of orbit.

The continent on the opposite side from his island was mostly covered with thick jungle which was home to many non-human life forms that caused his life detector to trigger almost continuously. He turned it off, relying instead on the other detectors: a pollution detector; an electronics detector; a fire sensor; and other similar devices.

It was not until the second rotation that one of the scanners emitted a warning tone. He was in the central portion of the continent, far from the oceans, flying over heavily jungled, mountainous terrain.

Somewhere not far away a scanner had detected an electronic circuit. The signal was weak, but it was also persistent.

He began to fly in a large circle, using the strength of the signal to guide him towards its source. Before long he found himself hovering over a small island in a midcontinental river. The island showed unmistakable indications of recent habitation. The electronic circuit was somewhere nearby, and doubtless it was in some way associated with the small encampment below.

His attention was attracted by a splashing movement in the river, and with a thumping heart he realized that a human was swimming from the shore to the island. The human swam clumsily and slowly. The water, muddy brown everywhere else, had acquired an unmistakable reddish tinge in the vicinity of the swimmer, who seemed to be using only one arm and one leg. Rum-Lem watched transfixed as the current carried the swimmer downriver. At first he was certain that the human was going to be swept downstream past the island, but at the last moment the swimmer seemed to find new strength and he struggled forward and beached himself on the island's downstream extremity.

The swimmer was a man, and he was clutching his chest with one arm, while he dragged himself forward across the muddy shore with the other. Now that he was clear of the water, Rum-Lem could see that his torso was bleeding. As Rum-Lem watched, trying to decide what to do, the man seemed to look apprehensively toward something not far away. Then Rum-Lem noticed for the first time an enormous reptile not far from the place where the man had come ashore. The reptile began to move forward. The man's head fell to the ground, and he stopped moving.

It did not take Rum-Lem long to bring the man aboard. He left the dead reptile where it was for the present; the body was not yet attracting flies, for the kill-gun had left no open wounds.

Rum-Lem wasted no time in speculating how the man had come to be in forward time. The man was dangerously close to death, and Rum-Lem was too busy trying to save the man's life to waste time in idle speculation. The man was very short and stocky for a human, but his skin color was close to Rum-Lem's own. He was youngish, perhaps thirty cycles old. There were a few rotations' growth of beard on the man's face.

The man was in a coma, and Rum-Lem wasted no time trying to pull him out of it. The man's wound was bad, and he was losing blood at a worrying rate. As Rum-Lem carried him up the ramp and into the sick room, the man began to shiver violently. Loss of blood was sending him into shock.

Rum-Lem placed him on the sick bed and switched on the emergency life-support machine. A translucent envelope slid silently up out of the floor, enclosing the man and the bed in a sealed environment. The panels on the life-support machine began to glow as it began to monitor the man's system, and almost immediately the machine began to alter the environment inside the envelope. Rum-Lem breathed a sigh of relief. Another couple of chrons and he would have been too late. Even as it was, the machine estimated that it would be a full rotation before the man was restored to health.

Rum-Lem gazed through the translucent envelope. The man's breathing was already deeper and more regular. The life-support machine injected a fine mist into the envelope, and almost instantly the bleeding from the wound halted. Rum-Lem smiled. The man was going to live.

But he had work to do. The man was now stabilized, but his wound would not heal properly without intervention.

Rum-Lem hurried from the room and consulted the research databox in the control cabin. A short time later he returned carrying several surgical instruments. He was no surgeon — the most he had ever done was to repair an ankle he had broken once when he was training on the treacherous slopes of the volcano field of Terellon — but the databox reconstructions had shown him exactly what to do.

Several decachrons later, Rum-Lem lifted his head from his patient's body. The worst was over now. The man would be restored to full health when the machine finished its work sometime tomorrow.

With a grunt of satisfaction, Rum-Lem stood looking at the man whose life he had saved, and wondered. The man came from a reasonably advanced society: he had been wearing a communicator device on one wrist. The screen on the device was small, but obviously stereographic, possibly even holographic. There was a small grill from which sound presumably emanated.

But the people on this planet were classified as primitive. While they might be able to produce the communicator, they could not possibly have discovered timeshifting yet. So how had the man come to be here?

He returned to the control cabin, and interrogated the research databox for details about the civilization that inhabited Tirsh. The entry was brief, but confirmed that Tirsh was classified as Primitive V, and had yet to discover either hyperspace travel or timeshifting.

Yet it seemed that somehow the man had been exposed to a timeshift field.

Rum-Lem gazed at the communicator, wishing that it could answer his questions. Well, the man would survive now. Tomorrow he would awaken. Then Rum-Lem would learn his language. And soon all would be explained.

21

HWANG

Hwang had never seen Earth from space. He had seen holograms, of
course, but never before had he left the planet in real life. There were
colonies on Mars and the moon, and a few commercial ventures on
some of the more profitable asteroids, but trips to such places were
beyond his means as a citizen and out of his field as a scientist. In
any case, he had no real desire to go into space. Living quarters were
cramped and lacked many of what people had come to think of as
necessities. No worse than his great-grandfather's cabin perhaps, but
at least that had the merit of being on Earth, and therefore relatively
safe.

Every few years there was a major mishap aboard a commercial
spaceship, and although it was now more than a decade since any lives
had been lost in space — not including the well-paid workers who
assayed the mineral-rich asteroids — still there was no doubt that
space travel was not yet wholly without risk. And what was there to
do once one reached one's destination? Not much, apart from taking
holographs to show one's friends and family back home. So all in all,
until this moment, Hwang Lee had had no cause to feel any regret
that he had never been in space. But now, as the alien ship hovered
high above central Africa and the holographic image of Earth floated
in front of him, he realized that perhaps he should have taken a brief

trip to the moon, just so that he could have seen this sight for himself before now.

The control cabin was in darkness, except for a few dimly lit bars on the panel in front of Rum-Lem. The hologram of Earth floated directly in front of Hwang in a sea of blackness. It was more stark, more impressive, more beautiful than he had ever imagined.

The dusk terminator was moving slowly across Africa. Behind the terminator there was nearly complete darkness; only the phosphorescent glow from the ocean and a dim reflected moonlight ameliorated the blackness of the night.

Earth was sometimes referred to as "the big blue marble" by those who were temporarily off-planet. Apparently a marble was a small glass ball, often highly colored with a swirling pattern embedded in the glass, and used long ago in a children's game. The word was archaic, unused now except as a means of referring to the Earth. "The marble" was often used colloquially as a synonym for "the Earth." Now, as he looked at the huge ball hanging before him in the blackness of space, it seemed only fitting that a sight so beautiful had a word all its own.

"The marble," he said under his breath.

Now he understood what people meant when they used the word. It was not so much a sight as an experience, and one never to be forgotten.

"It's a pretty planet," Rum-Lem interrupted Hwang's thoughts with a more prosaic evaluation.

"Don't a lot of planets look like this?"

Rum-Lem laughed.

"Far from it. Most inhabited planets have much less ocean, a well-defined cloud system that follows the edges of the continents, and larger areas of desert. There are a few planets, the ones where it is always raining, that are almost completely cloud-covered. But there aren't many planets that look like this, comfortably between the two extremes. It's really rather unusual, especially when you consider that Tirsh... Earth has such a circular orbit. A few planets look like this for part of their cycle, but I can't think of one that matches this all the time. Your home planet must be one of the most beautiful in the galaxy."

The beauty of his birth planet was hardly a matter for which he could be held responsible, but even so Rum-Lem's words gave Hwang a warm feeling. Surely it was something to know that one's home planet, even if it was regarded as technologically primitive, was one of the most beautiful in the entire galaxy?

"Ready to go?" Rum-Lem asked.

Hwang nodded reluctantly. He could look at this view for hours.

Rum-Lem spoke some words of his incomprehensible language while pressing buttons on the panel before him. The image of the Earth disappeared, and Hwang felt momentarily disoriented. It was difficult to get used to the fact that the ship had not a single window. External views such as the one over which he had just been marvelling were simply holographic reconstructions of what the scanners were detecting.

Rum-Lem explained what was going to happen. They would begin by moving far enough away from the sun to reach a place where the spacetime curvature would allow them to make a hyperspace jump.

According to the opnav computer, they would reach about 92% light speed before they reached their jump point. All spaceships were fitted with devices to cancel internal acceleration fields, but Rum-Lem explained that the generation of such fields was a rather difficult affair, and the acceleration which a ship could sustain was a major factor in its price.

Hwang's interest was piqued at Rum-Lem's mention of the acceleration-canceling field, for he knew that, fundamentally, acceleration is no different from gravity. In a sense, what had caused his jump into forward time was his own attempt to construct an acceleration-canceling field. But Rum-Lem moved his hand in his equivalent of a shrug when Hwang asked how the field was generated.

"It's probably in the research computer. We can look it up later," the alien said.

Rum-Lem declaimed further on the advanced nature of his ship. "In most craft, it would be madness to consider crossing a third of the galaxy in a single jump, but in this ship it is perfectly feasible, provided one has the time to let the computers calculate the jump parameters. In fact, it's probably the best and safest way."

"Safe? Is it dangerous to travel through hyperspace?"

"In this ship? No — it's as safe as anything done by man ever is. Hyperspace jumps are dangerous only when you lack accurate galactic maps or the time to let the computers calculate the jump trajectory properly.

"Most ships carry accurate maps for every major gravitational field in the galaxy down to the level of brown dwarves. This ship contains precise maps for every field down to the size of an asteroid. So hyperspace travel in this ship is almost completely safe.

"The only danger associated with making a hyperspace jump lies in the possibility of materializing inside a solid body, or extremely close to a star. You see, a hyperspace jump is a kind of metastable mapping function. If the opnav computer makes a very small error in its calculations, you will end up close to the place you were aiming for, but if the computer makes a larger error, the distance between your actual exit position and the intended one can become quite sizeable. As a result, the better one's maps, the more computational power is needed to make a jump, but the safer the jump will be."

Hwang nodded. He understood, more or less.

"Also," Rum-Lem continued, "the likelihood of error increases for very short and very long jumps. So most ships jump about a thousand of your light years at a time. We are about to jump thirty thousand light years; but it will be at least as safe as a thousand-light-year jump in an ordinary ship. We have plenty of time to chart our intended course on our way to our jumping-off point.

"Now settle back. You will feel a slight acceleration. It is only a fraction of our true acceleration, but it can be uncomfortable until you get used to it."

The alien issued a series of commands to the opnav system, and Hwang felt a firm pressure pushing him backward into his seat. Rum-Lem was right: the acceleration was enough that it would have been difficult to walk around the cabin.

Rum-Lem said, "I'll turn on the holoimage screen. You might enjoy seeing what happens as our speed increases. It will take a while for the relativistic effects to appear, but they will become obvious as we begin to travel faster."

All around them, a view of space suddenly appeared. Whichever way he looked, he could see pinpricks of light. Behind Rum-Lem's shoulder was the bright ball of the sun. The Earth was the next-brightest object in the sky, directly behind them and growing visibly smaller and dimmer as he watched. The ship was moving almost perpendicular to the ecliptic; Hwang soon found himself looking down on the Earth-Moon system.

"I'll magnify the view of the Earth-Moon system for you so that they stay the same size," said Rum-Lem.

The Earth and the Moon, and the distance between them, stopped shrinking.

Hwang watched intrigued as the ship's speed increased, and relativistic effects began to appear. The colors of the Earth and Moon changed, as did their relative geometry. The sun reddened. The stars appeared to move, clustering ahead of them in a phenomenon known as aberration. Hwang wondered whether the stellar gravity fields also moved, pulling them forward ever faster.

His reverie was interrupted by Rum-Lem.

"The computer has finished its calculations. It's safe now to make the hyperspace jump. Are you ready?"

"Will I feel anything? What will it look like? And how long will it take?"

Hwang had many other questions — questions about the physics of hyperspace travel — but he already knew that Rum-Lem was probably unable to answer those. He would have to wait until the alien could translate the reference materials for him.

Rum-Lem laughed.

"What's the matter?" Hwang asked.

"Those are the very questions I asked the first time I made a hyperspace jump. I was twelve at the time."

Hwang grinned sheepishly, and Rum-Lem continued, "You will feel just a slight jerk and maybe a tingling sensation in your nerve endings and in the pit of your stomach. You won't see what it looks like because the ship automatically disables its sensors during a jump. And it will be over almost as soon as it has started. This is an excellent ship, and the jump will be almost undetectable. In fact, you probably wouldn't notice it if I hadn't warned you. Now, are you ready?"

Hwang nodded. Despite the alien's assurances, he gripped his seat tightly. Rum-Lem said something in his own language, and Hwang felt a barely perceptible shudder pass through the frame of the craft. He felt a momentary desire to shiver and an equally fleeting feeling of something like fear in the pit of his stomach. The view projected around them blanked out momentarily and was almost instantly replaced by a sudden bright confusion of stars. For a few seconds Hwang felt like vomiting, not from of any physical cause, but because the starfield in which he was now embedded showed in the most graphic way possible that he had just been transported a third of the way across the galaxy in little more than the blink of an eye. They were now much closer to the central core of the galaxy. Probably not a single one of the myriad points of light floating around his head had been visible just a second earlier. The thought was enough to make anyone nauseated, and he swallowed hard several times.

Rum-Lem said, "That's all there is to it. And if you look at that bright star directly ahead, you'll soon be able to make out its planet, which is where human life originally began.

"At least, in normal time it's where human life originally began...," he added as an afterthought.

The ball of Kivra appeared and slowly grew. After an hour it filled the cabin before them. The planet was larger than Earth, and it orbited its cool orange-red sun at a greater distance. According to Rum-Lem Kivra was considerably warmer than Earth because of the high percentage of greenhouse gases in its atmosphere.

Rum-Lem placed the ship into orbit, and Hwang gazed at the alien planet, searching for similarities and differences. Kivra had oceans, but they covered no more than a third of the surface. Most of the rest of the planet seemed to be covered by ocher desert. Dark strips of vegetation were visible where the land met the sea and along a dozen or so large river courses. There were only a couple of small mountain ranges. The few clouds were thin and wispy, and followed the outlines of the continents.

"It should be easy to find traces of the timeshifted humans, if there are any to be found," said Rum-Lem. "The original timeshift work was performed at a research base located at a place called Tel Dahn, over there." He pointed some distance away, near the place where Kivra's large sun was rising over the limb of the planet.

"We'll land there and take a look around. As I told you before, there's no trace of people living there now. But perhaps you're right and those early timeshift experiments left some evidence."

The alien laid his hands on the control panel, barked a few words, and Hwang immediately had the uncomfortable sensation that the enormous ball of the planet was falling towards him.

22
LYSTRA

When Lystra Ten-Wer woke, it was dark.

On Kivra, close to the galactic center, the sky was never fully dark. But Soam was far from the center, and too small to possess a moon of any consequence, so here there were vast empty spaces between the stars. The night sky here was stark, alien, and oddly scary.

But as Lystra tried to sit up, she discovered something worse than the unaccustomed darkness: her hands were tightly bound.

She tugged, but it was pointless; her wrists simply chafed against the binding. But at least her legs feet were still free. Maneuvering herself onto her knees, she peered into the tenebrous surroundings.

The exiguous starlight cast a ghostly pallor over what little she could make out. In the distance, across the downward-sloping silvery-gray grass, she could see the calm ocean, reflecting the starlight so that it was difficult to tell where the horizon lay.

She listened. Behind her, the forest was unnaturally quiet. The only sounds were gentle soughs as branches moved ever so slightly in the barely moving air.

She called out, quietly at first, half afraid that whoever had tied her hands was still somewhere nearby.

"Teberill, are you there?" Then, when there was no response, she called more urgently, "Teberill! Teberill Gandeer! Where are you, Teberill?"

She peered toward the place where the hovercar had been parked, and an icy fear gripped her stomach. The hovercar was no longer there.

With a new urgency, she yanked at her bounds. To no avail.

Something scratched against her hand, and in the near darkness she could just make out what looked like a piece of paper tucked under one of the bounds, trapped next to her hand. Flexing her wrist, she managed to extract the paper.

It was folded into quarters. With difficulty, she opened it out. There was writing on it, but there wasn't enough light to read the note.

Suddenly, she became aware of a sound. She caught her breath and stopped moving.

It was quiet and distant: an engine of some sort. Its timbre was too deep for a hovercar; it sounded more like a spaceship. The sound was coming from somewhere between herself and the ocean. She heard the Dopplered pitch of the engine change as the ship passed directly in front of her. She searched the sky, then spotted a star that was briefly occulted. Another star briefly disappeared. The ship was travelling without lights and hugging the ground, passing from right to left in front of her. It was not very far away.

Lystra wanted to stand up and scream at the ship, but reason told her that that would be pointless. She scrambled awkwardly to her feet, the scrap of paper forgotten, and began to run desperately down the grassy slope. Perhaps the ship carried a life detector and would spot the movement.

She had taken five steps when she slammed into an invisible wall.

She fell to the ground, momentarily stunned. Something was dribbling down her face, and she tasted the sharp flavor of blood. She swallowed something small and hard: a fragment of a tooth.

By the time she had recovered, the ship was gone. Once more she could hear nothing except the gentle movement of the trees in the forest behind her.

For a moment, she felt an almost overwhelming desire to burst into tears. She had trusted Teberill. Why had he done this to her? What possible reason could he have for tying her up and leaving her? What was he up to? And where had he gone?

Or was it someone else? Had someone overcome Teberill while she slept? But no, that did not make any sense. Why take him away and leave her here? This must be Teberill's doing. But why? *Why?*

193

She took a hesitant step forward towards the sea; her way was blocked by a hard, transparent barrier. Clumsily, she began to walk sideways, pressing against the invisible wall.

The barrier forced her to walk in a circle whose diameter was perhaps a dozen paces. She was being held captive inside a small, locally generated force field.

She rested against the barrier, trying to think coherently. *If the field completely surrounds me*, she thought, *then the field generator must be in here with me. If I can find it, I might be able to switch it off.*

It was an eminently sensible plan, and Lystra lost no time in putting it into action. She limped to the place where she estimated the center of the field to be. Then she dropped to her knees and began to feel the ground with her bound hands. Almost immediately, she found a spot where the grass had been disturbed. Digging frantically in the soft soil, she quickly found what she was looking for: a metallic cylinder no larger than her thumb, humming so softly that she could barely hear it even when she pressed it against her ear.

She moved her hands over the cylinder, trying to find some indentation or protrusion that might act as a switch. There was nothing.

For a moment, her heart sank. Of course there was no switch. Doubtless the field generator was activated by remote control. Teberill — or whoever had buried the generator (she still could not quite bring herself to convict Teberill without more evidence) — would have realized that there was a good chance she would find the generator, and he would have made sure that there was no way she could switch the force field off until he returned.

But hadn't she seen a few pebbles earlier in the day amongst the grass? Perhaps she could find one large enough to damage the generator.

She picked up the device and carried it toward the edge of the trees, where she thought she remembered seeing the pebbles. As she moved, the force field moved with her, and it occurred to her that she was no longer trapped; but almost certainly the device was transmitting some sort of homing beacon, and if she went far it would lead Teberill — or someone else — straight to her.

No, she had to find a way of destroying the field generator; once she had done that, she would get as far away as possible.

She began to scrabble around on the ground. Almost immediately her hand landed on a stone. It fitted easily in her hand. She felt its weight: it had a comfortable, heavy heft.

Putting the generator on the ground, she smashed the stone down as hard as she could. Again and again she hammered the cylinder. After a while she picked it up and pressed it against her ear. It was still humming.

She shifted her weight, and her knee scraped against a partially buried rock. Placing the generator on the rock, she pounded it again with the stone.

She checked the generator again. It was still humming. She swore. Then she listened more carefully. Hadn't the note changed? Wasn't it a little higher in pitch now?

And just as she permitted herself the first glimmer of hope that perhaps her pounding was having an effect after all, she heard the sound of the ship returning.

She turned to face the sea. The sound was fainter than before, but with a burst of hope she could think of only one reason why a ship might be making a series of passes over this uninhabited area: someone was looking for her.

And if they were looking, that meant they didn't know where she was. And *that* meant that whoever was in the ship wasn't the person who had tied her up and trapped her in a force field.

She steadied the generator and brought the stone down with all her strength. And there was a distinct *crack!*

She pounded again, and this time, at last, the case of the generator split apart. One last pound, and the field generator was smashed to smithereens. She took a couple of deep breaths and stood up. She was shaking, and she could barely stay upright as she began to walk across the grass. Now that the field was gone, she should be visible on any life detectors in the vicinity.

Where was the ship? She saw a star disappear and, a moment later, flick back on. She began to run, her hands, still bound, high above her head as she shouted: "Help! Help me!"

She tripped and fell.

Then the sound of the ship's engine changed, and it began to come closer.

———————

Amril Gdrena was not worried about Lystra's disappearance — unlike Rum-Lem, the woman calling herself Lystra Ten-Wer knew nothing that could threaten the Empire — but she was angry at the prospect that Lystra might be dead.

The man known as Teberill Gandeer had returned alone to the tourist center. It should have been easy to find Lystra, if she was still alive. One simply set the thresholds on the life detector so that a human anywhere nearby would trigger it. Then one flew over the area in which the person was last seen. Simple. But despite circling the area several times, there was no sign of Lystra Ten-Wer. Worried that her quarry was dead — either at her own hand or that of Teberill Gandeer — Amril Gdrena ordered Veel to search in a widening spiral. Still the life detector registered nothing except a wandering herd of ruminants on the grassy plain between the jungle and the ocean.

Veel brought the ship around for another pass.

The ship raced above the plain, almost over the ocean now.

Suddenly the life detector emitted a piercing whine and began to flash urgently. A moment earlier there had been nothing; but now there was a human not far away, on the very edge of the jungle. The human was moving out on to the plain at a run.

Brynt Veel cut the power and brought the ship to a halt. The figure stopped moving. He turned the craft and slowly began to move toward the jungle; the human also began to move again, more slowly now.

Gdrena turned on the external lights, and in a few moments the view screen showed a human female standing not far away, looking up at them. Her face was bloody and her hands were tied. She winced in the glare of the lights.

"Lystra Ten-Wer," the minister said to herself. "What on Kivra has happened to you?"

It was a question to which the woman would soon supply the answer. Lystra Ten-Wer was going to tell the minister everything she knew, whether she wanted to or not.

———————

Lystra watched in relief as the ship descended. She felt almost like crying. Safe at last. But she did not cry; she simply walked up to the craft, raising her bound hands to shade her eyes, and waited for the access door to open.

The light from the craft was so bright that she was unable to see its markings. She assumed it was a search and rescue ship.

The access panel opened, and a ramp slid down. A man descended the ramp, holding out his arms in greeting. For a moment she wondered why her rescuer was dressed in the uniform of a P&S security officer.

As he put his arm around her, she saw that his uniform carried a small flash of maroon, gold and black stripes near the shoulder. The colors of the Minister of P&S.

"You are all right?" the man asked.

"Yes, yes. I am now."

"Good." The man took a step backward and regarded her. "You are Lystra Ten-Wer?"

She nodded.

The man pulled his stun-gun from its holster and pointed it at her.

"Wha...?"

He moved forward and grabbed her arm roughly. Ignoring her protests, he pulled her up the ramp and into the ship. It was unlike any ship she had ever seen: luxuriously appointed, with trimmings of maroon, gold and black everywhere. The man pushed her into the control cabin, inside which was a woman: a tall woman with short, graying hair, who turned to look at the pair as they entered. For a moment, Lystra did not recognize her, but she did see that the woman's face radiated a cold malevolence.

Lystra tried to shrink back from the malice in the woman's expression. But the man pushed her forward so hard that she fell on her knees before the woman. And now Lystra recognized her.

"Minister? Minister Gdrena?"

The minister ignored her. To her pilot she said, "I don't think she's any threat to us. Home, I think."

The man nodded and put away his stun-gun. As he settled himself in the pilot's seat, he glanced at Lystra. Lystra saw a hint of a smile at the corners of his mouth. It was the kind of smile to freeze one's blood.

23
LYSTRA

Lystra Ten-Wer's reaction when she was rescued was simple gratitude; but gratitude quickly became puzzlement; and then, finally, fear and confusion. She had always had a deep respect for the law and an unshakable faith in the benign and caring hands of those who guided the Empire. How could she have been so wrong?

The minister forced her to sit at the rear of the cabin with her hands still tied while the ship returned to Kivra. Whenever Lystra tried to speak, Gdrena told her to be silent, accompanied with a glare that made it clear that Lystra had better obey or else.

She tried to understand what was happening. Obviously, the gardener, Teberill Gandeer, was some sort of fugitive, and the minister had jumped to the conclusion that Lystra was an accomplice of some kind.

When the ship docked on Kivra two security guards in P&S uniforms entered the cabin, brandishing stun-guns.

Once more she tried to protest that a mistake had been made, but the minister slapped her viciously and told her to be quiet.

Smarting from the force of the blow, Lystra Ten-Wer was escorted by the grim-faced guards down a short corridor and then placed in what could only be described as a cell.

It was a small, spartan, windowless suite of two rooms. Primitive sanitation facilities were in the second, smaller room, but the rooms contained nothing else: no furniture, no vidbooks, no holoimage screen, not even any running water — nothing. She hesitated in the doorway, but one of the guards pushed her roughly inside. By the time she turned to face the guards, a barely audible hum was issuing from the doorway, indicating the presence of a deterrent field. The doorway was still transparent and apparently empty, but a slight random twinkling showed where dust motes were being vaporized.

She walked towards the doorway and extended her bound hands.

"I wouldn't do that," one of the guards warned.

The moment her index finger touched the invisible barrier pain shot up her arm, as if she had touched a hot surface. Reflexively, she pulled away. The guard who had spoken shook his head sadly, as if marvelling at her stupidity. He and his colleague took up positions in the corridor, facing the doorway.

Lystra looked at their grim expressions and knew that it was pointless to try to convince them that she was the innocent victim of a mistake. Their job was to make sure that she remained confined, and there was nothing to be gained by arguing with them.

She slumped on the floor in a corner of the cell. Pulling her knees against her chest, she waited.

Gdrena watched from her office as the medical technicians examined the woman.

They had given her an injection to make her sleep. Now they unbound her hands, undressed her and examined her body, looking for any signs of subcutaneous suicide triggers, homing implants or communications devices. To the minister's surprise, they found nothing suspicious at all.

The technicians gave her another shot and left the cell, taking the woman's clothes with them as she began to emerge from her drug-induced coma.

For some time, the minister continued to watch the vidscreen, waiting for the Union spy to realize that it was pointless to continue her act. Over her shoulder Brynt Veel also watched, his eyes narrowed like the minister's, looking for the least sign of anything suspicious.

But the woman who called herself Lystra Ten-Wer simply remained huddled in a corner. Her eyes looked blankly out across the cell toward the doorway in which flashed tiny flecks of gold.

Eventually, Gdrena tired of waiting. She turned to Brynt Veel.

"Let's go talk to her. She must know she's beaten. Perhaps she'll be sensible."

Lystra looked up as the whine of the deterrent field was interrupted. The minister and the man who had piloted her ship walked into the cell.

Lystra shifted slightly, drawing herself into a tighter ball in the corner, trying to comport herself so that the man — Brynt Veel, she assumed, who was rumored to be the minister's lover — would be unable to see her nakedness.

The two intruders stood on the far side of the cell, close to the doorway. Veel — if it was he — drew a stun-gun and pointed it at her.

For a while, nobody moved. Lystra glared belligerently at the pair, as if daring them to come closer. They had stripped her of her clothing, and thereby her dignity. Lystra saw the removal of her clothes as the act of a coward, and now she was filled with a steadily rising righteous indignation. No one, not even Amril Gdrena, had the right to do this to her. Lystra was a citizen of the Empire, and innocent until proven otherwise — not that any charge had yet been levelled against her.

Indicating the cell with an expansive gesture, the minister said, "I'm sorry about this, but this is the price you pay for losing."

The words made no sense to Lystra.

"You're Minister Gdrena, aren't you?"

The minister nodded.

"There's been a mistake. I don't know who or what you think I am, but my name is Lystra Ghetrol Ten-Wer. You took my clothes, but my ID card was in the pocket. You can check it. My citizen number is 465-987-098-125. Thank you for rescuing me on Soam but please let me go now. You know that it's illegal to hold me against my will. And I haven't done anything. This is all just a horrible mistake of some kind. I had nothing to do with that man, Teberill Gandeer...."

The minister raised her hand.

"So, the prisoner knows her rights. There's no mistake, and you can stop this pretense now. It's becoming tiresome."

Her voice was gentle and reasonable. She shook her head as she continued.

"We know exactly who you are. You are not Lystra Ghetrol Ten-Wer; you are just the woman who has passed as Lystra Ghetrol Ten-Wer for many cycles. We know who your real mother is, and who her parents were. We know everything about you. That means we know that your birth name is not Lystra but Per-Lem, and that you are a citizen, not of the Empire, but of the Union. You have no...."

Something snapped.

"No, it's not true," Lystra shouted.

She lunged toward the minister, uncoiling like a wild animal launching itself against larger prey.

The next thing she knew, Lystra was spread-eagled on a hard surface. She was in agony. Her first coherent thought was: *I've been hit by a stun gun.* She shook herself, fighting off a wave of nausea. She let out an involuntary groan.

She closed her eyes and counted to ten.

Feeling a little better, she opened her eyes and saw that the minister and her companion had departed while she was unconscious.

A gray pile of clothes was now on the floor nearby. The guards still stood impassively on the far side of the doorway. Neither of them showed any reaction to her groans.

Moving slowly, she sat up and put the clothes on. They comprised a kind of primitive two-piece garment, woven from some kind of ugly gray fiber, not the usual adaptametal, and they hung loosely from her frame instead of conforming themselves to her figure. She must look dreadful. She glanced toward the doorway and saw that one of the guards was watching her.

"There's been a mistake," she said.

Her voice was hoarse, her throat scratchy and dry. She looked around. There was nothing to eat or to drink.

"I'm thirsty," she said.

The guards ignored her.

She limped across the cell until her face was almost touching the deterrent field.

"I'm hungry and thirsty. Please get me something."

Neither of the guards moved.

She took a deep breath, opened her mouth and screamed as loudly as her parched throat would permit. The closest guard blinked, but that was all. But he *had* blinked, and that was a victory of sorts. Lystra stumbled back to the far corner and slid to the floor, whence she looked sullenly at the motionless guards beyond the doorway.

For a long while, nothing happened.

Eventually, the minister and her companion returned. The doorway briefly ceased sparkling and they stepped through, Veel pointing his stun-gun at the prisoner. The minister looked thunderous. She wasted no time in preliminaries.

"I trust you have learnt your lesson, Per-Lem."

Lystra's objection to the name was confined to a shake of the head, which was ignored by the minister.

"What's the meaning of this?" the minister continued.

She opened her hand, and a piece of paper fluttered to the floor. Lystra looked at the paper, then at the minister.

"I don't know," she said hoarsely, making no effort to move.

Somewhere in the recesses of her mind, Lystra realized that she recognized the paper. She made an effort to think, and after a moment she remembered: the note had been stuffed between the vine and her wrist when she had woken on Soam.

"Have you read it?" the minister asked.

Lystra did not respond.

"One of my operatives found it on Soam, in the place where you were hiding before we picked you up."

"I wasn't hiding...."

"Why are you being so stupid?" The minister sounded genuinely puzzled. "The last thing I expect from an agent of Tcharn's is stupidity. More than once...."

"Tcharn?" Lystra interrupted. "You mean the Union's chief of defense? I don't work for the Union. I'm a loyal citizen of the Empire. I tell you, madam minister, there's been a mistake. A terrible mistake. Please, you must believe me. If it was the gardener who told you this, he's lying. Perhaps he's a Union spy, I don't know. But I've never met him before. I see him occasionally on the hoverbus to and from work, that's all. He was on his way to Soam and just happened to be on the same ship as me. It was just a coincidence. Please, madam minister, honestly, I don't know what you're talking about."

It was a long speech, and her dry throat was raw by the time she had finished it. She looked up at the minister like an animal pleading for a favor from its master.

Amril Gdrena considered her for some moments. "I should applaud you, Per-Lem. If I didn't know the truth, you'd almost have convinced me. Unfortunately for you, the evidence is irrefutable. Your choice of companion on Soam merely confirms everything else."

"But there can't be any evidence. I've never done anything to harm the Empire. And like I told you, I'd barely met the gardener before. He's usually on the same hoverbus as me, that's all. I'd barely spoken to him before the trip to Soam. I know we spent the rotation together on Soam, but he was an interesting person to talk to. That's all we did: talk and sleep."

But as Lystra listened to the sound of her own voice, she knew she didn't sound convincing.

"Then perhaps you'll explain the note?"

Lystra picked it up and read:

Please don't be afraid. I'll be back for you later. Trust me. Soon we'll be together again, forever.

Teberill.

"Doesn't look like a note from a stranger, does it? What information have you have been feeding him? The reports from 35/CW perhaps?"

"I don't know what you're talking about. I've never heard of anything called 35/CW. What is it? It sounds like some kind of monitorship."

Suddenly she remembered.

"Oh! You mean the red reports. Is that it? I don't remember anything about those. They were just meaningless numbers. I know I forgot to report the first one; I'm sorry, but surely it wasn't all that important? And anyway I passed the second one on to Supervisor Qwilm. He said he never got it, but I sent it, I know I did. I told him there must have been a databox programming error or something. That must be why he never received the second report. Mindprobe me if you want; you'll see I'm telling the truth." She coughed; her throat felt as if it were on fire. "Water, please. I must have some water."

The minister contemplated the prisoner for a while, then she said, "Veel, get her some water."

Brynt Veel nodded and left the cell. The minister took a step backward and drew her stun-gun, covering the prisoner.

Lystra tried to think of something she could say that would convince the minister.

"What does the gardener say?" she asked. "If he's told you that I'm some sort of spy, he's lying. I don't know why he left me this note. I don't know why he tied me up that way. I don't know why he went away and left me inside a force field. I don't know anything. None of it makes sense...."

She was on the verge of tears.

The minister remained impassive and Lystra lapsed into silence, struggling not to cry. After a while, Brynt Veel returned with a container of water. He handed it to Lystra, who thirstily emptied it. The water was cool and sweet. By the time she had finished it, she felt considerably better.

Lystra repeated, less hysterically now: "If the gardener says I'm involved in something illegal he's lying, trying to trap me for some reason I don't understand. Honestly, I don't know the man. Look at my record. Surely that should make it clear I'm not a spy...."

She stopped. The minister was looking at her oddly.

"What's the matter? What did I say?"

"You told me to look at your record. That, Per-Lem, is exactly what I have done. You are quite correct. It is your record that makes it perfectly clear exactly what you are."

The minister abruptly turned to the two guards. "Give her food and more water, and let her sleep. When she is rested, I am to be notified."

She turned back to her prisoner. "When you are feeling better, we shall have a long talk, Per-Lem. And then you will tell me everything. Everything."

It was not a threat; it was simply a statement of fact.

With Brynt Veel at her heels, the minister strode out of the cell.

As Lystra watched her leave, she felt an ominous fear descend. What was the minister going to do? She had already told the minister the truth; so why did Amril Gdrena seem to believe she was hiding something? And why did she have the feeling that the minister was never going to let her leave this place alive?

She looked down as something touched her leg. A wet dribble was running down it. It was only then that Lystra Ten-Wer realized she was crying.

24
VAL-DOR

Val-Dor's hovercar lifted off and moved quickly away from the place where Per-Lem rested peacefully in her hypnotic sleep. As the vehicle gained altitude, he turned westward and headed out over the sea.

By now it was late afternoon and the yellow sun reflected from the blue ocean in a way that reminded him pleasantly of Dalith, so unlike the angry color of Kivra where sky, sea and sun all carried the pervasive reddish-orange tint of the Mother Planet.

After a while, Val-Dor slowed the hovercar, turned through 180 degrees and began to retrace his path. He turned off the jammer. They would be able to see him now.

Less than a chron later, a hovercar appeared on the scanner, travelling on an intercept course and closing quickly. He maintained his heading and speed, and very soon the other vehicle dropped into position close behind. The pursuing ship maintained visual contact and followed only a few centichrons in his wake; there was no chance of shaking his tail a second time. But Val-Dor had no intention of losing his pursuer again. He crossed the shore and the strip of coastal grassland. Altering course slightly, he headed for the tourist center.

He landed in the hovercar park; his pursuer followed suit moments later. Val-Dor looked out at the number and disposition of the enemy forces in position around the brightly lit park. There were several guards in P&S uniform scattered around the periphery of the park; all were looking in his direction. With a muted smile, he wondered how they would react when they observed that he was alone.

He clambered out the car. Out the corner of his eye, he could see that the fact that he was unaccompanied had precipitated an animated discussion in a knot of guards. He ignored them as he walked back to his room.

The sun set with a rapidity that was never seen on Kivra, and by the time he had waterdoused, the short, dark Soaman night had begun. He turned off the lights in his room and looked out the window. There was only one obvious guard, lounging against a tall, spreading tree with a wide trunk. There might be others whom he couldn't see, but there was no time to worry about that possibility. He did not have long. Per-Lem's absence had caught them by surprise, but by now the guards would be in contact with Amril Gdrena, asking for instructions. He was not going to allow her to take the initiative.

He opened the door, slipped quietly outside and began to amble toward the guard. As he approached, he observed that the guard was more or less his own height and build. Good. That would make things easier.

A few moments later, he was close enough to make out that the guard was a young woman, hair cropped short in regulation manner, her uniform carrying a sergeant's blaze. Val-Dor continued walking. Three more paces. Two. One. And he was level with her.

His left hand balled into a fist and smashed into her pliant stomach. She doubled up silently, caught unawares. His right hand chopped down on the top of her spine. With barely a break in his stride, he pivoted sharply, took the weight of her fall, and ducked with his burden behind the cover of the tree against which she had been leaning.

Barely ten chrons later, a man wearing a P&S uniform displaying the insignia of a sergeant strolled into the hovercarport of the Marsûk tourist center. The sergeant walked past the hovercar that Val-Dor had rented the previous day, exchanging salutes with two men who were examining the vehicle, but otherwise ignoring them.

In the corner of the park was a cluster of half a dozen hovercars guarded by a pair of young privates. Neither of them seemed likely to give him much trouble. Their faces were youthfully handsome, cocky, inexperienced: nothing to worry about.

He exchanged salutes with them, then halted in front of one of the vehicles.

"Is it OK for me to take one, or do I need special authorization?" he asked uncertainly. "The minister wants me to collect one of the scientists from up north and bring him in for questioning."

"I'm not sure, sir, I...," one of the privates began, but he was interrupted by the sound of a communications link.

The same voice came from all their personal communications devices: "All personnel, all personnel. This is Captain Voorg speaking. The subjects are to be apprehended on sight. It has just been reported...." There was more, but neither of the guards was in any condition to take any further interest in the pronouncements of Captain Voorg. One was laid out on the ground, groggily trying to get to his feet. The other was occupied by the pain emanating from his expertly-broken nose.

As the guard on the ground tried to rise, Val-Dor's foot swung forward with so much force that even though its path was impeded briefly by the man's head, he nearly fell over.

"Groo...," mumbled the second guard incoherently as he held his nose against his face. Val-Dor grabbed him firmly by his cropped hair and pulled his head sharply back. The guard would have screamed, except that a gloved fist entered his mouth at that moment, carelessly removing five teeth.

Val-Dor drew his hand back and punched the man's neck. Then he pulled the man's head down at the same time that he jerked his knee upward, crashing into the guard's face.

There had been no sound audible ten paces away, and the whole thing had occupied barely two hundred millichrons. Val-Dor let go the bloody mass that had been a handsome young face only moments before. The guard's body fell inert to the ground.

The voice of Captain Voorg continued speaking as Val-Dor clambered into a hovercar. He switched on the jammer in his pocket, and lifted off.

And now Val-Dor made a crucial mistake. If he had headed directly for the place where Per-Lem had just woken and was trying to come to terms with a world in which nothing made sense, he would have reached her before she destroyed the force field and ran out on to the plain chasing after Amril Gdrena's spaceship. But he did not.

Instead, he reasoned that it made more sense to ensure that the spaceship that had long ago been hidden to provide an escape back to Dalith was still viable. If the spacecraft was still operational, then all he would lose would be a little time. But if it was not, he would have to steal a ship from the spaceport before collecting Per-Lem and taking her back to Dalith.

Val-Dor's hovercar raced northward for the better part of fifty chrons as he travelled almost halfway around the small planet. The Skyward Mountains, Soam's only significant mountain range, had just appeared on the horizon when he received the first intimation that he was being followed.

On the scanner appeared a cluster of three hovercars, on a course that would intersect his path within a few chrons. He swore. But he knew that he should have expected that somewhere on this planet was a ship with the capability to penetrate the primitive wideband jammer in his pocket. Possibly one of the approaching hovercars possessed the capability. More likely they were being guided by commands from a spaceship in orbit. It didn't matter. However it was being accomplished, it was going to be a close thing. He tried to estimate times and distances, but it was impossible to be sure if he was going to make it. He opened the throttle to maximum.

The mountains came closer; so did the other hovercars. Slowly he began to lose altitude.

There on the scanner was the jagged peak he remembered from long ago, coming quickly closer now. From his pocket he removed a thin, pliable card.

The card was small enough to fit snugly in the palm of one hand. It was white and carried no design except, in the center of each face, a small box whose edges were marked by thin lines. He placed the thumb of his right hand inside the box on one side of the card, and squeezed. Almost instantly, he was gratified to see one corner of the card turn green. The tunnel into the cave was open. Now he just had to reach it without being caught.

The mountain range drew closer. So did the triangle of hovercars. Then he abruptly fired the reverse thrusters; in moments he was barely moving. He switched off the wideband jammer. He waited, watching the display screen, looking to see how quickly they would react. They were slow. It was almost a decichron before they changed course, making directly toward him now instead of intercepting his old course. He waited, ignoring the part of his brain that urged him to try to outrun them.

He looked out the window. The navigation lights from the hovercars were clearly visible now, clustered together in a multicolored matrix that grew as he watched. He followed the locus of the lights with his eyes, waiting for the moment when the hovercars would change course or slow down to avoid a crash. He held his breath.

It happened. One of the pilots must have realized that Val-Dor was not going to make a run for it. With a visible flare of thrusters, the hovercars broke formation, simultaneously wheeling and slowing. Val-Dor watched, awaiting his moment as they raced past not far away, turning and losing speed. And then Val-Dor opened his throttle wide and pulled back on the altitude lever.

Val-Dor's hovercar shot forward, climbing rapidly. He doused the navigation lights. The hovercar raced up the slope of a ridge and, the moment he was safely on the other side, plunged downward. The bulk of the mountain range hid the other cars from his scanner, but he could predict what they were doing. They were accelerating and turning, trying to follow his sudden maneuver. He kept his throttle wide open.

There they were: one..., two, three, shooting over the top of the ridge. He would be on their screens now. They began to spread out, so that one remained directly in his wake and the other two spread out to east and west as he flew north.

He slowed slightly, and began to climb again. Their throttles were wide open, and they edged closer.

Once more he waited. Very soon, the one directly behind was forced to slow down so as not to overtake him. The other two pulled level with him, one on each side. Gradually, he opened the throttle until it was wide open. The others accelerated, matching his speed until all four hovercars were hurtling northward at full speed.

Val-Dor counted slowly to three, then cut power to the main thruster. Instantly, his hovercar began to fall in a flat parabola. As Val-Dor's hovercar fell away from the others, he fired the maneuver thrusters and spun the craft through 180 degrees, then applied full forward thrust. He was pushed back heavily into his seat as the hovercar jumped forward. His finger slid over the switch on the jammer and turned it on. Every moment of confusion would help.

He climbed quickly, shot over the ridge and instantly disappeared down the far side of the mountains. He turned, flying parallel to the mountains. This time he did not even glance at the monitor. He was too busy looking for the tunnel.

At almost the last possible moment he saw the hole in the side of the mountain. He shot into the tunnel. The instant he was inside, he pressed his thumb against the white card. Behind him, a slab of rock slid smoothly into place, sealing the tunnel. The mass of the mountain now hid him from any detectors. As he fired the reverse thrusters the tunnel opened out before him to reveal a cavernous area flooded with light, in the center of which stood a small spaceship.

He landed beside the ship and killed power.

Outside, he had left a trail of confusion and consternation. Captain Voorg, orbiting high overhead, screamed his frustration as the blip that represented the spy's hovercar on his monitor dimmed and went out.

Voorg smashed his hand against the screen.

"You!" he shouted at the unfortunate woman operating the detector, "What happened? Where is he?"

The operator was desperately entering commands into the discriminator circuits, but with a sinking feeling in the pit of her stomach she knew that the spy had somehow outsmarted them all.

"I don't know, sir," she admitted. "I've lost him. He must be carrying some kind of device I can't cut through."

She knew that with that admission her promising career had just come to an abrupt end.

The pilot of one of the hovercars came on the commlink channel, "We lost him again. Where is he?"

Voorg swore, but his heart was not in it. He was already imagining what would happen to him when Amril Gdrena discovered that he had allowed a Union spy to escape.

25

LYSTRA

The room was surprisingly large. It had the clinical aspect of a hospital, although Lystra knew that she had not left the building that contained her cell. Near the center of the far wall was a boxy device, large enough to hold a human and unnervingly reminiscent of the coffins that were used on some of the more superstitious Outer Planets. A scurry of activity seemed to be centered around the box. There were half a dozen technicians clustered around it, running checks. A large panel hugged one wall, and two more technicians hovered nervously near the panel, pressing buttons and consulting indicators. Behind them and watching their every movement stood a stout man with his back to Lystra.

Lystra was feeling better than she had done at any time since the nightmare had begun back on Soam. She had been given plenty to eat and to drink, and not fifteen chrons ago she had woken from a long nap. As soon as she was awake, her guards had brought her to this place, and now they were standing a couple of paces behind her as she inspected the room.

The room was windowless and lit with a cold, even light emanating from the ceiling. There were several holoimage screens arranged on the walls. The screens were blank, but indicator lights showed that they were switched on, awaiting input.

Amril Gdrena and Brynt Veel stood near one of the screens, watching the bustle of activity. Their attention was diverted by Lystra's arrival. The minister greeted her prisoner with surprising politeness.

"You are feeling well, I hope?"

"Yes, much better. Please, what is this place?"

"Oh, you need not concern yourself with that. Don't worry; you will be quite safe, isn't that so, Gherran?"

The stout man turned to face them. He was in late middle age, balding, stout almost to the point of obesity, and remarkably dishevelled. He grinned widely when he saw Lystra.

"Oh, yes, madam minister. She'll be quite safe in my care. No need to worry about that."

He laughed in a manner that suggested that in Gherran's hands Lystra was anything but safe. She took a step backward.

"Is everything ready?" Amril Gdrena asked Gherran.

"Yes, yes, madam minister. Just some final checks. But everything is working. We are ready whenever you say the word."

"Then we shall begin."

The minister gestured toward the coffin-like box. As the guards ushered Lystra towards the box, the technicians moved discreetly away. There was an expression on their faces that Lystra could not quite place: not pity exactly, nor fear; something close to both, yet not quite either. With a rising sense of unease, she wondered what the box was for.

It stood vertically, a little forward of the wall. Its insides were cushioned, and there were several probes on the inner walls. The guards settled her against the cushioned interior, which quickly conformed to her contours and held her firmly in position. The box rotated slightly about a horizontal axle, leaving Lystra leaning backward at an angle. It was surprisingly comfortable. The technicians returned and applied sensing pads to various parts of her head. No pads were put on any other part of her body. For the first time, she began to suspect the purpose of the box.

"What is this machine?" she asked one of the technicians.

The technician ignored her question. He quickly turned away as soon as his work was done. But she had seen the look in his eye.

Lystra was sure of it now. Everything fitted: the holoimage screens; the number and the quiet efficiency of the technicians; the control panel beside which the minister and the repulsive Gherran were standing, conversing in quiet tones while Brynt Veel stood nearby, his eyes not on them but on her.

She was being prepared for an active mindprobe.

Mindprobe technology had been discovered many hundreds of cycles before, long before the War of Secession. Mindprobing was not regarded as a weapon, and its use was not restricted — indeed, it was not even mentioned — by the Treaty of Empire and Union.

The word "mindprobe" as it was commonly used referred to a machine more accurately known as a passive mindprobe, which was used to ensure that people with access to sensitive information did not abuse that privilege.

A passive mindprobe was essentially a benign device, whose worst effect was a temporary disorientation. It acted by guiding the mind along certain pathways, so that the operator could see how a person responded, and the overall effect was not very different from a kind of hypnotically-controlled dream. In its commonest use, the person being probed became receptive to ideas implanted from outside and would willingly describe feelings and memories that otherwise might be suppressed either consciously or unconsciously. Under the influence of a mindprobe, it was believed to be impossible to hide the truth.

Passive mindprobes were essentially harmless. It was not possible to damage or permanently affect a person with a passive mindprobe. It had been demonstrated many times that if a subject's mind was violated too much, the subject's subconscious simply refused to cooperate: the "dreams" ceased and the mindprobe was rendered ineffective.

But there was a second kind of mindprobe, one whose use was technically illegal, although it was widely believed that the government routinely used it on hardened criminals. This was the active mindprobe.

If a passive mindprobe was gentle examination — looking but not touching — an active mindprobe was lifting the brain's covers — an opening, poking and, one hoped, a careful closing again afterwards. In an active mindprobe, it was not simply a matter of asking questions and recording the dreamlike responses. Instead, the memory of the patient lay open for inspection, exploration and even modification. Memories could be extracted and, in the hands of a sufficiently skilled practitioner, altered. Or completely new memories could be implanted. Even the emotional character of a person could be changed, hence its usefulness in treating criminals.

Although Lystra was scared at the prospect of an active mindprobe — who wouldn't be? — she tried to convince herself that at least this would settle everything: the probe would confirm what she had been telling the minister all along: Lystra Ten-Wer was a model citizen of the Empire. But even so, the thought of someone wandering around inside her head was terrifying. There were rumors of active mindprobes that had gone wrong, probes from which criminals had emerged as mindless creatures, incapable of thinking for themselves. Lystra began to tremble at the thought of what might be about to happen to her.

Amril Gdrena concluded her conversation with the man Gherran, who bowed obsequiously and moved across to the control panel. The minister stood in front of Lystra. The expression on her face was colder than ever.

"You know what this is?"

"I think so. It's an active mindprobe, isn't it? Do you have to do this? I've heard stories...."

"Don't worry. Gherran has never lost a patient. For all his repulsive looks and mannerisms, he is the finest probe controller ever to serve the Empire. You will be safe. But nothing you have ever experienced will be hidden from me. I shall go inside your mind and take it apart piece by piece until I find what I am looking for."

Lystra did her best to return the minister's stare, but could not. Her eyes dropped to the floor as she said, "You won't find anything I haven't already told you, madam minister. I've been telling the truth."

"Pah! I shall talk to you again when this is all over."

Amril Gdrena turned and signalled Gherran. Gherran spoke to a technician, who pressed something on the control panel. The last clear memory Lystra had was of Brynt Veel, standing next to the control panel but looking across the room toward her, an expression of open curiosity on his face.

She opened her mouth to say something... and lost consciousness.

One moment Lystra was awake, looking across the room at Brynt Veel, thinking that the look of curiosity on his face was downright morbid; the next thing she knew she was groggily waking from a deep, dreamless sleep. She had the impression, even before she was fully awake, that a very long time had elapsed. Her stomach was tight with hunger and her lips dry with thirst. And somewhere at the back of her mind was something important that she knew she was supposed to remember.

She blinked her eyes and shook her head to clear it. She felt no pain, just a heavy fatigue.

She concentrated, trying to remember what it was that was niggling at the back of her mind. Panic seized her; then, with relief, she grasped the thought. Active mindprobes could alter memories.

Who am I? she thought. The answer came back immediately: *I am Lystra Ghetrol Ten-Wer, citizen number 465-987-098-125, born on the planet Eb.* She flitted through her personal history, looking for anything that did not seem quite right. She had grown up on Eb. She had come to Kivra to attend the university. She currently held a job as an upper-mid-level bureaucrat in the Ministry of Peace and Security. She remembered the strange events that had brought her to this room: the decision to get away from Kivra for a couple of rotations; meeting up with Teberill Gandeer; the rotation they had spent together; the horror that had followed. Everything was clear and consistent. Nothing seemed to be or fuzzy or lost.

But wouldn't they be clever enough to make sure that the memories were self-consistent? Wouldn't she remember it all that way even if the memories were all implanted? Perhaps she *wasn't* Lystra Ten-Wer. Perhaps she was someone else entirely. She wanted to scream.

But that way lay madness. She tried to control herself. *Take things slowly. Look for inconsistencies, but don't assume that just because you've been under an active mindprobe you aren't what you remember yourself to be. Assume that your memories are accurate. Only doubt them if they seem inconsistent.* It was the only way to stay sane.

She slowly realized that people were moving around her. The box in which she was encased had pivoted back to the vertical. A very tired-looking male technician was removing the pads from her head. Lystra looked for the minister and Brynt Veel. She could see neither of them. The man Gherran glanced at her from his post near the control panel. On his face was a smile of satisfaction. A momentary panic filled Lystra. Was he smiling because he had implanted memories that weren't really hers?

The technician finished removing the last pad and he stood back to look at Lystra.

"How did I do?" Lystra heard herself asking. Her voice was broken and raspy.

"Try not to talk," he admonished. "They tell me you did fine. Try to eat something. You won't feel much like it, but it'll do you good."

He held out an arm; Lystra leant on it and walked unsteadily out of the coffin-shaped box.

The man guided her to a table in a corner. Lystra sat down and a woman placed a tray of food and drink in front of her.

Despite her hunger, the thought of eating made Lystra to want to vomit. She swallowed drily several times, then lifted the container of liquid. It tasted like plain water, although her throat was so raw that it was hard to be sure.

"Well done," the woman encouraged her. "Now, just a bite or two to eat. It'll help you recover."

Lystra toyed with her food for a couple of chrons while the room slowly began to empty around her. The technicians, no longer needed, were leaving. Eventually she managed to eat a couple of mouthfuls of food.

Lystra realized that a pair of guards had entered the room while she had been eating. One of them stepped forward and asked quietly, "Are you all right?"

Lystra recognized the guard who, a lifetime ago, had warned her not to touch the deterrent field. She nodded her head uncertainly.

"Yes, I think so."

"Then if you would come with us."

The guard held out his arm. Lystra tried to take a couple of defiant steps without support, but she was weaker than she had thought, and nearly fell.

"You'll get your strength back soon," the guard encouraged her.

The other guard was watching carefully, his face grim and his unholstered stun-gun pointing relentlessly at Lystra.

For Kivra's sake, she thought, *What does he expect me to do? Jump them and make a run for it?*

But she said nothing. She was suddenly too tired. All she wanted was to collapse on a bed and go to sleep.

She left the room, supported by one guard, watched suspiciously by the other. They walked down a corridor, went up in an elevator, then passed along a series of hallways. It was slow progress, and Lystra was astonished at how weak she felt. Her muscles did not hurt, they simply did not want to function. More than once she nearly fell in spite of the guard's support.

For some reason, she never thought to ask where they were going. She simply assumed that their destination would be a room with a comfortable bed where she could collapse and fall into a deep sleep. She was shaken out of her mindless reverie only when they halted outside a doorway that she recognized.

"What are we doing here?" she asked groggily.

"I'm sorry...," said the guard who had been supporting her.

Gently he eased her from his arm and pushed her forward through the empty doorway back into her cell. The deterrent field came on.

There was a tray of food and drink on the floor in the center of the room, and over in one corner there was now a mattress. But otherwise the cell was no different from when she had left it.

She turned slowly to look at the guards. Their expressions were unreadable.

"What is this?"

They knew the truth now. They knew she was no spy. So why had they brought her back to her cell? Why weren't they releasing her?

The guards did not reply.

"Why did you bring me back here? You know I'm innocent." Her voice was rising angrily.

"What did I say? What did I say? What did I say?" She was screaming.

The grim-faced guard who had covered her with his stun-gun shook his head slightly; but it was the look on the other one's face that haunted Lystra's dreams when finally she collapsed and fell asleep.

It was a look of pity.

26
Amril Gdrena

The room was dark; not a sliver of light showed anywhere.

Amril Gdrena was seated in a comfortable chair near the center of one wall. The other three points of an imaginary square were marked by chairs near the other walls, invisible in the darkness. In the chair to Gdrena's left sat Gherran, the psychoanalyst who had performed so brilliantly during the prisoner's marathon session under the active probe. To her right sat Missen Hai, the middle-aged, highly ambitious man who was the deputy minister for Peace and Security and who one day soon would have to be removed. In the chair opposite her sat Brynt Veel.

Each of them wore on his head a complicated apparatus that was connected to the chair in which he sat. The room was cool, almost chill. The only sounds were the muted sounds of breathing.

The minister waited, gathering her thoughts, trying to prepare for what was about to happen. In a few moments she would give the order, and then the playback would begin. And each of them would become Lystra Ten-Wer.

The minister watched coldly as Lystra glanced toward Brynt Veel and then opened her mouth to say something. Whatever she had wanted to say remained unspoken, for at that moment the probe began, and its first act was to put Lystra Ten-Wer to sleep.

Images began to appear on the holoimage screens on the walls. At first there was only a confused jumble of pictures and sounds. Everyone in the room, except the psychoanalyst Gherran, fell silent as they looked at the screens, trying to be the first to spot the gelling of a coherent picture. At the control panel, two technicians followed instructions from Gherran, whose eyes were fixed on the closest holoimage screen. In response to his orders, the technicians turned controls and pressed buttons, and after a short while, the first recognizable image began to appear on the screen. It was a pair of hands, bound by a vine.

Without taking his eyes from the screen Gherran said to the minister, "You understand that the projectors will show us only the superficialities. They will allow us to see and hear the images and sounds that have left the deepest impressions on the subject, but the recorders are recording the entire experience in its full depth. Later, I shall play back the recordings and experience fully what the subject herself is now experiencing. But for now, I rely on the superficialities to guide me through her experiential web."

"I understand," said the minister.

So began the longest active mindprobe ever undertaken by the Empire. When it was over, Amril Gdrena was shaken to the core, the man Gherran was drained and sweating odiferously, and Lystra Ten-Wer — although Gherran had meticulously replaced the memories exactly as he found them, and therefore she was unaware of the fact — had been exposed for who she really was.

The interrogation had lasted for several hundred chrons, far longer than expected, because it had been much more difficult than anyone had expected to break through to the truth.

In one sense, Lystra was exactly what she had always maintained and what the passive mindprobes had confirmed. The passive mindprobes had not lied, they had merely been subverted. The probes had reflected accurately what the patient remembered. Lystra remembered being a student; she remembered her youth on Eb; she remembered friends, infatuations, lovers, trips with the family who had brought her up, and she remembered them all just like anyone else, sometimes with startling clarity and sometimes barely at all; and sometimes with a vivid precision that turned out, on inspection, to be wholly inaccurate.

For a long while, Gherran smoothly directed the probe, prodding here and there, finding nothing unusual or suspicious as they ransacked her memories.

After about eighty chrons, Gherran turned to the minister, who had not moved from his side, and remarked, "I don't know what you were expecting to find, madam minister, but there's nothing out of the ordinary here. Certainly no evidence that the subject is a Union agent. Everything here matches the results of the passive probes. She is exactly what she seems. Do you want me to continue?"

The minister looked up at the holoimage screen. It was showing an image from Lystra's childhood on Eb: her adoptive father playing ducks and drakes with flat pebbles on a pond. Lystra's father turned and smiled, the kind of encouraging smile that a parent gives to any young child bent on mastering a skill that is still beyond them.

She turned to Brynt Veel.

"What do you think, Veel? Was I wrong? How could she be a Union spy? The probe cannot lie."

Veel turned away from the screen and regarded the minister. His black eyes looked predatory.

"I suggest," he said quietly, "that perhaps it might be profitable to look more closely at a discrepancy."

"Discrepancy? What discrepancy?"

"Well, it strikes me that we have one solid piece of evidence against the woman. She has been confronted with it, and she denied any knowledge of it. Perhaps it would repay our efforts to look at what actually happened."

It was a moment before the minister understood. "You mean the signals from 35/CW?"

"Exactly. The ministry records indicate that on two separate occasions red reports from 35/CW reached her databox and were not sent to her supervisor. She has admitted to an error on the first occasion, but she insists that on the second she forwarded it. Her suggestion of a databox error is fantasy. We know there was no such error. Therefore she is lying. She deliberately deleted the red report without forwarding it."

The minister turned to the psychoanalyst. "He's right. Gherran. I want to look at a couple of events in detail."

And then came the first troubling indication that indeed something was gravely wrong. The holoimage screens showed Lystra's memories of the events surrounding the red reports. Both times, her memory was clear. The first time she simply forgot about the Standing Order; the second time she forwarded the report to her supervisor, just as she claimed."

"But the records show that that's not what happened," said the minister. "She deleted the second report. Could someone have tampered with the databox records?"

"Perhaps it's her memory that's been tampered with," said Brynt Veel quietly.

"That's not possible. Is it, Gherran? To alter her memory, I mean."

"Ordinarily, I would say no, without hesitation...."

Gherran's brow was furrowed and there was a worried look in his eye. He did not finish his thought. Instead, he said to one of the technicians, "Run through that sequence again, slowly. There's something not quite right. The memory looks OK, but its not in the right place. It's not in sequence."

The technician replayed Lystra's memory of the second report. This time Gherran himself stepped to the control panel and concentrated on a small display showing an apparently random jumble of colors that changed continuously as the memory replayed itself.

"There," he said grimly, freezing the replay.

He turned to the minister.

"You've found something?"

"I have," he nodded, "and it's the nicest piece of work I've ever seen. I would have sworn it was impossible to implant memories so perfectly. It's here, see." He gestured toward the multicolored display. "This shows how the memories are stored in the subject's brain. And this memory, beginning with the moment that she sees the screen of her databox, and ending here a couple of chrons later, is not right. It should form part of an associated sequence, but it doesn't. You see, all the memories surrounding the event are stored over here." He jabbed a finger at a gray area. "But this one, it's way over here. The pointers are stored here, in sequence as they should be, but for this short interval, the pointers have been altered. The original memory is still there in that gray area somewhere, but the pointers have been changed to point at a memory that was fabricated later, over here in this green portion. I wouldn't have believed it possible. This has been done by a genius, a true master."

Amril Gdrena cut him short. "So you're telling me that when this woman says she doesn't remember much about a red report, but that she knows she forwarded it to her supervisor, she's telling the truth, because her memory of the event has been altered?"

"Exactly, madam minister."

"But when? By whom?"

"That I cannot tell you. At least not yet. And perhaps never. If he covered his tracks as well as he changed this memory pointer, we may never find him. We'd have to go through her memories too carefully; it could take several lifetimes."

"All right, all right," she held up a hand to interrupt him.

She fell silent, thinking. Once more it was Brynt Veel who offered a suggestion as to what to do next.

"Something like this could not have happened without her knowledge and permission. It's all in her head somewhere. Large chunks of her memory must have been altered. Surely it shouldn't be too hard to find evidence of such large-scale tampering?"

"That's true," said the psychoanalyst. "I wasn't looking for it before. I never suspected that work like this was possible. I've been looking at what her memories *are*, not how they are stored and accessed."

Gherran turned to a technician. "Replay everything we have down-loaded from when we started, showing me the physical activity maps."

He found what he was looking for no more than five chrons later. And when he did, he whistled in awe.

"The whole thing is a fabrication." Disbelief — and admiration — was audible in his voice.

"The whole thing?" the minister echoed.

"Yes. Her past. It's not real. At least, it's not hers. Let me work at this for a while, and I'll see if I can reconstruct some of the original mapping. I probably won't get the sequence right, but we should be able to extract at least some of her real past if we're careful enough."

Over the course of the next two hundred chrons, Gherran worked as he had never worked before, restoring the memory pointers that had so carefully been changed many cycles earlier.

So the truth came out. And it was worse than Amril Gdrena had ever imagined.

––––––––––––

Now they were going to replay the memories in sequence, not just on holoimage screens, but inside their own heads. It had been Gherran's idea. He had insisted that it was the only way to gain a true appreciation for what was inside Lystra's brain. The minister privately thought that what he really meant was that it was the only way to gain a true appreciation for Gherran's skill. But for once she was feeling magnanimous. No one else could have done the job half so well as he. He had even returned all the memory pointers to their original values, so that Lystra herself retained no memory of the truth. More sessions under the probe would follow, but he had made an excellent beginning.

Amril Gdrena took a deep breath.

"Go," she said into the silence of the void-black room.

"About to begin. Memories rolling," a voice said out of the darkness.

The minister tried to relax, but almost immediately she broke into a sweat as a curious schizophrenia sundered her mind.

Part of her was still Amril Gdrena, imperial minister of Peace and Security, seated in the probe playback room with three others who were sharing her experience. But part of her was someone else entirely.

The darkness did not really change. The only discernible difference was a sort of mistiness, a haziness that was not so much seen as felt, as if her mind was filled with wool. Then things began to focus, and both the darkness and the silence were banished.

She was back in the mindprobe room, her eyes closed, with a vague woolliness to her thoughts as if she were lightly drugged. Around her she could hear the sounds of the technicians moving, talking quietly as they checked the progress of the probe into her skull. Into her skull! The thought flashed into her head and for a second she was terrified. She felt a sudden urgent pumping of adrenalin, but it was gone almost before it had started.

The tranquilizers, she thought vaguely. *The machines detected my agitation and tried to restore my chemical balance.* Then, approvingly, *They are doing a good job.*

She began to think back over her life. She wasted little time on recent experiences: the rescue on Soam; the strange rotation spent in the company of Teberill Gandeer, of which she remembered little except a pleasant chat and then falling asleep in the warm Soaman sun. There was a vague, shadowy memory somewhere in there, something not quite right, but it did not seem important, like a dream that was only half remembered. Although she momentarily thought that she really ought to make the effort to remember it properly, she decided that it was not worth the effort after all, and the memory was lost forever.

She recalled the journey to Soam, and before that to Prantys, and before that the forlorn feeling as she looked out the window of her apartment and wistfully watched the heavy ship lift off in the distance.

The pace accelerated. The thoughts flicked backwards, only the occasional memory standing out. And suddenly everything came crashing to a halt.

"You will experience both of the subject's memories of the second report from monitorship 35/CW," a voice said. "First the current memory, then the memory that was replaced."

The minister could not tell where the voice came from, nor whose it was. It was part of the experience, yet not part of it. Before she could puzzle any more over it, the memories began again.

She was in her office, feeling harried as she tried to catch up after the passive mindprobe. She retrieved the day's reports on the databox. At the top was a red line. Her first thought was the painful recollection that on the only other occasion when a red report had been routed to her databox, she had forgotten to forward it to Supervisor Qwilm, leading to the only negative entry in her file. She would not forget this time.

She pressed the line and the report expanded. The report was from a monitorship identified as 35/CW, which was, she thought, the same monitorship that had produced the earlier red report.

She looked at the report itself. It comprised five apparently meaningless numbers:

$$3546285{\cdot}12, \; 5{\cdot}2, \; 7{\cdot}159$$
$$19764{\cdot}3217 \; 361{\cdot}47$$

She wondered briefly what the numbers meant. But it did not matter. Her job was simply to bring the report to Supervisor Qwilm's attention. She forwarded it to him. The red report was his problem now.

Putting the incident behind her, she continued with her work.

Then there was a sudden strange, intense, unsettling feeling of having her mind violated, and she was once more slipping into her chair at the office and looking at the databox screen, just as she had done moments before. In red at the top of the screen was the line indicating that a report had arrived overnight from monitorship 35/CW. She felt a vague sense of excitement mixed with trepidation. She touched the red line and instantly the report appeared in full. It was brief, but she looked at it carefully. The numbers were meaningless, but she knew that someone back on Dalith would know how to decode them. The thought flashed through her mind: *I've got to get these back quickly. The last time a red report came from 35/CW was after Rum-Lem disappeared. Perhaps this report is somehow connected to his disappearance.* Associated with Rum-Lem's name were feelings of attachment that had their roots far in the past. She deleted the report without forwarding it, and continued with her work.

"We will now continue with the subject's earlier memories," a disembodied voice announced.

Lystra's memory continued going further and further back, ever more quickly: to her mindprobes, her promotion, then beyond, passing quickly now through the cycles: changes of rank and of apartment; her studies at Kivra Imperial University; experimentation with partners. There was a sudden aching emotional emptiness, and before that its cause: the crash that had killed her adoptive parents and from which she had barely escaped with her own life. There were pleasant memories of her youth and childhood, including one of her father trying to teach her ducks and drakes; and then there was a gradually fading into nothingness.

For a while there was nothing more. Then the voice that had spoken before intruded into the silent darkness.

"It was done so well that even though I know where the break occurs, I still can't detect it experientially. It was shortly after the time of the crash. Her memory of surviving the crash that killed her parents is real. But Lystra, the real Lystra Ten-Wer, was spirited across the demilitarized zone to the Union, and there her memories were extracted and placed inside the subject. Now we shall experience some of the subject's true memories of the time prior to the crash."

For a while, the dark and silent void continued to fill her mind. She began to speculate: *who exactly am I? Am I Amril Gdrena? or am I Lystra Ten-Wer? or am I Per-Lem, the Union spy?* She could find no answer, and slowly she began to become aware of a strange tickling somewhere inside her mind, as if something was trying to escape. Then there was something else, something reaching in, trying to touch whatever it was that was trying to get out.

The two... what were they? forces? objects? ideas? concepts? Whatever they were, they seemed to close and then move apart several times, never quite touching, never quite coming close enough to release whatever was struggling to escape. Then, in a single epiphanic moment, they touched, her mind was opened, and a new universe was revealed.

For some indeterminate period there was confusion as new images flooded her mind. A scream came from somewhere, maybe even from her own throat, as her brain rejected what was being revealed. But the images persisted, and along with the images there were sounds, aromas, palpations. They could not be denied; and, slowly, she began to realize that *this* was who she truly was.

It had been agreed as far back as she could remember. Her mother had drummed the message into her and her twin brother over and over and over, until it was accepted unquestioningly as truth: her life had but one goal, one achievement that would bring it meaning: Per-Lem — and *that* was her name, not Lystra Ten-Wer — Per-Lem and her brother Rum-Lem were to bring down the Empire once and for all.

She remembered the rotation when she had seen her mother for the last time, the rotation when she and Rum-Lem walked into the office of a man named Tcharn, who had recently been promoted chief of the Bureau of Defense. The memories of what followed flashed past, leaving only superficial impressions: the twins were separated, each entering a separate training regime. She entered a long nightmare of confused disorientation. An image kept recurring: an image of a room in which technicians looked at her with concern in their eyes. There was a machine under which she was forced to lie, a machine that somehow attacked her very mind. There were long periods of darkness, about which she could remember nothing, no matter how desperately she tried. The next clear memory was as a nineteen year old, arriving at Kivra Imperial University. But by now she was Per-Lem no more — she was Lystra Ten-Wer.

Suddenly it all dissolved. She felt a terrifying disorientation as the images and emotions were swept away and their place was taken by complete darkness.

A light came on somewhere and only with great effort did Amril Gdrena remember that this had all been no more real than a dream; these were images not from her own life, but from the life of the woman who was safely confined in a nearby cell. The relief that swept over her was more intense than any feeling she had ever known.

The light spread, and slowly her eyes focused on the scene around her. She was in a room. A door was opening and a technician was hurrying towards her. There were three others seated nearby. Two of them looked as confused as she felt. The third, an obese man in late middle age, seemed more relaxed. After a moment's desperate concentration, she remembered their names.

She lifted her hands and began to remove the mindprobe playback helmet from her head. A technician helped her and the helmet swung clear. Gdrena shook her head, blinking hard. It had all been far more real than she had anticipated, and she was finding it difficult to believe that her own mind had not been violated, that she was not somehow one with, and as guilty as, Per-Lem, whose history she now knew in the most intimate way imaginable.

It was some time before they all recovered sufficiently to discuss the shared experience. Deputy Minister Missen Hai had shown indications of incipient psychoshock, a condition that could produce permanent damage, and he had been given a tranquilizer whose effects were only now beginning to wear off. Gdrena, Veel and Gherran were provided soothing drinks, and slowly and more naturally their world returned to normal.

Now it was evening. They were seated in Amril Gdrena's office, a holograph recorder in the ceiling recording the discussion. Gdrena turned to the psychoanalyst.

"Gherran, I'll let you begin. What do you have to say about what we experienced this afternoon?"

"Well, the first thing is to congratulate you all. Even though I have experienced mindprobe playbacks before, this one was both disturbing and intense, and it is not everyone who could come through such an experience unscathed. As you discovered, the emotions and experiences associated with an active mindprobe are enormously powerful. One's whole being is subsumed in the imposed memory, so that one can no longer differentiate between oneself and the memoretic experience. In fact, I would go so far as to say that the individual in a very real sense ceases to exist for the duration of a mindprobe playback. I will take this opportunity, if you will permit me, madam minister, to inform you that you can expect to receive in the near future a request for substantially increased funding for mindprobe research. It is obvious that the Union has made this a priority and is far ahead of us in this field. We have a lot of catching up to do."

"Any request that appears reasonable in light of our shared experience this afternoon will be granted without delay."

Gherran nodded. "Thank you, madam minister. Now, let's consider what we've learned. It's obvious that the Union has capabilities in this area that we had never dreamt of. Apparently, they have succeeded in taking a subject — admittedly a well-prepared subject who for sixteen cycles was fed a continuous stream of anti-imperial propaganda — but they have taken a subject and changed her memories to an extent I would not have thought possible, so that the subject is now a functioning, intelligent member of imperial society capable of passing scrutiny by passive mindprobe. The change is so deep that the subject herself has no conscious memory of who she once was. The reason she protested her innocence so violently, the reason she has been so trusting of imperial justice, is that she truly believes she has nothing to fear. She thinks that the Empire can do no wrong and she believes that she is exactly who she says she is: Lystra Ten-Wer, a bright, motivated and successful bureaucrat in the Ministry of Peace and Security."

Gdrena said, "So my understanding of the situation is that she has no idea that she is really Per-Lem, and a Union agent?"

Gherran nodded. "That is precisely true, madam Minister."

The deputy minister intervened. "But if her past life is inaccessible, then what possible use can she be to the Union? Haven't they simply provided us with a useful member of imperial society?"

"Yes, that question bothered me too for a while," agreed Gherran. "But there were some memories I noticed this afternoon, a couple of events that I think might give us a clue to the answer. To be certain, I'll have to replay the memories a few times. I'll try to do that tomorrow. But I'm reasonably sure that the playbacks will bear me out. What do you remember of the afternoon on Soam, the one she spent with the man calling himself Teberill Gandeer?"

The others considered, trying to separate that memory from the others with which their minds had so recently been flooded.

"She slept, that's all. But there was some sort of dream, wasn't there?" Missen Hai said.

"That's what I thought at first, but I went over it several times when it was still fresh in my mind, because I was sure that it somehow held a clue.

"You're quite right, deputy minister: she was asleep, or at least she thought she was asleep, but the vestiges of what really happened are still there, remembered as a dream. What I think we will find actually happened, once we have gone through the mindprobe recordings more thoroughly, is that there was a discussion between the gardener and Per-Lem; something about a timeshift pulse, I think. I didn't understand it all. If I can't recover it from today's records, I'll have to perform another probe to reconstruct the lost links to the memories of that afternoon."

"Perhaps, but you're not cleared for information about timeshift devices," said Amril Gdrena.

The psychoanalyst sighed.

"Madam minister, you have to realize that starting tomorrow I will spend my time picking that woman's brain apart: looking for details, trying to form a coherent story from the memories stored inside her head. It will take a long time — a very long time — and many sessions with the probe before we get everything. We made a good beginning today, but that's all it was: a beginning. I am afraid you will have to get used to the idea that whatever she knows, and a lot more besides, I too will eventually know. If her work brought her in contact with secret material, I will know at least some of it by tomorrow evening. There's nothing I can do about that if you want me to do my job."

The minister nodded unenthusiastically. "I suppose I have no choice. Well, I think we've done enough for one rotation. Contact me when you have something, Gherran. I want to know everything there is to know about Per-Lem and her mission."

She looked around the room. No one had anything to add, and she dismissed the group for the night.

But for a long time she remained at her desk, thinking. Something didn't make sense. Per-Lem clearly remembered the first visit to Tcharn's office with her brother, Rum-Lem. It was odd enough that Tcharn had agreed to meet them, but what was even stranger was the way he had accepted their proposal to undertake their mission to undermine the Union. It was almost as if he had been expecting it.... But there was no memory of prior contact between Tcharn and Per-Lem. It was the first trip she had taken to Dalith from Qintir....

Qintir; something about that name snagged in the minister's memory. She consulted the databox, looking for a connection between Tcharn and the planet that was Per-Lem's home. She found it almost immediately. She performed a quick calculation: the dates fit. So *that* was the missing piece of the puzzle. She smiled, then laughed.

She had captured Tcharn's daughter.

27

HWANG

It was hard to believe that this was the planet on which all human life had originated. The Mother Planet was nothing like the hot, steamy combination of swamp, jungle and vicious thunderstorms that the scientists back on Earth had for so long insisted were necessary to the formation of the precursors to conscious life.

More than nine tenths of the land surface of Kivra was desert, and the narrow strips along the coasts where the green of vegetation could be seen were covered by thin layers of wispy clouds. Only in two places was extensive cloud cover visible.

Rum-Lem pointed to one of them and commented, "It's the rainy season. Under those clouds is where Kivra City exists in normal time. It's the largest city in the galaxy."

"Is this really where human life began?" Hwang asked, still not quite able to grasp the fact. "It looks so barren. Does it look the same in normal time?"

Rum-Lem laughed. "It would, yes, if it weren't for all the people. Well over ten billion people live on Kivra now. A billion of those live in Kivra City. Almost all the land is used for living and working. The place we are heading for, Tel Dahn, is one of the few places that is relatively untouched. It's been an imperial research facility for hundreds of cycles, with a wide buffer of desert between it and the nearest city.

"You are right, though: Kivra does seem a forbidding place once one strips it of its human trappings. But there it is: the birthplace of humanity."

Hwang nodded absently, still trying to take it in. They flew high over a coastline and headed inland, descending at a steep angle. Their course took them over the patch of cloud that Rum-Lem had identified as the location of Kivra City, but there was nothing to see: just a mass of gray cloud surrounded by a wide circle of low hills.

They touched down about five minutes later. The place where they landed reminded Hwang of the unpopulated portions of Mars. The ground was a mottled thirsty red desert, strewn with ocher boulders. The sky was an unsettling cloudless pinkish red.

Hwang gestured toward the sky and Rum-Lem said absently, "High level sandstorms. They're very common. The sky of most planets is more or less this color. Dalith, the most important planet in the Union, is one of the few populated planets with a blue sky like yours. Most citizens of the Empire say that the thought of a blue sky gives them the creeps. Personally, I don't really care either way. Now, are you ready to go outside?"

"Will I be able to breathe?"

"Certainly. The composition of the atmosphere is somewhat different from Earth's, but the physiological tests run by the healing machine indicated that you should have no difficulty breathing on any of the planets normally regarded as habitable. You might find it uncomfortably warm and dry, but not dangerously so. If you start to feel unwell, we'll come back inside and get you something to drink."

Rum-Lem lowered the ramp and preceded Hwang out on to the surface.

As Hwang followed him on to the Kivran desert, he could not escape a burdensome feeling that he really ought to say something intelligent. Neil Armstrong's famous phrase, "One small step for man; a giant leap for mankind," even if trite, was memorized by every child in elementary school, as was, "In peace we arrive, and take another step toward our destiny," the first words radioed back from the surface of Mars. But billions of people had been watching and listening on both those occasions. There was no one else here but Rum-Lem, and the import of the moment was obviously lost on the alien.

In the end, Hwang Lee merely mumbled, "Nice to be here," and stepped off the ramp.

"I'm sorry. What did you say?" asked Rum-Lem, turning to look at him.

"Nothing important. It doesn't matter."

Rum-Lem shrugged with his hand.

"Well, if there's anything around here, it's certainly well hidden."

Rum-Lem lifted a small hand-held instrument, a kind of hand-held metal detector. On board the ship the alien had already run a battery of tests designed to look for evidence of life, without success. Now he was reduced to looking for signs that there was metal nearby, perhaps buried under the surface of the desert.

"We'll try over there," he said, pointing to a clump of rocks. But the tone of his voice made it clear that he was not hopeful. He headed for the rocks.

Hwang did not immediately follow. He felt like he had walked into an enormous oven and was being baked on all sides. He squinted in the glare from the burning orange-red sun. Already a layer of sweat covered his body, and he had not yet taken five paces. Half an hour of this would be plenty.

They remained on the surface for slightly less than that. There were no signs of life, nor any indication that there had ever been any. The Mother Planet was lifeless. They returned to the ship and sat in the dining area, drinking fruit-flavored water.

"But there *has* to be something here," Hwang insisted for the fifth time in as many minutes. "We have the most persuasive evidence imaginable that timeshifting is not dangerous. You arrived safely in forward time even though you were fired on from a fast-moving ship a long way away; and I got here even though my equipment is probably the most primitive timeshift device ever built. If it was a dangerous process, at least one of us wouldn't have survived. So if you're right and this is where the early timeshift experiments took place, then there has to be something here. There *has* to be. Either the metal detector or the electronics scanner should have picked something up."

"I told you: before I found you I scanned every inhabited planet with every scanner on the ship. There's nothing anywhere. I can't explain it either, but it's a fact: the only two people in forward time are the two of us. I'm certain of it."

"What if all the tests were performed underground? Perhaps something awful happens when objects are timeshifted forward into solid matter."

"It probably does, but surely they would have taken that into account? Even if no one really understood what was happening in those early experiments, still they knew that they were moving people through time. They would have tried to make sure that the people didn't materialize inside anything solid."

"I suppose you're right. But then why can't we find any traces of the experiments?"

Rum-Lem shrugged again with his hand. "I don't know. You're the physicist. I was hoping you'd be able to tell me."

Hwang fell silent. His brow furrowed more deeply than ever, as if Rum-Lem's off-hand comment had opened a new and even more puzzling line of thought.

"What did I say?" asked Rum-Lem, but Hwang lifted his hand for silence.

After a while, he said, "Perhaps that's what we've been doing wrong. We haven't tried to understand the physics of timeshifting. Perhaps the reason we can't find any evidence of life is that when the timeshifting experiments were performed here, halfway across the galaxy from Earth and hundreds of years ago, the boundary conditions were somehow different from the ones that applied to us. Perhaps the two of us only ended up in the same forward timestream because we were shifted so closely together in time and space. I'm sorry. I'm not sure I'm making sense. I guess what I'm saying is that perhaps there's a fundamental reason, something to do with the physics of timeshifting, why only the two of us are in this timestream.

"I think we need to stop running around and start using our brains. It's time I looked at your research computer. You can translate and I'll try to understand what timeshifting is all about. I really don't understand any of it yet, and the lack of evidence of the old timeshift experiments here on Kivra doesn't mesh with the theory I was beginning to construct. That's telling us something important, if only we knew how to interpret it.

"You admit yourself that you have never been trained as a physicist, so maybe some of what you've told me about timeshifting isn't quite right. Don't feel bad. Physicists run into that all the time. Most advanced physics is not hard to understand if you've had the proper training, but what people forget is that the basic training may take fifteen or twenty years. Even elementary physics like 4-vector spacetime operational calculus requires several years to master. I just hope that your research computer will have enough information about timeshifting that I'll be able to understand it properly."

Rum-Lem nodded. It seemed like a sensible plan.

So they got down to work, and for two or three days they remained on Kivra while Rum-Lem first explained the basic organizational logic of the research computer, then began the task of trying to translate the entries for such diverse and incomprehensible subjects as *Timeshifting*, *Quantum Bubble Theory*, *Hyperspace*, *Spacetime Manifold Transla-tions*, *Spaceship Propulsion Systems*, *The History of Ten-Dimensional Calculational Tools*, *Twenty-Dimensional Action Principles* and many others.

After a couple of days, though, tempers were beginning to flare. Rum-Lem was increasingly frustrated at his inability to find precise terms in Hwang's language for words of whose meaning he was not ex-actly certain even in Galactic Standard. Hwang was similarly frustrated at Rum-Lem's inability to explain concepts that were fundamental to Kivran physics. By the end of the third morning, following a partic-ularly frustrating attempt to translate the introduction of an article on antigravity fields in which fully a quarter of the words had proved untranslatable, the two of them were almost ready to exchange blows.

Rum-Lem offered a suggestion.

"I am afraid this is going to take much longer and be much more difficult than I had anticipated."

Hwang grunted his agreement.

"Then perhaps instead of working at this all day every day, we should try to take things a little slower. Perhaps we should return to Earth. Maybe it would help you if you were in more familiar surroundings. I told you about the island where I was living; I think it might be sensible for us to go back there and work out a schedule that allows both of us time to be alone and to relax. That way we will be refreshed when we get down to work each day, and perhaps everything will move along more smoothly. Another couple of days like this and one of us is going to say something he regrets, and then things will go downhill from there."

"You're right," admitted Hwang. "I'm sorry. I know this must be difficult for you as well. It's just been so frustrating that I haven't been able to get to grips with most of the concepts. So yes; let's go back to Earth and try to approach this whole thing less urgently. After all, I don't suppose it really matters if it takes a week or a year. The important thing is to find a way back — if one exists."

And so they returned to Earth, and within minutes Hwang recognized how sensible Rum-Lem's idea had been.

Rum-Lem's island lay off the northern coast of Australia. Around it a gentle ocean was kept at bay by a coral reef. Beyond the reef Hwang could see the dark triangular shapes that could only mean that sharks were around, but there seemed to be no way for them to cross the reef and reach the warm, shallow water of the lagoon.

The island was close to the equator, and both sunrise and sunset came with the same rapidity as in Rabundi City; but the climate could hardly have been more different. The temperature remained balmy during daylight hours and was only a few degrees cooler at night. A gentle wind blew almost constantly from west to east. The island was perhaps ten kilometers in circumference, and was covered in vegetation; it had a broad periphery of sharp, pinkish-white coral sand. There were no large animals, although small and medium-sized mammals seemed plentiful. On the horizon to the north and west they could see other, larger islands on which were visible hills and even mountains, but Rum-Lem's island was a simple, large, circular atoll on which coconut trees grew in profusion.

Under other circumstances, Hwang could have been sublimely happy. The island reminded him of Ekbu Tbamti's Tongan retreat. After a couple of days, Hwang discovered that the cloud of depression that had been hanging over him since they failed to find evidence of life on Kivra had almost completely evaporated. Now, Hwang found himself strangely relaxed and almost ambivalent; it was difficult to worry overmuch in such paradisiacal surroundings. One look at the freewheeling birds soaring and diving over the pools of the reef, or the majestic palms swaying softly in the breeze, or even something so simple as running the pink coral sand through his fingers, was enough to put everything in a new perspective.

But still he knew that no matter how perfect this place was, things could not go on for ever. One day something would happen: an accident, or an illness that could not be treated by the healing machine. Besides which, a new thought was beginning to play around the periphery of Hwang's mind. It occurred to him that he was learning enough new physics that, if there was some way to keep the source of his knowledge secret, he ought to be able to convert the contents of Rum-Lem's research computer into several Nobels.

Rum-Lem had his own concerns and a quite different reason for wanting to return to normal time. Despite the fact that more than half a cycle had elapsed since the timeshift weapon had thrust him into forward time, Rum-Lem knew that he still carried information that had to reach the Union. Somehow, no matter how long it took, he had to return or die trying.

So they settled into a rhythm, on the surface relaxed and easygoing, while underneath, unspoken forces urged them onward.

They began each day with a short period of leisure when Rum-Lem would swim in the lagoon and Hwang would saunter along the beach for a kilometer or two. Then they settled down to work, with Hwang asking questions and Rum-Lem trying to coax comprehensible answers from the computer. They would break for lunch, after which Rum-Lem would spend the afternoon relaxing, often going for an extended swim or fishing from the reef. He stayed in sight of the ship, so that Hwang could signal for help. Meanwhile Hwang would lose himself in calculations, trying to make sense of the universe of alien physics that was slowly yielding its secrets.

Hwang quickly discovered that the research computer was less helpful than he had hoped, for the entry under *Timeshifting* contained little more than a potted history of the development of timeshift weapons. So he was reduced to researching around the subject as he tried to understand the mechanics behind the phenomenon. Although he progressed slowly and the work was the most difficult he had ever undertaken, it was also the most satisfying. Gradually he began to form an understanding of the web of physics that undergirded the intertwined subjects of timeshifting, gravity cancellation, hyperspace and translations across spacetime manifolds.

Nearly a month after they had arrived on the island, and after an uneasy night of dreams in which mathematical symbols were imbued with a life of their own, dancing to the sounds of popular tunes from another age, Hwang was taking his usual early morning stroll along the beach, thinking about the problems he would tackle that day, when he stopped in mid-stride with his eyes wide open and his jaw suddenly slack.

He jogged back to the ship, and when Rum-Lem arrived from his swim Hwang was already hard at work.

He said to the alien without lifting his head from his work, "Go away. Don't bother me now. I'll tell you later what it's all about if anything comes of it."

Rum-Lem left him to his calculations.

When Rum-Lem returned to the ship for lunch, Hwang was still hard at work, but this time he paused long enough to say, "I have an idea. It probably won't work out, so don't get your hopes up. In any case, the mathematics are tricky and I'll need at least a few days before I'll be able to see where it's all going to lead. But maybe there's something there."

Hwang refused lunch, remaining instead hunched over the table in the dining room at which he was doing his calculations. Rum-Lem retrieved a bar and a drink from the synthfood machine and silently stole out of the ship.

For three days Hwang lived in a world of his own. Then, in the early afternoon, a movement in the corner of Rum-Lem's eye attracted his attention, causing him to look up from the line that was dangling in the ocean at his feet. Hwang was walking down the coral beach. Rum-Lem watched to see if Hwang was going to signal for help with the computer, but instead Hwang stripped off his clothes and waded into the lagoon. Hwang swam slowly out to the reef until he was treading water only a few paces from the alien. He was smiling.

"I think there's a way home. I haven't finished everything yet, but I'm pretty sure that, except for the last set of calculations, it's all done. I understand the theory now."

Rum-Lem smiled. "I knew you could do it," he said.

It was almost not a lie.

"Well, I didn't," admitted Hwang, clambering on to the reef and taking care not to cut himself on the coral. "But it's all quite simple once you look at things from the right perspective. The trick is to stop thinking of time as... time. You need to think of it in terms of its conjugate variable, then it all begins to make sense, and the mathematics become far simpler — almost trivial, really."

"Conjugate variable?"

"Sorry. There was a theory developed on Earth by a man called Heisenberg about four hundred years ago. It's the only piece of physics from that time that hasn't been superseded or transformed out of recognition. We call it the Heisenberg Uncertainty Principle, and it seems to be one of the few truly fundamental, unbreakable laws of physics. Your research computer includes a discussion of it, calling it *The Universal Law of Inexactitude*; you remember translating that entry for me a couple of weeks ago?"

Rum-Lem nodded.

"Well, to put it simply, the Uncertainty Principle says that there are certain pairs of properties associated with objects which, if measured simultaneously, cannot be measured with arbitrary accuracy. For example, one such pair is a particle's position and momentum. What the Uncertainty Principle tells us is that the more accurately we know a particle's position, the less accurately can we know its momentum. It's not simply a matter of needing to build better equipment; the Uncertainty Principle states that even with perfect equipment, one cannot know both a particle's position and its momentum simultaneously with arbitrary precision. Two properties that are related in this way are called a conjugate pair. Basically it's because what we think of as two distinct properties are really just one fundamental property, manifesting itself in two different ways.

"Another conjugate pair is time and energy...."

Rum-Lem interrupted: "But I don't see...."

"...what this has to do with us? Simple — and obvious in retrospect, although it took me nearly a month to see it. What it means is that time and energy are really two aspects of the same thing. In a way it's sort of like a multiplication problem. If I know that the product of two numbers is ten, then the two multiplicands are deeply interrelated. Changing one will force a concomitant change in the other. In fact, you can think of the two numbers as being two aspects of the same thing: the geometric distance from the square root of ten."

Rum-Lem shook his head. "You lost me."

"Well, never mind. Take my word for it. Time and energy are two ways of looking at a single underlying concept that is actually quite distinct from both time and energy.

"My problem was that all along I had been trying to understand timeshifting in terms of exactly that: the shifting of time. What I should have been thinking about was energy shifting."

"You mean that forward time operates somehow at a different energy level than normal time?"

"Yes, in a way. The best analogy I've been able to think of is an atom. Think of the simplest atom in the Universe."

"Hydrogen," said Rum-Lem promptly.

"That's right: hydrogen: one proton and one electron. If it helps, you can think of the electron as orbiting the proton, although that's not really what happens, but for now imagine that a hydrogen atom is made of a single electron whizzing around a single proton, rather like a spaceship in orbit around a planet."

"OK."

"Now, what happens when a chunk of energy hits this atom? I'll tell you. If it's the right amount of energy, it gets absorbed. And when that happens the atom changes state. To a good approximation, the proton remains unchanged as the atom gains energy: all the energy goes into the electron. But an energized electron behaves a little differently from an unenergized one. One way of describing what happens to it is to say that its orbit around the proton changes. We can say, for example, that when a chunk of energy hits the atom, its response is to shift the electron up into a higher orbit."

"All right. I think I follow that."

"Now, the thing is that, except in its initial, unenergized state, the atom is unstable. After a period of time, the atom will release the energy it absorbed — the energy which was used to put the electron into a higher orbit — and the electron will jump back down to its original orbit, which we call the 'ground state'.

"Now it turns out that an electron in a hydrogen atom can't absorb arbitrary amounts of energy. It can absorb only certain well-defined amounts, which depend on its initial orbit. It's as if you had a hierarchy of orbits around a planet and you could be in any one of them, but never between them. If too much energy comes piling in, you jump to a new orbit and then release the excess energy, because you can't use it."

"All right, but I still don't see what this has to do with timeshifting."

"But, you see, that's exactly what's happened to *us*. Normal time is just like the hydrogen atom in its ground state, when the electron is in its lowest possible orbit, the one with least energy. Here in forward time we are just like the electrons in the hydrogen atom. We've absorbed a certain amount of something that acts like energy and we've been forced into the equivalent of a higher energy level. We call it forward time. You remember those particles you told me about?"

"Chronons?"

"That's right. Those are like the excess energy that is released after an electron jumps to a new orbit."

"I think I see," Rum-Lem said cautiously. "So it's just a matter of somehow getting rid of our excess energy and returning to the ground state?"

"Yes, I think so, although I'm not at all sure yet how we can actually do that. But at least it's beginning to look possible that there might be a way back to normal time."

"You really think we might be able to go back?"

"I think so, yes. I still need to finish my calculations before I'll be absolutely certain, because there's still a lot I don't fully understand — like why we didn't find anything on Kivra, for instance. And we'll probably have to modify my equipment a good deal; but yes, I think there's a good chance we'll be able to find a way back to normal time."

It took a moment for Rum-Lem to digest the import of what Hwang had said, but when he did, he let out an uncharacteristic whoop. He dropped his fishing line and hugged Hwang.

"Thank you," he eventually said. "Thank you, Hwang, for giving me hope."

28
VAL-DOR

It had all gone so terribly wrong.

Never, in any of the innumerable and interminable simulations, had the databoxes devised such a malicious scenario. And to make it worse, he had come so close to getting them home safely.

The artificial cave in which Val-Dor had gone to ground was well equipped. Apart from the spaceship — the twin of Rum-Lem's — there was a sophisticated communications center and enough raw material for the synthfood machine to create food and water for a lifetime. The thick, metamorphic rock surrounding the hollowed-out cavern ensured that he was undetectable by prying scanners. He was safe; but he was also a prisoner.

Val-Dor could monitor communications with impunity, so it was easy to follow the progress of the imperial search. The three hovercars that had been chasing him swept the area for several tens of chrons. Eventually they went away, heading for the tourist center, but not before Val-Dor had watched the disaster unfold.

He saw the ship flying over the grasslands to the west, near where he had left Per-Lem safely hidden in a force bubble. But the bubble must have failed, because a blip representing Per-Lem suddenly appeared.

"No!" he screamed.

But he was powerless to do anything. He watched helplessly as the distant ship halted, then turned towards Per-Lem.

The blips merged as Per-Lem was taken aboard. Then the ship sped away and disappeared out of range.

He contemplated giving chase. After all, his ship was more than a match for any imperial vessel. But it would be suicide; they would never let him get close. Even if he eluded the hovercars, he would never escape the circle of ships orbiting the planet. His ship was fast, but he couldn't outrun a photon missile. And now that P&S had captured Per-Lem, they would be less careful about sparing his own life.

So he watched, and waited, and felt more helpless than he had ever done.

The hovercars returned at dawn. They spent most of the rotation flying in formation, searching the region near the Skyward Mountains. After noon, the hovercars were augmented by three spaceships equipped with atmosphere-propulsion units and enhanced scanners. The hovercars disappeared back to the tourist center as night fell, but the spaceships continued searching all night, slowly extending the radius of their search farther and farther from the mountains.

For a second night, Val-Dor stayed at the console, watching the blips and listening to the occasional chatter on the commlink channels. Now and then he nodded off, but never for very long, and he never slept very deeply.

Soam's yellow sun rose once more and still the imperial ships searched for him, always extending the pattern, so that by the time night fell again the three ships had overflown the entire planet. He heard Captain Voorg give the order to abandon the search. The three ships returned to space and were soon lost to his scanners.

That night he slept uneasily, his sleep filled with nightmarish dreams that receded into blankness every time he woke, calling Per-Lem's name and sweating like a vagren in molt.

Eventually the night was over, and with the morning came a change in circumstances. He noticed it with his first bleary glance at the communications console. Commlinks were being made from the research centers to Prantys and to other nearby planets: the communications blackout had been lifted. The ships that had been in orbit began to peel away in ones and twos, heading away from the planet so they could hyperjump.

By nightfall, they had all gone.

He pondered what to do. He supposed it could all be an elaborate trap. It was possible that the fleet had simply retreated to a point beyond scanner range; perhaps they were waiting out there, paused to launch a salvo of photon missiles as soon as he tried to make a break for it.

But it didn't seem likely. It was much more probable that they were content to have captured one of the spies. What would they do with Per-Lem? If they contented themselves with a simple passive mindprobe, or truth drugs, or the services of an aletheologist — assuming that the Empire used such people; the discipline had been invented on Dalith only after the War of Secession and its existence was a closely guarded secret — then Per-Lem should be safe, because the truth as she knew it might be confusing but it was not dangerous. But what if they went beyond that? What if they used an active probe? He could not suppress a shudder at the thought. He needed help. He was too drained, and too close to the problem. It was time to go home.

Twenty chrons later, a small hole appeared in the mountainside. From it flew a spaceship. The ship was of an indeterminate design, not exactly imperial, not exactly unionist. It carried no markings; its color was a vague, nondescript brownish black. It hovered for a moment just beyond the end of the tunnel. Then it shot upward into the blue Soaman sky.

A huge explosion rocked the mountain, setting off rockslides along the length of the Skyward range. A fireball shot out the hole in the mountainside. The heat from the blast would have set the jungle alight, were it not for the fact that the shock front ripped up the trees and flung them ahead of the heat barrier, depriving it of fuel.

Val-Dor simply noted with grim satisfaction that the fusion device had completely destroyed the sanctuary.

Then he turned his attention to the journey home.

29

TCHARN

Tcharn looked up irritably as the holoimage screen beeped, breaking his concentration. The irritation changed to surprise when he saw who was calling him.

President Rahl looked furious.

"I want you in my office in twenty five chrons, Tcharn."

The president waved a piece of paper angrily in front of the holoimage camera, but Tcharn was unable to make out the writing, and before he could gather his thoughts the president terminated the commlink and the image faded.

Tcharn had been caught by surprise — just as, no doubt, the president had intended. What had Tcharn done? And what was on the paper that the president had been waving?

The door of his office slid open and Deputy Strenk entered unannounced.

"What do you...," the defense chief began to protest, but his deputy forcefully interrupted him.

"A signal from Val-Dor, sir. He's in the demilitarized zone, on his way home. Per-Lem has been captured."

Tcharn stared at Strenk for several moments before he found his tongue. When he spoke, his words were a colorful oath. He closed his eyes and tried to calm himself.

"How did it happen?"

His mind was already running ahead, making connections. Somehow the president already knew what Strenk was about to tell him. That's what the president's call had been about.

"We have no details yet. A transmission from Val-Dor arrived in my office about five chrons ago."

Strenk thrust a sheet of paper toward him.

The message was terse and to the point:

Agent 65-876; Op: Kālek; Code: Ultra

Returning in Soam escape vehicle. Kālek terminated. P captured by imperial forces, believed prisoner of Gdrena. Capture occurred minus two rotations.

Tcharn read the message twice, then looked up.

"That's all? Do we know what led to this, and do we know anything else about Per-Lem's capture?"

"No, sir. The signal originated inside the demilitarized zone near the imperial border, probably after his first jump. It will be a while before he arrives; until then we just have to wait."

The flood of events — first the president's call, now this — was too much for Tcharn, and a full chron passed before he spoke again. When he did, his voice was grim.

"Who else knows about this?"

"No one, sir."

"What if I told you that just before you came in here, the president said he wanted me in his office immediately?"

Strenk considered this for a moment, then shrugged.

"It can't be anything to do with this, sir. The signal was still encrypted when I received it. You and I are the only people with the keys to decrypt signals pertaining to Kālek. In any case, even if the message was intercepted and somehow decrypted by someone else, there wouldn't've been time to tell the president. I came as soon as I had read the signal."

Tcharn shook his head dubiously.

"Perhaps you're right, but I've never liked coincidences. Someone has penetrated Kālek and that someone is feeding information to the president. I'm sure of it."

"But who could it be, sir? You and I are the only ones who know about Kālek. The aletheologist knows a little, but certainly not enough to piece it all together. The same goes for the technicians who prepared the operatives. It must be a coincidence."

Tcharn glanced at a clock. "Well, I guess I'll know for sure in a few chrons." He stood up. "I'd better be going. If Val-Dor returns before I get back, I want you personally to take him to a debriefing room. I want every word and gesture recorded. Have Dunnis Delrun with you when you meet him. Let him talk, but don't interrogate him until I'm present."

"You know, sir, if Amril Gdrena really does have Per-Lem, then Kālek may be about to be blown wide open. We've got to get her back before that happens."

"The thought had not escaped me," Tcharn said irascibly. "You want to do something useful? Get me a list of all known imperial agents operating in Union territory. I want it ready by the time I get back."

Now for the president.

———————————————

Tcharn halted in front of the door to the Study while the security scanners checked his retina imprint and the pattern of pores on his cheeks. After a few moments, the door slid open and he entered the president's presence.

The president was alone, seated behind the new pawlwood desk that had replaced the one Tcharn had damaged on his last visit to the Study.

"Ah, Tcharn. Do come in. Sit down."

The president was uncharacteristically jovial. His mien was quite different from the anger which had been so obvious on the commlink just a short time earlier.

The president continued, "Are you carrying a weapon? Do you intend to threaten the leader of the Free Union if he does not bend to your will again?"

The words were direct, but the tone in which they were spoken was almost carefree, as if he was uninterested in Tcharn's answer.

He has something on me, thought Tcharn.

Tcharn sat. Their eyes met and locked. Eventually, Tcharn broke eye contact. From his pocket he withdrew, not a jammer or a weapon, but a square of paper. He placed it on the smooth pawlwood surface in front of the president.

"It is dated tomorrow, sir. I wrote it in the hovercar on the way over. I will take the necessary steps to ensure that it does not trigger any actions against your person. It is my resignation, sir."

"Your resignation?" The president's astonishment was obvious. "Why now? Last time we met you made it clear you weren't going to resign."

"Don't misunderstand me, sir. This has nothing to do with you. It is my job to protect the Union, not against only *some* threats but against *all* threats. And that includes the threat of a well-meaning but overzealous president who believes that the emperor and the Inner Council would rather have peace than overrun the Union. My loyalty is to the Union, not to its president, nor even to the misguided populace who voted you into office. But I can no longer function objectively. Now I find I must resign, to protect the Union from... me."

"You're making no sense."

"Per-Lem, sir. The agent who's been captured."

"What about her?"

So he does know, thought Tcharn. Out loud, he dropped his bombshell: "She is my daughter."

The president was speechless.

But there are some things he doesn't know. He knew an agent had been captured, but not that she was my daughter. Tcharn continued, "I've given the matter careful thought, and I believe that in the current situation I can no longer function objectively. Therefore I should be replaced. I hope you will replace me with someone who will stand up to you as I have done. And of course I am willing to offer advice. But I no longer believe that I am the right person to make the final decision."

"You never were the right person to make the final decision, Tcharn. Not for the first time you seem to have forgotten that final decisions are the prerogative of the president, not the chief of his Bureau of Defense."

Tcharn shrugged.

"It's not worth arguing about now. If you value my thoughts, I'd be glad to give them directly to you or to my successor, whichever you think most appropriate."

He slouched in his chair, beaten not by an enemy but by circumstance.

It was some time before the president spoke.

"If this agent, Per-Lem, is your daughter, then that means that the other one, the one whom we lost, her twin — what was he called?"

"Rum-Lem, sir."

"Yes; Rum-Lem is — or was — your son?"

"Yes, sir."

How does he know that Per-Lem and Rum-Lem were twins? Where is he getting his information?

"I think it's time you told me everything about Operation Kālek, Tcharn."

"Yes, sir. You're probably right...."

After a moment to gather his thoughts he began: "Article nine, section three of the Treaty of Empire and Union establishes our boundaries. It also provides for a buffer zone in which both powers may operate only under clearly circumscribed conditions, the most important of which is that no vessel capable of offensive action may enter the zone without the express permission of the other side.

"In recent times, this demilitarized zone has generally been honored, but it has not always been so. Records show that until quite recently the Empire routinely made incursions across the zone and into Union territory. Hit-and-run raids on systems near the border were for a time rather common, until the Union under President Sha-Chong ambushed one such incursion and embarrassed the Empire into ceasing its proscribed activities.

"One of the last incursions before President Sha-Chong acted was a raid on the planet Qintir. During the raid, several civilians were killed. Two of those were the parents of a small boy by the name of Var-Lem. The boy apparently escaped injury but, not surprisingly, from that time on he nursed a deep hatred of the Empire.

"The boy became a man and, as is the custom on some of the Fringe Planets, pledged himself for life to live with a single woman.

"As I am sure you are aware, sir, life can be very hard on some of these planets. Var-Lem, whether through ill-fortune or bad management, was not a successful farmer. The harvest failed for two successive years, and the banks began to make preparations to repossess his farm. Something inside Var-Lem snapped, and he somehow got the idea of crossing the demilitarized zone and attempting to assassinate the emperor, whom he seemed to hold responsible for all his troubles.

"He reached imperial territory, but was stopped before he could kill the emperor — who was the father of the current emperor — by a young operative for the Ministry of Peace and Security. The operative's name was Amril Gdrena. She is now the head of the ministry. Nothing more was ever heard of Var-Lem.

"Back on Qintir, Var-Lem's farm was sold off and his wife and their one young child, a girl, were forced to move into one of the planet's many impoverished villages. The wife did not live many more cycles, but in the short time before her death, she inculcated into her daughter the same hatred of the Empire that had caused her husband to go on his solitary mission to kill the emperor.

"In the fullness of time, this daughter became a rather extraordinary woman. I met this woman, sir, when I was stationed as a young man on Qintir as the security advisor to the planetary governor.

"I was intrigued by the stories I kept hearing about a strange young woman known as the Yern. This woman had a peculiar — indeed, a unique — reputation, which was only enhanced by the stories of her beauty and her mystique.

"No one seemed to know her real name. She was always referred to as the Yern, after a mythical beast that was supposed to inhabit the polar regions of Qintir and which combined, according to legend, traits of gracefulness, cunning and strength. The mythical yern was a solitary creature, but it was never clear whether the woman worked alone or with a small group of like-minded renegades.

"The Yern did not restrict her hatred only to the Empire. At the time I was on Qintir she had claimed responsibility for several raids on banks. While no one had been killed in these raids, a number of buildings had been destroyed and considerable sums of money lost. Still, it was widely understood that her ultimate target was the Empire, and it was rumored that she claimed that one day she would bring the Empire to its knees, if necessary by killing the emperor himself.

"Naturally, as security advisor, it fell within my purview to learn as much as possible about this strange woman, but that turned out to be far more difficult than you might think.

"As on any Fringe Planet, there were on Qintir a number of cell groups whose purpose was to foment discontent and generally remain a thorn in the side of the unionist government. My agents infiltrated all the known groups, but it soon became apparent that the Yern was not a member of any of them.

"As time passed, I gradually began to incline toward the idea that the Yern was no more real than her mythical namesake, and that the acts perpetrated against the banks were actually the work of a cell group that we had failed to penetrate. It was easy to see how the myth of a lone avenger, intent on destroying the Empire, would be attractive on a planet such as Qintir which had suffered for so long under imperial hit-and-run border incursions.

"I was on the point of forwarding my thoughts to my superior back here on Dalith when my theories were demolished by the simple fact that I met the woman in question.

"It was at a reception for President Ypp, who was on one of those tours of the Fringe Planets that precede presidential elections. As usual, I was hovering in the background, trying to conform to my official position, which was the advisor on artistic affairs, about which of course I knew absolutely nothing. I was nursing a drink...."

The room was overly warm. The largest reception room on the planet had been commandeered for the event, but it had never been designed to hold all those who wanted to meet the president of the Free Union face to face. He was not a particularly good president, everyone knew that, and his chances of reelection were not high. But he *was* the president, and it was the first time a sitting president had visited Qintir in fifteen cycles. Last election, President Vissič had mistakenly been so sure of reelection that he had foregone the usual pre-election tour of the Fringe Planets. The election before that, Qintir had been regarded as too unimportant to merit a visit; and all the native Qintirians in the room were well aware that were it not for the fact that President Ypp needed every vote he could get, the planet would have been omitted from this tour as well.

The president had arrived directly from Dalith early that afternoon. He had spoken briefly at a gathering of the Farmers' Trade Coalition. Then he had spent eighty chrons closeted with the planetary governor, the governor's cabinet, and some of the members of the unionist government who were stationed on Qintir. Now he was at the official reception, and here in this one enormous room were nearly fifteen hundred people, every one, it seemed, intent on speaking personally with the president and, if possible, touching his hand.

Tcharn's attendance was mandatory. Although the president was protected by a detachment from the Bureau of Defense, Tcharn was uncomfortably aware that if anything were to happen to the president on Qintir, he would be the scapegoat. Accordingly, among the throng of well-wishers and hangers-on were scattered fifty of his own men, armed and alert for the first sign of trouble. He noticed with some amusement that several of his agents were standing in the line that was slowly filing past the president.

He had no desire to touch the president's hand. He had already met the president in the relative privacy of the governor's mansion before the reception began. Now he stood near a corner of the room, trying to make himself invisible, watching the body language of the guests, trying to spot trouble before it happened, and studying the president as he warmly greeted the *hoi polloi*.

This afternoon, the president had been relaxed and affable, smiling and joking, putting the governor of this inconsequential Fringe Planet at his ease. Now, greeting his electorate, he was every bit the President of the Free Union, magisterially dressed in purple, and by some politician's trick he looked larger, and the governor at his side smaller, than earlier.

Tcharn noticed that nowhere else in the room was even a trace of purple. The unwritten rules of the Union were sometimes no different from the rigidly enforced ones of the Empire. In the Empire, by law only the emperor was permitted to wear purple. Here there was no such law, yet the result appeared to be no different.

He studied the president as he touched hands and exchanged a few words with each person in the line that passed before him. He could see the look on the faces of the people as they walked away from the encounter. Tcharn could not suppress a hint of a smile: he knew how they felt.

Tcharn had no respect for politicians, and certainly not for the incumbent president. This afternoon he had watched bemused as high-level bureaucrats were introduced to President Ypp; the president never failed to smile ingratiatingly; he briefly exchanged inaudible small-talk with each person. When it was Tcharn's turn, he had been astonished to discover that, even though he had watched the formula operate on more than a dozen functionaries, the moment the president touched his hand, smiled, and said, "Ah yes, Qintir's resident art advisor who perhaps is not everything he appears to be. Tell me, what do you think of my opponent's stand on the issue of mandatory mindprobes for government employees in the interest of enhanced security?" he was as swept away as all of them, believing, at least for that moment, that the president was genuinely interested in his opinion.

A quarter of a cycle later, President Ypp had lost the election in a landslide. Tcharn had always felt sorry about that. It was the only time he had ever troubled to cast a vote.

But now the second drink of the evening was in Tcharn's hand, and he was watching the president perform his magic and mulling over how someone might attempt to attack the president when he was suddenly aware that a woman was at his elbow. Tcharn turned to greet her.

For what seemed like a very long time he just stood there, drinking in the sight. Her dress was white: not the dirty off-white of eggshell or milk, but the purest white of virgin snow. A dazzling particolored necklace of glittering pseudo-jewels hung from her neck, guiding his eye downward. The bodice of the dress was low, so that the jewels lay against the skin of the upper part of her breasts. He had to stop himself from succumbing to the urge to stretch out a hand to feel the hard edge of the jewels against the smooth softness of her skin. A second necklace, a thin chain of lustrous gold, lay underneath the jewels, weighted down by some small charm that was hidden in her cleavage under the fabric of her dress.

Tcharn realized that he was looking rudely at her cleavage. Embarrassed, he raised his eyes.

Until that moment, Tcharn would have scoffed at the thought that a woman could be so beautiful that she could physically take a man's breath away. But now all the air seemed to have been pulled from Tcharn's lungs, and it required a conscious effort to refill them.

Her face was unadorned with makeup, and that fact alone differentiated her from every other woman in the room. Her hair was auburn and cut almost boyishly short. Atop her head was a small tiara such as was worn by many of the women, except that this one was smaller than most, and its deep red pseudo-jewels drew attention not so much to themselves as to the hair of the woman who was wearing the piece. It was only much later, as she slept next to him, that he had the opportunity to study her face, and even then he could not decide what it was that made her so beautiful. Like countless men before him, Tcharn was forced to conclude that true beauty could neither be prescribed nor described: it simply *was*. Almost everything about her face was average. But perhaps it was that very ordinariness that made her beautiful, for her averageness was flawless, and because of that she was as distinct as is a gem from a pebble.

Tcharn knew that he was lost.

She was talking to him, but he had heard nothing she had said. He leaned closer. She was wearing the merest trace of scent. He remembered reading somewhere that if a single perfume were to be worn by a hundred different women, each one would make that perfume her own as the odors commingled with her own natural scents. He could well believe it, for the faint odor that now reached his nostrils was enough to drive a man to distraction, and if it could be bottled and sold every woman in the galaxy would be wearing it.

She brought her face closer to his, and it was only with the greatest difficulty that he refrained from bridging the gap and kissing her on the cheek. He tried to concentrate on what she was saying.

"I believe your name is Tcharn and you have been looking for me."

"All my life." The words slipped out without premeditation.

She laughed. There was no trace of coquettishness in her amusement. Her laughter was gentle, soothing, understanding: the laugh of a long-time friend — a friend who understands and forgives the foibles and weaknesses of a man's folly.

He wondered for a moment what was happening to him. It could hardly be the drink: he had barely started his second. It had to be her. He was baffled and embarrassed that a woman could have such an effect on him.

He tried to think coherently, but merely blurted out, "I'm sorry; that was silly of me. Please forgive me."

The woman looked at him thoughtfully, then shook her head impishly. Tcharn could not help thinking how enchanting was the color of her hair as the reflections and highlights moved in response to the shake of her head.

She said, "I have to go now." She smiled to soften the blow. "I'll be in the garden at midnight. Goodbye... for now."

Tcharn opened his mouth to protest, but she was already moving away.

"Wait a minute," he said. There was a touch of desperation in his voice. "Who are you? I don't even know your name."

She halted, just for a moment, and turned to face him. Her hand went to the gold chain around her neck and she lifted it. The charm that weighted the chain arose from the bed of her breasts. Tcharn looked at the charm in puzzlement. It was the last thing he would have expected: a claw, or perhaps a tooth, from some sort of animal.

She smiled at him as if it explained everything.

"I don't understand," he mumbled.

"It's a claw," she said.

"Yes, I can see that; but...."

His voice trailed away. What was she trying to tell him?

"It's from a yern."

She turned and somehow, magically, disappeared into the crowd.

Midnight came. The reception was winding down now; many guests had left, but the president still had several hundred people to greet before he could gracefully slip away from the scene, steal a few hours' sleep, then grab a bite to eat and repeat today's show on another Fringe Planet.

Tcharn was in the garden. He was as nervous as a schoolboy as he stood in a secluded kālek arbor, trying to look casual but inwardly tense and expectant, as if he were waiting for his first date. His heart and his stomach were palpitating with nervousness. He half expected to be stood up.

He looked at the oddly shaped kālek trees, and to take his mind off *her* he tried to estimate how old they were. They must be far older than the buildings nearby, for these were mature trees, well over a thousand cycles old. There was one young tree, the single brown fur-covered vertical primary trunk almost as tall as Tcharn himself. At a thumb-width's growth per year, he calculated that the young tree was perhaps a hundred cycles old. The trunk would continue to grow for another nine hundred cycles, a brown stalagmite reaching for the sky. Only then would the trifold fast-growing secondary trunks appear at the base of the primary trunk: new trunks that branched and supported the foliage and the fruit of the kālek.

The sound of laughter floated out a window and wafted across the garden. As it died away, a clock somewhere struck midnight.

There was the swishing sound of fabric. He turned and saw her maneuvering around a low bush. There was little light by which to see her — Qintir had only a single, diminutive moon, and it cast an exiguous, pale light on the garden. He strained to see clearly as she walked the last few steps, imprinting her graceful movements on his memory.

She stopped in front of him.

The thought occurred to him that with almost no effort he could lean forward and kiss her. His heart beat even faster. She smiled.

"Well, I must say that you aren't exactly what I expected, Advisor Tcharn," she said.

Tcharn was flustered. "I'm sorry," he mumbled, feeling more than ever like an inadequate schoolboy.

"One expects security advisors to be — well, I don't know — rather military and overbearing. Tall men with hard faces that never smile and hands that hover over their holsters. But you seem rather nice."

Tcharn basked in the glow of the woman's words for several moments until he realized that she not only knew his name, but also his true position on the governor's staff.

"How did you know who I am?"

The possibility of denying the accuracy of her information did not occur to him.

"Trust me," she said, and he almost melted as her smile broadened, "there's not much happens on Qintir I don't know about. My name is Tan-Lem."

She held out her hand to be touched. He lifted his own hand and as they made contact Tcharn felt a distinct tingle pass the length of his arm. It was like nothing he had ever experienced.

They were lovers for nearly three cycles. Their meetings were frequent but clandestine, since Tan-Lem steadfastly refused to agree to an official partnership. They were the happiest, most joyous cycles of Tcharn's life. Towards the end of their time together, Tan-Lem gave birth to twins, a boy and a girl. Tcharn, who had always secretly prided himself on his stoicism, melted the first time he held them in his arms. At that moment he would happily have bound himself by oath forever to Tan-Lem and a life on Qintir. But she refused him and insisted instead that he must pursue his career with the Defense Bureau because, as she said, "You love the Union and hate the Empire, and Defense needs people like you. You will rise high, Tcharn, but I hope that no matter how high you go, you will never forget your time here with me."

Tcharn shook his head.

"Never. I will never forget because I will never leave."

But soon afterwards he was offered a promotion that would require his return to Dalith. He tried to cajole Tan-Lem into going with him but she refused.

"We've had a wonderful time, Tcharn," she said as they lay side by side, "but I would only be a stone around your neck on Dalith. With me at your side you could never go far. And in any case, the cost to me would be too great. My home is here on wild Qintir, not among

255

the cities of Dalith. The Yern may have ceased her irritating raids on the banks, but now she has a greater task ahead of her: raising her children."

Tcharn did not argue. He was tired and on the verge of sleep, and they had covered this ground before.

A while later she said his name quietly: "Tcharn?"

"Hmmm." He was more than half asleep.

"Would you promise me something?"

"Anything, my dearest."

"One day, if the twins come to you of their own free will, and it is in your power, would you agree to send them into the Empire to kill the emperor?"

"Of course, dear." The promise was made without thought. Indeed, it was only later that he realized what he had agreed to. For now, he hugged her closer, kissed her, and fell asleep.

When he awoke, she was gone, and the twins with her.

There were only two rotations left before he was scheduled to leave for Dalith, and he spent them in an insane frenzy scouring the planet for Tan-Lem and the children. It was a futile effort: he knew Tan-Lem well enough to know that if she did not want to be found, no amount of searching would uncover her.

He left Qintir with a heavy heart.

For several cycles, Tcharn spent every leave on Qintir, searching for any news of the woman he thought of as his wife, and their children. But he never uncovered any trace of them — they had completely disappeared. Even the inhabitants of Cullen, her home village in the far north, seemed to know nothing of her. Wherever he went, no one admitted any knowledge of the woman who had once been the Yern.

It took a long time for the hurt to heal.

He never forgot her, of course — that would have been impossible, unthinkable — but slowly time healed the wound of her absence, until it became no more than a cicatrice in his memory, a scar that ached sometimes when he was alone at night and had had too much to drink.

His career prospered. His obvious love of the Union, distrust of imperial motives, and considerable native intelligence saw to it that he was promoted quickly. Seventeen cycles after Tcharn left Qintir, the president of the Free Union appointed him chief of the Bureau of Defense.

He had been Defense Chief for barely half a cycle when his secretary appeared on the holoimage screen to inform him that there were two teenagers in her office wanting to see him.

"Why don't you send them away?" he asked irritably.

The secretary was apologetic. "I'm sorry, sir, but they insist that you will agree to see them."

"Well, who are they?"

And suddenly, before his secretary could reply, he knew the answer.

"They won't give their names. All they'll tell me is that their mother sent them and that you'll agree to see them."

Tcharn's secretary, looking expectantly at her holoimage screen, saw that her boss looked suddenly deflated.

"Send them in. Thank you," he said curtly. He closed the link.

His children walked into the office. They halted hesitantly by the door, seemingly unsure of their reception. Tcharn regarded them levelly, evaluating what he saw. They appeared to be strong and healthy, products of an outdoor life, perhaps on a farm. It would have been too much to say that he recognized them. He could see nothing of either himself or Tan-Lem in the boy, who was of medium height and rather undistinguished, except perhaps for his thick shock of dark hair. In the girl he could see something — just a trace — of her mother. Something in the cut of her hair and the suppressed fire in her eyes. She was pretty, but not remotely as pretty as Tan-Lem must have been at her age. But there was something about her that warned that here was a person not to be trifled with. The boy looked more nervous than the girl, but it was he who eventually broke the silence.

"Are we being monitored?"

Tcharn shook his head. "I turned off the recorder."

"You know who sent us?"

"Yes. How is she? Is she all right?"

The boy ignored the questions.

"You know why we are here?"

"Tell me."

He had been asking himself the same question, thinking that perhaps they had come with news of their mother's death. But suddenly he remembered the promise he had made the night before Tan-Lem had left him, and the memory seemed to chill the room — so much so that he actually shivered.

It was the girl, Per-Lem, who confirmed it.

257

"The Empire killed our grandfather and his parents. We came to avenge their deaths. We want to kill the emperor. Our mother said that long ago you promised to help us."

That was all. Just simple statements, but the matter-of-factness with which they were delivered sent a chill down Tcharn's spine.

He wanted to ask if they knew that he was their father, but something stopped him. What did it matter whether they knew? It made no difference to his promise. Only much, much later did he regret failing to ask.

And so Operation Kālek had begun. They named the operation after the slow-growing, long-lived, oddly-shaped tree from the planet Qintir. The theory was simple, the execution deadly dangerous. Kālek called for a two-pronged approach, utilizing three operatives — like the three secondary trunks of the kālek tree. Rum-Lem and Per-Lem would play the central, most dangerous rôles. The third part was taken by a young man a little older than the twins, the nephew of Tcharn's deputy, Strenk.

Per-Lem and the boy, whose name was Val-Dor, quickly became lovers, a situation that was fraught with difficulty because of the nature of Operation Kālek. But the lovers knew that their arrangement could be only temporary, that once the operation got under way the relationship would necessarily be broken.

Per-Lem's rôle in Operation Kālek was the most dangerous — not physically, but because of what must happen before the operation could begin.

Tcharn watched Per-Lem as she approached the mindprobe for the first implant, and he saw not even a momentary hesitation as she neared the machine that would alter her very being. There was no doubt that she was the Yern's daughter.

Per-Lem was given a new personality and a new past. An accident was stage-managed on the outskirts of the Empire involving a farming family from the planet Eb whose adopted daughter, who closely resembled Per-Lem, had won a place to the Kivran Imperial University. The parents were killed in the accident; the daughter was abducted and her memories copied and implanted into Per-Lem. Per-Lem was sent across the demilitarized zone to begin her new life as Lystra Ten-Wer, her future mapped out by a series of implanted hypnotic commands to be obeyed as the cycles passed.

Rum-Lem and Val-Dor adopted their undercover rôles. They began research stints on Soam with the intention of taking up posts tending the imperial gardens on Kivra. While they were on Soam, a surreptitious mining operation hollowed out a cavern in a mountain in the remote Skyward range. Into the cavern was placed one of the most powerful spaceships ever built by the Defense Bureau, along with a sophisticated communications and scanner center and a supply of food and water. The last item emplaced was a small thermonuclear device.

Operation Kālek unfolded according to plan.

Lystra Ten-Wer was an outstanding scholar at the university. After graduation, she was admitted into the Ministry of Peace and Security, where she rose quickly and singlemindedly through the ranks. In the meantime, Val-Dor and Rum-Lem acquired jobs working in the imperial gardens.

Now the plan called for them to wait until Per-Lem reached a sufficiently high level in the ministry for her to have access to the databoxes that stored maintenance information about the security devices at the imperial palace. She would tell her contact, Val-Dor, whenever a maintenance period would allow brief access to the palace. Afterward, she would have no recollection of having said anything. Assuming that Rum-Lem was successful in his mission, he would immediately return to Dalith while chaos descended on the Empire. Val-Dor would then awaken an implanted desire in Per-Lem to visit the planet Soam, where he would escort her to Dalith, and there her false memories would be removed.

Until the very last moment, Operation Kālek had given every indication of success. The reports from Val-Dor had been positive and the forecast databoxes had predicted an unprecedented likelihood of success. But they were wrong.

This was Tcharn's story, and most of it he now laid before President Rahl. The president listened in silence as the tale unfolded. When Tcharn finished, the president asked, "Was any president ever made explicitly aware of Operation Kālek? And if so, did he approve it?"

"President Branx and I discussed the possibility of something like Kālek. We talked about it only once, and only in broad terms. At the conclusion of the interview, he said to me, 'You realize, Tcharn, that if ever you were to come to me with a concrete proposal to do anything like this, I would have to order you to desist, don't you?' I understood that to mean that he approved as long as he was not told anything more about it. I still believe that was the correct interpretation."

The president nodded. He was all too familiar with presidential double-speak.

"So tell me, Tcharn. What would you have done if he had explicitly told you not to proceed?"

"A direct order? I would have obeyed, sir. Operation Kālek would have been canceled."

"I see. And what if, instead of President Branx, it was I who had ordered you not to go ahead? Would you still have obeyed?"

Tcharn hesitated before answering.

"Sir, I will not lie. If the order had come from you, it is possible I would have ignored it. Under President Branx there was no threat that we would lower our defenses."

The president picked up Tcharn's letter of resignation:

I, Tcharn Hwellon Tcharn, believe that under current circumstances I am not competent to perform the duties of chief of the Bureau of Defense. Accordingly I resign from that position, effective immediately.

It was handwritten. Tcharn probably *had* written it in the hovercar, just as he had claimed.

The president looked at the note for some time. Then he carefully ripped it in half, then in half again. He let the pieces fall to the desk.

"Your resignation is refused, Tcharn. The Union needs people like you, and, at least for now, I can think of no one better to see us through the crisis that has been precipitated by your actions. I am giving you a chance to redeem yourself. We will discuss your resignation again when the crisis has been resolved. Now, it is obvious what must be done: your daughter must be recovered. How much will they discover if they subject her to a mindprobe?"

"If they restrict themselves to an ordinary passive mindprobe, they should discover nothing, sir. But I doubt they'll stop there; I know I wouldn't. And if they use an active probe on her, they'll discover everything she knows. Worse, unless they're very careful, they'll destroy her mind in the process. She will oscillate violently and unpredictably between her two personas. My medical experts tell me that once that begins to happen, there is little hope for her. Imperial technology is far behind ours in the area of memory modification."

"I see. Well, we must try to get her back before that happens, mustn't we? Preferably without starting a war. Now, how do you think we might do that?"

Then, before Tcharn could respond, the president added, "I suppose I could try just asking them to hand her back. They might do it if I make a personal request. You never know."

Tcharn looked at the president, trying to decide if the man were serious. Was he really so deluded as to think that Amril Gdrena would willingly agree to give up Per-Lem? Simply conceding that she was a Union agent would be bad enough, but to go down on one's knees and beg for her return? What kind of president would do that?

And then he understood. All this time he had been blind to the president's priorities. He had mentally accused President Rahl of being so blind (or stupid) that he did not understand that to negotiate "peace" with the Empire would be to run the risk of losing everything the Union had won in the War of Secession. Now he realized that the president had understood this all along — but it did not matter. The legacy he wanted to leave was the end of the Status Quo. In the president's mind, that was more important than maintaining face, more important even than winning.

Tcharn had been right all along: the Union had to be protected against the man sitting on the other side of the pawlwood desk.

"It might be better if we offered them an exchange, sir," he heard himself saying, "although quite frankly if I were in Amril Gdrena's position I wouldn't accept it."

"An exchange?"

"Yes, sir. We know of perhaps a couple of dozen imperial agents in place inside the Union. My deputy is compiling a list. We could offer to exchange them for Per-Lem. But if they start taking my daughter's brain apart, they'll learn so much that it will take us a generation to recover. Everything she has ever experienced, whether she remembers it consciously or not, is buried inside her head, and they'll get it all. If I were Amril Gdrena, I wouldn't trade that for anything."

"I see. Still, we can try. Do you have any other ideas?"

"Not really. I suppose there's a chance they don't realize what they've got, but I'm not sanguine about that. They've held Per-Lem for several rotations now, and at the very least they'll have put her under a passive mindprobe by now. At first they'll be confused, because her memories won't match what they know has actually happened. It all depends on how much evidence they have against her. If she's been seen passing secrets to Val-Dor, she's as good as dead. Or perhaps they've come up with an inconsistency in her past. Maybe they've even discovered that we made a substitution, that she's not the real Lystra Ten-Wer. She'll deny it and they'll put her under a passive probe to get at the truth. Then they'll become confused because they'll see that she really believes she is telling the truth. At that point it's only a short step to using an active probe, and then the whole thing will begin to unravel. Any competent technician will spot the fuzzy areas in her brain and home in on them, and when they do that they'll see the changes we made to her memory links."

"I see. And what happens then?"

"They'll take her mind apart, and in the process they'll probably destroy it."

"All right." The president's voice carried the snap of a decision made. "Stay here while I make a commlink call. I may want you to back me up or to provide additional data. Do not be surprised at anything I say. Our priority now is to get your daughter back before any more damage is done to the prospect of peace."

He pressed several buttons on a keypad inlaid in the pawlwood surface of his desk, then looked up expectantly at the holoimage screen.

It was some moments before the dull gray of the screen was replaced by the image of a room in which the color purple predominated. A middle-aged man with thick, graying hair and penetrating gray-blue eyes was looking at them from behind a desk not dissimilar to the president's. Tcharn recognized the man immediately. He sucked in a shocked breath, but was wise enough not to say anything.

"Your Highness," the president began. "Excuse me for the interruption, but some facts have come to light regarding that matter we discussed earlier."

Discussed earlier, Tcharn thought. Now he understood. *So this is where the president has been getting his information.*

The emperor smiled. He indicated his desk, on which stood two piles of paper, one on his left and one on his right.

"I am always pleased to be called away from paperwork, Mr. President. Tell me, do you have the same trouble with endless mountains of paper in the Union? Sometimes I wonder if I would not prefer it if I could retire honorably from my post, as you will."

He smiled engagingly.

President Rahl agreed: "Paperwork seems to be the bane of any leader. That's one thing I certainly won't miss when I leave office."

The emperor leaned forward and peered at his holoimage screen. "But I see you are not alone, Mr. President. That is not usual for our discussions, especially on such a delicate matter." He frowned his disapproval.

"Ah, yes, your Highness. May I introduce Tcharn, the chief of my Bureau of Defense."

Tcharn nodded tersely at the holoimage screen, trying too late to arrange his features into the semblance of a smile.

The emperor beamed at him. "So glad to make your acquaintance, Chief Tcharn. I have heard much about you. It is always good to meet one's... shall we say... adversary? I understand that you do not always see eye to eye with your president on the matter of the relationship between the Empire and the Union?"

"No, sir, I do not. Nevertheless I am pleased, if surprised, to meet you."

"The pleasure is mine. Well, Rahl, enough of this. To what do I owe the pleasure of this unscheduled meeting?"

Tcharn picked up one of the scraps of his resignation notice and scribbled a note on the back of the piece of paper: *Is this communication being recorded?*

While the president was speaking, he thrust it across the table. The president glanced down and, without interrupting his speech, nodded cursorily.

"I wish to request that mercy be shown to the agent whom we were discussing earlier."

"I am sure she is being treated appropriately by my minister of Peace and Security, Amril Gdrena."

Tcharn, with the best will in the galaxy, could not prevent his eyes from narrowing at the mention of Gdrena.

"I quite understand, your Highness. However, Chief Tcharn is quite embarrassed about the matter. The agent in question should have been recalled some time ago, and because of his failure to do so he sees himself as being responsible for her capture. He as asked a favor of me, and I in turn am now asking one of you. We propose an exchange. In return for the safe and immediate return of this agent, we will immediately repatriate all known imperial operatives functioning within Union territory. We urge you — *I* urge you, as a personal favor — to consider our proposal. I hope that on reflection you will find it reasonable."

"How so?"

"In the first place, for the return of a single prisoner, you will be told which of your agents the Union has uncovered. I am sure that Chief

Tcharn's organization, no matter how efficient, has failed to identify all your agents, and those whom we do not return can be confident that they remain undetected. You have my word on that.

"Secondly, this would be a further step towards peace, a sign that two men of honor can do business regardless of the machinations of their underlings who try to subvert the process at every step."

Tcharn felt the brunt of the reprimand, although the expression on the president's face was unchanged.

The emperor's face wrinkled. There was a long, stretched silence as he pondered the proposition. Tcharn looked at the man in the holoimage screen, then at his president, then at the screen once more. He was asking himself questions: what promises had been made by these two men? what agreements had been reached? was Amril Gdrena as unaware of these conversations as he had been?

The emperor's face cleared.

"I'm sorry, Mr. President." Tcharn's stomach churned. His daughter was not going to be returned. "I cannot give you an answer right now. You are an honorable man — I am convinced of that — but even honorable men may surround themselves with dishonorable advisors. What you have told me may well be true, but while I am perfectly willing to accept your word, I have no reason as yet to accept that of your chief of Defense."

The emperor gave Tcharn a deferential nod, almost a bow.

"I apologize if I have offended you, Chief Tcharn, but you are fundamentally a military man with a military mindset and therefore a military way of looking at things. While the situation may indeed be as President Rahl has indicated, it may also be that the truth is quite different. It would be irresponsible of me to bind myself to a specific course of action until I have conferred with my own minister of Peace and Security.

"I will give this matter my immediate attention and you have my word that I will contact President Rahl tomorrow with my answer. I apologize to you both that I cannot make an immediate decision. I must be fully briefed before agreeing to an exchange. However, Chief Tcharn, if the facts indeed are as they have been stated, you have my sincerest assurance that I shall do everything in my power to return your agent unharmed and at the earliest opportunity of mutual convenience.

"Now, if there is nothing else, I have my paperwork to attend to." The emperor gestured ruefully at his desk.

"That is all, your Highness," said the president. "Chief Tcharn and I thank you for your time, and I look forward to receiving your response."

"Until tomorrow, then."

The holoimage screen went blank.

The president looked at his chief of Defense. "You see, Tcharn, he's not the monster you make him out to be."

If the president was expecting thanks, he was disappointed,

"How many of these conversations have there been, sir?"

The president laughed.

"Sorry, Tcharn. I suppose it does undermine your cause rather, doesn't it? But you must understand: in the first place I was elected on a platform that included a promise to work towards a normalization of the relations between the two powers; and in the second place I am sufficiently old-fashioned to believe that there is little that two men of honest intentions cannot accomplish if only they will learn to trust one another. Fortunately, the emperor appears to share that belief."

"Sir, with all due respect, you have not answered my question. How many of these conversations have taken place?"

"I'm not sure. Fifty or more, I would guess."

"And all of them have been recorded?"

"Yes; why? I hope you aren't going to ask to see the recordings, because you can't have them. These are private conversations, not for viewing by third parties."

"Sir, please, is it really too much to ask you to turn them over?"

"Yes, Chief Tcharn, it *is* too much to ask. These were private discussions and I am afraid that I simply cannot release the discs. They could be damaging both to the emperor and to myself if they fell into the wrong hands."

Tcharn nodded. "Yes, I suppose they would. I understand."

He understood all right.

"Now, unless there is anything else?"

Tcharn stood.

"I'd like to thank you, sir, for your efforts on my daughter's behalf. I am willing to admit directly to you, face to face, that I misjudged you, that you are truly a man of rare honor and compassion." *And terrifying naïveté for a president.*

The president flushed. He said brusquely, "That will be all, Tcharn. Don't thank me until we've seen how it turns out. And one more thing:

265

just because I tore up your resignation doesn't mean you are safe in your job. You're on probation until this affair with your daughter is over. Then we'll revisit the matter. Do I make myself clear?"

"Yes, sir, you do. And thank you again."

Tcharn turned and walked thoughtfully from the Study. He had a lot to think about.

Tcharn was so deep in thought that his return flight was over almost before he realized it had begun.

"Find Deputy Strenk," he said to his secretary as he swept into his office. "I need to see him. Now. Tell him to drop anything else he's doing."

Strenk appeared at the door less than two chrons later. He halted in the doorway, surprised at the grimness of Tcharn's expression.

"You wanted to see me, sir? If it's about Val-Dor, he hasn't arrived yet, but the scanners indicate that he's made his last hyperjump. He should be on the ground in about twenty five chrons."

"Forget Val-Dor and come in," barked Tcharn.

The door closed silently behind Strenk. Tcharn pressed a button on his desk.

He said, "This conversation is not being recorded and we are now screened by a jamming field."

Strenk nodded. Such statements were not an unusual prelude to conversation in Tcharn's office.

"Fact." Tcharn held up the thumb of his right hand for emphasis. "President Rahl has been holding unmonitored private conversations with an unknown person who claims to be the emperor.

"Fact." The index finger joined the thumb. "The president believes that this person really is the emperor.

"Fact. These conversations have been continuing for some time — there have been about fifty of them — and they would prove, on the president's own admission, to be embarrassing both to himself and to the putative emperor if their contents were known.

"Fact. The person claiming to be the emperor appears to be the source of the president's information about Operation Kālek.

"Fact. The conversations have been recorded."

Tcharn slammed his open palm against his desk and leaned forward.

"I want those recordings, Strenk. If we are to maintain the security of the Union, we have to know what our president has been saying and what agreements he has made behind our backs. I know you agree with the president's ridiculous ideas about the Status Quo, but even you must admit that there is no room for secret negotiations between the president and his counterpart. For all we know, Amril Gdrena is using the emperor to feed the president a stream of self-serving lies.

"As soon as we have the recordings, I want them viewed by a competent aletheologist, preferably Dunnis Delrun. I want to know if the man at the other end of the commlink really is the emperor, and, if so, I want to know how much of what he is telling the president is true. Got it?"

For several moments, Strenk was rendered speechless. So the president had been trying to out-maneuver Tcharn by holding secret discussions with the emperor. He could hardly believe it. Good for President Rahl. Strenk hadn't thought he had it in him.

But Tcharn was right. Someone had to review the recordings, to make sure that the president was not being sucked into disadvantageous agreements.

"You're asking me to locate, copy and analyze a set of secret presidential recordings that I didn't even know existed when I walked into this room? How long do I have?"

"Until yesterday. Sooner if at all possible. As soon as an initial report is available, I want to see it, no matter where I am or what I'm doing. Drop everything else. This has priority. Do whatever is necessary."

He looked meaningfully at his deputy and repeated: "Whatever is necessary."

"I'll do my best, sir. But what about Val-Dor? He'll need to be debriefed."

"Tell Delrun to meet me at the spaceport immediately. Delrun and I will debrief Val-Dor together. You just get your hands on those discs."

"Yes, sir. And by the way, we're still working on locating all the imperial agents we know about. Looks like there'll be a couple of dozen. I'm not sure it'll be enough to convince them to exchange Per-Lem, if that's what you had in mind."

"Tell me, Strenk: if you were Amril Gdrena and you'd already discovered at least some of the truth about my daughter, would you exchange her for a hundred times a couple of dozen low-level agents?"

Strenk shook his head. "No, sir, I would not."

"Neither would I. My daughter is as good as dead. Now, get those discs."

Deputy Strenk hurried out of Tcharn's office.

30

STRENK

Ter Shariq, head of communications security for the Bureau of Defense, paused momentarily outside Deputy Shrenk's office to arrange his uniform one last time. In the twenty five cycles he had worked at the Defense Bureau — the last four as head of his department — never had he been summoned so peremptorily to the office of a superior. "Ter Shariq, in my office. Now!" had been the command, and Deputy Strenk's face on the holoimage screen had looked thunderous as he issued it. Ter Shariq wondered what he could possibly have done to warrant such an obvious display of wrath.

He swallowed nervously; then he pressed the panel and the door slid open. He stepped into Deputy Strenk's office.

The door had not even closed before Strenk began to speak.

"Sit down, Ter Shariq. For security reasons, this conversation is not being recorded."

"Yes, sir. Thank you, sir."

Deputy Strenk continued: "I've just come from the office of Chief Tcharn."

"Sir?"

"It seems that President Rahl has been holding covert conversations with the emperor, or at least someone who claims to be the emperor. The conversations have been recorded. I have been ordered by Chief Tcharn to obtain copies of all the conversations. I want to know if

269

there is any way to recover those conversations. Is it possible that we have them archived somewhere?"

Ter Shariq thought quickly. "These are ordinary holoimage comm-link conversations?"

"I believe so, yes."

"Then almost certainly we have copies of the transmissions in the archives. The transmissions must have passed through the demilitarized zone. We routinely record all traffic into and out of the zone — there isn't very much of it. Unfortunately, even if we have a copy of the transmissions, it won't help us."

"Why not?"

"Because such sensitive conversations would be fully encrypted. Complete encryption of commlink communications by private individuals and corporations is illegal, but commlinks from the presidential palace are automatically classified Governmental-Ultra, whatever their content. Messages from the president are therefore always fully encrypted. We cannot decode them."

"You're sure about that?"

"Yes, sir."

Strenk swore.

"But you would at least be able to reconstruct a record of the times and durations of the conversations?"

"Yes. We should be able to recover that information."

"All right, then; get to it. We don't know how far back these conversations go. It seems unlikely that the prior president was involved, so probably you will find transmissions only in the last half cycle or so, but go back a complete cycle anyway just to be sure. I want a report detailing the time and duration of every communication, and I want it before the end of the rotation."

"I'll do what I can, sir."

"No, Ter Shariq. You'll get me the report. Before the end of the rotation."

"I'm sorry, sir. That's what I meant to say."

Ter Shariq pulled himself out of the chair, his mind already busy with the problem he had just been set.

————————

A man in his mid sixties disembarked from a hovercar in the public hovercar park in Telborn's Borough 23. His clothing was streaked and ill-fitting, the adaptametal nearing the end of its useful life. The fabric at the elbows was thin, and there was a rip on the right shoulder through which bare skin could be seen.

The man locked his car and walked the short distance to the elevator. His shoes, which were in rather better repair than the rest of his clothing, were silent on the pot-holed surface of the underutilized park. He surveyed his surroundings as he walked, registering the sights, sounds and odors of this most disreputable of all boroughs.

Lounging next to the elevator was a uniformed guard who eyed the stranger dubiously; his hand hovered over the holster that held his stun-gun.

Deputy Strenk nodded politely as he halted in front of the elevator and called the car. The guard returned the nod suspiciously. Neither man spoke.

The elevator car arrived. As the door slid open, Strenk said quietly, "If anything happens to my car, you'll wish I had killed you."

Before the guard could respond, Strenk stepped into the elevator and the door slid closed.

The elevator stank of urine and other less mentionable body products. Scrawled on the walls were obscene slogans, usually misspelled and uniformly executed in barely legible handwriting.

As the elevator rattled downward, he could see through the windows vandalized vehicles on most floors — some battered into twisted shapes like parodies of the hovercars they had once been, some simply set on fire and gutted. It was impossible to guess how long they had been there.

The elevator reached ground level and the door opened wearily, allowing the reek of the car's interior to leak out and the oily smell of the ground floor to enter. The guard at the entranceway was standing nearby, watching the door as it opened, his hand on his weapon. Strenk nodded, and the guard visibly relaxed at the sight of the solitary stranger, getting on in age, who obviously posed no threat. Strenk took a deep breath, then strode away from the hovercar park and into the jungle that was Telborn, Borough 23.

Small animals of wolverine and feline ancestry gathered and began to trot some way behind him, their cruel eyes following his movements hopefully. The streets here were narrow, little more than alleyways between six-story tenements that blocked the sun. The sweet stench of decay filled the air, its source the refuse and filth that met Strenk's gaze everywhere he looked. As his eyes adjusted to the gloom of the alley, he became aware that from the windows and the tenebrous shadows of the doorways he was being watched by a multitude of pairs of eyes, some human, some animal.

He had walked two and a half blocks when there was a sudden sound behind him, followed by a yelping cry. He turned and observed that the animals that had been following him had been involuntarily dispersed. One of the wolverine creatures was limping away, looking sorry for itself; the others had scattered.

In their place stood a man dressed entirely in black. His mask-covered head looked directly at the deputy chief of the Bureau of Defense.

The man was tall, very tall; he intimidated Strenk, who momentarily felt like turning to flee like the animals. He forced himself to hold his ground as the man approached. Affecting unconcern, Strenk turned and resumed walking.

The man's footsteps were as silent as his own; Strenk had no idea whether the man was following him and, if so, whether he was gaining or falling behind. Strenk turned a corner, and only by a supreme effort of willpower refrained from looking behind. He continued onward.

His destination, an ancient, grime-covered, grafittied stone building with broken windows, was visible not far ahead.

"You. Stop."

Strenk obeyed the command without thinking. It had been a woman's voice, not a man's, and it had come from close behind. Strenk turned slowly and regarded the figure in black.

She stood about three or four paces away, and was even taller than he had first thought. He had never seen such a tall human before; she seemed to tower over him and, despite himself, he was intimidated both by her sheer physical height and by the impenetrable blackness of her clothing. She was dressed in a kind of body suit; the only gap in the black adaptametal was over her eyes, where two small ovals permitted him to feel her malevolence. Her eyeballs were a red-veined yellow. They left an impression of lascivious lust: for trouble; for blood; for torture; for death.

In her right hand, the woman held a long, narrow knife whose blade was hard to make out in the gloom. At the sight of the knife, Strenk felt more confident: at least her chosen weapon was not a kill-gun.

She took a single pace forward, the knife rising until she was brandishing it barely an arm's length from his torso.

"I told you to stop. I didn't tell you to turn around, old man. Face the way you were walking."

Strenk's eyes moved slowly down the length of her body to her feet, then, equally slowly, back to the mask that covered her face. He said nothing, staring instead at the twin slits through which her eyes stared back at him. He did not turn away.

The woman took another step forward. Now he was within range of the knife. A single, quick thrust, and he would be mortally wounded.

"Are you deaf? I told you to turn around, old man."

She moved the knife, not yet to use, merely to instill fear in her prey.

Strenk kept his eyes fixed on hers. He could see the thin blade coming slowly toward him out the bottom of his eyes. The blade halted a handspan from his stomach. He counted silently to two. Then he moved.

The woman was caught by surprise. She had no idea who the man was; all she knew was that he was a stranger, and that was enough for her. If he was carrying a weapon somewhere on his person, it was not in his hand, and that could be a fatal mistake in Borough 23. It had been a boring afternoon until this nearly-elderly man had promised to enliven the day by his unexpected presence. She did not think she would kill him — not unless he gave her cause — but she would certainly make sure he never returned to *her* part of Borough 23 again.

She could have laughed out loud at the man's obvious terror when he had first seen her, and the way he had forced himself not to look behind, as if by appearing nonchalant he could somehow overcome his fear; she *would* have laughed, except that she had seen it too many times before.

She made less noise than a feline as she followed him. When she commanded him to halt, she felt an almost sexual frisson of pleasure at his obvious surprise: she had deceived him; he had thought her much farther away than she actually was.

The man seemed to think it was clever to challenge her, first by turning around when she had not told him to, and now by hesitating when she told him to turn back the way he had been going. Perhaps she would kill him after all. He was too stupid to live.

And then everything changed.

His eyes did not move; they remained locked to her own, but his right hand moved quickly upwards and sideways. The woman caught the motion of the hand out of the corner of her eye and she swivelled towards it. As her eyes slid away from his face, Strenk's left hand came up. His hand locked around her wrist and he applied a sudden jabbing pressure on the inside of her wrist with his thumb. Her hand opened reflexively, and the knife fell.

His leg thrust forward explosively, his foot connecting with her solar plexus. She bent forward, her breath exploding in a muted shout of surprise. Strenk slammed his palms against the side of her head, causing her head to swim. He twisted violently, then abruptly let go. The woman lost her balance and lurched sideways.

She shook her head, trying to clear it.

He raised his left hand in front of her face. In it was the knife. The blade was near her right eye. He saw a flicker of fear.

Then he stabbed the knife forward, just far enough to destroy the eyeball, not far enough to penetrate the skull.

A scream rent the silence of the narrow street as a brief fountain of red and white erupted from the eyeslit of her costume. He withdrew the knife. She was still screaming, holding her hands to her ruined eye. Strenk turned and walked away. The knife in his hand dripped a glutinous mixture of blood and humor.

Her cries turned to whimpers. He halted outside the building that was his destination.

"Good to see you've still got it in you."

Strenk tried to make out the source of the remark, but the shadows in the doorway were too deep. He waited for the person who had spoken to show himself. After a few moments, there emerged from the shadows a short, wiry man clad in a bodysuit that had seen much better days, a very long time ago. The man wore a holster, although Strenk could not make whether it held a stun-gun or a kill-gun. The man threw his arms around Strenk.

They greeted one another briefly. Occasional self-pitying noises came from the woman in black, half a block away. They turned to look at her. She was standing, dabbing gloved hands at her ruined eye. She looked toward them, screamed ferally, then began to stagger away.

"You don't think I was too hard on her?"

"You're too soft. You always have been. She's killed one man and maimed two others in the decarotation she's been in this part of the borough, claiming it as her territory. I've had several complaints and I'd already decided to put her out of commission myself. Thanks for saving me the trouble. We don't want the neighborhood to get a bad name, do we? Otherwise the Bureau of Housing and Transportation might take it into their heads to try to clean up Borough 23, despite the subtle pressure I understand the deputy chief of Defense puts on them to leave us alone."

Strenk smiled and embraced the man again. "It's been a long time, Sintaar."

"Aye, that it has. Still holding down that bureaucrat's job then?"

"I'm afraid so."

"Well, at least Mom would have been pleased at the way one of us turned out. Now, come on inside. What's the problem? That son of mine got himself killed yet?"

"No. In fact he's just back from his mission. I'll tell him you'd like to see him, if you want."

"Don't bother. He knows where to find me if he feels the need. Now, come inside and tell me what this is all about."

Strenk followed his brother into the building. The ancient house looked unsafe, and in any other borough it would have been demolished at least fifty cycles ago. The walls of the building were damp, their surfaces covered with a layer of ancient paint, blotchily faded, peeling and blistered.

Sintaar led Strenk into a room whose ceiling glowed dully with an unnatural light, giving the room a strange, surreal ambience. The furniture in the room was old and battered. There was no holoimage screen on the wall.

"Have a seat," offered Sintaar. "Want a drink?"

Strenk settled himself uncomfortably in one of the chairs. The contouring mechanism was broken, so that he had to adjust himself to the shape of the chair, rather than the other way around.

"No, I can't stay. We have a rush job on at the bureau and I need to get back as quickly as I can."

Sintaar shook his head as he studied his brother.

"You should learn to relax, Strenk, otherwise you'll be dead before you're fifty five."

Strenk smiled. "I *am* fifty five, and then some, as you well know."

What was left unsaid, because both of them knew it, was that Sintaar, who was ten cycles the younger of the pair, looked considerably older than Strenk.

"So what can I do for you?"

"This conversation isn't being recorded, is it?"

Sintaar looked with bemusement around the dilapidated room and through the cracked window to the street beyond.

"Right, and who would be stupid enough to come to Borough 23 to plant a recorder in a place like this?" He shook his head. "No, I think it's safe to say that this conversation is not being recorded."

"Sorry. I had to ask. It's a delicate matter."

"Aha! My brother, the master of diplomacy. The man who gouges out the eye of a woman before they are even introduced. Her name was Malenna, by the way. You might want to look her up in your records. She claims to have been responsible for that explosion in the orphanage in Borough 20 a couple of cycles ago. I've heard it said that she got bored one afternoon and wanted to spare the kids the burden of growing up to be as bored as she was.... Anyway, what is this 'delicate matter' of yours?"

"It concerns the president...."

Strenk went on to explain about the conversations between the president and the emperor.

"What I want is those recordings," he concluded. "Here's a list showing the exact date, time and duration of all the conversations we know about."

From his pocket he withdrew a torn scrap of paper on which were several columns of figures.

"Phew! He's been busy, hasn't he?" said Sintaar.

"Sixty two of them."

"All of them behind your back?" Sintaar was smiling. "He's not such a fool after all, is he?"

"No comment, Sintaar. Just get the discs, that's all I'm asking."

"Originals, not copies?"

Strenk shrugged. "I don't care."

Sintaar pondered for a moment. "Sounds simple enough. I'm surprised your own people can't do it."

"I can't use them because they can be bought. And there are things they won't do."

Sintaar smiled.

Strenk continued: "But why do you say it sounds easy? It sounds difficult to me."

Sintaar's smile became a laugh.

"That's because you have a pure and innocent mind, brother of mine. Comes of being a bureaucrat instead of earning an honest living,

I suppose. Just tell me where I can find the president's personal head of security, and I'll have the recordings in your hands before you can say 'Empire and Union'."

"What are you going to do: bribe the man?" Strenk asked dubiously. "You'll want money for that."

"Just give me his contact information. I'll take care of the rest. And you can keep your money. I'm not that crude."

Strenk shrugged and gave his brother the information. He stood to leave, glad to be out of the broken chair. "All I want are the recordings. I don't care what you have to do to get them."

"I know that, otherwise you wouldn't have come to me." Sintaar embraced his brother one last time. "Stay in touch, eh?"

"I'll see myself out," said Strenk.

No one bothered Strenk as he walked back to the hovercar park.

31
GHERRAN

It was early evening, and Gherran, chief psychoanalyst for the Ministry of Peace and Security, was so weary that it took a conscious effort to haul his overweight frame to its feet.

Despite his fatigue, there was a haggard smile on his face. Until now, he had never been sure how Amril Gdrena viewed the services he provided, but his work of the past two rotations should ensure that his value was never again in doubt. And there was so much work still to be done: the Union was so far ahead.

With an effort he brought his thoughts back to the here and now. He had to tell the minister what he had discovered; only then could he go home and collapse in bed.

He glanced at the chair in which he had been sitting for the last five hundred chrons, with its attached playback helmet and the control panel at its side. Five hundred chrons. No one had ever spent half so long working on a mindprobe playback before. But it had been necessary; and, he admitted to himself, it had also been exciting as, layer by layer, he had pulled the spy's mind apart. He could hardly wait to get her under the active mindprobe again. Next time, he would be less gentle. It was too important that everything be extracted as quickly as possible. Whether the woman herself survived was irrelevant. He would suck her dry.

He smiled, then stopped. His thoughts were wandering. He really was very tired. He leaned forward and pressed a button on his desk.

"Madam minister, it is imperative that I talk with you immediately."

———————

The four had gathered again: Gherran, the minister, deputy minister Missen Hai, and the slightly mysterious and always ominous Brynt Veel. The psychoanalyst held a soothing drink. The others waited patiently while Gherran made a show of recovering from a harrowing experience. The drink gradually pervaded his system, and he visibly relaxed. The aroma of his sweat was faint but definite.

The psychoanalyst glanced up at the ceiling. This time the holographic recorders were not running; the minister apparently wanted no record of his report.

Amril Gdrena observed his glance and interrupted his thoughts.

"Well, Gherran. You did a wonderful job with the probe, I think all of us admit that. Tell us, what have you uncovered now?"

Gherran tried to look modest, but was not particularly successful.

"First of all, I must thank you for agreeing to see me at such short notice. I understand how valuable your time is, madam minister.

"I apologize for my tiredness. I have just spent five hundred chrons under a playback helmet. As you all can attest, undergoing a mindprobe playback can be a shattering experience, one from which the mind does not quickly recover. A playback is traumatic because of the constant state of schizophrenic dichotomy. Separation of one's self from the thoughts and emotions of the subject is often difficult and always tiring. The impact of being inside another person's head, the sensation of having their thoughts and emotions and memories completely overpower one's own, so that, for a time, one *becomes* that person — well, it is a draining experience."

Gdrena, obviously impatient, opened her mouth to speak.

"But you know all this," Gherran hurriedly concluded. "I'm sorry. It's been a long rotation."

He took a long draught of his drink; then he breathed deeply, tried to collect his somewhat haphazard thoughts, and continued.

"As I told you yesterday, a couple of scenes didn't seem quite right, and I also wanted to take a better look at some periods that we skipped in the interest of brevity. I must tell you that I am shocked at how much more advanced the Union is at manipulating minds than we are. What I have seen today will take us decades to reproduce."

He paused to let this sink in, but if he was expecting any reaction, he was disappointed. The only face that showed any readable expression was that of the deputy minister, and that registered only an incompletely stifled boredom.

He continued, injecting his voice with a greater enthusiasm. "The first point that attracted my attention was the scene I mentioned yesterday: the period the subject spent with the man calling himself Teberill Gandeer, the imperial gardener. Incidentally, if I might be so bold as to ask: what has happened to him? He would make a wonderful subject for an active probe, if he is available."

"He is not," the minister snapped. "You said you had something important to say. I'm still waiting to hear it."

"Yes, yes, of course, madam minister. I'm sorry. The reason I mentioned the gardener is simply that he also is a Union spy."

He paused to see if anyone would react. No one did.

"But apparently his memories have not been altered, at least from the evidence I could glean from Per-Lem. He is the subject's conduit back to the Union.

"If you remember, I pointed out that there was something, a dream of some sort, that seemed to have occurred while the woman slept that afternoon they spent together on Soam. It transpires that it was not a dream. In fact, it was merely the most recent example of something for which we have no name as yet, but I am tentatively calling preburied memory."

"Preburied memory? What do you mean by that?" interrupted the minister.

"I'll try to explain. The way it seems to work is this: the mind of the woman calling herself Lystra Ten-Wer, whom we know to be the Union agent Per-Lem, has been so altered that she really believes she is Lystra Ten-Wer. That much we knew yesterday; but, if you remember, we were wondering what use such a person could be to the Union. After all, Lystra Ten-Wer is a productive, dedicated citizen of the Empire, and she would never willingly pass any information to the Union. So what was the point of installing her in the ministry?

"Well, it seems that there are certain trigger events buried in her mind which will place her into a state similar to a kind of hypnosis, where she will pass on information she has collected to the man we know as Teberill Gandeer. Once she has finished telling him her news, the memory of what she has done is erased and replaced with what I call a preburied memory, something whose outline was long ago inserted into her mind. Her mind takes the outline and builds a coherent memory of events to fill in the time that was spent divulging secrets. On Soam, that memory was of a brief but pleasant conversation followed by a nap. What actually happened was that she was interrogated by the so-called gardener and then he triggered a hypnotic suggestion that sent her to sleep while her mind short-circuited the memory of what had actually happened and replaced it with something constructed from the preburied outline. Now she has no recollection at all of what really transpired that afternoon. She would deny that she told the gardener anything, even under torture, a passive mindprobe or the influence of a truth drug. For her, the conversation simply never happened."

He paused, waiting for his words to sink in.

Brynt Veel asked, "What if she needed to send an urgent message to the Union? From what you said, it sounds like she can't initiate contact."

"That's perhaps the cleverest thing of all. Part of her mind monitors everything that happens to her. If there is any indication that she is suspected of being an agent, she makes an unconscious sign, a simple body movement, to her contact, whom she sees almost every rotation on the hoverbus. Then, when her contact gives her a signal in return, she is programmed to take a flight to Soam — don't ask me why Soam, but there must be a good reason buried somewhere in her past that I haven't uncovered yet. That seems to be the extent of her programming, so I assume that her contact is supposed to take over on Soam and either give her new orders or get her safely back to Union territory. Something must have gone wrong on Soam and she ended up in our hands."

He shrugged and drained the glass. He looked pleased with himself.

"The gardener, Teberill Gandeer," the deputy minister began, "what about him? When we went through the playback yesterday, there were all those scenes back on Dalith. The same man was there. What have you been able to find out about him?"

"I must apologize; there simply hasn't been time to look into that yet. You must realize, deputy minister, that this is painstaking work. I have barely scratched the surface. The five hundred chrons I spent under playback today took me back only a few rotations. To thoroughly analyze the events on Dalith will occupy me for many cycles. And in any case we need to probe her many more times before we have a complete record of her experiences."

"Tell me," interrupted Amril Gdrena, "What did she tell the gardener that afternoon on Soam?"

"Ah, yes," said the psychoanalyst. "I was coming to that. You remember those red reports from a monitorship in the demilitarized zone?"

"35/CW. Yes."

"Well, it seems that after she forgot to forward the first report — an omission, incidentally, that I suspect was the result of a preburied command — her supervisor instigated an automatic periodic audit of her databox. The most recent such audit disclosed the fact that a second red report had come in and she had deleted it without forwarding it. He called her in to explain that fact. In the interview she emphatically stated that she *had* forwarded the report; as of course she would, since that was her memory of the event. She suggested that perhaps it was a databox programming error. That interview triggered her subconscious monitor program, warning her that perhaps she was under suspicion, and set in motion the events that followed. She signalled the gardener, and he responded with a signal that provoked a sudden and deep dissatisfaction with life on Kivra. The following rotation she took a ship to Soam. The afternoon in question she spent recounting the details of her meeting with her supervisor."

"So why was she tied up and left inside a force field? It makes no sense," said the deputy minister.

Gherran shrugged. "I have no idea. And neither does she. Perhaps the answer lies further back, somewhere in her training, but I'm inclined to doubt it. As far as I can tell, she was genuinely shocked, at all levels, when she woke up and discovered her situation. She honestly doesn't know whether it was the gardener who did it, although she can't imagine who else it might have been."

A heavy silence fell, as everyone mulled over what that the psychoanalyst had told them.

Eventually, the minister thanked Gherran.

"You've done well. Good work."

"Excuse me for asking," Gherran said, "but what happens to the subject now? We've barely scratched the surface of what she knows. If you want to know everything, I need to put her under the probe and suck her dry. Of course, the effects on her brain would likely be catastrophic. She would almost certainly be subject to such large psychic stresses that she would lose her faculties. But once you have no further use for her...."

"You'd like that, wouldn't you, Gherran?" said the minister. "She's a challenge, isn't she? You want to undo all the Union's work."

She waited for him to acknowledge his lust. But he did not. He simply looked at her with a faint smile, as if challenging her to deny that she felt the same way.

She shrugged.

"What happens to her is unimportant as long as we can be certain we have extracted everything. Her knowledge is far more valuable than the life or faculties of a single spy. Do what you have to, Gherran, but be sure to keep me informed of your progress."

"Thank you, madam minister."

The prospect of the delights in store almost overcame Gherran's tiredness.

32
DUNNIS DELRUN

Dunnis Delrun was dreaming.

The afternoon had been long, difficult and traumatic. He had spent it in the company Chief Tcharn debriefing an agent who had worked undercover in the Empire for more than a decade. And what the agent had revealed was enough to give anyone nightmares.

The full debriefing would take many rotations. But Chief Tcharn had been in a hurry to get answers to some specific questions, and so the three men — Tcharn himself, the agent Val-Dor, and the aletheologist — had spent the afternoon and much of the evening in a small room while Tcharn went down his list of questions, Val-Dor did his best to answer them, and Dunnis Delrun gradually pieced together Operation Kālek.

The worst part of the investigation was the desperation in Val-Dor's voice as he pleaded for Tcharn to do something to help Per-Lem.

"Please. They'll destroy her mind. You've got to do something."

Val-Dor's voice was on the verge of breaking and his eyes were moist with unshed tears. Tcharn too seemed unusually affected, as if he shared his agent's desperation.

Now Dunnis Delrun slept fitfully, and as he slept he tossed and turned and made wordless sounds that might have been calls for help or shouts of terror. In his nightmare he was under a mindprobe, and the technicians were placing him in impossible, horrific scenarios: a hovercar losing power; a spaceship rent by a meteor; a nearby star suddenly going supernova. He would be pulled out from under the mindprobe just at the moment of death; and the voice of a faceless technician somewhere behind him would say: "Good. Now let's do it again." And a new horror would begin. He had died six times already. He was drenched in sweat, and the night was barely half over.

From somewhere a low-pitched, urgent buzzing intruded. For a while, his brain sought to assimilate the noise into the structure of his nightmare, but the buzzer continued and eventually his brain gave up the effort, and Dunnis Delrun began to waken.

A hand shook his shoulder.

"Uuuuhhhh...," he groaned.

He opened his eyes. A man dressed in the black and silver uniform of the military branch of the police was standing at his bedside.

"Dunnis Delrun?"

Delrun nodded as he wiped the sleep from his eyes and tried to ignore the layer of sweat covering his body..

"I'm sorry to intrude like this, sir. I tried the door buzzer, but there was no reply. I am afraid you are needed immediately at the Bureau of Defense. Deputy Strenk's orders."

The officer shrugged, informing Delrun more clearly than he could possibly have known that he knew no more, that he was truly sorry, but, well, it was his job.

Delrun nodded again and blinked his eyes awake.

"It's all right, officer. I understand. Give me a few chrons and I'll be with you. If you'd be so good as to wait outside."

The officer left the room, and the door closed behind him. With a long sigh, Delrun climbed out of bed. He wondered what Deputy Strenk wanted. Did it have anything to do with Val-Dor's shocking tale? What else could be so urgent that it could not wait until morning? He put the questions forcefully out of his mind; he would find out soon enough.

Thirty five chrons later, Dunnis Delrun was ushered into the office of the deputy chief. The military officer accompanying him bowed and then left, leaving the two men alone. A tired-looking Deputy Strenk greeted Delrun.

Delrun read the face and the slump of the body as other people might read a print-book. Strenk had not been to sleep yet tonight. More than that, Delrun observed, yesterday had been a more than usually rigorous day, both mentally and physically.

"I'm sorry to wake you Delrun," Strenk began, "but it's something that can't wait. Do you need a stimulant?"

Delrun shook his head. He noticed a container of recorder discs on one corner of the deputy chief's desk. Strenk glanced at the discs nervously.

"Delrun, we have an important job that needs to be done as quickly as possible. It's these discs. They are two-way holographic recordings made from a series of communications links over the course of the last half cycle. None of the commlinks lasts very long — the longest is a little over fifteen chrons. The same two people appear on all the discs except the last where, as you will see, they are joined by Chief Tcharn.

"The two people in question are President Rahl and the emperor. I want you to view these recordings and tell me everything you can about the state of mind of the participants. You are to permit no one else to view the recordings, or even to know of their existence, and you are to bring your conclusions directly to me or, if I am not available, to Chief Tcharn. I cannot stress how urgent this is. Chief Tcharn wants to know if there's anything on these recordings that indicates...."

Strenk's voice trailed off as he considered his words. He finished lamely, "Well, if there's anything abnormal at all."

"Are the discs genuine?"

"Yes. They came into my possession only in the past few decachrons and I've not had time to review them, but it's more important for you to see them than for me to do so. I can look at them later. For now, we need to know if things are really as they appear on these discs."

"By which you mean you suspect they are not?"

"Perhaps." Which meant: "Yes."

Delrun stood. "I'll go to a screening room, get a voice recorder from my office for my notes, and get to work."

"Thank you. Report to me or to Chief Tcharn as soon as you have something. I'll probably be here. It's going to be a long night for all of us."

Delrun nodded. Strenk was suffering from the early stages of sleep deprivation, but he obviously thought that whatever was on the discs was more important than sleep. Delrun picked up the discs and left.

He seated himself comfortably in the screening room and sorted the discs into reverse chronological order. Slipping the most recent disc into the player, he dimmed the lights and stared at the holoimage screen. He spoke into the voice recorder: "Dunnis Delrun. Comments on disc number sixty two." The disc began to play.

Anyone else would have concentrated on the conversations between the two men. But Delrun was an aletheologist. Only later, on the second or third viewing, would he pay any attention to the words; in the meantime he concentrated on the body language of the president and the emperor. Later on, the words would merely fill in the minor details and complete the picture that had already been drawn.

The president was seated behind his pawlwood desk at one side of the screen, the emperor behind a similar desk at the other. Off to one side of the president was Chief Tcharn, astonishment written on his face. The emperor looked at the president, his eyes flicking momentarily as he registered Tcharn's presence; his attention returned to the president as the latter began to speak.

The remnants of his tiredness dropped away from Delrun like a castoff cloak as he concentrated on the movements of the people before him. The eyebrows, the curls of the lips, the tilt of the shoulders, the eyes: these and the other hundred and one details of body language spoke to him far more eloquently than the words that issued from the mouths of the two heads of state.

By the time he was on the fourth disc, Dunnis Delrun was beginning to form worrying convictions about the Union's president.

He had never bothered to analyze the president's body language before because he had long ago realized that such an attempt was pointless. The body language of every successful politician screamed just one thing: "I'm prevaricating." Sometimes the spoken words weren't a complete lie, but never had he watched a politician for any length of time, whether in a debate, or making a speech, or during a campaign, and failed to discern endemic duplicity. After a few cycles of observing politicians on the news broadcasts, he had given up looking for one that was honest, and since then he had steadfastly refused to exercise his right to vote, ineffective and pointless though this protest was.

But the body language of President Rahl in the commlinks told quite a different story, and Delrun was sufficiently surprised that he began to pay attention to the president's words. And as he listened the aletheologist began for the first time to worry about the president's state of mind. President Rahl was determined to go down in history as the man who had brought an end to all war. That was the indisputable message conveyed by his body language. And the president firmly believed that this impossible goal was within his reach. He believed that the two powers could sweep aside centuries of history, that they could end the Status Quo and begin a "new age as partners in an economically based peace," if only the emperor and he were given free rein.

Delrun understood now why he had been told to look at these recordings. It was not so much that peace in itself was dangerous, although of course peace might eventually mean the dismantling of the Bureau of Defense and the loss of many jobs, including his own. What was more immediately dangerous was the president's mistaken belief that he and the emperor could create peace by themselves, simply by imposing it from above like some sort of edict. The president seemed deliberately to be ignoring the vast machinery of state that must be involved in any steps towards a meaningful and long-lasting peace. There were so many details that needed to be worked out: how to de-arm the two sides in a fair and rational way; how to build commercial ties; how to regulate travel; how to control the production of weapons. None of these seemed to be of any consequence to President Rahl. He simply wanted to declare peace by fiat and then take his place in the history books. He would not stand for reelection once the task was accomplished, for what could ever equal the attainment of galaxy-wide peace? He would simply retire and accept the neverending adulation of a grateful galaxy.

All these observations and much more Dunnis Delrun dictated into the voice recorder.

But there was something that he did not record. For some time something had been nagging at him, just below the edge of conscious-ness. When he came to the end of disc number forty two he paused, stood up, and stretched several times, trying to clear his mind. He sat down and replayed the disc, watching the president's demeanor carefully. Still he could not see anything wrong, but as the disc ended for the second time, he was more certain than ever that he was missing something. He pondered for a while, then moved unhappily on to disc number forty one.

Until this point, he had been concentrating on the president. Now he began to watch the emperor, and the next disc was barely halfway through when he finally realized what had been bothering him. For almost a full chron he sat without moving, unable to believe the ramifications of what he had just seen. The disc came to an end and for a while he simply stared at the blank holoimage screen.

He said nothing into the voice recorder.

Abruptly, he ejected the disc and reinserted the first disc he had played, the most recent one to be recorded. This time, he watched the emperor and ignored the president and Chief Tcharn. By the time the disc ended, he was certain. The president, even with his strange obsession with peace and his place in the history books, was at least who he appeared to be. But the person at the other end of the link was not the emperor.

In fact, the person at the other end of the link was not even a real person.

His heart beating rapidly, Delrun returned to the beginning of the disc and set the controls to replay it at one hundredth of normal speed.

33
TCHARN

The holoimage screen on the wall of Tcharn's office flashed once then
lit up with the image of the president. Tcharn looked up from his
work. With the first barely perceptible shake of the president's head
he knew what was coming.

"Chief Tcharn, I'm sorry. I just talked with the person with whom
we both spoke yesterday."

President Rahl was being prudent; he would not mention the emperor
by name because this commlink was being recorded by the bureau's
automatic recorders.

"The gentleman in question says that his hands are tied. He has
spoken with the minister concerned" — Amril Gdrena, and she had
done exactly what Tcharn would have done in her position: insisted
that there could be no deal involving Per-Lem — "and she apologizes
but says that no deal can be made along the lines we suggested."

The president shrugged and shook his head. "I'm sorry. Truly I
am. But I don't see what else I can do. It's out of my hands."

Tcharn nodded. "Yes, sir. I understand."

Yes, it's out of your hands, he thought. *But is it out of mine?*

"Feel free to contact me on this matter if you have any further
suggestions. I think that we should meet again to discuss matters.
Say, tomorrow at noon?"

Tcharn agreed to the appointment, the president cut the commlink, and the screen flickered to gray.

Tcharn leaned back in his chair, which adjusted itself as he shifted his weight. His eyes remained locked on the gray screen, but he was deep in thought, his mind far away, planning, trying to concoct some way to extricate his daughter.

For a long time he remained motionless as he turned plans and possibilities over in his mind, seeking some way out of the situation.

He started with surprise when his secretary suddenly appeared on the screen and announced: "Dunnis Delrun to see you, sir. He says it's urgent."

"Send him in."

Tcharn was still struggling to collect himself when Delrun entered.

The aletheologist looked just about all in. Dark semicircles accented his eyes; his hair was unkempt and hung in straggles down the sides of his face; his eyes had the vacant look of a man deprived of sleep, and his movements were abnormally slow, as if they required conscious effort. The door slid closed behind him.

Tcharn stood to touch hands. There was a clammy patina of perspiration on Delrun's skin.

"Have a chair, Delrun. What can I do for you? Is it about Val-Dor?"

For a moment Delrun was at a loss; then he remembered. It seemed like so long ago.

"I don't want this conversation recorded, sir."

Tcharn frowned and then slid a finger silently across the touch-sensitive panel inlaid in the surface of his desk.

"The recorders are off."

"Thank you, sir. I'm sorry if I'm intruding, but this was so important that I thought I had to tell you immediately. It has nothing to do with Val-Dor. It concerns the conversations that have been taking place between the president and the emperor."

"You've seen the discs then?"

"Yes, sir, I have. I've been looking at them half the night and all this morning. Deputy Strenk gave them to me. Ordinarily I would have reported to him, but in the circumstances...." His voice trailed off.

"The circumstances?"

"Yes, sir. I must emphasize that a complete investigation of the discs will require a lot more time. But what I've seen already is too important to wait.

"There are sixty two discs, each containing a record of a single conversation between the president and the emperor. In only one disc, the most recent one, does a third person appear. That person, of course, is yourself."

Tcharn nodded.

"I have looked at every one of the discs, but most of them only cursorily. There has been no time to examine them all in detail, I just wanted to be certain that my diagnosis was not in error. It is not."

Get on with it, thought Tcharn wearily. The thought reflected in a twitch in his face. The aletheologist saw it, and pressed hurriedly on.

"For the first few discs, I concentrated on the president. It is my opinion, on the basis of what I've seen so far, that the president is speaking without guile. He believes everything he says. He is driven by a deep desire to go down in history as the man who ended the Status Quo and initiated a true and sustained peace between Union and Empire. He also believes that together, he and the emperor are on the verge of bringing this change about."

He paused.

"But...," supplied the chief of Defense.

Delrun nodded.

"Exactly. But. But the emperor is a different matter entirely. Once I turned my attention to the emperor's body language I saw immediately that there was something wrong, something very wrong indeed. Not to put too fine a point on it, I believe that not only is the image on the discs not that of the emperor, but that image is, technically, not of a human at all."

He stopped, waiting for Tcharn's response.

It was some time coming. Tcharn seemed to consider several possibilities before he eventually said: "What do you mean: 'not of a human'?"

"Once I started observing the emperor, it was obvious there was something wrong, although it took me a while to realize what it was. It was the eyes that finally gave the game away. It was well done. It has certainly fooled the president all this time, and it seems to have taken you in on the one occasion you saw it. I believe that the image of the emperor on the recordings is a model generated by a databox.

"They could not risk using an actor, because an actor's body language might have given him away, even to someone as unskilled in reading it as President Rahl, and in any case they could never be sure that no one else was eavesdropping or reviewing the discussions later. It would require a remarkably skilled actor to convincingly maintain the body language of someone like the emperor, someone who for twenty five chrons has ruled a third of the galaxy. Instead, they decided on a simpler and less risky course.

"You will see that the emperor is always seated behind his desk. You will also observe that he is parsimonious with his body motions: he rarely gestures with his hands, he almost never alters his position in his chair; almost the only movements he makes are changes of facial expression as he speaks. By limiting the view, they — whoever 'they' are — they gave their databoxes enough time to manipulate the features of a digital image to match what might reasonably be expected from the real emperor. Somewhere out of sight, a real person speaks the emperor's lines. These are converted into a facsimile of the emperor's voice."

"Is that really possible?"

"Certainly, given sufficiently powerful databoxes. There would always be a slight delay while the necessary calculations and transformations were being made, but the procedure is eminently practical. In fact, once I realized what was happening I looked for traces of the delay that the procedure must insert into the emperor's movements, but I could find no trace of it. That, I think, points more to the quality of the databoxes being used than to any defect in my reasoning."

"You seem very sure of yourself, but I don't really understand. Why couldn't it be the emperor?"

"Simple, sir. They made a mistake with the eyes. I'm sure you've heard it said many times, mostly by poets and lovers, that the eyes are the most expressive part of the body. In fact, although the statement is not technically correct — the most expressive parts of the body are the muscles of the face and the motions of the hands — the eyes do give away far more than the uninitiated would guess.

"Actually, they really did quite a good job, which was perhaps why it took me so long to spot their mistake. They varied the blink rate correctly, matching it to the changes in the emperor's emotional state as he spoke and listened. What they forgot to do was to vary the details of the blinks.

"I've examined several of the discs in detail, and the emperor's eyes always blink in synchronism. To put it in layman's terms: whenever one eye blinks, so does the other, exactly at the same moment. That's unnatural. Especially under any kind of stress, there is always a slight preference of one eye over the other. Either the blinks of the two eyes last for a different length of time, or one eye habitually closes or opens fractionally before the other. There is no such pattern on the recordings. The blinks in the two eyes always match one another exactly, starting and ending together. Someone forgot to include natural blink behavior when they wrote the program that constructed the emperor's image.

"To test my theory, I went to the archives and retrieved a disc of the emperor's coronation.

"As I'm sure you remember, the emperor was just six cycles old at the time of the coronation. In fact, the emperor's coronation is one of the very few times he has been seen in public and recorded in close-up. I discovered that all the recordings we have of him since then are long-distance shots. But during the coronation the imperial newscast service broadcast a clear shot of the emperor's face that persisted for almost three full chrons.

"I am sure that if you submit the recordings to a gerontologist, he will tell you that the face on the recent discs could conceivably be the same as that of the boy at the coronation. But there is not the slightest shadow of a doubt that they are not the same person. It is simply not possible. The languages of the two faces are totally different. The boy's face is not only far more expressive, but its blink behavior is perfectly normal. In particular, the right eye takes a fraction longer to blink than the left, closing marginally earlier and opening slightly later. Almost every blink recorded in the three-chron transmission shows that pattern. The face in the coronation images is indeed that of a young boy being crowned emperor. The face in the recent recordings is an artificial construction depicting someone's idea of what that boy would look like now."

The aletheologist halted, waiting for questions.

Tcharn ruminated for some time. The question he eventually asked was not one that Delrun had anticipated.

"Resources," he said. "How much in the way of resources would it take to pull something like this off?"

"This took careful planning over a long period. The face seems to be a good match for what I would expect the emperor to look like, although, as I said, you really need to check with an expert in aging. But the real-time construction of the digital image would require both unusual computational power and quite remarkable programming expertise. Then there is the matter of the commlink circuit. This was obviously a direct link between the Study and the imperial palace. No, I would say that this could only have been done by someone with extraordinary resources at his command. Indeed, it is hard to see how it could all have been managed without the emperor's connivance."

"Suppose that sometime soon after his coronation the emperor was in an accident that left him permanently disfigured — disfigured so badly that for some reason the damage could not be repaired. Might he not then arrange for a digitally reconstructed image of his face to be superimposed on his body? I admit it seems a bit farfetched, but it's possible, isn't it?"

"I had the same thought, sir, but it isn't likely. I looked at the commlink recordings made shortly after the telebroadcasts informed us of the death of the empress."

"A bacterial infection, or so they claimed. Yes, I remember."

"Well, sir, I looked especially closely at the disc made immediately after the empress died. The president, as you would expect, began by offering his condolences, but the emperor's body language as he responded was no different from what it was on any of the other discs. I grant that we know nothing about the relationship between the emperor and the empress, but I do not believe it possible that there would have been no change in his body language after her death. He should have held his body differently, reacted differently — more slowly — but in fact there was no difference at all. The program they are using emulates very well the way a person responds to stresses and to changes in emotional state in the course of a conversation; what they forgot to do was to change the baseline after the empress's death. It's an easy mistake to make, but one that simply strengthens my conviction that whatever is at the other end of those commlinks, it is not the emperor."

"You sound very sure of yourself, Delrun. How certain are you really? What's the chance you are mistaken?"

"When I suggest that it's a computer image instead of a live person?" Delrun shrugged. "Small but finite, I suppose. One in ten thousand, perhaps, although I think that's conservative. I'm all but certain that the facial expressions are artificial. When I say that it is not the emperor? None. I haven't made a mistake about that. I'd bet my life on it."

"And the life of the Union?"

"Sir?"

"Never mind." Tcharn shook his head. "It wasn't a fair question. Thank you, Delrun. You've given me a lot to think about."

"Shall I continue my analysis of the recordings? Or do you want me to attend any more sessions with Val-Dor? And do you want me to tell Deputy Strenk my conclusions? He told me to report to him."

"No; go home and get some sleep. You've earned it. And by the time you wake up, it probably won't make any difference what you do."

Delrun looked at him quizzically. For once, Delrun found it impossible to interpret the meaning behind the chief's words.

34

Amril Gdrena

It was not often that Amril Gdrena allowed herself the luxury of smugness, but for once she permitted a slight smile to play around the corner of her lips — for it was rare that such an unlooked-for opportunity could be turned so much to advantage.

President Rahl was putty in her hands, and had been ever since he first attempted to contact the emperor half a cycle ago. Not for the first time, she found herself amazed that the inhabitants of the Union could have been so corporately stupid as to elect Rahl to a position of such power. He was so weak, so grasping, so transparent, and therefore so easily manipulated. His election was a textbook demonstration of a fact she had known intuitively long before it was explained in her political science courses at the academy: that while democracy was popular with the people, it was fundamentally flawed because under it people were governed by a leader who pandered to popularity.

The benign dictatorship under which the Empire operated was infinitely superior. The people who lived in the Empire knew that their leader, like the advisors whom he chose, was responsible not merely to them but to something far more important — the very notion of the Empire.

And now that the fundamental rottenness of the democratic system was eating away at the very foundation of the Union, it engendered the smug smile on her face. How appropriate it all was.

Today's commlink transmission had gone easily enough, although scheduling conversations with the idiot Rahl on two consecutive rotations had been a little difficult. The transmissions required Gdrena's presence, for it was her words that came out of the emperor's mouth.

She wondered how the president would react if he ever discovered that when he thought he was speaking to the emperor he was actually discussing peace with a digital representation of Amril Gdrena herself, her voice and facial patterns masked by instantaneous digital editing to simulate those of a thirty-one-cycle-old male emperor. Her smile became a grin, and she almost laughed out loud. The fool would probably fry his brains with a kill-gun. He was that kind of man. Insufferably weak. If it weren't for the fact that he was titular head of the Union, she would never have wasted as much as a chron's effort on such a pathetic creature. But his position made all her work worthwhile.

The fool thinks history is going to remember him, she thought. Well, he was right about that.

It was a short walk from the communications room to the laboratory where Per-Lem was being debriefed. Today was the third session. Gherran was already standing beside the control panel, awaiting her arrival. Next to him stood Brynt Veel, his eyes on the comatose figure in the coffin-like box that confined the subject while she was under the probe.

Gherran smiled tightly when the minister entered the lab. Now that she was here he could begin. He turned to the control panel and began to press buttons. The technicians became more alert.

Gherran himself controlled the probe, as he had done during the second session. He had explained to the minister that the probe needed a more delicate touch on these runs. On the first run, intended simply to provide a glimpse into the spy's brain, it had been more important that he oversee the operation than that he be in direct control. But now that deep-seated memories were being revealed, Gherran would entrust the controls to no one else. One false move, a momentary lapse in concentration, and irreparable harm could result.

But what he had not shared with anyone was his fear at what he had seen when Per-Lem came out of her coma after the second run. He was worried that Per-Lem's mind was already beginning to react to the intrusions, even though he had barely begun to mine the lode of information that was stored inside her skull. Ninety nine hundredths of what she knew was still locked up inside the cells of her brain, and Amril Gdrena wanted him to extract all of her knowledge — *all* of it — and place it safely in the mindprobe databank. Worse, after the first run he had all but promised that he could do it. But could he? How much longer could Per-Lem survive?

He watched the minister nervously out the corner of his eye. She crossed to Per-Lem. Per-Lem looked like she was asleep, relaxed and emotionless under the metallic cap of the active mindprobe. Gdrena turned away and approached Gherran. Gherran transferred his attention to the display of Per-Lem's brain activity. As he slowly steered the probe towards a drab gray-green area, he became tense.

Gherran tried to ignore the presence of the minister, but it was impossible. Brynt Veel he could just about deal with, but Amril Gdrena herself.... He felt a sudden excretion of sweat coating his hands. Lifting his hands from the steering mechanism to wipe them on his uniform, he realized that they were trembling. He hurriedly wiped them and replaced them on the control.

Somewhere deep inside his head a doubting voice insisted: *Gherran, you're the best there is. But you're not good enough for this. You're going to damage her before you can get much out of her.*

It had begun during the second session. He had watched carefully the signs of confusion when the spy, still thinking she was Lystra Ten-Wer, woke from her coma. The signs had not been obvious — at least not yet obvious enough for anyone else to see that something was amiss — but he had seen them clearly enough. Psychoshock-induced schizophrenia was already beginning. Another session, perhaps two if he was both careful and lucky, but after that her brain would, for all practical purposes, be useless.

And he dreaded to think what the consequence of that would be for himself.

So he had formulated a desperate plan. Today, instead of extracting memories, he was going to try to join the two ids that shared Per-Lem's skull. He was going to break down the barrier between Per-Lem and Lystra Ten-Wer.

Nothing like this had ever been attempted and he did not know if it was even possible. He would try to ensure that the self that was Per-Lem remained in control, so that she would understand all that had happened to her. She would remember her programming and her life as Lystra Ten-Wer; but she would know that she was really Per-Lem, Union spy.

He stabbed at the magnification button and his eyes narrowed as the probe approached the greenish wall that represented the barrier between her two selves.

Gherran had made good use of his time since the last run. He had programmed the simulator with the map of Per-Lem's brain they had obtained from the first exploratory probe, letting the machine fill in the unresolved details with random but internally consistent links. Then he had performed this operation on the simulator a total of eight times. Twice he had killed Per-Lem. Three times, the simulation had included unexpectedly complex chains of links and he had had to withdraw the probe, unable to master the complexity. Out of those three times he had only once succeeded in withdrawing the probe without damaging the subject. The other two times he had impossibly scrambled the contents of the simulated brain. In only three of the operations had he succeeded in removing the wall between her two selves. And only once had the result been what he had hoped for: a more or less complete and functioning Per-Lem. In the other two cases, full and immediate schizophrenic psychoshock had been induced. All told, then, only one out of eight attempts had been successful. Little wonder that the layer of sweat reformed when the minister asked, "What's that area you're heading for, Gherran?"

He swallowed. His mouth was dry, and his voice was a shade too hoarse as he replied, "It's a kind of wall between her two halves, the Per-Lem half and the Lystra Ten-Wer half. I've been thinking that it will make memory extraction much easier if we can breach that wall. That's all I plan to do today, but if it works out it should make the rest of our job much easier." It was almost the truth. "It shouldn't take long," he added.

And indeed it shouldn't. This was, theoretically, a brief exercise. It was a simple matter of going into Per-Lem's brain and removing a blockage. That was all. Nothing to it.

She was warm. She was pleasantly tired. She was comfortable. She was asleep. Somehow, she knew that she was sleeping, and the thought struck her as slightly odd, because wasn't one normally unaware that one was dreaming when a dream was actually taking place? But she wasn't dreaming, not really. She was simply asleep, wallowing comfortably in a gentle, reassuring lack of consciousness.

She tried to remember how she had come to be here; but then decided that she did not really care. There was a faint familiarity to the feeling. Somewhere, some part of her brain told her that it was like being in a light drug-induced coma. Yes, that was it. Perhaps she was undergoing a surgical procedure. But no, that did not seem quite right....

She became vaguely aware that she was supported by some sort of inclined bed, warm and giving. She decided that she preferred unconsciousness, and slipped away once more.

The next thing she was aware of was peculiarly unpleasant. She was still asleep, but now there was a harsh edge to everything. Her heart was beating wildly — she could hear the blood throbbing in her ears: *ker-thud, ker-thud, ker-thud*, as if she had been frightened, although she could not remember what it was that had frightened her. Or perhaps she was anticipating something that was about to happen. She could feel her breath coming in short, shallow pants. From some place outside herself she heard a voice issuing loud, abrupt commands. Even though the voice was loud, in her anœsia she did not understand the words. She slipped away again....

"Watch out now. Here she comes. We'll know in a chron."

This time she understood. At least, she understood the individual words, but the meaning behind them escaped her: who will know what in a chron?

She had been asleep, she knew that much, but now she was waking up. It had not been an ordinary, natural sleep. The room around her was brightly lit; she could tell that from the yellow-tinged red of her closed eyelids. There was an unpleasant taste in her mouth, as if a residue of burnt food had been lying in it for a considerable period of time. She breathed deeply and, with an effort, swallowed. It felt as if there was something stuck in her throat. She swallowed again, a little more easily this time. She bunched her eyes tightly then tried to open them. The sudden brightness engendered an instantaneous headache. She closed her eyes again, and forced herself to breathe deeply. One... two... three... four... five. She opened her eyes again.

She blinked several times. She was in a room that was ablaze with artificial light. She was leaning backwards against something soft: a bed, a stretcher, she could not tell. Gathered around were a number of people, most of them wearing a uniform she didn't recognize. She knew it wasn't a hospital, but could not consciously follow the logic that had led her to that conclusion.

One of the people in uniform, a rather overweight, unpleasant-looking man in late middle age, was close enough that she could see a sheen of sweat on his face. She did not recognize him.

"What's your name?" he asked with an odd belligerence.

She knew her name, of course, and struggled to say it.

It was difficult to speak. She swallowed again, but her throat remained dry and constricted. She could still taste the overwhelming flavor of something burnt; it seemed to come from somewhere deep inside her body.

"Per-Lem."

It did not sound like her voice, but she knew that it was she who had spoken. She listened to the sound of the word, rolling it around inside her head. An age went by while the word reverberated inside her skull: *Per-Lem, Per-Lem, Per-Lem.*

Then she thought: *But that's not my name.*

She closed her eyes to concentrate, and something inside her head gave way.

She opened her mouth.

She screamed.

35

AMRIL GDRENA

"Put her back in her cell for now."

The minister issued the order brusquely, then turned and let her furious glare fall on Gherran. Nobody moved as they waited to see what form her anger would take. To the surprise of everyone — except, perhaps, Brynt Veel — she adjusted her features, the anger ebbing away and a calm determination taking its place.

"This is not the place to discuss what just happened. Come to my office, Gherran. You too, Veel."

She pivoted on one foot and swept out of the room.

The technician who had stood over Per-Lem while the operation had been underway extended his hand to the woman with the confused, vacant stare who was now standing motionless next to the coffin-like box.

"Come with me," he said gently, as if he were talking to a young child or a favored pet. "We won't hurt you."

The woman hesitantly stretched out her hand and grasped his arm. She looked directly into the technician's eyes. The technician turned his head away. He was not strong enough for the look of confused helplessness in those eyes.

"Please," she said. "Where is this place? And who am I?"

"Never mind. We can get to that later. Please come with me now. I expect you're tired. Wouldn't you like to rest?"

She nodded vacantly.

"Rest.... Yes. I am tired. So tired. It would be nice to sleep."

Then she paused, and, as if she had no memory of having already asked the questions, she said, "Where is this place? And who am I?"

The technician led her gently from the room.

"So, Gherran. A drink?"

The three of them — Gherran, Brynt Veel and the minister herself — were in Amril Gdrena's office. The minister was standing next to a hatch recessed in the wall, her fingers hovering above a control panel. Gherran wiped his face. Despite the controlled climate of the building, he had been feeling uncomfortably warm for the past few chrons, and sweat was beginning to trickle into his eyes. He wondered how he was going to explain what had happened. Brynt Veel was already seated, slightly apart from the others at the rear of the room, where Gherran could not see him without turning around.

"Yes, please," said Gherran. "It's not too early for a Solaris Special, is it?"

"No. Good idea. I think I'll have one as well."

Gherran was surprised. He had not known that Amril Gdrena drank. He began to feel a little more comfortable. Perhaps this wasn't going to be so bad after all. And it really wasn't his fault, was it?

For a dreadful moment after Per-Lem had emitted that awful scream, he had thought he had read his death on the minister's face. But she seemed to have calmed down now. Doubtless she understood that he had been doing his best. Now she wanted to discuss the situation to see what might be salvaged. All the stories about her anger were probably just that: stories.

Amril Gdrena collected the drinks from the machine and handed Gherran his red fluorescent Solaris Special in its transparent cup. She carried her own drink around to the other side of her desk and sat. Gherran took the opportunity to begin to make inroads into his drink. He immediately felt better, and his brow began to cool. The relaxants in the Solaris Special were exactly what the situation required.

Gdrena placed her drink on the desk.

"Perhaps you can answer a few questions for me about what we just saw," she said.

"Yes, yes. Certainly. Most unfortunate," said Gherran.

He took another mouthful. The drink was already half gone.

"So what happened?"

"I'm not exactly certain. I thought I had succeeded. I removed a small part of the blockage that was holding her two personas apart. I tried to do it in a way that would permit the Per-Lem persona to recognize and overcome Lystra Ten-Wer. Everything was looking good when I removed the probe. Her mind was adjusting, transferring links, trying to form a single coherent self-image. I don't know what went wrong. The symptoms aren't quite like anything I've ever seen before. It's not classical psychoshock or schizophrenia; it's something else."

"Can anything be done to save her mind?"

Gherran waited a long while before answering. In the lacuna, he finished his drink. Gdrena's Solaris Special remained untouched on the desk.

"You know," Gherran began thoughtfully, "it's not really that anything is lost. All the memories — the real ones of Per-Lem and the implanted ones of Lystra Ten-Wer — they're all still inside her head. It's just that what we call the memoretic pointer sequence, the parts of her brain that tell her where to find memoretic information, are scrambled. All the information is still there, it's just that she doesn't know how to access it properly."

"Could we put that right?"

"No. Perhaps there's a way, but I don't know how to do it. Possibly the person who implanted the persona of Lystra Ten-Wer would know how to reconstruct something useful out of the mess. I certainly don't. As I mentioned before, minister, the Union seems to be far ahead of us in this area. They might be able to bring order to the chaos, but I'm afraid it's beyond us."

"But if the information is there, couldn't we extract it even if she doesn't know how to do so herself?"

"No."

Gherran began to speak quickly and confidently, partly because of the Solaris Special and partly because of his familiarity with the subject.

"When we extract memories, our system relies on the presence of a more or less valid memoretic pointer sequence. That's what makes memory extraction in her case rather more difficult than usual. In her case, the ordinary series of pointers is occasionally broken, and where those breaks occur are the places where her memory has been changed. For example, you remember the reports from the monitorship in the demilitarized zone? There's a break in the pointer sequence there, and that's how I could tell there was something amiss. But such breaks are rare, and it's because they are rare that they stand out. What's happened now is that the sequence of pointers has become chaotic. There's no obvious pattern. Which means that we can no longer reconstruct anything useful. You understand?"

"I think so, yes. And her condition is permanent? She won't get better?"

"No. Entropy tends to increase. Breaks in the pointer sequence often occur naturally as we age. Things get worse rather than better. The only reason that our memory systems don't break down completely is that there are checks built into healthy brains, so that when a pointer is damaged it can often be reconstructed from undamaged information. If everything is damaged, as has happened to her, then I'm afraid there's nothing that we, or the brain itself, can do. Her condition is permanent."

Amril Gdrena said nothing. She lifted her drink and eyed the vermillion liquid thoughtfully through the transparent walls of the container. The silence in the room became heavy.

Suddenly, Gdrena threw the drink violently against a wall. The container cracked loudly, and the drink spilled out in an ugly rhodamine splash. Gdrena looked at the mark on the wall.

"Kill him," she said, not moving her eyes from the stain.

By the time Gherran's mind had processed the words for the third time, searching for some meaning other than the obvious one, he was aware of a sound behind him. He began to rise from his chair, turning towards Brynt Veel. His last sight was of Veel's unsmiling face. He never did see the kill-gun in Brynt Veel's hand.

Amril Gdrena was alone in her office. After Gherran's body had been removed, Brynt Veel had decided that only a fool would remain in the minister's presence, and he had suddenly remembered an urgent task that required his presence over at the Kivra Space Military Academy on the far side of the city. Now the minister sat unmoving behind her desk, her hands steepled in front of her face, staring at the stain of the Solaris Special on the wall.

The holoimage screen suddenly flickered into life. The minister's eyes slid listlessly toward the face of her secretary. Too late, she realized that she had not issued an order that she was not to be disturbed.

"Excuse me, madam minister. There is an incoming commlink for you."

"Go away."

"I'm sorry, madam minister. Brynt Veel did give orders that you weren't to be disturbed..."

If Amril Gdrena had been in a better mood she would have smiled.

The secretary was still talking. "...but the commlink is encrypted with imperial cipher Θ-6, yet it seems to originate inside Union territory."

The secretary sounded confused, as well she might. How could a transmission encrypted with the Empire's most secure cipher be coming from beyond the borders of the Empire?

"And it's for me?"

"The commlink request is directed to you by name, madam minister."

"And there's no indication of who initiated the request?"

"No, madam minister."

"Let it through."

The face of her secretary disappeared, to be replaced moments later by that of a large man in his late fifties.

"Chief Tcharn. This is an unexpected pleasure. And using our own cipher. How thoughtful."

Tcharn nodded in greeting. "Minister, you have my word that this transmission is not being recorded at my end. Since it crosses the demilitarized zone, it is doubtless being intercepted by Union monitors and, I presume, imperial ones. It is, however, as you have noticed, Θ-6 encrypted and therefore immune from decipher. I urge you to turn off your personal recorder. You will not want a record of this conversation."

Gdrena raised an interrogative eyebrow. "You have a flair for the dramatic, Tcharn. Or perhaps merely the melodramatic. However, I am prepared to trust your judgement."

She pressed a button on her desk.

"The recorder has been turned off. You may now speak freely."

"Minister, I would have spoken freely anyway. It was for your own protection that I suggested no recording be made."

"My protection? And from what do I need protection?"

She sounded relaxed, but Amril Gdrena could feel the hairs at the back of her neck beginning to rise. There was something wrong here, something very wrong.

Amril Gdrena was unused to having the initiative lie with someone else. Before Tcharn could begin to explain, she continued: "I expect you've heard from that moron Rahl about the decision regarding your daughter."

The shock on Tcharn's face was obvious. He hadn't guessed that she knew about the agent's relationship to him.

"I am sorry, Tcharn. We both know the decision was mine. President Rahl was trying to convince the emperor to agree to an arrangement that would most decidedly not have been in the best interests of the Empire. Fortunately, the emperor recognized that the matter was sufficiently delicate that he needed to discuss it with me before rendering a decision.

"I am sorry, but I could not in good conscience agree to such a one-sided exchange. I'm sure you understand when I tell you that your daughter is the greatest prize to fall into our hands in a generation or more. I am afraid there's nothing you can offer in exchange that we are likely to find acceptable.

"I've just come from interrogating her, Tcharn. You can do whatever you like with our agents; it doesn't make any difference, she's worth more than them all."

She smiled benignantly. At the other end of the link, Chief Tcharn made no attempt to hide the fact that he was rattled. He leaned forward.

Always a mistake, thought Gdrena. *It shows you aren't in control.* The initiative had passed safely to her. These unionists, even the few like Tcharn who were not fools, really were easy to handle.

"You know she's my daughter? How?"

"Of course I know, Tcharn. I'm not a fool."

"I never thought you were, Gdrena. How is she?"

"As well as can be expected."

"What does that mean?"

"We had her under the mindprobe. Some temporary disorientation is to be expected." She smiled pleasantly. Or at least as pleasantly as Amril Gdrena was capable of smiling. "Now, why did you call? Was it simply to plead for your daughter? Or was there something more? I'm sure you are busy; and if *you* aren't, I'm afraid *I* am."

She looked at the screen expectantly, secretly certain that the defense chief would have nothing more to say. She was surprised when he appeared to collect himself.

"Yes," he said, more quietly now. "I wanted to tell you that I know about the emperor."

It was Amril Gdrena's turn to be rattled.

"The emperor? What do you mean?"

"I've been reviewing recordings of the discussions. How do you think the president will react when I tell him he's been discussing peace with a digital figment of someone's imagination? I don't think he'll take kindly to the deception, do you? I assume you're the one behind it?"

Amril Gdrena responded without missing a beat: "So you've discovered our little deception, have you? Well, it's only to be expected, I suppose. To be honest, I'm surprised it's taken you this long."

She hoped that the lie had been delivered smoothly enough to convince the defense chief. It would be most unfortunate if her deception were to fail through the interference of one of the president's minions.

"The Inner Council advised the emperor that it would be a mistake to engage in direct negotiations with the president; his body language might give too much away. The emperor is not a skilled negotiator, so we initiated this harmless deceit. Actually, I expected your side to do something similar. I know that the president insists he is acting alone, without the knowledge or consent of his advisors, but of course we have never believed that. No one could be that stupid, not even President Rahl."

Tcharn grunted.

Gdrena continued, "Anyway, we decided to use a combination of digital superposition and voice masking. Is that what you wanted to tell me? That you've only just realized that your president has been talking to an image?"

She smiled at him; her sweetest smile yet.

One look at his face was enough to tell her that she had him. He was confused and spent, and for a long time he just sat there, impotent. When he finally did speak, he returned disjointedly to the subject of Per-Lem.

"My daughter. You'll kill her, won't you?"

Gdrena pondered her answer. Tcharn was a defeated man. Her spur-of-the-moment explanation had convinced him that his great insight about the commlinks was worthless. No doubt he had been expecting to take his revelation to the president and use it to convince him that throughout his conversations with the "emperor" Amril Gdrena had been simply trying to lull him into lowering the Union's defenses. Now that the use of a digital image had been explained, his evidence was worthless. And the conversations would continue.

"I make no promises, Tcharn, but I see no reason why your daughter should be harmed. She will tell us everything, of course."

Tcharn nodded dejectedly. He understood. Amril Gdrena was in the process of learning all about Operation Kālek, and much more besides.

Gdrena was still talking, and Tcharn struggled to pay attention.

"Your mindprobe technology is much more advanced than ours," she was saying. "I have already ordered an increased budget for mindprobe research to try to catch up. It was only through the skill of our best technician that we succeeded in entering your daughter's true memories. He told me he was in awe of what your people had accomplished. But it's all undone now. The last time I saw her she was being taken back to her cell. She won't be mistreated. You have my word on that."

"You'll keep using mindprobes on her, though, won't you?"

"Yes, as soon as she is strong enough. Though I'm told that it may even be possible to do everything with a passive probe now. She still doesn't consciously know anything about her true past, but her Per-Lem persona is now close to the surface, and it might be accessible to a passive mindprobe. I'll talk with our experts. If there's a way to avoid using an active probe, we'll do so. I'm sorry; that's the most I can promise.

"In fact," she brightened, as if an idea had just occurred to her, "perhaps when we've finished we'll be able to return her. I can't promise that, of course, and it will be several cycles before we would be ready to negotiate on the matter."

She paused, and a frown crossed her face as if a serendipitous possibility had just occurred to her.

"But, you know, maybe there is one thing you could do that would spare her all the mental trauma."

She waited for him to nibble.

"What do you mean?" He was leaning forward again.

"It's just a suggestion." She paused. "There is one person who would be even more valuable to us than your daughter."

She stopped, letting him work it out.

"You mean... me?"

"Exactly; we'd swap her for you."

For a moment, just for a moment, she thought he was going to bite. But then the defense chief wearily shook his head.

"No. Much as I love her, that would be to betray the Union. I can never do that, not even to spare my daughter pain. You win, Gdrena. If she remembers that I'm her father, please give her my love. If she doesn't, at least tell her that Chief Tcharn is very, very sorry for everything that has happened. Will you do that for me?"

Gdrena nodded. "Yes, of course. It's the least I can do. Now, there really are other things I should be doing. Good rotation, Chief Tcharn. Feel free to contact me again if you change your mind."

"Good rotation, minister."

The screen went blank. For a long time Amril Gdrena stared at it, lost in thought.

36
HWANG

The whole process took considerably longer than Hwang had expected. Before any of the practical work could be started — testing components, constructing converters so that the ship could power the terrestrial electronics, running simulations — he had to plod through the vital but tedious calculations and recalculations necessary to define completely his theory of timeshifting.

It was only slowly that a full theory began to emerge. He was fortunate that the onboard computers were available to perform and check most of the abstruse calculations, although even for this relatively mundane task he required Rum-Lem's assistance, for the computers functioned in ways that Hwang did not fully understand and their interface was aural, so his inability to speak Rum-Lem's language made the devices inscrutable to him.

The task of checking and rechecking Hwang's emerging theory of timeshifting occupied the pair for nearly a full week. It would have been completed in half that time were it not for the fact that, with Rum-Lem's unwitting assistance, Hwang used the opportunity to ask the research computer many questions that were plaguing physicists on Earth back in normal time. Hwang did not always completely understand the answers, for he did not limit himself to questions that were in his own narrow field of expertise, but by the time he was satisfied that his theory of timeshifting was more or less complete, he was as certain as he could be that if their attempt to return to normal time was successful, his mentor's record of two Nobels (three if one included the award that was certain to come as a result of the very experiment that had sent Hwang into forward time) would soon fall.

For while he had been standing on the burning, desertified surface of Kivra Hwang had come to the conclusion that, were he ever to return home, there was little to be gained and much to be lost by trying to convince the world of what had happened to him. Even a spirited defense of the reality of non-terrestrial intelligent life would be enough to brand him untrustworthy as a scientist — all reputable scientists had long understood that the lack of contact with other intelligent species was all but definitive proof that no such species existed. To tell the truth would confine him to the life of an eccentric outsider. Instead of becoming an outcast, Hwang's plan would ensure that he became the very opposite: the most revered scientist of all time. If he ever made it home.

Getting ready was painstaking work. While Rum-Lem fabricated a power converter Hwang tested every subsystem in what had once been the quantum bubble antigravity experiment and now was called by the two of them simply "the Device."

Larger and larger subsystems were tested. Everything seemed to be working as Hwang expected. Eventually, everything had been checked and re-checked. The theory was complete. The problem was that there was no way to test it adequately. They would get only one chance.

The trip back to normal time was going to take far more power than the journey into forward time, and he soon realized that the experiment would destroy the Device. If it didn't work the first time, there would be no second chance. The Device might work once, but it could never be made to work a second time without access to spare parts.

It was not until the eve of the run that Rum-Lem asked Hwang to explain his theory of timeshifting in simple terms, if that was possible.

They were seated in the dining area, trying not to think of the morrow. A heavy uncertainty hung in the air. Hwang gathered his thoughts for several moments, then opened a notebook that had been in the lab when it had been thrust into forward time. He flicked past pages filled with neat, compact equations until he reached a clean sheet. Quickly he sketched a diagram on the page. Then he began to explain the outline of his theory, making reference to the picture.

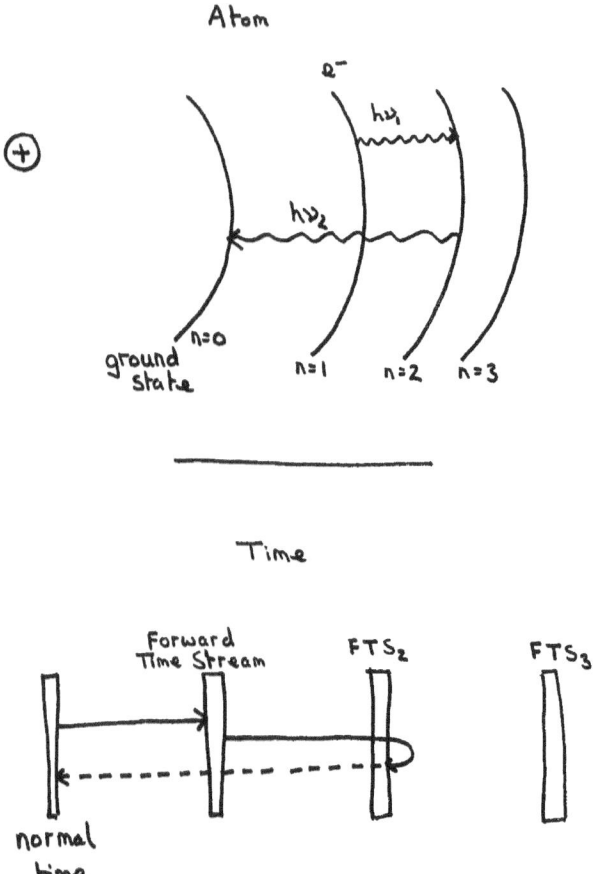

In principle, what Hwang was attempting was quite simple. When the Device began to operate, it would generate a timeshift field which should expand rapidly to include the entire space ship before it became unstable and collapsed, sending everything it contained to a different timestream.

At the moment of collapse, he explained, everything inside the field would be sent, not backward to normal time, but forward.

Rum-Lem protested: "I don't understand; I thought we had already moved forward through time. Normal time is behind us. We need to go backward if we want to get back to normal time."

"Quite right. But just as it is theoretically impossible to build a time machine that will go backward in time, so it is impossible for us to generate a field that will send us back to normal time."

Rum-Lem, baffled, began, "But...."

"There's a trick," Hwang interrupted with a smile.

He referred Rum-Lem to his notebook.

"You remember my analogy with an atom?"

"Yes."

"Well, think of an electron orbiting a nucleus. Suppose that the electron is not in the orbit with the lowest energy, the ground state, but we want to force it somehow into that state. We can't take energy away from the electron, there's no way to do that, but what we can do is to *add* energy. And if we add the right amount of energy, we can force the electron into a new state that is less stable than the old one. Very quickly, then, it will radiate away not only the energy we just gave it, but also the extra energy it already had. You see, by *adding* energy, we permit the electron to *lose* energy. The energy is radiated away and the electron ends up in the ground state, just as we wanted."

Rum-Lem nodded. He understood now.

"And time for us is like energy is for the electron? If we are exposed to a timeshift field, we will be sent forward to an unstable timestream, where we will immediately fall back all the way to normal time. Is that right?"

"More or less, yes. The entire Universe in normal time is in the ground state. But at every point in the Universe there are a number of accessible stable states of forward time. The position of those states — that is, their location in forward time — depends on the local spacetime curvature. It took me a long time to realize the importance of spacetime curvature, but I'm sure now that's why the two of us ended up in the same timestream but we could find no trace of those early experiments on Kivra."

"The spacetime curvature on Kivra is different," supplied Rum-Lem, "because the gravity is different."

"Exactly. The experiments on Kivra worked, and all those people and objects were thrust into forward time, but not into *our* stream of forward time. In fact, if my calculations are correct, there is no direct way for us to get from our forward time to theirs. The only way to do it is by returning to the ground state — normal time — then travelling to Kivra, then moving into forward time once more. If we were to do that, we would be projected into their timestream. Of course, we'd arrive there many centuries after them, so there'd probably be no one alive, but we would at least be able to find the evidence we looked for and didn't find. Sorry; I'm not sure if I'm explaining this very well. Does this make sense?"

"Yes, I think so. But you still haven't explained exactly how we are going to get back."

"Well, I think I've been able to calculate the relative stability of the various timestreams. There do seem to be some differences between an atom and forward time. For example, the amount of time an atom stays in an excited state is a function of the stability of the state. If the level is not completely stable, the electron will eventually decay to a lower state, emitting energy as it does so. Forward time doesn't work quite that way. Each timestream seems to be completely stable. In other words, once one arrives in a forward timestream, one need not worry about the stream suddenly disappearing. Instabilities manifest themselves, not *within* a timestream, but during the jump *between* streams. If one tries to jump into an unstable stream, the probability of success is low. If the jump fails, then one simply falls all the way back to normal time, and a burst of energy in the form of chronons is released. If the jump happens to succeed, one simply finds oneself in the new forward timestream.

"What we have to do, therefore, is to try to reach a timestream that is highly unstable. We have to put at least enough energy into the timeshift field for us to reach the stream. Any slight excess will be radiated away as chronons if we happen to be unlucky and end up reaching the forward stream. But if we don't reach it, all the energy will be radiated away and we'll fall all the way back to normal time.

"The vital calculation, then, is the placement and stability of all the timestreams available to us. Right now we are — I think — in the closest timestream to normal time. That's like being in the lowest-energy state above the ground state. I calculate the stability factor of this state to be somewhere between 97% and 100%, meaning that attempts to reach this timestream almost always succeed. We need to find an accessible stream with a much lower stability level — as low as possible — if we are to have a reasonable chance of getting back to normal time.

"Our biggest problem is going to be power. The Device used ninety percent of the energy cube just reaching this timestream, and even that was enough to burn out a few of its circuits. According to my calculations, there is no limit to the number of streams accessible to us, but the more distant a stream is from this one, the more energy it will take to reach it. As a general rule, the more distant timestreams seem to be the least stable. The limiting factor is not going to be the power your ship can supply; it's going to be the ability of the components in the Device to withstand the excess current. I think, if my calculations are correct, that we have a good chance of reaching a stream with a stability somewhere between 8% and 12%. That's the best I can do. It means that if everything works perfectly, the probability of returning to normal time is roughly 90%. I don't think we can improve on that."

"I see."

For a while there was silence. Then, without saying anything, Rum-Lem walked out of the room; he passed through the cramped central compartment filled with the Device and its ancillary equipment, and down the ship's ramp.

Hwang followed him outside.

Rum-Lem was standing at the water's edge, looking across the lagoon at the line of low breakers where the swell broke against the reef with a distant susurration. The sun was setting. Wordlessly, Hwang halted beside the alien. Tomorrow they would know for sure. If his theory was wrong, they would probably know nothing about it. They would be instantly killed. But if he was right... what would they do if the worst happened and they successfully made the jump forward into a distant timestream? Would the electronics survive? Might they get a second chance? What would they find there? Would it look more or less the same as this timestream? Or would it look quite different? There was no way to know.

The sun set. After a while, Hwang turned and without a word returned to the ship.

For a long time, the alien remained at the shoreline, staring at the darkening reef.

The two of them were seated side by side on the coral sand beside the ship.

There was a fire nearby, from which emanated the smell of roasting meat. A boarlike animal had disturbed Rum-Lem in his reverie on the beach, and the alien had drawn his kill-gun and killed the creature without compunction. He had built a fire and Hwang, attracted by the smell, had left the ship and now sat beside Rum-Lem while the animal roasted.

A small heap of tropical fruits was piled between the two of them. Hwang picked up a mango. He removed a section of the fruit's skin and bit deeply into the yellow-orange flesh. A gentle breeze blew off the ocean and brushed their faces before losing itself in the jungle behind them.

Rum-Lem stirred; he removed the carcass of the boar from the fire, then stripped off portions for the two of them. There was enough meat for several days. But they would simply eat their fill and then leave the rest of the animal on the beach, along with the uneaten fruit. Time would do the rest.

Hwang finished the mango, tossed the remains on the fire, and accepted the meat from Rum-Lem.

As they ate, the breeze died down. They peered out towards the phosphorescent line of breakers. If all went well, this would be their last evening together.

But what if Hwang had made a mistake — some simple, stupid oversight? What if it wasn't possible to go back? Wasn't it better to stay here? At least he was alive, and Rum-Lem provided companionship. Why risk what he had for something that might be forever inaccessible?

He knew that his mind was only playing tricks on him; he reminded himself that had already made his decision, and deep down he knew that it was the only possible one. If they stayed here, there would come a time when one of them died or became incapacitated. Then the other was doomed to a life both lonely and alone, the sole intelligent creature in a neverending ocean of stars. That way lay madness. No; better — far better — to take one's chances now in a single glorious moment of risk. If the Device failed, they would probably not even know it. To use it was the only way.

They retired early, but Hwang could not sleep. He got out of bed and padded soundlessly into the cramped central portion of the ship. The Device stood there, silent and menacing, waiting for the morning.

He walked around the guidance block that was surmounted by the fragile glass cylinder. He touched the glass gently.

Hwang was not a religious man; in fact, he now realized, religion was something that he and Rum-Lem had never discussed. But he found it impossible now not to pray, although he would have been at a loss to identify the object — or Person — to which — or Whom — he made his supplication.

"Please, let it work" — he whispered the words out loud.

He looked up at the curved ceiling. If something or Someone up there had heard his prayer, it could only be an entity that existed outside the physical world, outside even time itself. Was such an entity possible? He did not know.

He lowered his eyes and walked around the Device, thinking of the electronics inside. He thought of every subsystem as he passed it, checking cables, looking, imagining the circuits that were waiting for the life-giving current to flow. Would it work?

Tomorrow, they would find out.

37
TCHARN

Tcharn did not know where the idea came from. Perhaps it was simply the fatigue of being for so long the man on whose shoulders the defense of the Union had rested. Perhaps it was a dormant memory stirred uneasily from its repose by the knowledge that his daughter was in the pernicious hands of Amril Gdrena. Whatever the cause, when the idea came to him, he embraced it without further thought.

Fifty chrons after his commlink confrontation with Amril Gdrena, Tcharn was seated at the controls of his personal ship, next in line for lift off, a flight plan to Qintir filed with intersystem traffic control. In the interim he had gone home and changed into the autoheat suit that would be necessary when he reached his destination. He was not incommunicado — that was a luxury denied the chief of the Defense Bureau of the Free Union of Independent Planets — but he had at least, however temporarily and tenuously, escaped the confines of his office, which was in itself a victory of sorts.

He watched a spaceliner ponderously lift off, promoting him to next in line. Moments later, Tcharn opened the throttle. He felt a sudden lightening of his spirit as his ship left the ground. It occurred to him that this trip was long overdue.

On the vidscreen was the painfully familiar image of the small, isolated planet.

Tcharn's destination was on the opposite side. He eased into a low orbit; as his destination came into sight around the limb, he saw that he had arrived around the middle of the morning sometime late in the northern hemisphere's autumn.

Qintir's axis of rotation was tilted at nearly 34 degrees. This, combined with the planet's relatively large orbital eccentricity, engendered a strong cycle of seasons. In particular, winters in the northern hemisphere, which occurred when the planet was at its most distant from its feeble orange sun, were harsh and unforgiving. Tcharn's destination, the village of Cullen, lay nestled between mountain ranges at a latitude of almost 70°N.

Qintir was originally a mining colony. Nature had seen to it that the richest deposits of pultinium were in the far north. Played out in the early cycles of the War of Secession, the mining villages had for the most part been abandoned long ago. But not completely so. Cullen was one of the few villages from those early times that was still inhabited. It was also the village in which the Yern had been born.

Tcharn fired the thrusters and began to descend into the thick Qintirian atmosphere.

It was autumn; the long, dark, cold rotations filled with winter storms had not yet commenced; but the calm, tranquil, warm rotations of the brief summer were over, and Tcharn knew how it would be in the village now: each rotation slightly cooler and darker than its predecessor, the feeble sun arcing slightly lower in the sky. If it was going to be a particularly bad winter, the first storm might already have occurred. And if it hadn't come yet, it soon would.

He landed in a large meadow southwest of the village. The grass was still green — greener than he remembered at this time of the cycle. Ancient kālek trees grew in one corner of the meadow, sustained by the pultinium-rich soil; they were still covered in their mantles of greenish-brown leaves.

Tcharn had spent most of the journey from Dalith trying to remember Cullen. He had been chagrined to discover that he had no clear memory of the place that once, long ago and in another life, had meant so much to him. Nearly thirty cycles had passed since then. It was a long time, but even so he had expected to remember something more substantial than that the village was a decrepit assemblage of old wooden buildings, many of them too dangerous for habitation, the ruins of many miners' cabins scavenged long ago, while those buildings that still stood unmistakably exhibited the effects of entropy's universal tendency to increase.

There were just a couple of distinct images in his mind: the cabin where the Yern and he had first coupled, and the smiling face of the old woman who was somehow related to her — an aunt, he vaguely remembered — to whom the cabin belonged. The memory of the noise the bed had made should have brought a smile to his lips, but it didn't.

He could remember no other details. And now that he had landed and was looking at the village on the holoimage screen, he realized why that was so: there was nothing else worth remembering.

He waited in vain for any indication that his arrival had attracted the attention of the inhabitants, but the village remained silent and unmoving.

Cullen lay in a wide, shallow valley between two mountain ranges. The peaks of the range to the east were hidden by a line of clouds that from this distance looked peaceful enough but which Tcharn knew from experience were flinging a cold, whipping snow at the hidden mountaintops.

The closer range, to the west, stood gleaming and painfully bright in the morning sunlight. The sight jarred a memory. How could he have forgotten their secret place, shared by just the two of them?

He had intended to disembark here, to walk into Cullen, to knock on the door of the cabin he once had known so well and then... then what? His imagination failed him. The aunt must have died long ago: even when he knew her she was old.

But would *she* be there in her aunt's place? After he had given up trying to find her, had she come back to Cullen to raise her children among friends and family? Was she, whose looks alone could have at one time garnered her a place in the grandest mansion in the Union, was she now living in a decrepit hovel in a forgotten village on a Fringe Planet?

Tcharn could not decide whether it was likely, or even possible. Even when he and the Yern had been undeclared partners, he had never been able to predict her actions or follow her thoughts very easily. After all this time it was impossible to guess what she might have done.

And if she *was* in Cullen, what then?

Did he really want to see her again? Until a moment ago he had been sure that he did, but now he was suddenly filled with indecision. She would be older now. Thirty long, hard, difficult cycles older. Her looks would long ago have been lost, eroded by the vicissitudes of simply staying alive in this harsh place. In his mind she had never aged, remaining always the beautiful creature she once had been. How would he react if he knocked at the cabin door to find himself face to face with the woman the Yern had become?

He tried to imagine himself thirty cycles ago, then pictured himself as he was today. He had aged reasonably gracefully and with a certain dignity, as befitted a man who had made a success of his life. But she... for her it would be different. Would he even recognize her?

The question chilled him so much that he shivered.

He looked up at the mountain range to the west, and made a spur-of-the-moment decision. It would put off the fateful moment a little longer. He applied power to the atmospheric thrusters, and the ship lifted off.

It was a short flight to the hideaway. It was little more than a ledge really, slightly more than halfway up one of the mountains. He surprised himself by finding it on the first attempt.

He landed smoothly, sending a fountain of virgin, early-season snow spouting skyward and exposing a flat slab of granite. The snow was not thick, for the ledge was protected by an overhanging rock that made landing tricky unless one had learned the knack of ducking underneath the overhang at the same time as firing the landing thrusters. The fine crystals of ice sparkled in the autumnal sun, turning the ledge briefly into a magical place of glistering diamonds. Gradually, the snow fell away, leaving the air clear and pure and blue.

He disembarked.

It was cold up here but his clothing compensated so that very soon he could feel the chill of the air only against his unprotected face: a sharp cold on the limen of pain that almost brought tears to his eyes.

Behind him was a small hole in the mountainside. The tiny opening led to an extensive natural warren of caves that occupied the entire side of the mountain. But he did not make for the opening; instead he turned and walked in the other direction, towards the edge of the shelf. His landing had swept away the snow, and the shelf was filmed with only the thinnest of coverings which squeaked as he approached the edge of the ledge; his boots left a short trail of clear, precise imprints.

He stopped at the very edge. In front of him, the mountainside fell away precipitously. Far, far below was the long valley in which the village of Cullen had grown and in which it had ever since been fighting a losing battle against decay. He let the view wash over him — the green grass of the meadow near the village; the perfect whiteness of the snow on the mountains all around; the clear, uncorrupted blue of the sky; the absolute silence; the majestic tranquility seemingly eternal and inviolate.

Tcharn and Tan-Lem had shared their most intimate moments here. This was not a place for the raw physicality of coupling, even in summer — they did that either in the cabin in Cullen or in the cave behind him. No, this was a place for stripping the veneer of pretense, for baring one's very soul, secure in the knowledge that what was said here would never be repeated.

Sometimes, they had simply stood or sat on the ledge, absorbing the peacefulness from the very air. During the brief northern summers, they had sat here looking out over the valley and discussing the future of the galaxy. He remembered that even at the time it had seemed surreal and arrogant to be talking about the fates of billions of humans spread over more than two hundred planets while the two of them perched secretly on a ledge overlooking a forgotten and almost deserted valley on a tiny and unimportant planet. And yet perhaps it had not been so arrogant after all, for he had eventually become one of the most powerful men in the Union, and she... she had given birth to children who, if only his plan had worked, might have been instrumental in throwing the Empire into chaos, allowing the Union to expand its benign protection, possibly across the entire galaxy.

If only Operation Kālek had not failed. If only....

He shivered — not from the cold, for his suit was protection against that — but from his memories, against which nothing could protect him. With a last look at the valley, he turned away and looked back, past his ship, to the cave where the twins had been conceived. He almost expected Tan-Lem to step out from the dark hole in the cliffside, waving and shouting joyfully in greeting as if the intervening cycles had been nothing more than a momentary inconvenient aberration.

But she did not appear. The only movement was a change in the pattern of reflected sunlight as snow crystals melted.

He began to walk towards the dark rent in the cliff. He approached within half a dozen steps before he halted, suddenly aware that if he went any farther he would be trespassing on all the cycles that had passed since he and the Yern had parted. It pained him to think it, but it was possible that Tan-Lem had shared this place with others. She had told him that he was the first, but who was to say that he had been the last? Once he had left Qintir, might she not have sought companionship — or even love — and brought others here?

Better to leave the cave unentered and his memories unsullied.

For a long time he simply stared at the cave, lost in his memories. Eventually, he turned away and walked the few steps back to the ship. His gait was that of an old man, defeated by life.

He flew back to the village and landed once more in the meadow just beyond the southwesternmost cluster of decaying huts. His second arrival provoked no more interest than his first. He disembarked and began to walk towards the village.

The buildings were in an even greater state of disrepair than he had remembered. Every window was either broken or cracked or covered. More buildings than he remembered had fallen down — or perhaps they had been pulled down, it was hard to be sure — and the wood scavenged for makeshift repairs to those cabins that were still standing.

As he walked past the dilapidated cabins, the only incongruity was the sight of the hovercars parked in leantos and sheds, and even, next to one relatively large house, a small garage. In Cullen, a hovercar was a necessity, for there was no other way to leave the village.

Even communications up here were sporadic. As on most of the Fringe Planets, the inhabitants of Qintir generally used simple radio transmissions for intraplanetary communication. But Qintir had an anomalously strong magnetic field, which combined with the frequent solar storms from its ancient, dying sun to cut off the polar communities from the rest of the planet, sometimes for many rotations at a time. The result was a community that was close-knit and insular.

No one greeted Tcharn as he walked along Cullen's major thoroughfare, which was simply a wide, unpaved stretch of hard, bare ground. Apart from the occasional flicker of movement at a window, he might have been in a ghost town. He turned a corner, expecting to see the small wooden structure in which Tan-Lem's aunt had lived, and his limbs froze in shock.

It was clear that a building had once stood here: debris was still scattered around the site; but it was also obvious that several cycles had elapsed since then.

Recovering, he walked slowly forward. Had he got it all wrong? Had she never returned here at all? After all, he had visited Cullen several times after she had walked out on him, and she had not been here then. The old aunt had answered his questions with a vague shrug and a smile, and had refused to discuss Tan-Lem's disappearance further. Perhaps Tan-Lem had never come back here; perhaps she had settled somewhere else entirely.

He stood gazing at the ruins of the primitive dwelling, his mind far away. He only became aware of a shuffling sound when it suddenly stopped.

"I remember you," an old, grating voice said.

Tcharn turned to look at the speaker. He was an impossibly old man, with a face deeply lined and beaten into submission by the harsh polar climate, and a stoop so pronounced that if it were not for the stout stick that he clasped with both hands he would undoubtedly have toppled. The man's eyes were strongly strabismic — perhaps the muscles of one of them had simply given up the effort of moving — and apparently myopic, for he shuffled forward another few steps and peered closely at Tcharn. He leant forward so much that they almost touched.

The stale, moldy aroma of the man's breath swept over Tcharn. He tried to ransack his memory for a name to go with the face, without success.

"Yes, I thought so. You're the one she loved, aren't you?"

"Am I?"

The old man straightened slightly and shuffled backward a couple of steps.

"You're the one who fathered her children."

He seemed to be waiting for some sort of response from Tcharn.

"The twins, you mean?"

"Yes; the twins. There weren't any more. Or perhaps you didn't know that. You came back a few times looking for her, didn't you? I remember that."

"I did. But they said they didn't know where she was."

"She wasn't far away."

The old man made an odd gurgling sound that might have been laughter. It turned into a cough and for several moments he was helpless as he fought to control the convulsions that wracked his body.

When he recovered, he said, "She was here all the time. We just warned her whenever you landed. She used to hide in my house."

The old man turned and tried to lift his stick to point towards a neighboring building, but as soon as the stick was off the ground he began to lean perilously. He planted his support firmly on the street once more and confined himself to a nod.

"That house, the one next door, that's where I live. I was born there and I've lived there all my life, and I reckon I'll die there."

"And you took her in whenever I showed up?"

"That's right. She'd grab the tykes and hurry on over to my place. Her aunt was careful never to let you into the house, otherwise you'd have discovered they were living there. Anyway it didn't last long. You stopped coming."

It was impossible to tell whether he was stating a fact or making an accusation.

Tcharn shrugged.

"I guess I gave up. There didn't seem much point."

It sounded like an excuse, and he suddenly wondered how things would have turned out if he had kept coming back, refusing to give up searching for her. Would he ever have found her? Would she have relented?

"Aye. But she loved you, you know."

"Did she? She used to say that she did, but since she left me I've never been sure. Why did she do that if she loved me? And why did she hide whenever I came looking for her?"

"She always said it was for both of your sakes. You had a career ahead of you that she didn't want to jeopardize. She loved Qintir and said she would never leave, not even for you. I don't say she was right, mind. I'm just telling you what she told us.

"She thought the world of those two mites, you know."

Tcharn nodded. "Yes."

He suddenly realized that the old man had been referring to Tan-Lem in the past tense. The bile in his stomach told him that he already knew the answer, but he asked the question anyway.

"Where is she?" He nodded towards the ruins of the cabin.

"Gone now. At peace, if there is such a thing. She died three winters since. We bury our people here. You remember where the cemetery is?"

Tcharn nodded distractedly, his suddenly-moist eyes still on the ruined building, his thoughts on rotations long, long ago.

"Aye. Well, that's where she is. Difficult burying people in winter, it is. We have to thaw the ground and there's not many of us around any more to help. Still, she's peaceful enough now, I suppose. When I saw you just now, I thought you might like to know that."

Suddenly the man, who until now had seemed to have retained all his faculties despite his advanced age, stopped speaking and a furious series of tics rendered him speechless for some time. When he recovered, one eye was looking glassily at Tcharn.

"I thought I recognized you," the man said; then he paused, and looked as if he was trying to dredge up a memory that was beyond his reach.

"She had two children, you know. She thought the world of them. Then they went away. She was never the same after that. Did I tell you we buried her? In winter it was. Awful job, thawing the ground. And not many of us left to help. Haven't I seen you before around here... a long time ago?"

Tcharn smiled at the feeble old man.

"Thank you, sir. I appreciate your kindness in telling me these things."

The old man looked uncertain, then he glanced up at the sky and said, "Aye, well, I'd best be getting on now. Snow will soon be here and there's plenty to do before it arrives. Give my best to the Yern if you see her around. She doesn't live around here any more, you know."

He began to shamble away. Tcharn could hear him talking beneath his breath, the words inaudible.

Tcharn watched the old man until he disappeared safely inside his home, then he turned and began to walk heavily in the direction of the cemetery.

Cullen boasted a large cemetery, the number of its corpses manyfold greater than the number of living inhabitants. He walked morosely towards the bleak, untended patch of land at the north end of the village. It was bounded on the west by low foothills and on the east by a long drumlin deposited eons before by the glacier that had created this valley. Between the drumlin and the foothills, the cemetery stretched northward, marked by a geometric tessellation of metallic plates bearing the names of the dead that was interrupted here and there by the occasional kālek tree. Closest to the village were the graves of the original miners who had been sent out from Kivra to live, to work and to die in this remote place. The newest graves were the most distant.

He passed the rows of graves, not looking at the metallic plates until he reached the very final row. There was her grave: nothing but a shallow mound piled with the dirt that her body had displaced, and on top of the dirt the engraved plate. A kālek tree stood nearby, the primary vertical trunk pointing directly at the sky overhead, the short stubby trifold secondary trunks no more than waist high. The tree was a youngster, no more than a thousand cycles old. Its proximity to the Yern's grave seemed to Tcharn one of those tricks that fate plays every now and then, as if it were winking conspiratorially at him and saying, "You see, I know your secret."

There was only one grave more recent than Tan-Lem's. One death in the past three cycles. He wondered what the population of the village was now. A hundred? Fifty? It had been three hundred when he had been stationed on Qintir.

Tan-Lem

daughter of Var-Lem and Pryn Haar

mother of Rum-Lem and Per-Lem

said the plate that marked her grave. That was all. No mention of the Yern. No mention that anyone would miss her. Was there no one other than Tcharn who cared? No one? No one at all? His eyes misted, then welled, then filled; then, finally, the tears began to flow.

He did not know how long he stood there. By the time he turned away, the sky was dark and a bitter wind had blown up.

He glanced up at the stars. He stopped, gazing upward at the abysmal empyrean. Tan-Lem was gone. And so was Rum-Lem. But somewhere out there was Per-Lem. His child. The Yern's daughter.

And he knew what had to be done.

38
HWANG

Hwang and Rum-Lem were up before dawn.

Neither of them had slept well, and Hwang almost wished that they had done all this last night when they had been merely anxious — now they were anxious and tired. But it was too late to change anything. They ate a breakfast of gluey bars and flavored liquid in the ship's dining area, eating in silence, each of them lost in his thoughts. Their eyes kept returning to the doorway through which the Device intruded into the room.

Until now, the Device had been merely a machine on which they were working; but today everything was different: its presence loomed ominously, and neither of them could keep his thoughts from it for more than a few moments at a time. Most of the meal went into the ship's waste destructor.

"I suppose we'd better get on with it; we can't put it off any longer," Hwang said.

Rum-Lem nodded. "Yes, I suppose so." He hesitated for a moment. "My friend, whatever happens, I want you to know that I thank you for everything. Even if the experiment fails and, well..., if this is the end, I want to thank you for our time together, and for giving me hope."

Hwang, although his thoughts echoed those of the alien, could not bring himself to say them out loud. Instead he said brusquely, "Come on, then; let's get it over with. I can't stand this strain much longer."

Hwang went to the computer console and Rum-Lem moved to stand beside the power supply. Hwang nodded, and Rum-Lem turned on the power. Hwang took a deep breath, and flipped a switch. An indicator began to glow green. He began to manipulate the controls.

The Device could not be operated manually. Only a computer could react quickly enough to keep the quantum bubbles trapped within the guidance tube, away from the walls of the cylinder. As Hwang pressed buttons on the control panel to supply power to the subsystems, he found himself wishing that he was in more direct control, even though it was he who had written the program that would run the Device. The basic program was unchanged from that final run in the physics tower of Rabundi University, but a multitude of incremental changes had been made in the course of the past month. The changes should enhance the efficiency and improve the accuracy of the program, but what if he had made a programming error? Such things were not unknown. People still occasionally died from simple software errors, despite the rigorous logic-testing that all software routinely underwent before it was placed into service. And he had had to do without logic-testing programs. He had checked everything as well as he could, but one couldn't think of everything. Given the complexity of the control code, there were bound to be interactions he'd never considered.

He pushed the thought aside. It was too late for any of that now. Just press the buttons and get on with it.

His finger rested on the button that would commence the run. He and Rum-Lem looked at one another across the guidance block. Hwang pressed the button, then took a step backward. It was out of his hands now.

On the power meter the control computer showed two graphs on a single pair of axes: expected power consumption in green and actual power consumption in red. The two were superimposed directly atop one another. The double line was climbing almost exponentially.

Hwang turned to peer at the long glass tube that ran the length of the guidance block. He realized too late that there was more ambient light in the spaceship than there had been in Ekbu Tbamti's shuttered laboratory. The quantum bubbles would be much harder to see in here — but it was too late now to rectify that mistake. The red waves of light on the side of the guidance block were beginning to move in their hypnotic pattern, starting at the ends and slowly moving in toward the center. A hum, increasing in volume, came from the Device. His eyes flicked back to the power graph and he saw that they had passed the kink that accompanied the formation of the quantum bubbles. The bubbles were still too small to see in the glare of the room, but they were in there somewhere, slowly expanding at each end of the glass cylinder as they absorbed power from the alien vessel.

He watched the proximate end of the tube, looking for the first visible sign of a bubble. For a few moments he could not be sure. He closed his eyes for a couple of seconds, then re-opened them. Yes, there it was: a tiny purple-blue area hugging the plug that sealed the cylinder. The first quantum bubble was visible.

The power curves still tracked one another; now they were in the featureless part of the curve, rising at an almost constant rate. The bubble was growing; it was perhaps a centimeter in diameter now, and easy to see. At the far end of the tube he thought he could just make out its twin.

The bubble continued to expand. His heart was pounding and his breathing irregular. He forced himself to breathe deeply and evenly: in... out... in... out. His hand moved to the power switch. In an emergency, if he was fast enough, maybe he could prevent a disaster.

Still the bubbles grew; the rippling waves along the side of the box indicated that phase lock was coming closer.

The closest bubble was almost filling the width of the tube. It was much larger than when it had detached itself in the lab. Hwang could not suppress a momentary self-satisfaction that his control program was indeed far more effective than it had been. The bubble reached the maximum possible size before it detached itself from the end of the cylinder.

The red waves repeatedly met in the center of the guidance block and reformed at the edges. At last the waves halted as they locked on to the position of the two bubbles. As lock was achieved, a high-pitched tone came from the control program, the audible signal that power consumption had peaked. He looked at the graphical display for confirmation: power consumption was falling rapidly. The bubbles had detached and power was no longer needed to sustain them. Now the only power necessary was what was needed to guide them down the cylinder towards one another. Back in Rabundi City, the bubbles had been unstable at this point; they had oscillated, blurring their surfaces and requiring enormous quantities of power to keep them confined to the center of the guidance cylinder. This time, the power consumption was less than half a megawatt, a mere trifle.

The bubbles were moving now. He could see the closest one travelling slowly down the axis of the glass tube. There was no side-to-side jitter as the bubble moved; there was no scope for such movement now, for the gap between the bubble and the walls of the cylinder was no more than a couple of millimeters. Hwang hoped nervously that his control code was up to the task, for if one of the bubbles were to touch the wall of the cylinder... well, if that were to happen he would never know it, because he would be dead before his brain had enough time to process the information.

The bubbles moved slowly, taking an eternity to cover the short distance to the center of the glass tube. Hwang held his breath as the bubbles approached one another. A deep, powerful sound, felt more than heard, began to come from the Device. There was a moment of hesitation and then the bubbles began to affect one another as their fields overlapped. They began to shrink. The sound coming from the Device rose in pitch, escalating rapidly through the audible spectrum. The bubbles started to deviate from their courses, and no amount of external correction could stop them as they began to move in a counterclockwise direction, still shrinking. The sound became louder, more intrusive, a sinusoidal wail.

Hwang was forced to cover his ears; Rum-Lem, despite being clearly discomfited, left his ears uncovered. Hwang began to wonder whether the Device was going to survive as the whole thing began to vibrate. His finger tensed on the power switch. Inside the tube, the bubbles were orbiting one another. Now Hwang saw something that he did not remember from last time: the bubbles were no longer spherical. Instead, each was elongated in the direction of its twin, like miniature blue stars in close orbit around one another, each sucking material from the other. The analogy hung in his mind for only a moment, because suddenly a violent shiver seemed to pass through the orbiting bubbles. They touched.

Afterwards, Hwang could not recall what happened next.

He remembered watching the two bubbles as they stretched out towards one another, but then it was as if he had been caught in an explosion.

He was lying on the ground with his eyes closed, quietly moaning.

At length he opened his eyes and slowly picked himself up off the floor. His mind was groggy and his muscles protested at every movement.

Somehow he had moved several feet away from the control panel and was now beyond the end of the guidance block. He could see Rum-Lem dragging himself upright with the help of the metal block.

Hwang hauled himself to his feet and looked around. The Device was now dead. The power switch on the front of the control panel was still in the On position, but no lights were lit, either on the Device itself or on the panel of the computer that controlled it. An uneasy silence filled the air, the hum of the experiment's control circuits noticeably absent.

The two men stood, leaning against the guidance block for support. Neither of them spoke as their eyes ranged around the room, looking for something that would tell them whether the experiment had worked. It was only after half a minute that Hwang thought of the obvious test.

Slowly, as if in a dream, he raised his left arm until he was looking at his wristcom. He stabbed at a button to receive one of the broadcast channels. There was a pause that in other circumstances would have been barely perceptible but now seemed to last half a lifetime.

And then the diminutive vidscreen on his wrist was filled with a smiling face that Hwang instantly recognized. The sound of speech filled the room.

"It's really quite simple," Ekbu Tbamti was saying with a jovial glint in his eye, as if he was sharing a secret with his viewers. "While it is possible for particles to travel faster than light, it is not possible for those same particles ever to travel slower than light. The speed of light is a kind of energy barrier. The only hope for those of us stuck on the slow side of that barrier lies in a phenomenon called the tunnel effect. The tunnel effect, unfortunately, is a viable method of crossing the barrier only for small particles, not large masses like a spaceship. And that, in a nutshell, is why this thing called hyperspace travel, which has been so beloved of science fiction writers for centuries, will always remain just that: science fiction."

For a moment, an olio of emotions competed to be uppermost in Hwang's mind. He burst into loud, hysterical laughter. Just as suddenly, he stopped laughing. He looked at Rum-Lem, who was regarding him with a broad grin.

"Well done, my friend," said the alien.

Hwang began to cry.

39

STRENK

"You're certain?"

"Yes, sir. Positive."

"I see."

President Rahl sighed deeply. For a long time he said nothing, his eyes fixed glassily on a holoimage on the wall.

Deputy Strenk was also silent as he waited for the president's decision. His future was in the balance, and his hands were sweating nervously. He wiped them on his clothes.

Finally, the president shook his head wearily.

"I'm sorry. I'm really sorry, Deputy Strenk."

For a moment, the bottom fell out of Strenk's stomach. The president was going to refuse to act.

But he had misunderstood.

The president continued, "I had hoped that Tcharn had put his scheming behind him. Apparently I was hoping for too much. He has already set up the exchange?"

"Yes, sir. We are due to leave early tomorrow morning."

"And no one else knows?"

"No, sir. Just him and me. And Amril Gdrena, of course."

"Gdrena. Tell me: what do you think of her? Is she also an impediment to peace?"

Strenk shrugged.

"I can't say, sir. Tcharn has always claimed that her aim is to overpower the Union by any means at her disposal. She certainly has a reputation for being ruthless, but whether she is really to be feared I don't know. Perhaps Tcharn merely projects himself on to her."

"I think we can be sure of one thing," the president said. "The emperor himself was willing to return Tcharn's daughter to us even though he was unaware of their relationship. It was only after he had spoken with Gdrena that he denied my request. I think, on balance, that we may therefore conclude that she is a danger to the relationship that the emperor and I have been cultivating." He paused. "It pains me to say it, but I am forced to the conclusion that the galaxy would be a better place without Tcharn and Gdrena."

He looked piercingly at Strenk.

"I understand, sir."

President Rahl nodded unhappily. "Then I wish to hear no more about this matter. You will report to me as soon as you return."

"Yes, sir. Thank you, sir."

Deputy Strenk rose to leave the Study. As he reached the door, the president said, "And Strenk?"

"Yes, sir."

"I thank you, not just for myself, but on behalf of the emperor and the entire population of the galaxy. Your dedication will not be forgotten, even though few people will ever know of it."

Strenk mumbled his thanks, and hurriedly exited the room. He was not proud of betraying Chief Tcharn.

40
AMRIL GDRENA

The minister stood in the doorway of the cell; Brynt Veel was behind her.

The woman in the cell looked up at them. She had been rocking backward and forward, humming to herself, lost in a world in which the cell did not exist, and neither did Amril Gdrena, nor the Empire, the Union, Tcharn, nor indeed the pool of urine in which she was sitting.

Now she stopped humming and, a moment later, ceased her back-and-forth motion. She looked at Amril Gdrena, but there was no expression in her eyes.

"Do you understand me?" asked Gdrena.

No response. The minister approached Per-Lem and stretched out her hand.

"Get up."

The minister pulled Per-Lem's hand, and Per-Lem got slowly to her feet. Brynt Veel's nose wrinkled at the odors released by her movement. The minister turned to the guards.

"Clean her up. I want her presentable and in my office in fifty chrons."

She said to the vacant face of her prisoner, "Thank you, Per-Lem. You are bringing your father to me; and he will deliver the Union into my hands."

337

She smiled.

Uncertainly, Per-Lem returned it.

The two ships faced one another across the void. It seemed a fitting place to enact the exchange: in the demilitarized zone, close to the planet Tirsh.

The two craft were close enough that, had the ships been endowed with windows, Gdrena and Tcharn would each have been able to make out the other's ship without the aid of the holoimage screens.

On the imperial ship were three people: Amril Gdrena, Brynt Veel, and the uncomprehending shell that was all that remained of Per-Lem. On board the Union ship were Tcharn and Deputy Strenk.

Gdrena inclined her head and Brynt Veel opened the communications circuit.

The ships' defensive shields were in place, which interfered with the commlink and rendered the video blurred and indistinct, although the audio was still clear.

"Everything is as we agreed?" said Gdrena.

"It is. We are alone, myself and my deputy. We filed a flight plan for Meglarin. By now they've probably begun to look for us. We don't have much time."

"I forget too easily that you don't wield the same power in the Union that I do in the Empire. All right. We are ready."

"My daughter. May I see her before the exchange?"

Gdrena frowned. "I'm sorry. She's already in the capsule. I give you my word that she is unharmed."

Tcharn nodded. "All right." He turned to someone off-screen, presumably Deputy Strenk. "You'll show her to me when she arrives?"

"Of course, sir. But with the greatest respect, we should have proof that she's really on board that ship before you get into the capsule."

Tcharn grunted.

"I'm afraid my deputy has a suspicious mind. He wants to see Per-Lem before he'll allow me to leave."

"Quite understandable. Please wait. I'll be back shortly. Remember when you talk to her that she still believes she is Lystra Ten-Wer."

She severed the commlink.

"I told you he'd want to talk to her," said Brynt Veel.

"Did you notice something about that deputy of Tcharn's?"

"What?"

"He called Tcharn 'sir.' You might do well to remember that, Veel."

"Yes... madam minister."

"Thank you. Now, are you ready?"

Veel nodded. The minister pressed a sequence of buttons; a light flashed on, and she reopened the commlink.

Tcharn looked at the indistinct image. In the background was the inside of a ship. In the foreground stood a woman whom he recognized only after scrutinizing her for several moments. She wore a featureless gray suit; her hair was cropped close to her skull. It was hard to be sure of the expression on her face. He was certain of her identity only when she spoke.

"Chief Tcharn?"

Tcharn nodded, fighting to keep his eyes dry. "Yes, Per.... Yes, Lystra Ten-Wer."

"Can you tell me what's going on? What do you want with me? They are treating me like a spy. Tell them I'm not. I barely knew Teberill Gandeer. We spent a rotation together, that's all. I didn't know he was one of your agents. What's going to happen to me?"

As she spoke, her voice rose in both pitch and volume, so that by the time she finished it was almost a screech.

"It will all be explained to you shortly. Please, trust me. You have my word that you are in no danger."

The woman leaned forward and spat at the holocamera; involuntarily, Tcharn winced.

"You're the enemy," shouted his daughter. "I wouldn't take your word for the color of the night sky."

"All right, I've seen enough," mumbled Tcharn, averting his gaze. He could not bear the raw hatred on his daughter's face.

Per-Lem walked off-screen and her place was taken by Amril Gdrena.

"I'm sorry, Chief Tcharn. That must have been painful. I wanted to spare you the knowledge that your daughter hated you. Are you sure your technicians will be able to restore her mind?"

"Yes. That was the last part of Operation Kālek: to extract her from the Empire and repair her memories. I'm only sorry that I won't be there to see it happen."

"Perhaps we can arrange something: commlink sessions perhaps."

"Yes. Thank you. That would be most kind."

"Now, I suggest we get on with the exchange." The minister smiled pleasantly.

"Yes, I suppose so."

Deputy Strenk severed the commlink. Chief Tcharn looked at him dully.

"It's time," said the deputy; and he held out an arm to support the defeated chief.

"Well done, Veel; now, put her in the capsule," said Amril Gdrena as she closed down the program that had converted Brynt Veel's image and voice to those of Per-Lem.

Brynt Veel approached the woman who was seated at the rear of the cabin. She was staring vacantly into the distance, rocking backward and forward ever so slightly, humming tunelessly so quietly that she could barely be heard.

Veel stretched out a hand, and she stopped moving. For a few moments she continued humming, as if it were vital that reach a sensible stopping point; then she grasped Brynt Veel's hand and permitted him to help her out of her seat. Veel observed that she had wet herself again.

He pressed his palm against a flat plate and a door slid open to reveal four glistening emergency capsules.

"You'll be all right," he said, guiding her forward until she was standing in the closest capsule. She was facing the far wall of the capsule. He carefully turned her until she was facing him, so that when the capsule closed she would be able to see out the window. Not that it would make any difference.

The logistics of the exchange had been worked out by Gdrena and Tcharn. Even though both had sworn that they would seek no advantage from the situation, neither side trusted the other. Tcharn and Per-Lem would enter emergency capsules aboard the two ships. The capsules would be released with zero velocity. Then the ships would exchange places. When the ships were both in position, the two capsules would be recovered simultaneously.

Tcharn and Strenk had recognized that this was the moment of greatest danger. Amril Gdrena might try to destroy the Union ship with a photon missile, or she might even use a timeshift weapon against them. Accordingly, Tcharn had given Deputy Strenk orders to fully cloak as soon as Per-Lem's capsule was aboard, and then to move out of range before releasing his daughter from the capsule.

The capsules were released and Strenk opened a commlink channel.

He inclined his head toward the blurred image of the imperial minister.

"Amril Gdrena, I am Deputy Strenk. May I speak to your pilot, please?"

The hazy image of Brynt Veel, unsmiling and dressed in black, appeared on Strenk's screen.

"I am Brynt Veel, the minister's pilot."

"I must warn you that I am carrying a zero-distance photon bomb, and at the first action that I interpret as aggression, I shall explode the bomb. The radiation will kill us all instantly. I shall give no warning of my intention. If I see something I don't like, I will simply detonate the bomb. So I suggest you pilot your craft with extreme caution. Do you understand?"

"I do."

Deputy Strenk pressed a button. "Sir?"

Inside the emergency capsule, Chief Tcharn tried to turn towards the speaker from which the sound of his deputy's voice emanated. There was not enough room.

"Strenk?"

"We are getting ready to make the exchange, sir."

"Just get on with it, Strenk. Let's get this over."

"Yes, sir. Goodbye."

"Goodbye."

There was a barely audible click from the speaker as the low-power radio transmitter was turned off.

Ever so slowly, the two ships began to move, each leaving behind a small elongated capsule barely large enough to contain a single human being. The ships passed each other. After five chrons they had exchanged places. Deputy Strenk re-opened the commlink channel.

"I am ready to retrieve the capsule."

"Likewise," said Veel.

"Together, then...."

The airlock doors opened and the ships slid sideways, swallowing the capsules. There was a clanging sound on board the Union ship as Per-Lem's capsule touched the innermost wall of the airlock. Brynt

Veel was a better pilot. The minister's ship stopped moving before Tcharn's cylinder touched a wall. On both ships, the doors of the airlocks closed.

Brynt Veel flooded the lock with air. His eyes flickered to the scanner, where a light had begun to flash.

"Strenk's cloaking," Veel said.

"Let him go," said Gdrena quietly. "He doesn't trust us. He knows he's vulnerable now. He'll want to get away."

The unionist ship became a fuzzy dot on the screen.

"He doesn't trust us, yet you seem to trust him," Veel said. "That's unlike you."

"No; I trust Tcharn. I know Tcharn's mind. To fire on us now would be dishonorable. He doesn't think like that. On the other hand, there's a chance he might commit suicide. Come, Veel, let's greet our guest before he gets any ideas."

––––––––––––––

Tcharn was relieved when he felt gravity returning. The capsule settled against the wall of the airlock. Gravity quickly increased from the zero of space to the standard gravity of the imperial ship.

Through the frame of the escape cylinder he heard the sibilant sound of air racing into the lock. Then all was silent. For what seemed like a long time he was alone with his thoughts as he awaited his release. He tried to empty his mind, trying not to think about what he had just done and what would happen next.

At last he saw the airlock door slide open through the window of the capsule. He recognized Amril Gdrena. She was somewhat taller than he had expected, and he had expected her to be grimmer. In all the pictures he had ever seen her mouth had been a taut, straight line. But now she looked positively gleeful as she entered the airlock and, peering through the window, saw Tcharn inside the capsule.

She touched the release mechanism. The door slid open and Tcharn stepped out. She held out her hand in greeting. They touched hands. There was an awkward silence.

––––––––––––––

Strenk decided that he had moved far enough away. He was out of weapon range now. He uncloaked. The imperial ship had not moved since Tcharn had been taken aboard.

Tcharn. He could barely suppress his rage at the man's arrogance. How could he dare set himself up as a higher authority than the president himself? President Rahl was a great man. Left to their own devices, President Rahl and the emperor would forge a strong and lasting peace between the two powers. But Tcharn would never allow it.

It was obvious now that Tcharn was an anachronism. Tcharn thought that peace was so dangerous that it must not be permitted except under terms dictated by the Union. Recent presidents had thought the same way. But now there was a new face in the presidential palace, one who was not afraid of what true peace might bring. One who had given his word that the act Strenk was about to perform would not be forgotten.

It had been easy to plant the bomb. Tcharn had never suspected. He had entered the emergency capsule without the slightest suspicion that he was sharing the metallic shell with a zero-distance bomb.

Well, better get it over with. Rid the galaxy of the two people who were keeping peace at bay. Strenk stretched out his hand and pressed the button. With a flash brighter than any star, the imperial ship ceased to exist.

It was over. Time for a new beginning.

Strenk blinked, trying to rid his eyes of the afterimage of the explosion. When he could see again, the holoimage screen was empty. The scanners showed that the place where the imperial ship had been was now the center of an expanding shell of fragments.

And then the silence of the ship was sundered by an alarm.

Strenk looked wildly around. A light was flashing: the chronon indicator. Somewhere nearby a timeshift field had been generated. He looked at the control panel, unable to believe his eyes. The chronon reading was off-scale. Someone must have fired a timeshift weapon at him. Fortunately, it had missed. But they wouldn't miss a second time.

"Cloak," he commanded the opnav databox. He fired the low-level thrusters, taking the ship away from the position where it had last been visible.

For a moment his mind was a blank. What should he do? There must be another ship nearby. But where? He peered at the scanner, searching. It had to be here somewhere. But there was no trace of a ship within scanner range.

The other ship must be cloaked. So neither of them could see the other. Stalemate. There was nothing for it but to wait.

———————————

Hwang and Rum-Lem did not dally over their farewell. They embraced awkwardly, and then Hwang simply walked down the ramp to stand on the pink coral sand.

"You're sure you'll be all right?" asked Rum-Lem.

Hwang was grinning wildly. He had hardly heard the alien's question. He was already savoring the thought of what was to come. Three, four, maybe five Nobels. An unassailable place in history. From this moment on, he could do anything he wanted. The world was at his feet. He turned and waved at Rum-Lem.

"I'll be fine," he said. "Now go, before someone picks you up on a scanner and starts asking questions."

Rum-Lem went back inside the ship.

Half a cycle late, but there was still a chance. Just wait until Tcharn heard the news. He'd never believe it at first, but a passive mindprobe or an interview with an aletheologist would show that he was telling the truth. Operation Kālek was doomed from the beginning. It was impossible to kill someone who didn't exist.

———————————

"You won't find him because there's no such person, you fool," the empress shouted gleefully.

She looked up at the camera to make sure that it was all being recorded.

"He was killed when he was still a child, soon after his coronation. Everything since then has been a sham. There is no emperor. He has no child. None of it is real... except me. I'm the only member of the imperial family who is ever seen in the flesh, because I'm the only one who exists. The others only ever appear in holoimage broadcasts and commlink circuits.

"When I agreed to join their scheme, I didn't realize what it would mean: that I would be forever a prisoner, doomed to making trite speeches, opening research institutes, meeting diplomats, and all the time knowing that if I so much as looked like I was about to give them away I would be shot instantly with a kill-gun.

"Amril Gdrena masterminded it all. She's the one with the power, the others on the Inner Council take their orders from her. She's the real emperor. If the people ever found out how she's been duping them all this time, they'd rise up and kill her. Listen: you came here to kill the emperor, but you can do something far more dangerous, far more profound. You can tell the Union that there is no emperor. They'll know how to handle it. They can make the Empire ungovernable. Gdrena won't be able to command a class of schoolchildren, much less the defense fleets. Don't wait. Get out of here. Get back to the Union. Tell the president he's our only hope."

There was the sound of running feet in the corridor outside. Rum-Lem began to move for the door.

"Please. Before you go, kill me. It will be less painful than what they'll do to me."

She nodded at the camera. Rum-Lem aimed at it and fired, but its security screen prevented any damage. It continued running, recording the scene.

"Quick! He's with the empress," said a voice not far away down the corridor.

Rum-Lem fired one shot at the empress, then plunged out the door, firing to cover himself as the empress collapsed.

Rum-Lem's ship raced away from Tirsh. He was deep inside the demilitarized zone, and did not expect to see anything on the scanners. But two fuzzy dots indicated that he was not alone. One signal resolved itself into a cloud of debris. The other was a Union ship, cloaked but adumbratively visible to his advanced scanners. The screen flashed the identification of the cloaked ship, and Rum-Lem exclaimed in surprise. What on Dalith was his father doing out here?

But questions could wait. Chief Tcharn was the person he most wanted to see.

He commanded the communications databox: "Establish commlink with cloaked ship at bearing 76·3, 32·4, 19·6."

Strenk watched nervously as the ship entered scanner range. It was moving incredibly quickly. No ordinary ship could travel that fast. It must have been hiding near Tirsh, waiting for the right moment to launch an ambush.

The scanner identified the ship: a private vessel with an imperial transponder. That must be where the chronon burst had come from

— the ship must have fired a timeshift weapon at him, and missed. The ship kept coming.

"Enemy ship within weapons range," the weapons system announced.

Almost simultaneously, the communications databox reported: "Commlink request from enemy ship."

"Decloak and fire photon missile," he barked.

———

The ship decloaked, and Rum-Lem smiled. It would be good to see his father again. How astonished he would be to see his son alive after all this time.

There was a flash, and the smile froze on his face.

"Warning: incoming photon missile, bearing 76·3, 32·4, 19·6. Evading."

Rum-Lem felt the sudden jerk as the emergency thrusters overloaded the gravity-cancellation field. But he knew it was hopeless. He had been through similar situations in the simulator too many times. He was too close, and there was no time....

———

Strenk permitted himself a smile of satisfaction. The pilot had done a good job of trying to evade the missile, but it had been futile.

Strenk got out of his seat and headed for the airlock, where Tcharn's daughter awaited inside her capsule. He thought fondly of his nephew Val-Dor, waiting back on Dalith for Per-Lem's return. He would not have long to wait now. The technicians were standing by to restore her memories, and then the two could resume their interrupted life together. Good for them. They deserved it.

It was all over now. Perhaps, if the president's talks with the emperor went well, there would never again be the need for a mission like this. Peace. It was hard to believe it was a real possibility. He reached the airlock.

"Now, my dear," he said to himself. "Let's welcome you home."

EPILOGUE

41
MISSEN HAI

Thirteen people were seated around the conference table. All of them looked nervous. The situation was unprecedented, and no one was sure how the meeting was going to end.

"As most senior member of the Inner Council, I call this meeting to order," said the Minister for Entertainment. "We have only one order of business: to determine how we will handle the current situation. I call on Minister Missen Hai for his thoughts."

Missen Hai stood. His nervousness showed in his shaking hands and raspy voice as he began to speak. He stopped, took several sips of water, then started again.

"I will try to be brief. The deaths of Minister Gdrena and her counterpart Chief Tcharn put us — and the Union — in a position to re-think our strategy. You more than anyone know that for many cycles Amril Gdrena effectively led the Empire. The Gdrena Plan — killing the emperor and allowing only a synthetic image to be seen by the public — has proved workable, and some, perhaps some gathered here today, would call it successful. More recently, the Union's election of a pacifist president was seen by my predecessor as an opportunity to mount a surprise attack on the Union. By engaging President Rahl in peace talks, she hoped to persuade the Union to lower its defenses to the point where a well-armed imperial fleet could wreak havoc, and possibly even completely overrun the Union. The death of Chief

348

Tcharn and his replacement by Chief Strenk with his known pacifist leanings makes this strategy even more likely to succeed.

"So that is one possibility: we can continue to implement my predecessor's plans, with the eventual goal of subduing the Union."

Several heads around the table nodded. Missen Hai's hands, which had stopped shaking, now began to do so again. He took another drink of water.

"Or we can take advantage of the situation to do something that Minister Gdrena, with all due respect, would have found unthinkable. We can engage in real peace talks...."

Other heads nodded.

The Minister for Entertainment interrupted, "We know the options, Missen Hai. Make a concrete proposal. What do you think we should do?"

"Two things, minister. Firstly we should end the deception we have played on our people. The Gdrena Plan should be eliminated. We are in a situation oddly like the one in which it began: the public believes that the heir to the imperial crown is a young boy. Effectively, we would continue to run the Empire just as we have done since the Gdrena Plan was implemented. We choose some suitable child to give life to the image that the people believe to be the emperor's son. Then we anoint him emperor. It will be a decade or more before he becomes an adult. By then he can be reduced to a figurehead, perhaps a permanent member of the Inner Council. The details don't matter. The point is that we have plenty of time to ensure that he is no threat to us."

The Minister for Sport interrupted: "I want to be clear about one thing. You aren't suggesting that we tell the people about the Gdrena Plan? Admit what the Inner Council has done? I couldn't go along with that."

From around the table came grunts of agreement.

"No," said Missen Hai. "I am not that naïf. There is nothing to be gained by admitting anything. No, I suggest that the Gdrena Plan be ended the way it was started. The people will be told that the emperor has met with an unfortunate accident. They need never know that he never really existed. The new emperor will be crowned. There is no need for the people ever to suspect anything."

He looked around the table. "It's the right thing to do. It's also the safest thing to do. If we continue, the deception is bound to be exposed eventually. Can you imagine the reaction when it is? We'd be vilified, perhaps even killed. Chaos would ensue. No, the Gdrena Plan should end now that its author is no more. The time for deception is over."

"And the talks with President Rahl?" asked the Minister for Human Resources. "They can hardly continue. Unless you're suggesting that after the emperor has been 'killed' we continue those talks ourselves?"

"That's exactly what I'm suggesting."

"But this time they'd be for real? We wouldn't be planning to invade the Union as soon as its defenses are down?"

"That would be up to this council. But yes, that's what I think should happen."

"Persuade me," said the Minister for Education. "The Union began as an insurrection, an uprising on the edge of the Empire. Why should they not be punished for that?"

"There is another choice," said the Minister for Human Resources. "The Status Quo has served us well for a long time. Why not just break off talks and continue the Status Quo? I see nothing wrong with that."

"You're right; that's an option too," said Missen Hai. "And let's be honest, if we choose to do that no one outside this room will ever know about the opportunity we missed. That would be the easy option, the safe option. But I am asking for something more than the easy way out. The people deserve more than that. They may not know that they've been deceived all these cycles, but *we* know it. We owe them something. Something more than just taking the simplest option. We owe them a chance for true peace."

He saw heads shaking in disagreement, and hurried to continue, "But that's not the real reason why it would be wrong either to take advantage of President Rahl or simply to return to the Status Quo. The real reason is that we have an unprecedented opportunity to bring permanent peace to the galaxy. The Union has seen fit to elect a president who truly believes that peace is not only possible but that it's to be preferred over the Status Quo. His new defense chief, Chief Strenk, agrees with him. So the decision is entirely up to us. The Union is offering its hand in friendship. Should we just brush it aside without at least giving it a chance?

"It's true that the Status Quo, at least superficially, has served us well. But at its core it is a temporary measure. It serves to emphasize that the basic posture of the Empire and the Union is one of belligerence. The Status Quo is simply a hiatus, albeit a long-lived one, in a state of war. To us, the Union is still the enemy and not to be trusted. It is to be taken advantage of whenever the opportunity arises. And as long as we treat one another as enemies, then always our principal goal will be, like theirs, to win the war.

"Surely we can do better than that. The Union has shown us the way. They took the first step to peace when they elected President Rahl...."

"That just shows their weakness," interrupted the Minister for Human Resources. "They are the ones who are tired of the Status Quo, not we."

Missen Hai ignored the interruption. "President Rahl took the second step when he thought he was initiating peace talks directly with the emperor. The Union has taken two steps. It's time we took one. We lose nothing by continuing the talks. Let's see what they have to offer. That's all I'm asking. To listen. Let's listen to President Rahl and Chief Strenk. Give them a fair hearing."

"All right," said the Minister for Entertainment. "As I see it we have two proposals before us. The first is to abandon the Gdrena Plan, and the second is to continue to engage in talks with the Union. If we agree to the latter, I think we can decide later whether we use those talks to take advantage of the Union...."

"Forgive me, minister, but I think not. I'd rather we settled the matter now. It would color our talks if we approached them with the possibility that we were going to betray the Union's trust."

"They betrayed our trust when they rebelled," said the Minister for Human Resources.

"Yes, perhaps they did. At least from our viewpoint. From theirs, though, perhaps it looked different."

"Enough!" interrupted the Minister for Entertainment. "All right. Since the Minister for Peace and Security wishes it, we will also consider this a binding vote on whether the peace talks, if we hold them, will be genuine. We will break the vote into two parts. First will be the issue of the Gdrena Plan. Second will be whether we negotiate in good faith with the Union."

The motion to end the Gdrena Plan passed 11–2.

Voting for the second motion was much closer. The issue was decided by one vote.

42
HWANG

Ekbu Tbamti said nothing. For a long time he just stared unseeingly at the party going on outside on the beach. His mind was far away.

"You do believe me, don't you?" asked Hwang when he could stand it no more.

Tbamti's eyes shifted to Hwang's face.

"Of course I do. You have no reason to make up such an incredible story."

"Then what do you think I should do?"

"I think you already know that, Hwang. Otherwise you would never have asked my opinion."

"I should keep it all to myself?"

"That would be my advice, yes."

Hwang pondered this for a while. "I'm not so sure. Surely something like this is too important to keep quiet about it?"

Ekbu Tbamti shook his head. "On the contrary, it's too important not to do so. What possible advantage is it, either to you or to the human race, to try to convince them that advanced aliens actually exist? The aliens will make themselves known when they think the time is right. If you go public with your story, at best you won't be believed and your career — despite the Nobel — will be tarnished; at worst you *will* be believed. Can you imagine the result? I can't. Governments won't know what to do, so they'll do what they always do: something far more stupid than we can possibly imagine. I shudder to think what idiocy will result if they believe that advanced aliens are on our doorstep. But whatever they do I guarantee that it won't be good. Much, much better to keep quiet."

"I see your point. After all, I have no real proof. But what about all the physics and technology I learned? When I was on Rum-Lem's ship it seemed obvious that I should take advantage of all that knowledge and then release it when I got home. But now I'm here it doesn't seem so clear-cut any more."

"From what little you've told me about the contents of Rum-Lem's research computer, you've learned enough for several Nobels, and possibly a Fields medal or two as well."

"I know. But I'd be getting them under false pretenses.... I'm torn. I just don't know what's best. Surely it would be stupid not to publish what I know?"

"Surely it would be stupid — or at least arrogant — to deny the human race the right to make the discoveries for itself. Would you deny them that?"

"You're saying I shouldn't publish any of it?"

"Not quite. That would be asking too much. But I think you can be more subtle about it than open publication."

"What do you mean?"

"Well, look at it this way. You've just won a Nobel — and one you thoroughly deserve — for your work on the quantum bubble experiment. You'll never have to look for work again. And there's a lifetime of work just investigating the details of that experiment, improving the technology, trying to make anti-gravity a useful tool instead of merely a proof of a theory in particle physics. So you don't *need* to publish what you learned on the ship. But look at the list of subjects you learned about: graviton aberration; the relationship between inertial and gravitational mass; spacetime manifold transfer; practical causality violation....Why not drop hints in semi-popular articles that these are fields in which research might pay off? Suggest the questions, not the answers."

"I suppose.... I'm still not sure. What about the whole theory of timeshifting? Admittedly I used the research computer as a basis, but the actual theory was all my own work. That didn't come from Rum-Lem's civilization. Probably it's the best piece of work I'll ever do. I can't let it go to waste."

Tbamti leaned forward; suddenly the customary glitter was gone from his eyes.

"You must never, ever even hint at the possibility of timeshifting."

"Whyever not? I don't understand."

"Think about it. Timeshifting is the most powerful weapon you could ever hand anyone. Frankly, I'm worried about your friend Rum-Lem; when he gets back to his people what he tells them may forever change the balance of power in the galaxy."

"I'm sorry. I still don't understand."

"The aliens — both sides — already know how to timeshift. Armed with your theory, they can project an entire battle feet into a future timestream, then hyperjump to a position behind enemy lines, and finally timeshift themselves back to normal time. Basically, you've thought of a way to just appear, out of thin air, wherever you want. Offhand, I can't think of a better weapon."

Hwang was shocked. "You're right. I'd never thought of that. There's no defense."

"Not at first, no. Whoever uses the weapon first wins. But if history has taught us anything, it's that there is no such thing as permanent peace. There will come a time when the winner has to fight again, but now against an enemy who has the same weapon. And *that* war will be fought across multiple timestreams." Tbamti shook his head. "No, Hwang. Your theory is brilliant. But you must forever keep it to yourself. Why do you think I concocted that ridiculous cover story about you losing your memory and simply wandering in from the jungle? There must never be any suggestion that you were in a different timestream."

"But what about Rum-Lem? When he tells his people about my theory...? He didn't understand it, but he can surely tell his scientists enough to help them look in the right places. Once they know that a person can safely return from a different timestream, surely they'll figure out the rest?"

Tbamti shrugged. "There's nothing we can do if that's what happens. You might be right. But I'm not completely discouraged. Terrestrial governments are notoriously inefficient. Perhaps theirs is just as bad. Your friend was on a secret mission. There's no reason to assume that anything he learned will ever reach the ears of a competent scientist. And if it does... well, like I said, there's nothing we can do except to hope that they don't involve us in their galactic war."

"If we started working on it though, we could defe...."

Tbamti held up a hand. "No! Don't say it. Look inside yourself, Hwang. Don't let me persuade you. You need to persuade yourself. Nothing good can come of publishing your theory. I know it's hard. It's too much for me to ask. You have to make the decision yourself."

Hwang looked out the window. On the beach, the party celebrating the announcement of their joint Nobel was in full swing. Hwang's colleagues were playing some sort of game they'd invented that involved a net, a ball, and drinking beer. The faculty members sat in beach chairs, some of them watching the younger ones at their games, some of them gesticulating as they made points in debates, some of them facing the sea, either watching the waves or simply dozing.

Hwang sighed. "You're probably right. You usually are."

"I'm sorry. Come on; let's go outside and join the celebration."

43

STRENK

Strenk looked out the window while his nephew fixed him a drink. The garden glowed in the late-afternoon sun. At the far end a grove of kālek trees seemed to be reaching up to catch the light, as if they knew that the warmth of the early autumn rotation would all too soon give way to the long, cold, gloomy rotations of winter. Just this side of the trees, a figure was digging.

"Your drink," said Val-Dor.

Strenk nodded towards the figure. "How is she?"

"Almost completely recovered. They've decided not to treat her any more unless the fits come more frequently."

"When was the last one?"

"Nearly a cycle ago now. And it wasn't a bad one. She recovered in less than a rotation."

"Do you think it helped, bringing her back to Cullen?"

"It's hard to say. It certainly didn't do any harm."

"And she remembers nothing of the cycles she spent on Kivra?"

"No. She's says all those cycles are like a big hole in her life. I think the gardening helps her to deal with that. Takes her mind off it."

The figure stopped digging. She bent down and lifted something from the ground. Turning towards the house, she lifted a handful of some kind of plant with green leaves and elongated yellow roots for them to see. She was smiling.

"I suppose she's going to make us eat those," said Strenk.

"Afraid so," replied Val-Dor with a smile.

"Give me synthfood any day."

They watched while Per-Lem walked back to the house carrying her spade and the vegetables.

"I have some news," said Strenk. "I was with the president this morning. He's not announced it yet, but he's not going to stand for re-election."

"Why not? He's the most popular president in history."

"He says his job is done. The Treaty of Peaceful Coexistence is signed. The borders are about to be opened. The only important remaining issue is how the demilitarized zone is to be administered: will we simply each take half, or will we co-administer it? Once that's decided, he feels a graceful retirement is in order."

"He'll be missed. And what about you? What happens to the Bureau of Defense?"

"For now it will continue to exist, but naturally its rôle will change. But I've decided to retire when President Rahl steps down. New times need new people. Which brings me to the reason for my visit. I've never appointed a deputy. I know that while Per-Lem was sick you felt it was important to bring her to Qintir, so she could be in familiar surroundings and far away from the stresses of life on Telborn. Is that still important? Or is there some chance I could persuade you to be my deputy? When I step down, you'd probably be made chief of the bureau. It's time for new blood. I can think of no one better. What do you say?"

They heard the sound of the back door opening.

"And things are going to be different around here," continued Strenk. "Kivra needs the pultinium that Qintir provides. There's a good chance that Cullen will soon be a thriving mining town. It won't be a peaceful backwater any more."

Per-Lem walked into the room. She smiled at Strenk; she was still carrying the vegetables.

"Kîrots," she said, lifting them up in triumph. "Hope you like them."

"Do I have choice?"

"No. Good to see you, Strenk. To what do we owe the pleasure?"

"He came to offer me a job," supplied Val-Dor. "He seems to think he'd like me to be his deputy. We'd have to leave Qintir, of course."

"What did you tell him?"

"I didn't answer yet."

A look passed between them. Val-Dor turned to Chief Strenk as Per-Lem poured herself some water. "We have some news of our own," Val-Dor said.

"I'm pregnant," said Per-Lem.

"Congratulations."

"It changes things," she continued. "Now we have someone else to think of. Cullen is no place to bring up a child. Especially if the rumors are true and the mines are reopened. The place will change, and assuredly not for the better. I suppose there are worse places than Telborn."

"So you accept?" said Strenk to his nephew.

Per-Lem nodded at Val-Dor.

"I think I do."

Strenk lifted his glass. "A toast," he said. "To the baby... the peace... and the future."

"The baby. The peace. And the future."

Colophon

The main body of the text of this book was typeset with the pdfT_EX digital typesetting system. The typefaces used are mostly from the Latin Modern family, set at 10·5/13.

The paper stock used for the body of the book and for the cover depends on the particular printer that created the book you are holding.

The VEDIT PLUS text editor was used to create the original text.

The cover was created with the Scribus desktop publishing system and the GIMP image manipulation program.

Computer processing for this edition of *Timeshift* was performed on an Intel quad-core system running the Kubuntu 10.10 64-bit distribution of the GNU/Linux operating system.